A BOOKKEEPER'S

# Practical Sorcery

## by Kate Russell

A BOOKKEEPER'S GUIDE TO

# PRACTICAL SORCERY

BY KATE RUSSELL

FIRST EDITION

First Published by Fantastic Books Publishing 2016

Cover design by Heather Murphy

ISBN (hardback): 978-1-912053-72-8

Kate Russell © 2016

All rights reserved.

The right of Kate Russell to be identified as the author of this book has been asserted by her in accordance with the Copyright, Designs and Patents Act 1998.

All rights reserved. No part of this publication may be reproduced, stored in or introduced into a retrieval system or transmitted, in any form, or by any means (electronic, mechanical, photocopying, recording or otherwise) without the prior written permission of the publisher or unless such copying is done under a current Copyright Licensing Agency license. Any person who does any unauthorised act in relation to this publication may be liable to criminal prosecution and civil claims for damages.

## Dedication

To the memory of Neil Davidson, who endured more in his lifetime than anyone should have to, but remained playful to the very last.

To Val, for delivering endless cups of tea.

And to all those of you who keep magic alive.

# Acknowledgements

With thanks to Dan and Gabi Grubb, who took my story into their hearts and encouraged me to make it the best that I can. To Mae, my tireless editor whose initial feedback filled me with pride and made me want to impress even more. To Heather Murphy for a perfect cover design that sat on my desktop to inspire me as I wrote the final draft. To Alex Campbell, for an honest read that revealed the last few flaws. And to my cats, Captain Jack and Tia for not walking across the keyboard to add their own footnotes (or should that be pawnotes?) to the prose.

# Author's Note

This story is my 'first album'; the story that's been brewing in my imagination since I first decided I was going to write a book. Some of the ideas and characters have been with me since childhood; others came along later. Some were even lost along the way, shaved off in ideas that went on to become something else or were lost out at sea. I finally started writing it seriously twenty years ago, completing the first manuscript four years later when I had a dry spell of freelancing and the characters demanded my attention.

I got a favourable response from some publishers when I touted the finished manuscript around. But this was 1999, and Harry Potter was happening. While my story was good there was, apparently, only room for one trainee wizard in the literary world. Since then I've learned a lot about writing; written close to a billion words I reckon. I've penned dozens of short stories, published two other books, and experienced a lot more life.

When my now publisher, the amazing Fantastic Books, said they loved the manuscript, I was thrilled. But I thought it deserved a rewrite. I did this applying all the knowledge and skills that I've gained in the fifteen-years since I last put it to bed. It's been almost two more years in the doing, but has been a rare opportunity to go back in time and look at a completed story with fresh eyes. During the rewrite it was often like reading a thing for the first time; such a lot has happened since I last opened the manuscript.

Oddly enough this obfuscation of time gave me real clarity. I'd be tempted to say I should put all stories away for twenty years before publishing, but at this stage of the game I'm afraid the boat might have sailed on that strategy.

It's hard to explain how much I've enjoyed spending time in this world again. It's been like redecorating a favourite room with all the finest materials I've saved up for over twenty-years for.

I hope you enjoy relaxing inside its pages.

For those who need to ask; this story is for children. Or parents to read to their children; or read to themselves surreptitiously after bedtime. But mostly it's for anyone, of any age, who enjoys letting their mind wander through the words of a damn good yarn. Like me.

# Chapter 1

Do you believe in magic? I see you pause for thought, perhaps to ponder 'what is magic anyway? Where is the proof of it around me?' But why must you see a thing for it to be real? Can you see the air you breathe? Deny its existence if you like but it will go on filling your lungs regardless.

Magic, let me tell you friend, is just as real.

It flows across the earth as blood flows through your veins. You don't believe me. I see it in your eyes; the tolerant look of someone humouring a fool. But I hope to change your mind tonight. Because unlike blood and the air that you breathe, magic does need faith to exist. Not much, just a trickle of belief from a special few; like the hidden roots of a cactus drawing life from deep below the desert floor. I wonder if your mind is open enough to become one of those roots, ensuring for another generation that magic survives?

I'd like to tell you a tale, if I may? About a time when magic would have died were it not for one brave soul who fought a monster to save it. Perhaps you'll think it's a pleasant story and go on your way, your life unchanged.

But I see more than that in your eyes. I see a deeper understanding that hints at something special.

So sit, be comfy as we travel, friend. Perhaps my tale will sow in you the seed of belief that magic needs to keep blooming.

...

Henry Noble wasn't a particularly remarkable-looking young man. Small for his age with a thoughtful face; the kind of face you'd skim right past if you were looking for trouble. Each morning at a quarter-past-six he would pick up his lunch pail from the faded kitchen table, kiss his mother's cheek goodbye and stride down the garden path, out through the neat little gate that leads on to the rest of the world.

At the end of the road he would turn right on to Market Street, skirting the shiny cobbles of the square before winding his way west through rows of cheerfully fronted cottages towards the looming stone walls of the castle. Henry loved the square at this time of day. The worn trestles and empty stalls still naked of burgeoning produce, stood in tidy ranks that seemed to march purposefully towards the frowning grey castle above. The cobbles glistened in the early morning emptiness, polished to an impossible sheen each day by a stampede of hungry bargain-hunters.

Henry paused to enjoy the scene as a swifttail looped down out of the clear blue sky to snag some morsel overlooked by night-time scavengers. In the distance he heard the faint echo of hooves and cart wheels as the first of the day's traders began making their bleary way to their stations.

Henry's walk to the castle wasn't very long, twenty-minutes at most, but he liked to allow enough time to stop by the north wing on his way to work. This majestic stone tower was home to Halcyon, the Wizard Royal, and Henry's only true friend. Together they would sit and drink tea chatting about the comings and goings in

Terratonia. But the conversation always ended up in the same neighbourhood.

'I *need* you to teach me Halcyon. I can't go on like this. It's killing me inside.' As usual, Henry's face was the picture of misery as he sat across the table from the wise old sorcerer.

'You know I don't do that any more, boy.' The old man stood, leaning on the back of the chair so he could reach a large clay jar labelled 'biscuits' down off the shelf.

'But it's so unfair. I've dreamed of this my whole life and instead I get stuck counting gold in the King's vaults.'

'At least you have work, dear boy, and shebbles to buy what your family needs. There are far worse fates than becoming an accountant.'

Henry huffed, a rosy blush rising in his cheeks. 'What about *my* needs? Don't they count too? I'm only sixteen years old. I should be chasing dreams not stuck in a dungeon counting someone else's money.'

The old man smiled at the earnest face before him. Henry had always been fascinated by magic. As a small boy he'd often come to the castle with his father, the Chief Accountant. At the first opportunity the boy would slip away from the counting vaults and seek out Halcyon in his chambers. The old wizard would charge up his wand with a colourful array of spells and charms to entertain the lad, whose eyes would grow as big as dinner plates.

Normally quite shy, Henry would come alive talking about how he would one day become a great and powerful sorcerer, leaping at imaginary monsters brandishing a wooden-spoon-wand to demonstrate. The King's Wizard would laugh and pat him on the head, turning an apple into a twirl of butterflies to the squealing delight of his small visitor.

'Your family needs you right now, Henry. Dreams can come later when the twins are older and your mother's heart has mended.'

Henry's cheeks flushed again, this time fuelled by guilt. He looked down sheepishly and dropped a lump of sugar into his tea. 'I know; you're right. I'm just being selfish. I realise we're lucky the King gave me work at such a young age, otherwise where would we all be now? It's just … I wanted so much more out of life.'

'Cheer up lad, your life is just starting. Let's have a biscuit and you can tell me what's going on in town.'

Henry watched as the old man wrestled with the cork lid of the jar, which seemed determined to keep the tasty treats to itself. Realising the futility of its efforts, it popped off flying out of Halcyon's hand to roll across the flagstone floor. Halcyon peered into the jar smacking his lips. He stopped abruptly, his expression changing from hungry anticipation to absolute rage as he sprang to his feet and slammed the jar down on the table.

'YOU!' he bellowed at the offending container, rifling with urgency through the folds of his robe.

Henry inched back his chair, staring at the jar. The jar squeaked and Henry saw a tiny, pink nose twitch its way over the rim. The nose was followed by a small pair of paws, and a mouse, rather fat and looking very pleased with itself, started hauling its tubby body out of the jar. Halcyon managed to untangle his wand from his robe and jerked his arm outwards, blasting a ball of crackling pink light into the jar. The mouse squealed and fell back inside. Henry gripped the edge of his seat.

'That troublesome rodent has been snaffling my snacks for far too long! Well, not any more!' Halcyon pulled the biscuit jar towards him and reached inside. He scooped out a plump, slimy and very cross-looking toad. 'You, my rascally little friend, are going to the pond!' Halcyon waggled his wand sternly at the toad.

The toad burped rudely and tried to squirm out of his grasp. But the old wizard held tight before plopping it in a wooden casket on the floor. He slammed down the lid with his foot.

Henry felt sorry for the mouse; a jar full of biscuits must be an awfully big temptation and it didn't look happy about being turned into a toad.

'Oh, don't worry, boy,' Halcyon said, seeing Henry frown at the casket. 'It's only a low level spell. Lasts a little over a week if you get the mix right. He'll be back up here, making off with my confectionery in no time I don't doubt.' Halcyon glared at the casket. '*But not before a good soaking in the pond!*' he said loudly, rapping the lid with his wand.

Another belch came from inside.

The old wizard looked pleased with himself. He sat back and pushed the jar across the table. 'Biscuit?'

Henry eyed the amphibious ooze now smearing the rim of the jar and shook his head. Halcyon raised his eyebrows and then dug deep for a handful of his own. 'Now, where were we?'

'You were reminding me my life isn't my own and refusing to teach me magic.'

Halcyon sighed, dunking a biscuit into his tea and swirling it around. 'It's for your own good, Henry. Magic is no living. Not nowadays.'

His voice was sad. There was a time many scores of years gone by when men and women of magic had been admired and revered. The Kings and Queens of yesteryear would consult with their mystical consorts on affairs of state and the heart. Halcyon would stride through the cool dark corridors of the castle with his head held high, his magnificent silken robes whipping importantly at the empty space he left in his wake. But that was then, and this was now. Magic had been getting a bad name lately and many of the best wizards had been driven into hiding; branded charlatans and fraudsters by mobs of scornful townsfolk. Halcyon was one of the lucky few. Were it not for the high regard the King's father held him in, he too would no doubt be living a lie; beating out a meagre existence as a blacksmith or a baker. His tall pointy hat and emerald robes tucked quietly away in some dark, secret cupboard. He shuddered.

'Besides, your mother would have my hat for a handbag if I led you off the straight and narrow. You're the head of the household, boy. Food and lodgings don't pay for themselves.'

Henry felt bile rise in his stomach at the injustice of it all. 'But if I had magic, I could *spell* them into existence! Or better yet go out and find the bandits that took my father and blast them into oblivion!' Henry's fists were balled on the table top now.

The old man reached across and patted one. 'I know lad. I know. Just give it time. It's only been two years and the loss is raw, for all of you. But right now, your family needs you.' The old wizard watched the young man sadly for a moment, then remembered the biscuit dunked in his tea and pulled it out to inspect it.

Henry relaxed his fists and sighed again deeply. 'Two years feels like a lifetime in my shoes.'

At that moment the tea-soaked biscuit decided it had also had enough of life, and a large chunk broke off the arrangement, diving headfirst back into Halcyon's cup. A droplet of tea sploshed on to Henry's nose.

'Oops. Sorry,' Halcyon said, but couldn't help smiling as Henry wiped at it crossly.

'Never mind.' He scraped back his chair and got up. 'I should head off now. I don't want to be late. That old misery, Mr Colloid, is just looking for another excuse to dock my wages.'

'Very well, boy.' Halcyon rose stiffly, crossing the room to open the shutters.

The bright spring morning burst rudely into the dusky old chamber, transforming it instantly from an intriguing cavern filled with secrets and promise, to just another stone-clad box containing a bent old man with a slightly odd dress-sense. The magic was gone, and Henry should be too if he was going to buy a chicken from the market that night. He'd already been docked five shebbles this week. If he lost much more his brothers would be tucking into roast accountant instead of chicken; a dish his mother would be more than happy to prepare.

The cool, damp corridor skirting the central courtyard was still deserted as Henry headed for the vaults, the sound of his heels tapping on cold, grey flagstones echoing in a most satisfactory way. Most courtiers didn't surface before ten o'clock and Henry savoured these moments of peace as he wove his way through impressive chambers filled with ancient treasures. Despite the prospect of spending the next eight hours under Mr Colloid's critical eye he allowed his face to relax and try on a smile. It wasn't such a bad life, he mused, running his hand along the pleasing curve of the white stone banister leading down into his place of work. And yet, he craved more. It wasn't that he disliked the people he worked with, besides his miserable boss of course. But the only magic they believed in down here was the magic of a carefully balanced ledger, and Henry found that stifling.

The Chief Accountant was already sitting at his desk by the door when Henry arrived. He looked pointedly at his pocket-watch, unable to conceal his contempt for the young man scurrying across the room. Henry's cheeks burned as he nodded polite greetings to colleagues left and right. Mr Colloid squeezed the pocket-watch shut and stood, his heavy oak chair screeching an ugly complaint across the floor. He tugged at the bottom of his sombre black coat and pushed steel-rimmed reading-glasses even higher up on the bridge of his nose.

'You are aware, Master Noble, that work begins at eight o'clock sharp in this establishment, are you not?' His voice was high and nasal, his face pinched into a ferocious squint as he tried to focus on Henry through the reading-glasses.

Henry stopped and turned to face his employer. 'Err, yes of course Mr Colloid. Eight o'clock. Is it past that now?' Henry was sure he'd arrived on time.

Mr Colloid's mouth curled up into a victorious sneer as he flicked the top off his pocket-watch again, examining it closely for several seconds. 'Simply being in one's place of employ is not to begin work, boy,' he said eventually. 'The time is now precisely forty-seconds past the hour of eight and you have yet to count a single piece of gold.'

Henry stood in the middle of the room, all eyes on him. 'Well, I've been standing here talking to you for about forty seconds, otherwise I would have done.' Injustice coloured his cheeks.

Mr Colloid gasped, snapping the watch shut and levelling his gaze on the young man. But the short-distance lenses in his glasses, which were in a particularly mischievous mood, hiked his aim off to the right ten-degrees and he wound up glaring at a table instead. The table shook nervously.

Mr Colloid snatched the treacherous glasses off their perch and stalked around his desk towards Henry, snarling, 'You are sailing perilously close to the edge of your world, sonny. I should hate you to fall off.'

Somehow Henry doubted that. 'I ... I'm sorry Mr Colloid, but ...'

His attempt at an explanation was brought to an abrupt halt by the clatter of coins bouncing across the stone floor. This sound was quickly followed by the frantic rustling of cloth as somebody tried to cover it up.

Mr Colloid's head whipped around and he glared at the red-faced clerk who'd caused the commotion. 'COSSET!' he roared.

Peter Cosset shrank back into his soft leather boots, cradling the wayward coins in his tunic as he cowered at the edge of the room. 'I ... I ... I'm sorry, Mr Colloid,' he stuttered.

Seeing his chance, Henry scurried to his station, settling down and immediately starting the process of transferring towers of glittering gold coins from one side of the bench to the other.

'Oh you will be boy,' Mr Colloid's sneer broadened into a smug smile, 'when you find your remuneration for today to be five shebbles *light!*'

He finished with a strangled squawk that roughly resembled a laugh, and curled spiny fingers into the turn of his lapels. His icy eyes focused on the cowering accounts clerk, which without the interference of the troublesome reading-glasses marked their target with devastating accuracy. Peter went back to studying the coins in the scoop of his tunic and eventually the Chief Accountant stalked back to his desk.

Henry felt sorry for Peter. The bullying overseer made him so nervous he was all thumbs and two left feet. He'd only been working in the vaults for a month and had already been docked twenty-five shebbles. Much more and the poor lad would be paying to come to work.

Henry watched as Peter pulled himself together, pouring the errant coins in his tunic on to a long wooden bench in front of one of the busily counting accountants. He dug in his pocket, pulled out a white handkerchief and blew his nose gently. Dabbing at his nostrils fussily he noticed Henry watching him. He blushed and folded the hanky neatly away into his pocket, then went back to collecting stray coins.

'Never mind, eh Peter?' Henry whispered as the young lad appeared from beneath his bench clutching the last few runaways. 'He's probably just having a bad day. Wouldn't you if you had to look at that face in the mirror every morning?'

The clerk's mouth gaped in horror, his eyes flicking between Henry and Mr Colloid from behind a mop of unruly hair that seemed to sprout in every direction, despite evidence of an attempt to tame it with rather too much hair cream. 'Shush! Henry, he'll hear you. My mother will ground me for life if I lose any more shebbles this month.'

Henry clamped shut his mouth. That was a feeling he knew only too well; expected to work like a man down here, yet still treated like a child at home. Perhaps he had something in common with one of his colleagues after all? Peter sniffed and put the back of his hand to his forehead, seeming to test its temperature.

'You OK?' Henry asked, with genuine concern.

Peter blinked and seemed to resolve some internal conflict. 'Yes. Sorry. I'm fine.' He tried on a tentative smile.

Henry smiled back, encouragingly.

'I'll go get some more coins.'

Then Peter scampered off towards the lower vaults.

Henry looked at his bench. Light from the paraffin lamps on the walls danced across the glittering stacks of gold. He went back to counting and allowed his mind wander through the hypnotic patterns they cast on the worktop, his imagination transforming the light display into swirling garlands of magic he commanded to do his bidding. A shard of light here to fix his family's money troubles; a shaft of brilliance there to bring his father back; and a blade of pink luminescence spun across the room to turn his employer into a toad. A chuckle rose in his throat as he imagined tossing the nasty man into a pond with all the other slimy creatures. His imaginary spell casting was broken when a shadow fell across the work surface, killing the shimmering reflections.

'Count?' Bob Frugal's chalk was poised above the grey slate cradled in his arm. Henry's face remained blank. 'Count?' Bob repeated, an edge of irritation creeping in. 'Henry. For heaven's sake, what count do you have?'

Henry glanced down at the stack of coins laid out on the desk in front of him, his face growing hot as the awful truth dawned. He had completely lost count! An entire morning's work wasted. Mr Colloid was going to have his head on an abacus.

# Chapter 2

The day outside was calm and hazy. The fields and woodland surrounding Terratonia seemed to be dozing the afternoon away, while in contrast clusters of cottonweed swirled busy trails across the lazy terrain. As Henry left the confines of the castle he pulled the soft leather wages pouch out of his pocket and tossed it up and down, frowning. Five shebbles light, again. Mr Colloid had waved him off with a look that seemed delighted to point out the subject was not open for discussion.

He sighed as he clumped along the road towards the market, kicking at any unfortunate small rocks that happened to lie in his path. The sun beat merrily down on his back, but Henry was too busy stewing over the deducted coins to pay it any heed.

'Oh, what's the point?' he asked a solitary cloud despondently. 'I'm going to be stuck in that dungeon for the rest of my life.'

The cloud replied by passing in front of the sun, spilling a miserable-looking shadow across the path Henry's feet were trudging. He aimed a vicious kick at another small rock, only to discover it was part of a much larger rock that had buried itself deep in the surface of the road, presumably to wreak vengeance for all the genuinely small rocks now scattered left and right.

'OUCH!' Henry hopped about on the spot, clutching his stubbed toe. His face was pink and cross. 'Oh, that's typical. Hit a man when he's down why don't you?' he accused the world.

The world offered up no reasonable explanation for its behaviour, so Henry turned his back on it and carried along his gloomy way. What was he going to do? He couldn't imagine the rest of his life being this dull. He could remember when he was seven-years-old, walking home along this very track with his mother after picnicking in the sun-drenched meadows behind the castle. She was so happy back then, full of life and radiance. He'd chattered away about his dreams of magic and what Halcyon had shown him in the castle that week. She'd laughed and ruffled his hair, stopping for a moment to fuss at the twins in the trolley she'd been pulling. They had only been a few weeks old and were just two gurgling balls of pink flesh.

'And what would you do if you met an ugly old witch?' She'd turned from the babies and raised a playful eyebrow at her older son. Dropping slowly into a hunch, her face contorting and her hands rising towards him like claws she said, 'One that wanted to cast a horrible spell on you?' Her voice was contorting too, into something scratchy and ugly. Henry remembered feeling the thrill of danger rise in his stomach as she advanced towards him with menace.

'Mum, stop it,' he'd giggled, unable to resist the urge to step back.

'A spell like ... the curse of everlasting tickle!'

Henry screamed gleefully as she leapt upon him with tickling fingers, tucking himself down into a tight ball in an attempt to keep them from their targets.

'Mum ... Stop!' Henry could hardly get the words out as giggles racked his body and he squirmed beneath his mother's searching fingers, seeking out those tickle zones that are so powerful it's a good job only mothers know where they are.

She'd stood, laughing and admiring her handiwork.

'Some wizard you'd make,' she teased as Henry recovered on the dusty track.

'Some wizard indeed,' the older Henry said sadly to the memory.

The road narrowed as it headed into town and the rough surface littered with deceitful little rocks reformed into a smoothly cobbled street. Row upon row of friendly-looking cottages lined up to greet the miserable accountant, their neat little gardens festooned with the all the happy, bright colours of summer.

Henry faked a cheery smile and waved at a spotless window, through which Mrs Flibbertigibbet (the town gossip, and unfortunately Henry's aunt) could be seen scrubbing away at some dirty dishes. She regarded him with suspicious contempt, a look she'd developed especially for her nephew, and then turned her attention back to the sudsy sink-load.

'Yeah, yeah, you ugly old bat,' Henry muttered through the clenched teeth of his unconvincing smile. 'Love you too Aunty Giblets.'

The woman in the window snapped her head up as if she'd heard him with perfect clarity. Her cold, grey eyes levelled on Henry, who blushed hotly, waved again, and then became terribly interested in his shoes.

Mrs Flibbertigibbet was Henry's father's sister. She was slim and fine-boned, much like Henry and his father, with a pointed, nosey-looking face and sharp eyes that never missed a trick. Her home was small and neat, strategically situated on the corner of the square to allow for optimum views of anything that might be going on. Regimented rows of floral plumage marched along the entire face of the cottage in brightly painted window boxes, breaking up the party only briefly to allow the front door to do its thing. Image was everything to Mrs Flibbertigibbet. It was terribly important to her what people thought. But it was even more important that they understood what she thought; and she had a thought on practically any subject you'd care to mention. Regardless of whether or not you actually cared to mention it.

She'd doted on her younger brother, and had never liked Henry or his mother. By the time the twins came along he didn't even think she'd bothered to notice them. It was perhaps the one thing he wished he could learn from the miserable old goose.

When she'd heard Henry was going to start work in the vaults to keep a roof over their heads after his father went missing, she'd wafted the idea away as if it was a bad smell, barking a laugh of cruel disbelief.

'He's fourteen for goodness sake. And he's *Henry*.' She'd squeezed his name out of her mouth like she didn't like the taste of it. 'I give him a week before he's back hiding behind your aprons.'

Henry bristled at the memory. Ironically she'd probably done him a favour as it was a determination to prove her wrong that had helped him get through the first difficult few months at work. He was a full year younger than even the most junior of clerks. Other kids his age were finishing off their school studies and planning myriad possible futures. His had been mapped out along a pedestrian path by dumb fate, and he had Mr Colloid as a boss to boot.

He tried to shake off the funk that had fallen on to him since leaving the castle and headed into the bustling business of the market square. He could still feel his aunt's stare burning into his back, so he veered sharply right, weaving in amongst stalls now overflowing with every kind of produce. He kept up his pace, chancing a peek over his shoulder once he thought he was out of sight.

BAM!

Henry's normally fluid, three-dimensional world was smashed into a two-dimensional sandwich. On one side; a large object he hadn't seen coming (due to the fact that he was looking in the other direction); on the other side the rest of reality, which apparently had also not expected him to stop moving so suddenly. Several grocery laden shoppers barrelled into him, squeezing his slight body against the doughy surface he'd slammed into before bouncing back in surprise, causing a ripple effect at least ten shoppers deep. There were gasps and exclamations of pain as feet were trodden on, bags dropped, and somebody elbowed a pyramid of oranges which went cascading across the pathway.

Stunned by the blow, Henry slid to the floor like an unwanted pickle.

As his brain clamoured to regain control of the situation it began to perceive certain sounds it recognised; the clatter of falling belongings; confused apologies and indignant protests.

Feeling a little more confident his brain decided to try out another sense. He opened his eyes and a large, round face swam into focus ... out of focus ... and then back into focus again.

'You all right little fella, yeah?'

The face shrank away, and was replaced by an over-sized pair of hands. Henry blinked as his brain gave up trying to understand what was going on and settled instead for attempting to remember where it was. The hands reached down and grabbed him by the lapels, pulling him up to his feet and brushing his coat down roughly. Finally, the rest of the body belonging to the face and hands swam into focus, and it appeared that Henry's observational abilities were fully restored.

'Th ... Thank you,' was all his vocal section could muster.

Henry sensed other hapless shoppers being pulled to their feet and dusted down, their strewn possessions smartly gathered up and poked into any available bag or large pocket to clear the path for other impatient shoppers. He stared as someone appeared with a broom and swept the river of tumbling oranges away. His cheeks prickled with guilt and he turned his attention once more to the object he'd just slammed into.

The round-faced man was in his late forties, and round was the most appropriate word to describe him. The benefactor (or victim, depending on your point of view) of many years of large second-helpings, he had pink, chubby cheeks that were currently wearing a pink, chubby grin. He nodded affably and continued the rough valet with his large, round hands. Henry stepped back, for fear of being knocked over again. He checked the side of his throbbing head for any signs of damage. The round man regarded him apprehensively.

'Sorry 'bout that 'lil fella, but you did kinda charge into me a bit there. Sure you're OK, yeah?'

Henry nodded, and instantly regretted it as this head spun.

'Yes, I'm fine thanks,' he said wobbling slightly.

'Oh good!' enthused the round man. He finished brushing off the worst of the dirt and gave the stunned accountant one last cautious look of appraisal, as if he half-expected to see him slide to the floor again. Satisfied this wasn't the case he thrust a piece of parchment into Henry's considerably smaller hand, patted him enthusiastically on the shoulder and then turned and disappeared into the chattering crowd. Henry watched his large, round bottom get swallowed up by the press of people as he continued to push pieces of parchment into their hands.

Henry looked down bemused.

*Are you stuck in a rut?*

the flyer asked in ornate, curly handwriting.

*Do you long for excitement, and crave respect from your fellow man?*

it enquired emphatically.

*Bring the magic back into your life … train for a new career as a Sorcerer today!*

it impeached.

Henry stared at the inoffensive piece of parchment as if it had just stuck out its tongue and blown a raspberry. He glanced about at the surrounding throng to see if anyone else had noticed. The throng seemed unconcerned and continued to shop, so he went back to the flyer in his hand.

*You are invited to enrol on a course of twelve classes, which will place the powers of magic and mystery, right into the palm of your hand.*

Henry read on eagerly.

*For an all-inclusive price\* of just fifty shebbles you could be mastering the art of magic and carving out a place for yourself in* *the annals of time as one of the greatest wizards ever to walk the earth! \*N.B. Fortune Telling modules not included.*

Henry stood there agog. Here it was; his chance to learn about magic. But fifty shebbles? He deflated further as he realised another stumbling block; there was no way his mother or Mr Colloid would let him take time off work for the classes, even if he could afford them. He stared down at the flyer miserably and spotted a footnote.

*This once-in-a-lifetime opportunity is brought to you by Gorman Dizing Enterprises; a member of the Council for the Respectable Advancement of Speculative Sciences. Evening and weekend course schedules on application. Credit available, subject to status.*

Henry nearly 'whooped' out loud. He clutched the slip of parchment to his belly, scanning the crowd again for any sign that they were on to him. No-one paid a blind bit of notice. Henry couldn't believe his luck. This was perfect! He could go to the evening classes and his family would be none-the-wiser. Once he had some magic he could go off on a quest, do some impressive spell casting, maybe thwart a criminal mastermind or two, then pay off the debt with his rewards. They'd have to take him seriously then! Henry pulled himself reluctantly out of this daydream and stuffed the flyer deep into his pocket, skimming the market with his eyes in the hope of catching sight of the round man. As it seemed almost impossible that a man of such a size would not be spotted immediately if he were still in the area, he quickly gave up looking. He resolved to fill out the application form that evening and walk across town after supper to deliver it. He smiled to himself, but the smile wilted as some part of his shaken brain sparked the rumblings of uneasy recall. There was something he was supposed to be doing ... With a zap his brain-circuits reconnected.

'Supper! I have to buy a chicken for supper! Oh, Mum will kill me if they've sold out!'

He turned on his heel and began fighting his way through the crowd toward his mother's favourite butcher, still grasping the amazing piece of parchment in his pocket. What a good day, he thought to himself as he trotted through the busy square, dodging left and right to avoid colliding with any more people. What a splendidly good day this was turning out to be.

# Chapter 3

Later that evening as Henry sat at the kitchen table watching his family tuck into the hearty chicken dinner his mother had prepared, he contemplated the curious events of the day. He pushed small mounds of mashed potato through a sea of gravy with his fork, trying to disguise how little he'd eaten by rearranging the scenery. Will and Bill, his nine-year-old brothers, were arguing over the ownership of a snakeskin they'd found on the way home from school. Their mother was beginning to look frayed around the edges.

'Oh for goodness sake boys, can't you just share the thing nicely?' she said wearily. 'Otherwise I shall have to ask Henry to throw it away, and neither of you will have it. Horrible, filthy bit of rubbish it is anyway.'

'Ha! He can try …'

Will, the eldest of the pair by three whole minutes, glared at Henry insolently as he held the snakeskin aloft. Henry never understood why his mother dragged him into these disputes. The twins clearly had no respect for him, and in a couple of years they'd be bigger than him too, taking after his mother's more robustly built side of the family. Following his brother's lead, Bill poked out his tongue at Henry and in that brief moment of united rebellion the squabble over the snakeskin was forgotten.

Henry ignored them as his mother started clearing away the dishes. He'd learned long ago that reacting to their taunts was about as helpful as placing a steak sandwich on your head to divert the attention of a starving crocodile.

They'd been just about bearable a few years ago, the usual annoying brother stuff. But when their father had vanished they'd run a bit wild; constantly getting into trouble around town and running circles around Henry when their mother, too wrapped up in grief to deal with it, had tasked him with reprisals.

Henry envied them sometimes as they'd seemed to bounce back so fast; hardly appearing to miss their father. He watched his mother transfer dirty plates from the table to a deep sink filling with hot, sudsy water. She moved almost mechanically, shoulders dropped with an air of defeat that had settled on her like a cast-iron shawl as it became clear that her husband wasn't coming home.

Henry shivered as ghosts from the past flitted through the shadows of the room. It had been about this time of night, right after supper that the dreadful news had come. His father had headed off on a business trip that morning, to buy exotic foods for the King from the port town of Amalga. Henry had been cleaning the dishes while his mother argued with the twins about finishing their greens, when there was a knock at the door. They all stopped and looked at each other, a thread of silent worry stretching out between them. No-one ever called round at this time of night.

Henry was jerked out of his reverie to find his mother peering into his face with anxious scepticism – a curious expression that only the mothers of exceptionally worrisome children can pull off with any real conviction.

'You haven't done very well with your supper Henry, are you feeling ill?'

'No, I'm fine mother.' Henry fibbed, pushing a loaded forkful into his stiffly smiling mouth to prove it.

The truth was he did feel sick; sick with anticipation brought on by the slip of parchment tucked inside his pocket. But he couldn't tell his mother that.

She turned back to the dirty dishes.

The mashed potato was almost cold and Henry could feel rich onion gravy clinging to the sides of his throat as the unwanted food parcel slid down to his stomach. Arriving at its destination it was churned up into an even more nauseous mess by the excited butterflies now swirling there. Henry didn't like lying to his mother, and the flyer burned guiltily against his left hip to remind him. He looked down at his overloaded plate.

'He's probably suffering some kind of brain embolism,' said Will matter-of-factly.

Well at least he's paying attention to biology classes, Henry thought vaguely as he continued ignoring them resolutely.

Frustrated by the lack or reaction, Will kicked him under the table. Bill sniggered into his hands.

'Ow! Will, stop it!'

'Ewww, Will stop it,' mimicked Bill, flicking a pea across the table while their mother's back was turned.

The pea ricocheted off a spoon and hit Henry square on the chin, depositing a splodge of gravy before falling into his lap. He swiped crossly at his face as the twins broke into gales of laughter. Henry glared and Will kicked again, harder this time. The toe of his boot connected painfully with Henry's shin and he leapt up from his seat, rubbing it.

'OW! Right, you leave it out right now or I'm going to …' Henry faltered. Or he would do what, exactly? Since his role as provider and head of the household didn't extend to him getting any respect from his brothers, and his mother was just too sad to notice their dissent, there wasn't a lot he *could* do. Suddenly enraged, Henry drove his fork into his own plate of food and catapulted a large wodge of cold potato right at Will's head. The older twin dodged left, barging into Bill who tumbled off his chair with a cry of protest, and the airborne mash splatted messily on a portrait of Mrs Flibbertigibbet hanging on the wall.

'HENRY!'

The three of them stopped fighting and looked at their mother, who was standing over the table fuming.

'They started it,' complained Henry, but his mother threw down her tea towel and put her hands on her hips, glaring.

'You're supposed to be the responsible adult here! For goodness sake Henry! You want me to run around doing everything for all of you, on my own, with no help … First you lose another five shebbles of income we badly need and now I have to clean up after a food fight too?'

Her voice was shrill, eyes brimming with frustrated tears.

All three boy's tempers blanched to see their mother's distress.

'I'm sorry. I'll clean it.'

Henry made to reach for the tea towel but his mother cuffed him on the side of the head, startling him back into his seat.

'No you won't. You'll go to your room. I've had more than enough of you for just now.'

Will and Bill smirked at Henry but their mother grabbed the tea towel herself and threw it across the table at them.

'YOU two will clean up this mess. And you can finish the washing up too. I'm going sit down and try to imagine I have three good, supportive sons instead of the monsters I see before me.'

Without another word she slumped into the chair by the stove and buried her face in her hands.

Will reached across to pull the tea towel off Bill's head where it had landed, glaring at Henry, who just sighed and headed for the stairs with a heavy heart.

So much for being a responsible adult, he thought, sent to my room like a school kid.

He climbed the stairs and pushed open the door to his tiny bedroom heading straight for the battered old writing desk by the window. Swooping his arm across the cluttered wooden surface he pressed the crumpled parchment flat on to the space he'd created. Settling himself on the edge of the bed he read through the flyer again. It all seemed pretty straightforward; he must complete the application form on the reverse side, then deliver it to the corporate headquarters of Gorman Dizing Enterprises and await response.

Henry scratched his details eagerly into the spaces provided and marked a heavy cross in the check box next to 'credit required'.

'There.' He sat back on the bed to admire his handiwork.

Now he just had to deliver it.

He looked at his closed bedroom door, chewing on his bottom lip.

There was no way this side of the Amalgam Sea his mother was going to let him go out tonight. So the smart move would be to drop it in after work tomorrow.

He chewed harder on his lip, eyeing the filled out parchment on the desk.

Smart was dull. Smart had got him nothing but boredom and drudgery, with the occasional bout of murderous rage towards his annoying siblings.

A different emotion started bubbling up. One he hadn't felt in years; adventure.

His gaze slipped to the window and his eyes narrowed as they began to debate with his brain whether he could make it out, and down into the garden safely or not. You read about people doing it in books all the time, his brain insisted. His eyes remained quietly cynical.

Before any more parts of his body could add to the discussion, Henry snatched up the parchment and folded it roughly into his pocket. He'd never even thought of escaping through the window before, so was unsure what he'd see when he looked out with the critical eye of a fugitive. He pulled up the lever and the window creaked open, coughing a rim of dust from the seal that suggested it had been a long time since Henry had looked out of it with any kind of eyes.

He waved the dust cloud away and peered down. A trellis supporting a sorry-looking yasmin vine was nailed to halfway up the front wall. He could probably swing his legs over the window sill and lower his feet down on to the top of it with his elbows still on the ledge. He could test the strength of it at least. He'd still be able to climb back in if it felt too flimsy.

His thoughts whirled, following dozens of possible scenarios to their end point as his heart beat faster and faster.

'I can always turn back,' he breathed eventually, and began easing his bottom up on to the window sill.

Heart now hammering as if alarm bells were going off in his chest, he braced himself in the frame and swivelled his knees out through the small window. Despite his feet's severe reservations about their role in this stage of the plan, they had no choice but to follow.

'Right. OK,' Henry said to himself, trying to sound confident. 'That's OK. Now I just need to grab hold of the window ledge,' he moved as he talked, his body almost mechanically following his mouth's instructions, 'and slide myself around and down ... Oof!'

The wind had been knocked out of him as his knees left the safety of the ledge and his stomach took the full weight of his body from a height of about twelve inches. After a moment he stretched his toes forwards to find the wall, breathing hard. They scraped against brick and he started slithering gradually down, feeling for the top of the trellis.

His left foot found it first, and Henry sighed with relief to realise he still had enough leverage on the ledge to pull himself back up without too much trouble.

'Right.'

He gave the trellis an experimental rattle with his toes. It seemed fairly secure. He allowed himself to put a little weight on the structure. It continued holding gallantly to the wall and Henry felt his confidence swell.

He could do this. He could really do this.

Sliding his body a bit lower, he began stepping his feet tentatively down the grid work until he could let go of the ledge with one hand and grab the top of it.

'There!' he cried triumphantly, then remembered he was supposed to be being stealthy and clamped his mouth shut.

He felt like a burglar as he climbed hand over hand down the wooden frame. It was cool and dark outside. No-one on the street, not an animal in earshot. He dropped the last few feet on to the lawn and landed in a crouch with a grace that surprised even him, then turned and crept into the shadows at the edge of the garden dragging a long string of bright white yasmin flowers from his ankle.

...

Half an hour later on the other side of town Henry stood across the street from the Gorman Dizing Enterprises' corporate headquarters with a sudden, inexplicable feeling of dread. He shuddered. His hands were slick with sweat; his heart still thumping in his chest after the excitement of the escape followed by a brisk walk across town.

Or was it thumping for another reason?

He had an irresistible sensation that something dreadful was about tap him on the shoulder and introduce itself. He checked over his shoulder; both shoulders just to be sure, then took a shaky breath.

'What is wrong with me?' he asked the night with an embarrassed little laugh before lifting up one foot and pushing it towards the building, banking on forward momentum and gravity to take care of the rest.

The interior of the building was plush and tastefully decorated. There were fine examples of art hanging from every marble-clad wall and the floor glittered with a mosaic of delicately coloured tiling that Henry felt sure must drive the caretaker to distraction. A massive marble desk sprawled elegantly in the middle of the entrance hall, with a long-legged girl a couple of years older than Henry sprawling equally elegantly behind it. She was thumbing lethargically through a pile of parchments in her lap, so Henry cleared his throat politely to announce his arrival.

The girl behind the desk looked up without much interest and Henry felt his cheeks flush. What with working in the vault all day and only brothers at home, he didn't have much contact with women. Apart from his mother and Mrs Flibbertigibbet, but he didn't think they counted as women. Henry had no clue how to behave when he came across a girl at close quarters. She looked from Henry's dumbfounded face to the slip of parchment in his hand, then back up to his unblinking eyes.

'Put it in the tray marked *in*, we'll get back to you as soon as we've processed it,' she recited in monotone, and then went back to thumbing through the parchment.

Henry forced his feet to move further into the room and stretched his arm out until it was long enough to drop the application form into the tray she'd indicated. He tried desperately to think of something witty and intelligent to say but it seemed like his brain was taking a break.

'Uhm ... I ... uh,' he stammered.

When it became obvious the power of speech had deserted him Henry gave up, turning and scurrying towards the exit. He suddenly hoped that his application would be rejected so he would never have to go through this humiliation again.

'HEY YOU!'

The shout echoed around the foyer like a wolf's howl across an empty mountain. Henry froze in his tracks, torn between the twin urges to sprint for the exit or turn round to address the challenge.

'SORCERER'S APPRENTICE, OR PRACTICAL WIZARDRY GRADE ONE?'

Now that Henry had come to a complete halt the voice had lost its edge of urgency, although it was still raised to a volume that suggested the owner was communicating from some distance. He turned and saw the round man from the market leaning precariously over a high banister at the far end of the entrance hall. Henry blinked, and the round man repeated his question.

'SORCERER'S APPRENTICE, OR PRACTICAL WIZARDRY GRADE ONE?'

Henry recognised these options from the tick boxes on the form he'd filled out earlier.

'ONLY IF IT'S SORCERER'S APPRENTICE, YOU'D BETTER GET A MOVE ON OR YOU'LL MISS YOUR INDUCTION LECTURE.'

Henry looked at the receptionist, expecting her to bark up at the round man about his application form not having been processed yet, but she continued her business without even registering a disturbance. Henry trotted over to the foot of the stairs underneath where the round man was standing.

'Uhm. Sorcerer's Apprentice I think.'

'You think? Got any previous experience with magic, yeah?'

Henry thought briefly about his early morning chats with Halcyon and how the old man would occasionally ask him to collect herbs and minerals for use in his spells. He knew where practically every magical property in the kingdom could be found. He wondered if this could be classed as previous experience with magic.

'What? Question too difficult? Come on lad. Do you know any spells? Got a wand?'

The face was still friendly, but the round man clearly had better things to be doing than watching Henry's impersonation of a moonfish.

'Uhm, no.' He really would have to break out of the habit of beginning every sentence with 'uhm', he thought to himself crossly.

'Then Sorcerer's Apprentice it is my little friend. Down the hall, take the second flight of stairs on the left to the third floor, then knock on the door marked D315, yeah? And try not to run into anyone on your way.' The round man winked one heavily lidded eye at Henry, and then disappeared back into the empty corridor behind him, chuckling to himself.

Another glance at the girl behind the desk suggested she saw no problem with these instructions, so he jogged off down the corridor.

Deeper into the building the obvious signs of luxury began to disappear. Tasteful works of art were replaced by boldly printed signs issuing instructions about where to go, what to remember, and how to avoid the wrath of the Gorman Dizing debt collectors by making sure your repayments were all received on time. The butterflies started getting fidgety again. He slowed as he took in his surroundings. The intricately tiled ceramic floor was now made of simple slabs, well-worn from the trampling of thousands of feet. At regular intervals on the left and right, starkly numbered wooden doors stood resolutely to attention ... B105, B107 ... a set of stairs ... Henry continued, scanning the dim corridor ahead for any signs of life ... B109, B111 ... and the next door on this side of the corridor was labelled simply CONFERENCE A. As Henry approached the door he noticed it was slightly ajar and he could make out the sound of muffled voices coming from inside. He drew closer and held his breath to hear what was being said.

'The board of directors are extremely unhappy with you. *I'm* extremely unhappy. Do you understand?' The voice that spoke was thick with distaste. 'This academy has been a severe drain on our bottom line for over a year now, and it's obvious to me that you've been more than a little creative with your bookkeeping. A fact I'm sure Mr Dizing would be most interested to hear.'

'My instructions come straight from the top. You can't threaten me.'

This voice was distressed, reduced to a squeak by the stranglehold of fear. But Henry would recognise that high, nasally whine anywhere. Mr Colloid! He pressed himself against the wall and edged closer to the crack in the door, hoping to catch sight of whoever his employer was talking to. The other voice was coming from behind a high-backed leather chair, the only sight of its inhabitant from where Henry lurked was a curl of grey smoke drifting up from the tip of a cigar rested out on one arm.

'I'm on to you Colloid. Do you hear me? It's not a game you know? This is serious business and your books seem to be more a work of fiction lately.' The menacing voice seemed to coil itself around Mr Colloid's throat, squeezing until the accountant's face turned beetroot. He struggled visibly to assert some authority.

'But ... but my instructions were quite clear. Mr Dizing said ...'

'MR. DIZING SAID!?'

Colloid recoiled like a snake as the hidden man roared at him.

'I don't care what you *think* Mr Dizing said. Since he never shows his face around here I have only YOUR word for it. And I don't take the word of worms. If you're so pally with the big, mysterious boss, why don't you roll him out here to back you up? Eh?'

Mr Colloid continued to cower through an unimpressive attempt to straighten confidently.

'Since you're on the board of directors,' he retorted unsteadily, 'why don't you roll Mr Dizing out here to challenge me?'

The unseen man gripped the arms of the chair and the whole thing shook with the force of his rage.

'Get out, Colloid. GET OUT!'

Henry's body went rigid. Mr Colloid was about to leave the boardroom. Henry didn't know the full story, but it was clear he was moonlighting for Gorman Dizing Enterprises. Henry was also pretty sure it wouldn't go well for him if he was caught out here snooping on his boss. Seeing the accountant stoop to collect his ledgers from the table Henry took his chance and dashed across the gap in the door. Holding his breath in anticipation of an angry shout, he bolted down the corridor, rounding the corner on to the second set of stairs just in time to avoid being spotted by the hastily departing accountant.

So, Mr Colloid had been fiddling the books at this big, impressive corporation? What a scandal that would cause if it got out. He smiled to himself as he scaled the stairs to the third floor and began searching for the door marked D315.

# Chapter 4

It wasn't hard to find room D315. Apart from the fact that the door sported a now familiar-looking silver placard that stated quite clearly 'D315', there was another sign tacked above it with the words 'SORCERER'S APPRENTICE INDUCTION' printed on it in big, patronising letters. Henry knocked gingerly.

'Enter,' came a thin reply. As Henry reached for the handle he was distracted by a loud clatter coming from the stairwell behind him. He turned to face the chaotic noise, and saw a red-faced girl come careering around the corner.

'COME IN ...' The voice inside the room was louder, and clearly annoyed at being made to repeat itself.

Henry turned his attention back to the door and twisted the handle. He stepped into the large room and the girl flung herself against the doorframe, struggling to stay in control as she rounded the corner juggling a stack of books. This erratic manoeuvre proved too much for the delinquent books, which made a break for freedom leaping and sliding from her arms in every direction. One skidded across the floor and came to rest against Henry's boot. He bent and picked it up.

*Quantum Numerology by Doctor Hyperbole*, it informed him haughtily. Henry stooped and collected a couple more of the wayward books before handing them back to the red-faced girl who was now scrambling around on her hands and knees collecting her belongings.

'Goodness me, what an entrance!'

Henry's attention was drawn back to the woman at the front, presumably the lecturer. The rest of the room was full of expectant faces tucked behind neat little desks, staring open-mouthed at the commotion in the doorway.

'Name?'

'Uhm ... Henry Noble ... Ma'am.'

'Hmmm.' The lecturer was running her finger down a long list of names on a scroll and Henry's stomach screwed itself up into an uncomfortable knot as he remembered his un-dealt-with application form still sitting in a tray downstairs. 'Well, never mind, we'll sort it out later. Go and find yourself a seat and try not to cause any more fuss.'

Henry clamped shut his mouth and headed towards an empty desk at the back of the room. 'And you ...?' the lecturer asked the catalyst of the disturbance with an air of exasperation.

'D.C. Hubbub,' she said hurriedly, finally perfecting the balancing act in her arms and scuttling off to the desk next to Henry.

The woman at the front of the room glanced down at her register and ticked a name off with a satisfied flourish.

'OK, I'll start again shall I?' She glared pointedly at the new arrivals and then settled herself on to the corner of her desk. 'My name is Mrs Don, and I'll be your course tutor for the first part of your studies here at G.D.E. Sorcerer's Apprentice, Grades A through D. Now, classes begin at eight o'clock sharp,' another spiky look towards the pair at the back, 'every Tuesday and Thursday night. All coursework and fees should be placed in the relevant pigeon-holes in LOWER ASSEMBLY ROOM C, before 6 pm on the day that they become due.' She said the room's name loud and robotically, as if delivering it that way might help it stick in their minds.

The list of instructions continued for some time as students diligently scratched away, noting down all the important information on pieces of parchment in front of them. Henry, who'd come completely unprepared, shrank a little further into the back row and tried to feign fascinated scribbling with a non-existent quill on the empty desk in front of him. He looked surreptitiously around the room. The faces he'd spotted earlier were now the backs of heads, all nodding vigorously to confirm their understanding, and occasionally dipping forwards to supervise the jotting down of another important note. On his left sat D.C. Hubbub. He wondered what the initials stood for. It seemed a strange way to introduce yourself.

She was still riffling through one of her many satchels looking for something to use on the crumpled slip of parchment she'd placed on her desk. She caught Henry's eye and smiled a broad smile from behind an untidy flop of auburn fringe. She shrugged in carefree resignation, sticking out her bottom lip to blow the wayward hair off her face with a huff that made Henry grin back. Dropping her uncooperative bag on the floor in an untidy heap she sat back in the chair and folded her arms across her chest. It was the most disorderly folding of a pair of arms Henry had ever seen; as if she had too many parts to them. Then she grinned again and turned to face the lecture being unravelled at the front of the room.

After droning on for almost an hour, Mrs Don threw the floor open to questions from her students. Everyone looked about expectantly but nobody raised a hand, so their teacher began the process of winding up the class.

'So! Our first module will be contemporary wand design. In preparation for Thursday's class, I want you to obtain a comfortably sized branch or twig, from a tree or shrub that holds some meaning for you. It could be from a tree in the forest that you used to climb as a child or a sprig from a longwaddle bush in your back garden. Just remember, this stick is going to be your wand, so make sure you pick something that will stand the tests of time and trauma. OK. Any questions?' Henry glanced across at the girl and saw her expression falter, as if she was stealing herself to raise her arm.

'Good!' Mrs Don steamed on, obviously keen to be rid of the class. 'Just drop your registration documents in the tray on my desk on your way out please. You'll find them in the welcome packs you got with your course acceptance letters.'

'Ah, Miss?'

All eyes turned to face D.C. who had her arm raised in the air.

The teacher looked at her with mild interest.

'Yes, ah ...' she looked down at the register again briefly. 'Daisy was it?'

The girl's face tightened and she lowered her arm.

'Actually, it's D.C. – as in the alphabet,' she corrected stiffly.

Mrs Don looked no more interested than she had been previously.

'You have a question?'

'Ah, yes. The project. Wands.'

'And?' A note of irritation crept into her tone.

'Well, I read somewhere,' D.C. ploughed on gamely, 'I think it's in one of these books here actually.' She turned to look through the precarious stack of books now balanced on her desk, then thought better of it and turned back to the teacher. 'I read that a magic wand has to be made of Malvern.'

'Malvern? Malvern what young lady?'

There was a titter from a few rows in front of them and Henry's cheeks flushed on behalf of the girl.

'Ah, the Malvern tree. Because, you know, the magic absorbing bark?'

The teacher levelled a contemptuous glare on the girl.

'Oh, you mean a tree from the mystical forest that burnt down a hundred years ago? Would you like me to arrange a field trip on Unicorns to go and gather it?' Several more students titter-guffawed and Mrs Don looked around the room sharply to silence them. 'Be careful what you read young lady. Magic has moved on. Evolved to be more efficient and streamlined. Now have you come here to learn, or to challenge?'

Henry could see D.C. swallow hard.

She said nothing.

'Right, that's that settled then. See you all on Thursday, eight-o'clock sharp. And don't forget your registration cards.' She had raised her voice over the thunder squall of scraping chairs, gesturing to the tray on her desk, as the whole class stood simultaneously.

Henry pushed himself into the back of the crowd and shuffled towards the exit looking as casual as possible, carefully circumnavigating the registration document drop-off point along the way. Out in the corridor the babble of new acquaintances being made enveloped him. The girl, D.C., who was still struggling with her unruly load, caught Henry's eye and headed over.

'Hi,' she said happily, jiggling her upper body from side to side as the books tried to escape again.

'Hello.'

The crowd surrounding them began moving slowly towards the stairwell, so Henry caught a handful of books as they slithered underneath the girl's right arm and fell into step beside her.

'I'm Henry.'

'D.C.' She grinned gratefully.

'What, that's your name? D.C.?'

'Yep. S'what people call me.'

'OK ... D.C. ...' Henry tested the moniker on his lips and smiled. 'Nice to meet you.'

'Exciting, huh?' D.C. said trotting along with the flow of the crowd.

'What?'

She looked surprised. 'This. Magic? Don't tell me you went along for the floor show tonight? That Mrs Don could bore the tail off a donkey.'

'Oh, right. Yes.' A solitary stomach-butterfly performed a loop-the-loop.

'Debrief? Could kill a ginger ale.'

'Sorry?'

'Drink. Fancy a soda in the tavern to compare notes? I realise neither of us took any notes, but I could certainly do with letting off steam before heading home. I'm buying,' she finished persuasively.

Henry blinked. The tavern? He'd passed it hundreds of times and had always been intrigued by the strange sounds and smells spilling out of the warmly lit doorway, but he'd never had the nerve to actually go in. He could practically hear his mother frowning all the way across town as he contemplated the invitation.

'C'mon on, just a swifty?' D.C. encouraged.

'Are we even allowed in there? I mean, aren't you too young?'

D.C. went pink. 'I just turned fifteen actually. Last week. But that doesn't matter. You can go in any time you like as long as you're with a grown up. And don't try to order booze,' she said as an afterthought. 'I'm only talking about a ginger ale. Not challenging you to a scumble dash.'

Henry looked around the rapidly emptying corridor. 'But we're not with a grown up.'

D.C.'s eyes glinted with a hint of mischief. 'The barman don't know that though, does he? The place will be rammed this time of night. I'll just say my dad sent me to the bar for a couple of sodas for the kids. Point to some guy noodling with his girlfriend, or starting up an argument. Someone they're not going to catch the eye of across the other side of the bar. Works every time.' She grinned hopefully.

Henry didn't quite know what to make of the sparky girl in front of him. She must be almost two years younger than him and a good foot shorter. Yet she was so brazen and gutsy.

'You do that a lot?'

Her cheeks flushed a deeper pink. 'No! I, well, just a few times. Look, it's hot, that was intensely boring. I just fancied a cold ginger ale and some friendly conversation. But it doesn't matter.' Her shoulders drooped in defeat and she went to take back the books Henry was holding .

Henry held them away from her, turning pink himself.

'Oh, no. I'm sorry. I just ... I've not been in there before. But I could do with letting off steam a little before heading home myself.'

'Oh, good.' She smiled with relief, wrinkling her nose as she concentrated on bringing the equilibrium back to the wobbly stack in her arms. 'Don't worry, been in there loads. I'll show you the ropes.'

Henry followed her down the corridor after the last few straggles of the dismissed class, who were funnelling down the stairwell. As they passed back through the impressive entrance lobby and out of the doors, G.D.E.'s latest crop of magical students dispersed into the night like smoke.

Henry fell into step beside D.C. and they headed towards the centre of town. As they walked she assaulted him with rapid-fire small talk. In the time it took them to reach the market square he had learned she was a middle child in a brood of seven, ranging from three to nineteen years old. Her mother and father worked long hours running a pottery business to feed them all, which she had been banned from helping out in on account of breaking more pots than she sold.

She grinned proudly at this revelation. 'Bless my clumsy feet, right? Who'd want to get stuck making potties for the rest of their life?'

Henry harrumphed in solidarity. 'I know that feeling. I have to work as an accountant because that's what my family expect. I can't stand it. Boring old stupid ledgers.'

D.C.'s mood turned solemn. 'Some people like them. I guess you can't break 'em though, so you haven't got an easy out like me.'

They fell into companionable silence, each contemplating their own fate; which in Henry's case meant imagining running amok in the vaults breaking every bit of counting hardware he could find.

'Still,' said D.C. suddenly, 'that's why we're here, right?'

'Here?' asked Henry, confused as they stepped up into the welcoming glow of the tavern porch.

'Well, not *here*, you daft goof.' She grinned and nodded for him to open the door. 'But where we met. Magic class. If that's what it was.'

Henry threw her a questioning look as she staggered through the door. It slammed shut behind him and the moist warmth of the hoppy air closed in like a beery hug. D.C. raised a cryptic eyebrow then leaned in to tip the stack of books into his arms.

'In a sec. Find some seats and I'll get the drinks.'

Henry staggered under the weight of the unstable load and edged round the crowd to find a table.

Inside the tavern was like nothing Henry had ever seen, or heard for that matter. The room was alive with the jabber of people talking, or laughing, or arguing loudly and waving their arms about. Bodies occupied every conceivable space; a sea of happy smiling mouths, which only occasionally ceased their stream of constant chatter to wrap lips about frothing tankards of ale. It seemed to Henry that every person in that large room was making a noise of some sort and the racket was almost unbearable. It reminded him a bit of his brothers' last birthday party, which had been bedlam. The musty aroma of fresh sawdust soaked with spilt ale hung in the air as he pressed his way through the chaotic crowd and found a space on the end of a bench that could fit two people, as long as they were small.

He poured the books on to a reasonably dry spot on the table and sat nervously waiting to be asked in no uncertain terms to leave.

'Two ginger ales!' D.C. shouted after ten minutes or so, slamming the cups down and squeezing in beside him on the bench.

She lifted up one mug and drank deeply before plonking it back down and grinning at Henry. Henry looked at his own drink. The frothy topping reminded him of dirty socks bubbling away in detergent on the stove. He hoped it wouldn't taste as bad as it looked, but as he drew the mug towards his lips the pungent aroma of ginger that barged its way up his nostrils set his taste buds watering. He drank feeling the heat spread as golden liquid fizzed under his tongue. Gulping greedily the fluffy head on top of the drink spilled from the corners of his mouth in rivulets that met in a mini fountain off his chin.

'Hits the spot, huh?'

Henry nodded enthusiastically and some of the bubbles escaped through his nose.

D.C. laughed as Henry coughed and spluttered into his sleeve. 'So, what brought you to G.D.E. then H?'

'G.D.E.?' Henry said, recovering his composure and making a mental note never to gulp ginger ale again.

'Gorman Dizing Enterprises? Blimey H, anyone would think tonight was a complete surprise for you.' She laughed, sipping her drink.

'Oh, right. Sorry ... yes. I just wanted to learn magic. I've always wanted to really, as long as I can remember.'

'Me too.' D.C. grinned, then a shadow cast across her expression and she looked seriously at him over the rim of her cup. 'Though I'm not sure how much we'll learn there.'

'Why not? The wand project?'

'Exactly! I've been doing a bit of reading, you know, to get ahead of the game? I'm sure I read that the only wood you can make a wand out of comes from an enchanted forest which, as the old battle-axe pointed out, was burned into extinction a hundred years ago. I can't remember all the details but it has something to do with the magic-absorbent properties of its bark.'

'Pardon me. Hello?' A smart-looking man sitting opposite was leaning across the heavily stained table, apparently addressing them. 'Far be it from me to barge in on a private conversation,' he said with the air of a man who did so frequently, 'I couldn't help but overhear. The tree you are thinking of, young Miss, is the Malvern tree; so named after one of the greatest wizards ever to walk this sweet earth. He was first to discover the magic-retaining properties of the bark, but was tragically killed not long after during benchmarking tests for the magneto spell; crushed between a large Malvern trunk and a blacksmith's anvil from three-hundred yards away. Such a tragedy.'

'Exactly!'

D.C.'s excitement caused the smart-looking man to glow and he stretched his hand out magnanimously. 'Doctor Hyperbole, at your service. I have written many classic tomes describing the mysterious art of magic. Perhaps you've read them?'

Henry felt irked by the smug tone in his voice, but the doctor didn't need any encouragement from him. D.C.'s reaction fed his ego quite sufficiently for both of them.

'Doctor Hyperbole? I don't believe it! I must have read every one of your books three times over! Here, will you sign my copy of Quantum Numerology?' D.C. was rummaging frantically through one of her bags.

Doctor Hyperbole, clearly delighted with this turn of events, glowed even more smugly.

'We've just started at G.D.E. We're going to be wizards too!' D.C. was beside herself with enthusiasm and Henry felt it rubbing off on him.

'So I heard,' the doctor rounded off his signature with a flamboyant swish and returned the book to its owner, 'which is why I feel compelled – nay, duty bound – to show you this.' He reached inside his jacket and pulled out a small brown bottle with a very grandiose label on it stating;

*Doctor Hyperbole's Memory Magic. *74 Patents Pending**

'You're very lucky to have met me tonight as stocks are dwindling fast, but I always carry a couple of spare bottles in my jacket,' he tapped his right lapel confidentially as he spoke, 'in case of emergencies just like this,' he added with a gracious nod to his audience of two.

D.C. took the little bottle reverently and turned it over in her hands as Doctor Hyperbole continued his sales-pitch. 'An invaluable aid to anyone embarking on an educational journey. No more cramming revision leading up to an exam. Put an end to desperate rifling through long-winded textbooks to find that gem of knowledge that's been eluding you. Just take one drop, orally, before each class, and you'll remember every single word that was said. Forever! But you must act fast! Little point in bolting the stable door after the horse has fled, so to speak.' He paused, allowing the impact of this statement to have its full effect, then; 'There are, of course, many other uses for this miracle elixir, several of which have been published in the recent editions of *The Complete Book of*

*Practical Spells and Incantations, Volume 2,* and *Professor Blanco's Idiots' Guide to Popular Wizarding.*'

If this was supposed to impress Henry, it didn't. But he supposed this had more to do with the fact he'd never heard of the books rather than the unimpressive-ness of the fact. D.C., he noticed, was so impressed she was practically drooling.

'So, how many bottles would you like?' Doctor Hyperbole unleashed his most winning smile on the young companions across the table and waited for a response.

'Wow, it certainly sounds like it could be useful. What you think, H?'

D.C. was cradling the little bottle in her hands as if it were a bird. Henry, however, was sceptical. He was certainly no scientific genius, but he felt sure a person's brain would quickly fill up with rubbish and have no space left for the important stuff if Doctor Hyperbole's potion were allowed to do as described.

'How much is it?' he asked to be polite.

Confident he was on the doorstep of a sale, Doctor Hyperbole redirected his carefully crafted smile so that it hit Henry with full force. 'Ahhh, what you must first ask yourself my little friend, is how much is it worth to you?'

Henry did so, but since he had no idea whether the potion would work, the exercise proved to be rather fruitless. He blinked and continued to look at the doctor.

'I see you're overwhelmed with the possibilities lad, and that's only to be expected. But it's my pleasure to inform you that I can let you have that bottle for an introductory offer of ...' Doctor Hyperbole's eyes flitted over his potential customers, appraising them for wealth and gullibility, then he lowered his voice and leant towards them conspiratorially, 'of just seventy-five shebbles.'

'*Seventy-five shebbles!?* That's outrageous!' Henry's comment left his mouth rather louder than he'd intended and people on the adjacent tables looked over to see what was happening.

Doctor Hyperbole blushed and snatched the bottle back from D.C. 'Or you can just waste my time. Genius doesn't come cheap you know?' He sat there for a moment, glaring at them. When no obvious signs of remorse were forthcoming he got stiffly to his feet, stuffed the bottle back beneath his right lapel and levelled a quite different expression on the pair across the table. 'Well, I can see I am dealing with the ignorance of youth so I won't take offence at such a tawdry exchange. I was merely attempting to do you a favour.' Still no-one made a move for their money pouch so he continued in a sulky voice; 'I'll bid you good evening then, and good luck with your mediocre lives.' He sniffed once, to punctuate the statement, and then turned on his heel and stalked out of the door.

'Wow, tetchy,' D.C. said in astonishment as she watched him go.

'Oh dear. I really put my foot in it.' Henry's face was hot with embarrassment and he could sense the curious onlookers whispering to each other scandalously about the scene.

'Don't worry,' said D.C. 'There's no way either of us could afford that price. Besides, I'm not sure I want to remember every single mind-numbing word that Mrs Don will speak over the next six weeks; forever!' Henry smiled at her rather comical impression of the doctor's sales-pitch, and the tension was broken.

They drank a bit more ginger ale and Henry felt the tension of the day ease out of his shoulders. Then he remembered his stealthy escape from his bedroom and began contemplating the climb back up. It gave him an uneasy feeling.

'So, your parents don't mind you taking up magic then?' he asked D.C. 'And not going into the family business?'

She snorted a laugh into her mug and ginger ale splashed up her nose. 'Goodness me, no. They have no idea. I told them I was taking a weaving class. I guess they just assumed I meant baskets rather than spells.'

Henry laughed. 'You're a sneaky one, aren't you? I wouldn't have the guts to lie. I think my face would give me away instantly anyway.'

'It's not exactly a lie,' she defended slyly. 'But I've found that being sparing with the facts can often work in your favour. People hear what they want to hear, as long as you don't give them too much detail.'

Henry mulled this over and filed it away in his brain under 'strategies to try sometime'.

'Come on,' D.C. said, glugging down the last of her drink, 'we'd better get out of here. I have get my little sisters dressed for school in the mornings and they get up at ridiculous o'clock. I guess you have work too, right?'

Henry nodded gratefully and downed his own drink, then helped D.C. stack the books a bit more stably in her arms.

Outside he took a deep breath of cleansing fresh air. He'd begun to feel a little light-headed sitting in that stuffy bar, and his brain welcomed the sudden flood of cool oxygen. He was glad he'd finally stepped through those mysterious glowing doors, but didn't really care much for the pungent odour it had left clinging to his jacket and the inside of his nostrils.

'Well, I guess I'll see you on Thursday night?' D.C. was grinning at him through the moonlit darkness.

'I guess so. Thanks for the drink.'

Henry had no idea if he would actually see D.C. at his next class, since he felt sure the un-dealt-with application form might not be so inconspicuous if he tried slip past Mrs Don's registration scroll again. He had a feeling they'd bump into each other though. After all, they were going to be students at the same night school, and Terratonia wasn't such a big place at the end of the day. He smiled warmly over his shoulder and waved at D.C. as she trotted off down the street towards home.

# Chapter 5

The next morning, Henry woke early. His head was still buzzing with the previous night's events, and he was eager to get to the castle and discuss them Halcyon. He sloshed cold water on to his face, scrubbing vigorously to expel the last clinging shadows of sleep, and then jogged downstairs for breakfast.

His mother was already in the kitchen, busying herself with the preparation of the first meal of the day, and making an incredible racket with the banging and clashing of pots and pans while she was about it.

'Morning,' Henry greeted her somewhat warily.

Silence, save for the invigorated rough handling of kitchenware.

Anyone who has ever found themselves on the receiving-end of a mother's scorn, no matter how unwittingly, will instantly recognise this kind of frosty reception as cause for concern. Henry tensed as a battered old frying pan took umbrage at the unsolicited abuse and leapt off its shelf in protest. He winced as it clattered noisily to the floor. Slowly, his mother turned to face him, her face pulled into a taut expression.

'And where were you last night?'

'Uhm.' His cheeks burned. 'In my room?' The lie came out like a question and he realised instantly from the expression on her face his mother was having no truck with it.

'Oh, so now you're lying to me as well?' Rage coloured her own cheeks.

'I ... no. I'm sorry. I, I just went for a walk.'

'For a walk? Through the window?'

Henry sat at the table and folded his hands contritely in in lap. 'Sorry.' He didn't really know what else to say and readied himself for the onslaught.

'Henry! Look at me ... have you any idea how worried I was?'

Henry gulped.

'First I go upstairs to check on you. Actually to apologise because I realised it was probably the twins who had started it and I'd been a bit hard on you. Gone!' His mother threw her hands up as if vanishing her son into thin air. Her expression turned intense and she leant on the table putting her face close to his. 'First your father and then you. That's what I thought all evening as I paced and worried and worried and paced. You've NEVER done anything like this before, Henry. I thought you'd been kidnapped and murdered and every imaginable kind of danger that could fly in through the window in the dead of night!'

Henry's heart sank as he realised how she must have been going out of her mind.

Her face still close to his, she sniffed the air suspiciously. 'Is that beer?' She stood bolt upright, her expression morphing from concern to outrage as she grabbed his arm and brought it to her nose so she could smell his jacket. She tossed his arm aside in disgust and planted hands on hips in total disbelief. 'It is! I smell beer on you! Did you go to the tavern?'

The look on her face told Henry there was little point in denying it. Mothers have a nasty habit of being able to smell a lie even better than they can smell stale ale. He dropped his gaze to the floor and watched his feet scuffing nervously from side to side.

'I ... I didn't drink. Well, only a ginger ale,' he offered lamely. During the silence that followed, Henry's cheeks turned the heat up three more notches, brightening his face to a burning guilty red. 'Sorry,' he mumbled again finally, unable to bear the stony silence.

His mother sighed and shook her head. 'I just don't know what to do with you boys any more. You need a father figure to guide you, damn it! How am I supposed to cope with all this?' She was becoming hysterical now, and Henry rose and took a few tentative steps towards her, hands outstretched as if to reassure a cornered animal.

'Mum! Mum I'm sorry.' She was crying now and Henry felt tears welling up in his own eyes. 'I hated it in the tavern. I promise I'll never go back there. Please, don't cry.'

Will and Bill had been roused by the commotion and made their way blearily into the room. Seeing the younger boys standing wide-eyed in the doorway his mother seemed to pull herself together. She blew her nose into a dishcloth and threw it carelessly on to a pile of dirty laundry in the corner.

'Well, I hope not Henry, I hope not.' Her tone softened as she saw how devastated Henry was at having made her cry. 'Listen love, I know you miss your father. We all do. When those ... those outlaws attacked him and poor Mr Colloid, they stole a lot more than gold.'

Bill sniffled from the doorway and Will elbowed him half-heartedly in the ribs.

Henry was reminded again of the night the messenger had come.

The Chief Accountant and his senior assistant had been a couple of hours into their journey through the dense forest between Terratonia and the Ribald mountain range, heading for the narrow passage that leads to the coast. According to a stricken Mr Colloid, who'd arrived back on foot, scratched and bedraggled late that evening, they'd been ambushed by criminals of undistinguished origin. The horses had panicked and fled in different directions, Mr Colloid tumbling off his mount as it ploughed through a tangle of grip-weed. He had never seen Ernst or the satchel of gold he was carrying again. In the weeks that followed the town's people had searched and searched for the missing Chief Accountant. With every empty knock on the door, another messenger brought news of nothing to report. Henry had watched his mother crumple further and further in on herself, just like she was doing now.

'Your father is gone,' she sighed eventually. 'We have to accept it, and deal with it the best we can.' She seemed to be lecturing herself more than anything now, and went back to absently gathering up the dishes for breakfast. 'Just please, try to stay out of trouble and never, *ever*, go running off like that without telling me again.'

'I know, mother. I won't. I promise.'

• • •

Across the other side of town at Gorman Dizing Enterprises corporate headquarters, a squat man with a squat face was sifting doggedly through a mountain of parchment-work. He gave each tattered piece a cursory scan before tossing it on to one of the haphazard piles growing on the desk in front of him.

'Here you are Curly, more cannon-fodder for the corporate machine.'

He flung Henry's application form across the bench to another stout man, with exceptionally straight hair.

'Aye.' Curly caught the slip of parchment and without even looking at it stamped it with big red letters declaring: CREDIT APPROVED.

...

Up at the castle an hour or so later, Henry rapped the knocker on the door that led into Halcyon's chambers. When the old man opened it he found a very excited young accountant standing in front of him. Henry wore a big, proud smile that stretched clear across his cheeks, threatening to push his ears right off the sides of his face. Halcyon took a step back and gestured for his animated visitor to enter.

'Well, don't we look pleased with ourselves this morning. Tea?'

Henry could barely contain himself. He'd had to sit sombre and remorseful through a most uncomfortable breakfast while his mother continued to lecture about the evils of drinking and gadding about late at night. He brushed aside such negative thoughts and plonked himself down in a chair by the table.

'Yes please ... two lumps,' he managed to squeeze out through his lunatic smiling lips.

Halcyon took an excruciating amount of time to fill two delicate teacups with steaming hot liquid. Henry had time to wonder whether D.C.'s family had made them. At last the cups were full, and Halcyon plopped two little rocks of sugar in each before settling back into his familiar old armchair.

'OK then, spill the potatoes. What's been happening in your world, Henry?'

'Well ...' Henry was breathless with excitement, 'you know how I'm always going on at you to teach me magic?'

Halcyon nodded pleasantly as he sipped his tea.

'And you know how you're always telling me that an opportunity will present itself, if that's the course I'm fated to take?'

Halcyon continued nodding and sipping.

'Well ...' Henry paused for effect. 'It happened!'

Halcyon's right eyebrow decided to liven up the placid expression on his face by raising itself in a quizzical arch, so Henry began regaling the story of the previous night's events with gushing enthusiasm. As he did, however, the expression of agreeable interest Halcyon's face had been wearing began to transform into a look of deep concern. At the mention of 'Gorman Dizing Enterprises', and the subsequent description of Mrs Don's wand-making assignment, his right eyebrow threw in the towel on its quizzical stance and opted to join the left eyebrow in creasing a deep furrow into the old man's forehead.

It wasn't until Henry had finished telling his tale that he noticed the disturbance on the old face opposite him. 'What's wrong?'

'I've heard this name, Gorman Dizing before,' Halcyon mused, 'and it's always connected with trouble.'

Henry's cheeks flushed with guilt as he remembered his promise to his mother to stay out of trouble, but Halcyon was too lost in his own contemplative thoughts to notice his companion's discomfort.

'And this business about collecting a meaningful twig, supposedly to make a wand? What utter codswallop!'

Halcyon paused, rubbing his scratchy old chin, so Henry chanced a question. 'What do you mean? Why is it codswallop? I don't even know what codswallop is to be honest.'

It was as if Henry's question had crept round the back of Halcyon's chair and jabbed him in the behind with a fork.

'Trash, twaddle, balderdash, bunk!' he burst out. 'You cannot make a wand out of just any old stick! Sticks, by their very nature, are good at being one thing only; and that's a stick! Unless of course we're talking about a stick from the Malvern tree, in which case it's possibly more unlike a stick than anything else it is not like! Do you see?'

Henry didn't see. He didn't see at all. But he knew about the tree that Halcyon was referring to. 'Uhm, I think so. The Malvern tree is the one with magic absorbing bark, right?'

Halcyon's eyebrows leapt up in unified surprise at his young friend's startling knowledge.

'That's right! And any fool knows you can't go making something out of nothing. So only a piece of wood from the Malvern tree will do if you want to create a wand. How did you know that?'

Henry wasn't sure he *had* known it, but gave the old man a quick synopsis of his interchange with Doctor Hyperbole in the tavern anyway.

'Hmm,' Halcyon mused when he'd finished. His tone was that of someone considering a delinquent youth who was bound to end up in trouble one day. 'A harmless enough wizard and he has some good ideas. Although I fear he is driven by profit and greed a lot of the time. Hardly in the spirit of good magic.' The old wizard tutted. 'Well, anyway,' he continued, 'there's little doubt that something very fishy is going on in that big, expensive building, so I suggest you steer well clear of Gorman Dizing Enterprises in future Henry.'

Henry blinked in disbelief. This was intolerable. It seemed the whole day people had been throwing water on his parade. First his mother and her fit about the tavern; and now Halcyon was telling him that he shouldn't attend the night classes he so desperately needed. And it wasn't even eight o'clock yet. He rounded on the old man, taking him by surprise.

'Now hang on a minute! You've been fobbing me off for years with your prophecies about being given the chance to become a wizard if it's written in the stars. "You'll know when the time is right Henry," you said. "There'll be a sign you can't ignore," you said. Well this is it! Talk about being hit in the face by a flying brick. Surely it doesn't get much more obvious than this? I AM READY TO LEARN ABOUT MAGIC! And I'm going to go to these night classes, with or without your support!'

Once he'd finished his outburst, even Henry was a little taken-aback.

Halcyon regarded him grimly. 'Your time will come, if it's meant. But *this* is not it.'

'But you say that every time! Why isn't this it? Why can't this be my time? Why don't you want me to learn about magic?' Henry punctuated each sentence with a balled fist on the table, making the tea cups dance.

'Look, don't be such a hot-headed fool, Henry. I'm not saying you can't learn about magic, but I don't think these people will be teaching you about magic. At least, not the right kind of magic.'

Henry recalled how D.C. had voiced a similar set of concerns. 'Then *you* teach me the right kind, Halcyon. *You*. I'll just die if I have to wait any more.'

'We've been through this before Henry. I don't take apprentices any more. Not after those scurrilous yobs threw eggs at me at the town fair. I gave up on people then, the way they gave up on me.'

The old man looked suddenly worn out and Henry's voice softened sympathetically. 'But I'm not *people* Halcyon. Have I ever disrespected you or not done as you've asked?'

'Until today, no.'

Halcyon's voice was defiant, but Henry thought he sensed the glimmering of contemplation, so he ploughed on hopefully.

'Then why give up on me? I *need* this Halcyon. I'm dying down there in the vault. Please … if the classes I've signed up for are altogether wrong, teach me the altogether right way. Help me become a good and honourable wizard like you.'

For a moment their eyes locked, and Henry could almost feel the old man's gnarly fingers working their way across the surface of his brain, like a hand grappling along the seam of a bag in search of some unseen trinket. Eventually Halcyon broke the stare and Henry remembered to breathe again. The wizard rose awkwardly from his chair and shuffled over to the window. He looked out wistfully.

'It's going to be hard work. Magic isn't all glamour and glitz you know?'

Henry couldn't believe his ears. After years of trying to persuade the old man to impart his wizardly knowledge Henry had finally hit the jackpot. He leapt up from his chair and rushed over to where Halcyon stood.

'I'm not afraid of hard work. You know I'm not. I'll be the best wizard's apprentice the world has ever seen. I'll make you so proud of me. Oh Halcyon, do you really mean it? Do you? Will you really teach me magic?'

Halcyon turned slowly, his face now filled with a gravity that hissed on the heat of Henry's excitement like cold water on a frying pan.

'This is no cause for celebration Henry. I do not undertake this responsibility lightly. There will be many dangers strewn in your path once you step along the road towards magic, and I cannot always be there to protect you.' Once again their eyes were locked, only this time Henry could feel the warmth of the old man's feelings for him filling up his soul. Halcyon smiled, and then placed a gentle hand on his shoulder as he ambled past towards one of the inner rooms of the chambers. 'But I can at least equip you with some of the more appropriate tools of the trade. Wait here while I see if I can find the right box.'

Henry stared after him, his curiosity peaking when he heard the banging and clattering of many falling objects coming from behind the door. It soon became clear that an almighty hunt was taking place next door, as the skirmish of riffling through boxes was punctuated with the odd, cryptic comment.

'No ... not there ... Ah, that's where you've been hiding, I'll deal with you later ... No, not that one ... Ouch! Was that really necessary? ... Ah-ha! Got you ...'

Halcyon returned and triumphantly handed a long, thin box to his eagerly waiting apprentice. It was perfectly smooth; made of hard, dark wood, and Henry could've sworn he felt it shiver as he ran his fingers along one polished surface.

He looked up at Halcyon, his eyes flooded with gratitude. 'Thank you. What does it do?'

'Tsk, not the box. Inside it, Henry. Look inside it.'

Henry returned his attention to the box and noticed a tiny clasp hiding along one long, thin edge. He slid his thumb across it and the lid jumped up, then came to rest not-quite-back as it was. The box shivered more urgently, as if some ancient spirit inside had just had its first whiff of freedom in a millennium. Henry pushed the dislodged edge of the box up and his eyes widened as they took in a long, thin, black stick. It was polished to a brilliant sheen and lay innocently on a swathe of lush, purple velvet. With a great deal of effort, he tore his eyes away from this glistening treasure to meet those of his mentor once more.

'Is it a wand? A real wand?'

'That it is, young Henry.' By now Henry's eyes had dragged themselves back to stare at the box and were greedily caressing the foot-long stick, so he set his ears the task of keeping up with what Halcyon was saying. 'It's *your* wand now. And one of the few true available wands left in circulation, so I believe. Guard it with your life for they have a nasty habit of going missing, though heaven knows why. If you lose it there will be no replacement as the enchanted forest from which it came was tragically ...'

'Burnt down a hundred years ago,' Henry finished for him.

The old man's eyebrows bobbed up in surprise once more. 'That's right. You really have been doing your research, haven't you?'

He sounded impressed so Henry decided not to disappoint him by explaining it was D.C. that had done all the research.

'No-one knows how or why the fire started. But until another source of Malvern wood is found, and many greater men than me continue to search, there will be no more magic wands.' Henry's gaze was starting to drift back to the box and Halcyon touched him lightly on the forearm to anchor his focus. 'And never, ever give your wand to untrained hands. It's one of the most important rules we have. Magic is like a wild animal and the wand, its harness. In untrained hands the beast can turn, or break free completely and then you're in trouble. Just how much trouble will depend on magic's mood.'

Henry nodded seriously and looked at the wand. Just a stick. A shiny black stick. Henry knew it was impossible, but it definitely felt like it was grinning at him. He reached inside the box and trailed his fingers down the length of it. They tingled pleasantly. The stick was tapered and he slid his thumb under the thicker end. It seemed to hop into his palm and he curled his fist slowly closed.

Without warning Henry was overcome by a powerful burst of energy, which felt as though it connected the very core of his being to the furthest tip of the stick with explosive electricity. The wand whooshed uncontrollably upwards. Henry's hand and arm could do nothing but follow obediently in its wake, and it was only the weight of his body that prevented his head and shoulders from doing the same. He hung helplessly off the end of the quivering wand.

'Oh dear, still charged is it? How careless of me.' Halcyon was reaching forward to unwind his new student's death-grip from around the harmless-looking stick. Once the wand was tucked safely back into the box he looked at the stunned accountant and added apologetically; 'One should always discharge a wand of any potent magical properties before putting it into long-term storage. There you are, your first lesson, well learned I think.'

'Wha ... wha ... wha ...' Henry spluttered, still reeling.

'Oh, you'll be learning all about that soon enough young man. One step at a time, eh? First we'll have to get you a few things,' Halcyon continued, warming to his new role as benevolent mentor. 'Grab a quill and some parchment Henry, I want you to jot down some notes.'

The list went on and on, and whilst Henry was fascinated by the incredible sounding shopping-list he was scribing, he was beginning to feel uneasy about the impending hour of his work.

'One set of magical robes; entry-level. They're a bit scratchy but you'll get used to them. One tall pointy hat ... size three I think. One disappearing text book; that's a book with disappearing text rather than a disappearing book for text. One small multi-channel cauldron – I think eight segments will be enough to start with. It took me years to admit that those things were worthwhile, now I can't imagine life without one. They work just like a normal cauldron, only divided into a number of smaller segments, depending on the size of your bowl, with a stand running right down the centre so that you can just plug your wand in to charge it up with multiple potents at once, do you see? It's really incredibly convenient when you think how it used to be, messing about with lots of individually prepared cauldrons of spells. Now, where were we?'

# Chapter 6

After that day, time went by in a blur of activity that shifted between memorising lengthy texts describing ancient magical rituals; traipsing all over the countryside collecting herbs and unusual talismans for preparing magical potents; and scurrying through the empty corridors of the castle trying not to be late for work. Henry felt as though he was trying to share eight slices of time-cake with a hungry rabble of thirteen bodies of responsibility. But he wasn't about to give up, no matter how hard it became.

After he'd been studying with the old wizard for about a week, he'd received a letter from Gorman Dizing Enterprises finance department, informing him of their gracious acceptance of his application for credit. It instructed him to bring the enclosed registration document along to the *Sorcerer's Apprentice induction lecture* the following Tuesday night at eight. Henry wondered briefly how D.C. was getting along as he crumpled the useless pieces of parchment into a tight ball and tossed them into the bin by his desk.

To cope with the time management issue he had devised quite a routine. He would get up even earlier than before, sometimes as early as five o'clock, and rush downstairs to make breakfast before the rest of his family had arisen. By the time his brothers had dragged themselves out of their pits and down into the belly of the house, he was usually on his way out of the front door, kissing his mother lightly on the cheek as he went. This extra-early morning activity had caused a few eyebrows to be raised in the Noble household, but he'd explained it away with an almost-truth about some additional studies at the castle that would facilitate advancing his career. Taking a leaf out of D.C.'s book, he'd left out the bit about *which* career, but his mother, who was probably just relieved he wasn't out drinking every night, had seemed satisfied.

'I'm so proud of you Henry. Your father would have been ... well, he will be ...' Her words drifted off as her heart wrestled again with the idea that her mind was starting to file Ernst away under 'history'.

Once he was safely inside Halcyon's chambers he would disappear into an untidy back room to put on his rough blue robes and jam the tall pointy hat on top of his head. Then, dressed and ready for action, he would admire his reflection briefly in the long mirror hanging on the wall before returning to the main chamber to join Halcyon.

Henry remembered the first time he'd put on his wizardly garb. He'd been none-too-impressed at the start. The robe, being made of pure, unlined wool, was intolerably scratchy. It was also far too long for Henry (apparently they didn't make robes for such slightly built young accountants), so he had to hitch it up almost a foot-and-a-half with a leather belt at the waist. He looked more like a sack of apples than a wizard. On its own this wouldn't have been too bad, but then there was the hat. What was all that about? It made him look ridiculous. So he'd challenged Halcyon about the necessity for such an old-fashioned get-up in this modern day-and-age.

'Look, it's tradition. OK?' the old wizard had replied. 'If you don't wear those uncomfortable woollen robes you'll have nothing to look forward to when you become a fully qualified wizard, other than the obvious benefits of knowing lots of powerful spells to fight evil and enhance your quality of life, of course.

'But why the robe at all? Can't I just wear my normal clothes?' Henry was plucking at the spiky cloth cinched in tight at his hips.

'Trust me Henry, the robe is an essential. First of all, for recognition. A good wizard only uses magic as a last resort, and if the bad guys can't see you're a wizard how are they to know they should surrender? Plus, if you do ever find yourself in a tight spot it's a lot easier to get your wand out of a specially tailored fold in your robes than an awkward little jacket pocket.'

Henry scratched his irritated armpit, eyeing Halcyon's slick, silken robes with envy.

'And the hat?" he muttered crossly. 'I mean, really. I look like I've just stepped out of a circus ring!'

'Only because of society's perception. Things have changed. Through all of this you must remember that, Henry. There was a time when that particular pointed accessory would have commanded a devastating amount of respect for its wearer; and with good reason too.'

'Oh, so it's like a status symbol is it? Kind of a "my hat's bigger than your hat" thing?' Henry straightened his back and stopped raking fingernails across his prickly ribcage so he could assume what he hoped was an imposing stance.

'No.' Halcyon looked at Henry like he was reconsidering the apprenticeship. 'It has a much more meaningful purpose than that, although it does make one easier to spot in a crowd it's true. The hat actually works as a hypostatic flux enhancer, affording a percentile increase in the wearer's potential for magic by the sum of the rim-circumference multiplied by the height of the total hat. It's not essential of course, but you'll never win a magical stand-off if you have a bare head, no matter how good you are.'

His words hit Henry like a barrage of illogical lemmings throwing themselves to their death in the raging torrent of his confusion. Halcyon noticed the young man's intellect was flailing so he threw it a flimsy rope of rationalisation.

'It's really very simple,' he lectured, snatching the hat off Henry's head and turning it over to illustrate. 'The inside of the cone is lined with an enchanted weave made mostly out of magnesium-phosphate and dragon-fly wings (only discarded ones, naturally), which once placed on the head of a person who is casting a spell, creates a powerful anti-stasism vortex, thereby increasing the brain's proactive-activity by an amount proportionate to the cubic volume of the cone. OK ...?'

Henry continued to look blank.

'Look, it works in exactly the same way as it would increase the volume of your voice were you to snip off the tip of the hat and put the resulting hole up to your mouth before you spoke.' The old wizard held the conical hat to his lips like a trumpet to demonstrate.

The penny was finally dropping inside Henry's whirling head.

'Oh ... like a brain-power magnifier then?'

Halcyon sighed deeply. 'If you must, yes. Like a brain-power magnifier. Now can we move on?'

The robes still itched like crazy and the hat, once removed, left an explosion of melon-shaped hair bouncing about on top of his head for almost half the morning. But when he was wearing them now, he felt like a wizard; and never more so than when he was casting a spell.

Henry remembered the first day he'd done that more clearly than any other event in his life so far. It had been during the second week of his studies with the old magician, the first week having been devoted entirely to basic theory and boring lectures about health and safety.

'OK,' Halcyon had said after Henry had completed a particularly nasty multiple-choice test about the magical properties of a bushwinkle fruit. 'I think you're ready to move on young man. Go and fetch your wand will you?'

On hearing this Henry jerked his head up in total surprise. He hadn't been allowed to even touch the wand since it had first sent its supernatural energy surging through his veins. To be perfectly honest he'd been dying to give it a proper test drive. Well now, apparently, that day had arrived. He dashed into the little back room where he kept all his stuff to retrieve the long wooden box.

When he returned he found Halcyon seated at the solid old oak table by the window, brushing great mushrooming plumes of dust from the covers of a huge, ancient book the like of which Henry had never seen before. The binding was of tattered and faded red leather, with broken gold lettering embossed across the front saying;

*The Complete Book of Practical Spells and Incantations, Volume 2.*

He sat silently in the chair opposite the old man, coughing slightly as an unruly crowd of dust particles made their way up his nostrils and tickled the back of his throat. Halcyon thumbed busily down the index at the back of the book and finally found the page number he was looking for.

'Ah! There you are!' He flipped the book open towards the middle and began riffling the bottom corners of the pages, counting them away in blocks until he found the right one. 'Three-thousand eight-hundred and fourteen, here we are. Perfect!'

He looked up at his wide-eyed student and spun the book around so that Henry could read the text.

*The Lifting Charm: This class fifteen spell can be used to facilitate the lifting and carrying of objects otherwise too heavy to be moved by hand.*

'All spells are classified according to their power-rating,' Halcyon explained as Henry took in the details of the enchantment. 'From the most harmless and well-meaning ones like this at class fifteen, all the way up to a life-threatening or death-defying hex at level one. But we won't be moving on to those until I know you can shoot straight.'

Henry read down the list of ingredients that went into making up the potent.

*Essential Ingredients;*

*1 cup, limp-weed extract*

*1 grain, feather salt*

*1 generous sprig, garden parsley*

He looked up at his mentor, eager to begin.

'Now,' said Halcyon matter-of-factly. 'I've prepared your wand for you ahead of time; we can worry about the charging process at a later date. Have you been doing your daily meditation exercises? Otherwise you're in for another rough ride at the hands of your wand I fear.'

Henry nodded vigorously. He'd followed every one of Halcyon's instructions to the letter, from the day they'd first started out on this adventure. He meant to keep his promise of being the best wizarding apprentice the world had ever seen.

'Good. Well, those exercises should help bring the powers of your mind and spirit into tune with the magic inside your wand, rather than the two forces simply colliding with each other willy-nilly; which is, I think, what you experienced before.'

'Willy-nilly. Right.' Henry was still nodding.

Halcyon frowned. 'When you grasp the wand remember to relax and breathe evenly. Don't fight it Henry, your magic will naturally want to merge with the wand so just let it flow freely from your body.'

'*My* magic?' Henry was concerned. He'd never done anything magical in his life. What if he didn't have any in him? 'From *my* body?' he looked down at his slim body swamped in deep blue material.

'Well, of course from your body, boy. How else did you think it was coming? By carrier pigeon from Bankerloo Bay?'

'I, I thought the ingredients? You know the limp-weed and parsley?'

'Who ever heard of magical parsley?' Halcyon scoffed. 'No, no boy. The potent merely *flavours* the magic so that it behaves in a certain way. It forms the magic from inside you into a spell; which are both entirely different things incidentally. It's surprising how few people know that.'

'What if I don't have any? I never felt any magic in me before, Halcyon.'

'We all have it, Son. Every living creature does; apart from those who forgot it, but we'll cover that later. Wizards of old had to soak rocks in their potents to absorb the spell casting properties, and then toss them at a target to cast it. That was a violent period in wizarding history, I can tell you. The discovery of the Malvern tree made things a lot more civilised, and safer for all concerned.'

'I can imagine.'

'Once you are holding the wand and it has settled down, you must try to connect with its energy and let your magic flow gently out through your fingertips, whereupon it will travel along the length of your wand towards the tip, gathering the properties it requires to turn it into a spelling force as it goes. Then do exactly like you've been practising with the wooden spoon; flip the ball of magic towards the subject of your spell.'

Henry glanced down at the box nervously, recalling the overwhelming burst of energy that had racked his body last time he'd picked up the wand. He tried to relate that experience to the relaxing sequence of breathing and flipping exercises he'd been practising whilst gripping the handle of one of his mother's wooden spoons.

Noticing his look of concern Halcyon placed a soothing hand on his forearm.

'Don't worry. I've discharged all the magical potency that was left in the wand from before. There's only a tiny portion of lifting charm ingredients soaked into the bark now, so the worst it can do is stick something quite light up on the ceiling for a while. Just try to avoid anything shiny. There's a different casting action if you want to mark a target with a reflective surface.'

Somewhat reassured, Henry reached forward and slipped the tiny clasp on the side of the box across. Like before, invisible hinges made the box-lid jump up on one side, so he inserted his finger and tipped it all the way open. The highly polished Malvern stick was lying on its plush velvet bed, looking all innocent. He paused for a moment, going through the calming breathing exercises Halcyon had taught him. As he sucked air in an out in long easy sighs he began to feel a faint tingling sensation starting in the tips of his fingers. Once he felt a little steadier, Henry slowly curled the fingers of his right hand around the thicker end of the stick. The instant his fingers closed on the wand he felt that sickening rush of power connecting his stomach to the wand. It was like taking the reins of a headstrong stallion. Henry's brain started filtering through these strange sensations trying to make sense of them, but it had been decades since the Malvern stick was last allowed to do its thing, so it wasn't feeling very patient. It jumped sharply out of the box and swung itself through the air until it was standing poised at a 45-degree angle to Halcyon. It hung in the air at the end of Henry's arm quivering with anticipation.

'OK,' soothed the old wizard, taking a nervous step backwards. 'That's OK. You're obviously still feeling a little tense, which is quite natural. You'll find that the little blighter will get easier and easier to handle the more you manage to relax. It can sense your nervousness, just like a horse will bolt with an unsteady rider if it has a mind to. It's a cheeky little wand that one, but I'm rather fond of it. Learn to be in control of it, Henry, and before you know it you'll be using it as if it were an extension of your own arm. Happy?'

Henry nodded vigorously again, forcing his breath to continue in long, rhythmic sighs as his heartbeat gradually slowed to a normal-ish pace. It was a good tussle, but eventually the wand had to admit that it couldn't actually do anything particularly magical without the help of a wizard, even a trainee wizard. In fact, if it were honest, it would have to confess that if Henry decided to uncurl his fingers right now, it would have no choice but to fling itself on to the ground with a clatter and lie there just being a stick. This decided, the pair of them relaxed a little. As they did, Henry became aware of a change in the sensation of electricity coursing through his body. The angry, excitable sizzle was becoming an exhilarating buzz somewhat similar to that which the butterflies in his stomach were prone to causing at moments of great excitement, only much more intense. He could practically feel the air about him fizzing as he continued to breathe deeply, willing the connection between himself and his wand to strengthen and become stable. Finally, he felt the wild, quivering thing in his hand begin to respond, allowing him to gently wave it about in the air from side to side as the unbroken stallion finally accepted its harness. Henry was mesmerised by its beauty. It really was a splendid looking stick. After a few moments Halcyon coughed politely, so Henry dragged his eyes away from it and looked expectantly up at him.

'OK. You two seem to be making friends. That's good. What I want you to do now is assume a steady position like this.' The wizard grabbed a fork from the table and held it out in front of him, planting his feet in a wide stance and raising his free arm out to the side for balance. He looked a bit like a fencer readying for a lunge.

Henry mimicked Halcyon's stance.

'Now, can you see the short verse printed just below the spell description? That's it. The words work like a mini-meditation, to help you focus your energy on the task at hand and to let your wand know what you're up to. It's a question of good manners as much as anything else, but also vital when you start storing the potents for more than one spell in a wand. You don't have to speak them out loud, though it might help the first few times you try it. But you and the wand are intrinsically linked now. As long as you stay in regular contact it will always know what you're thinking.'

Henry raised an eyebrow. He might have to start moderating his thoughts.

'Ideally you should be the only one to hold it from now on too. You'll find the bond between you grows stronger the more you get to know each other. Using another wizard's wand will not only confuse the poor little blighter, but in truth is rather impolite.'

Henry nodded sagely. There was no way anyone was taking this wand off him now.

'Right. Now, I want you to decide what you're going to lift. Perhaps one of the logs over there by the fireplace? When you're ready, begin to repeat the words of the incantation. You should see a small ball of yellow light gather about the tip of your wand. It'll take you longer to release the energy at first so don't worry if it doesn't seem to be working immediately, just keep going.'

Henry picked out one of the logs lying in a heap by the fire grate, then looked back down at the ancient lettering in the book and began to mumble the mystical words. At first nothing happened, but as he started to repeat the verse for the third time, Henry felt the tingling in his fingertips beginning to increase. The invisible bond between his hammering heart and the powerful stick seemed to be pulling itself taut, like the elastic of a sling-shot being readied for an attack. The wand quivered. A fourth time through the verse and the sensation in his fingers intensified, then his eyes widened incredulously as he saw impossibly fine drifts of light beginning to trickle out of the pores on the end of his fingers. Fine glowing white wisps licked their way up the sides of his wand gradually taking on a yellow hue as they neared the tip, where they tangled together to form a bright yellow ball of light. Henry blinked, just to make sure that it wasn't his imagination, and then looked back excitedly towards Halcyon, who nodded at his young apprentice approvingly.

'Very good Henry,' he encouraged. 'I've yet to see anyone master that art so quickly. You are a natural.'

This made Henry glow almost as brightly as the spell, which was now a tight ball of golden light about the size of a pea.

Halcyon watched his student proudly. 'Pretty soon you'll be releasing your magic so precisely that the spell will seem to pop into existence on the tip of the wand the moment you thought of it. Obviously very useful if you ever find yourself in a magical shoot out. I've seen many a powerful wizard brought down by lesser magic because they weren't quick enough on the draw. But again, that's all a long way down the line for you, my boy.'

Henry squinted at the pulsating yellow ball on his wand.

'Right,' said Halcyon stepping away from him. 'All you have to do now is fire it off towards the target. OK? Just a quick flick of the wrist, like I showed you with the wooden spoon.'

Henry turned his undivided attention towards the wand. He flipped his eyes towards the fireplace to sight the hapless log once more, and then jerked his hand forward with a flowing movement of the wrist, before snapping it sharply back. The ball of light remained resolutely clinging to the end of the stick. Henry frowned.

'Try again Henry, with a little more authority. You have to take control of the spell.'

Henry sighted the log across the room again then performed the flicking action with the business end of his wand. This time the yellow pea of light stretched out and away from the end of the wand for about an inch-and-a-half, before recoiling smartly back into place like a clingy child refusing to leave its mother's arms.

Again Henry frowned, winding himself up for a more vigorous third attempt to launch the spell. This time he succeeded, jerking his hand back with enough force to dislodge the glowing orb, which promptly fled away from the tip of the wand like a startled rabbit. Henry watched it go in wide-eyed amazement. He'd cast his very first spell and it felt great. There was no stopping him now.

There was no stopping the spell either, which Henry realised with some dismay had been knocked off target by the additional effort he'd used to release it. He watched apprehensively as the angry little pea of light streaked across the shadowy room towards the fireplace, unsure quite where it might end up. But the pea knew exactly where it was going. It went careering into a large brass plate resting against the wall, whereupon it rebounded and continued its careering path straight towards the old wizard by Henry's side.

'LOOK OUT!' Henry shouted as he realised where the light-ball was headed.

But Halcyon's arthritic old bones couldn't possibly move him fast enough to avoid the approaching spell. It hit him on his left hip with a billow of emerald cloth, before dissipating into his silky green robes with a shimmer. The robes, now enchanted by the magical properties of a lifting charm did exactly that; they lifted themselves smartly upwards and over the old man's head, floating away until they were pressed against the whitewashed expanse of the ceiling. Halcyon was left standing in the middle of the room wearing nothing but his faded red long-johns and a tall, pointy hat. Henry suppressed a snort of amusement and coaxed his face into a look of concern.

'Sorry,' he offered lamely.

'Hmmm, yes. Well your aim needs a little work, but the basic principles are in place. Now you can wipe that smirk off your face and get back into your ordinary clothing. Lessons for today are over. I need to find something clse to wear. It'll be a good ten minutes before that wretched spell has worn off and my robes come back down to earth.'

Five minutes later, Henry came back into the main chamber-room, buttoning up his sombre accountant's jacket and desperately trying to tame the explosion of hat-hair jiggling around on top of his head in a most un-accountant-like way. He was grinning from ear to ear as he approached the table where Halcyon sat wrapped in an old curtain, staring impatiently up at his bobbing robe.

'Wow! That was incredible! I could feel the power coming from right down deep inside me ... It was like ... it was like ...' Henry faltered, searching for the right analogy. 'Well, it was like nothing else on earth!'

'Yes, very astute,' Halcyon replied sarcastically, still miffed about his floating attire.

Henry admired the ancient spell book.

'So, when do I get one of those? A spell book?' he asked as casually as possible.

'Not for a very long time, Henry. You'll have to be proved fully proficient in the art of accurate spell casting before you can be granted access to such a powerful collection of potents and incantations. This book contains details of every magical discovery that there has ever been, as well as some very tasty recipes. There are exams to pass; you'll have to perform perfectly in your casting-test. Not to mention an intense psychological evaluation to make sure you're the right *sort*. You can't just get one of these things out of a Christmas cracker you know? Their distribution is regulated by very bureaucratic people. But we'll cover all that in the coming in weeks I'm sure,' Halcyon trailed away vaguely as he watched Henry run his fingers covetously over the tattered, dusty binding of the book.

'The spells in this book must be older than time itself,' he mused as he stroked it. 'Volume 2 … I wonder what volume it's up to now?'

'Volume 2,' Halcyon informed him matter-of-factly.

'But this book looks ancient. Surely there must have been new spells since it was made? What about all the modern discoveries in the world of spell casting? Doctor Hyperbole said that his memory enhancer had recently been included so I thought …'

'And it has," the old man interrupted. 'The publishers distribute regular update-spells to all of the registered owners on record, and the book re-writes itself. Ingenious when you think about it. Since the beginning of time there has only ever been one spell book, apart from that cheap and tacky 'idiots guide' thing by Blanco but I hardly think that counts. The insufferable old fool. Having just one spell book saves a lot of confusion, you know? And apart from anything else, it's great news for the trees, considering how many pages there are in a volume and how frequently magic changes.'

'Ah, but there must have been more than one spell book at one time. Otherwise why did they call it Volume 2?' Henry challenged, feeling quite pleased with himself.

'That's a misprint,' Halcyon countered simply, and at that moment the whitewashed ceiling finally gave up its hold on the silky emerald robes, and they flumped on to the floor in a crumpled heap.

# Chapter 7

There aren't many people who know how to distil the sap from a discarded feather until they're left with a fine, crystalline substance that can be ground down to make feather salt; a key ingredient in many of the popular spells in use today. In truth, there aren't that many people who would know how to get the sap out of a discarded feather in the first place. If you're sitting there thinking to yourself 'feathers have sap?' then join most of the rest of humanity in pleading complete and utter ignorance to the fact. Henry Noble knows. But after three-and-a-half months of intensive studies with the King's magical consort, Halcyon, there are a lot of strange things Henry Noble can boast he knows.

For example, he knows how to light a torch without any flames, or how to get water out of a stone by turning it into a glistening ball of ice before melting it. He also knows how to trap a rare semorphic-fly without even upsetting it, then delicately comb its tiny leg-hairs to extract the precious oil that's found on them; one of the essential components of any successful co-operative spell such as the *loose tongue hex* or the *compliancy curse*.

He also knows how to cast a semi-permanent *intellect deflector*, so that he can safely prepare his potents and recharge his wand in his bedroom without being rumbled by his brothers. This is one of Henry's favourite spells; so simple, yet so effective. It works to deflect the attention of prying eyes by conjuring an object of such fascination to the prier that they never even notice the thing you're concealing. They just stand there, ogling whatever object has been enchanted to enthral. Yet the moment they turn away to point out this amazing discovery to someone else, they instantly forget there's anything out-of-the-ordinary there to begin with. It wasn't an absolute guarantee of privacy; the higher the intellect of the observer the less chance it had to work. But it was certainly sufficient to bamboozle the quite simple minds of Henry's nosey brothers.

Another particularly useful spell when it came to 'brother management' was the tagging spell. It had been one of the first spells Halcyon had taught him, and by the look on the old man's face when he'd given his lecture, it was clear he'd had some considerable degree of satisfaction in using it throughout his unusual lifetime.

'I first learnt the tagging spell when I was at school. Very handy it was too, as I recall,' he'd said. 'You see, not only does the spell allow you to track any person or object that's blighted by it to the ends of the known earth – and possibly beyond, but nobody's had the chance to test that yet – but whenever your ill-fated subject approaches within twenty-or-so-feet of you, your wand will become most agitated.' At this, he'd chuckled to himself, obviously remembering some childish folly, and how utterly dumbfounded the teachers were to have been so unlucky when it came to catching the culprits red-handed.

So, the tagging spell had been one of the first of his newly acquired magical aids that Henry had put to practical use. Seeing the twins playing out in the garden he'd opened his bedroom window and jammed the pointy hat on his head ready to cast the spell. His first shot had been off target, hitting a tree, which wasn't much use to anyone since the tree clearly wasn't going to be going anywhere. But the next shot had been on target, slapping Bill squarely on the rump with a sharp slap. The startled lad had spun around, outraged, and promptly booted Will on the backside in reply. Will, understandably confused by this unprovoked attack, had decided to let the matter lie, but had launched himself at his twin in a full-on fury when he turned his back a moment later and felt the force of Henry's second tagging spell find its mark on the seat of his pants. The ensuing scrap had been a happy bonus, and now he was equipped a twenty-foot warning when either of his brothers was about.

All in all, Henry was rather pleased with his progress as a wizard's apprentice. It had taken a couple of weeks to fully master his rampant wand, but once he had, using it had become like operating his own hand. The magic for a spell now glided effortlessly out of his fingertips and along the length of the wand as soon as he started thinking the incantation, and it was resolving into a tight ball on the tip faster and faster the more he practised. He'd even managed to perfect the flicking and snapping action required to finally launch it. His aim still left a little to be desired, but that would come with practice so he'd been using every opportunity he could to disappear into the forest surrounding Terratonia and spend time turning colliwall-nuts into field mice and suchlike.

The opportunities to do this weren't as frequent as he'd have liked. This was partly down to how little free time he had and partly because since the school holidays started it had been harder and harder to shake off his brothers. With no homework tying them to the house they were becoming more and more curious about his mysterious trips into the forest. He could pull it off occasionally though, often with the aid of a cunning magical diversion such as a *scramble dew* spell cast on to a pair of shoelaces. This temporary spell made it impossible to keep anything tied, buying Henry a valuable few minutes to make good his escape.

On one such weekend towards the end of the holidays, Henry was strolling along the path that led out of town with his satchel stuffed full of all the usual trappings of magic admiring the late summer scenery as it flowed past him. Sensing the weather would soon be turning, the prolific cottonweed bush was spewing great billowing clouds of seedlings wrapped up in fluffy white coats across the rolling, golden fields. As he strolled, the flat open landscape surrounding the town was interrupted more frequently by bold clusters of trees wearing long white beards of cottonweed fluff. Before he even realised it, Henry was treading easily over the soft peaty soil of the forest floor.

'What a perfect day!' he said to the trees.

'Yes, isn't it?' came an unexpected reply.

Henry stopped in his tracks, not quite sure whether to believe his ears, which was a bit unfair given that they'd done such a diligent job up to now. There was a rustle in the undergrowth to his left and he whipped round to see a head pop up out of the top of a thick longwaddle bush.

'Hey! Oh my god. It's Henry isn't it?'

As the figure stood he recognised it immediately as the girl he'd met at Gorman Dizing Enterprises. It had been months since he'd seen D.C. and he felt such a pang of guilt at not following up on their budding friendship that he totally forgot to wonder why she was standing in a longwaddle bush.

'Hi D.C.' He waved awkwardly. 'How are you?'

'Oh, you know … Not too bad. Still breaking my mother's heart and my father's bank balance with all the pots I fumble in the workshop … I've often wondered what happened to you. Why didn't you come back to G.D.E.?'

Henry flushed. 'Oh, yes. Sorry not to get in touch with you about that. You see, I had second thoughts at the end of the day. The credit thing you know? Well, since I hadn't actually given in my registration documents I decided to pull out … if you see what I mean?' Henry clamped his mouth tight shut to prevent any more words tumbling out in a rush of remorse. He hoped that D.C. wouldn't press him further on the subject. He really was the most appalling liar. But it seemed his fears were unfounded, since he'd clearly hit a sore point with the young girl standing in the bush.

'Oh! Tell me about it! You're well out of it to be honest, H. The classes were a load of rubbish! I mean, most people seemed kinda satisfied by the end of the course. Though I think everybody was surprised at how little magic was involved in making magic. I'm not convinced myself. Seemed to me all they were teaching was cheap parlour tricks and basic illusions. Total rip off.'

'Really?' Henry hoped he looked suitably aghast.

'Yep. Honestly … they had the most elaborate and expensive selection of equipment on offer to help us perform their 'supposed' magical feats. Just one big money-guzzling corporate machine churning out cheap magicians to entertain at parties. What a con.'

She looked momentarily crest-fallen. 'Can't believe I paid fifty shebbles for that. Well, at least I *will* have done after five years of repayments plus interest.'

'Oh, I'm sorry.' The satchel full of magical garb on his shoulder was getting heavier and heavier.

'Not your fault, H. You were smart to get out when you did. Wish I could say the same. After the ridiculous wand-making task I realised I'd probably been had, but there was no getting out of the agreement. Signed is signed, so they said. They even had the cheek to offer a reduction in debt for every new student we recruited. Can you believe that? As if I'd recommend anyone throwing away fifty shebbles on that twaddle. Still, you've got to admire the sustainability of the business model.'

The two stood looking at each other for a few moments.

'So, you decided against magic did you? Still plugging away on the ledger books?'

Henry wrestled with his conscience about what to tell her. On the one hand, she'd been nicer to him than anyone he could remember of his own age. On the other hand, he felt sorry about how things had worked out for her. But on a third hand, part of him didn't want to risk having to share Halcyon with anyone. Thinking this made him feel shamefully selfish.

'Oh. You know,' he muttered noncommittally. 'How about you? What are you doing in a longwaddle bush, by the way?'

D.C. looked down as if surprised to find herself there. 'Oh. Lily. My littlest sister. Dropped her favourite doll when we were out in the woods yesterday. Been squealing like a trapped piglet about it all morning so I said I'd come out and look. More to get away from the house than anything. Gets messy with six girls all bouncing off the walls wondering what to do with the school holidays. You know?'

Henry didn't know at all and the idea made him feel slightly queasy. But he understood the need to escape your siblings. 'So did you find it?'

D.C. looked confused.

'The doll? Did you find it?'

'Ah!' She held up a tiny pink coat with pretty lace trim. 'Only her coat I'm afraid.' She affected a mournful gloom. 'Yet another disappearance we'll have to chalk up to the demons in the forest.'

This casual reference to whatever had ambushed his father took Henry aback. He blanched visibly and D.C. went to step towards him, concerned. But she'd forgotten she was standing in the tangle of a longwaddle bush and promptly tripped face first into the underbrush. In the time it took her to resurface Henry had managed to regain his composure. He even felt slightly vindicated not telling her about Halcyon.

'What about you?' D.C. asked, looking around. 'What brings the mild-mannered accountant way out here into the forest?'

The bag on Henry's shoulder grew heavier still as his brain ransacked its alibi bank for a suitable excuse. 'Uhm, just walking. Enjoying the last throes of summer … you know?' was all it could dispense on such short notice.

Henry made a mental note to have a long, hard think about some more plausible untruths at the earliest possible convenience, and flushed pink in the face. But it seemed to be fair enough to D.C.

'Oh, well. I'll see you around then?' She smiled.

'Yes. Nice to see you again D.C.' As he turned and continued along the track Henry made another mental note to look her up in the next couple of weeks. He might even reconsider telling her about his apprenticeship. He had to admit, it would be nice to have someone to show off all his amazing new skills to.

Half an hour later all thoughts of D.C. had vanished as Henry stood in a small clearing about a mile or so into the edge of the forest. The trees were still quite sparse here so there was plenty of light shining down through the leaves, which were just beginning to turn to Autumn with a sprinkling of red and orange. Now dressed in his robes and tall pointy hat, he was preparing himself for a spot of target practice with his wand.

Halcyon had taught him that the higher the level of the spell the more magic it took to carry it, and consequently it was more effort to release. For Henry, the amount of effort required was directly proportionate to his accuracy, or rather the lack there-of. So, Halcyon had suggested he adapt the level fifteen *temporary changeling* spell he'd been working with so far into a slightly more ambitious level fourteen version that allowed for a greater body mass of transformation. Instead of turning colliwall-nuts into field mice he was going to be changing uglimelons into geese.

Feeling his spirits lift at the prospect of making some magic, Henry skirted the perimeter of the clearing looking for a fat, undulating uglimelon to use as a target. He'd chosen this particular clearing not only for its abundance of the wild-growing fruit, but also for its total seclusion from the business of the town. There was also a large pond on the edge of the clearing, which he felt he owed to any resulting geese since it would be about a week before they went back to being uglimelons.

He pushed aside a tangle of bracken with his foot, and it hit something with a hollow clunk. He'd found what he was looking for. He bent and pushed the rest of the weeds aside to reveal the shiny orange skin of an uglimelon. He wrinkled his nose at the smell as he slid both hands underneath the large, knobbly fruit and lifted it out of its bed.

Henry carried it over to a fallen log at the edge of the clearing, and took ten paces backwards to set himself up with a good shot. He'd already memorised the incantation and his wand was fully charged up with all the necessary ingredients, so he assumed the spell casting position. Almost immediately he began to recite the words of the verse he saw fine wisps of light leaking out of the tips of his fingers, turning green as they curled their way up the shaft of his wand. He smiled to himself as he worked. It really was a most pleasing sensation, and he hadn't forgotten what Halcyon had said about him picking up this part of the spell casting process so quickly. When there was enough energy dancing about on the tip of his wand to complete the spell he glanced towards the uglimelon lying peacefully on the log and wound himself up for a shot. He deftly flicked the end of the enchanted stick towards it, but then something unthinkable happened.

As the ball of swirling greenness left the tip of his wand, there was the crashing sound of something lumbering through the undergrowth, and Mrs Flibbertigibbet exploded into the clearing behind the log. 'I saw you! You wicked child, I saw you! What devilish work are you …?' But she never got the chance to finish her sentence, at least not in any language Henry could understand, as the pelting missile of light that went streaking across the clearing was completely off target. Henry watched in horror as it slapped his charging, red-faced aunty right on the front of her neck.

Mrs Flibbertigibbet's hands flew up to grasp at her throat, her face racing through a series of expressions one after the other ... Accusation became realisation, which promptly switched to a look of blind terror, followed sharply by a contorted grimace of confusion. Then she vanished.

Henry just stood there for a few seconds, his chin unravelling to let his mouth dropped open. What had he done? And where on earth had she disappeared to?

'Nwack!'

Henry clapped his mouth shut with a plop.

'Nwack, SQUWACK!'

This angry sound was coming from just behind the log, with the unaffected uglimelon still propped on top. Henry dashed over to take a look.

Behind the log was a biggest, fattest goose he'd ever seen, standing indignantly in a crumpled heap of clothing.

'Squack!' it shouted at him.

'Aunty?' Henry ventured uncertainly.

'Squack, NWACK!' the goose retorted crossly, and charged at him out of a billow of petticoats.

'Yikes!' Henry jumped up on to the log to avoid the furious pecking beak. The goose attempted to flap its considerable wings to fly up and continue the assault, but thankfully a blouse was buttoned up tight around its neck so it just flopped around in the swathe of white cotton, seething.

'Aunty!' Henry was waving his hands at the angry bird. 'Please.

Look, I'm sorry. OK? It wasn't meant for you. What are you doing out here anyway?'

The goose unleashed a litany of squawks and quacks that Henry thought it was probably a good job he couldn't understand.

Henry watched it, biting his bottom lip. It would be a week or more before the goose would become Mrs Flibbertigibbet again. As tempting as it was to leave the nosey old bat like this, his brain had enough sense to realise there was going to be one hell of a fuss if she went missing for that long.

'Aunty, listen,' he shouted over the furious quacking. 'I can turn you back!'

The goose stopped lumbering about inside the blouse and looked at him with livid blue eyes ringed in bright orange.

'OK, good. That's good. Now, I'm going to step down from the log.' He did so and the goose remained still, but regarding him with deep suspicion. 'Now,' he continued in a soothing voice, beginning to gather up Mrs Flibbertigibbet's belongings, 'I don't have everything I need to do that right now.' The goose squawked and he took a step backwards. 'But it won't take long!' He hoped this was the truth. He knew there was a reversal spell for most low level enchantments, but he didn't know what it was, or what ingredients he'd need to make it. He wouldn't be able to ask Halcyon until tomorrow morning as he only had castle access for work days, so she was going to have to spend at least one day as a goose. He decided it might not be prudent to tell her this just yet though.

He looked about the clearing dubiously. It didn't feel right leaving his aunty out here to fend for herself. He was going to have to try and take her back to her house and stash her away safely. This was going to require some cooperation on her part.

'Hey again!'

Henry let out a small cry of surprise as he saw D.C. trotting along the path into the clearing. She stopped and took in the scene; Henry standing there in an over-sized blue sack holding an armful of lady's petticoats with a tall pointed hat on his head; the goose standing before him wearing a blouse and a furious expression.

Henry blushed deeply. 'Uh, D.C. ...' He was totally lost for words.

Her eyes took in the black stick in his hand and he could see realisation dawning.

'You're doing magic!' she cried, overjoyed. 'You are, aren't you?'

'I ... uh ...'

She dashed over to him, checking out his clothing and the mesmerising black stick. 'Is that a wand? A *real* wand? Goodness H, wherever did you get one of those?' Her eyes lingered on the grasp of petticoats and then she looked down at the goose. 'Who is that?'

'I ... uh ...' He pushed coherent thought back up from the dustbin of his surprise. 'D.C. I've had a bit of an accident.'

The goose quacked, surprising them both.

Henry looked ruefully down at the bird. 'This is my aunty, Mrs Flibbertigibbet. I was doing some target practice when she popped out unexpectedly.'

D.C. laughed. 'Really? That nosey old bat?' The goose squawked with rage and dove at her ankles with a pecking beak. 'Yikes!' It was her turn to take refuge on the log, still giggling.

'It's not funny D.C. She's going to be mad as hell when I turn her back. I'm never going to hear the end of it. Not to mention she's going to tell everyone and Mum will most likely forbid me from continuing my studies.'

D.C. looked at him. 'Yes, well we can get on to you telling me all about that later, you sneaky devil. Learning real magic? H, I'm so happy for you.'

Henry was slightly taken aback. He'd expected her to be jealous. Or cross with him for not sharing his secret earlier. It made the colour of embarrassment rise in his cheeks again.

'Can I watch?'

'I ... uh.'

She wrinkled up her nose. 'Please? I promise I won't get in the way. I'd love to see real magic done. Oh, Henry, please say I can stay.'

'Well,' he managed once more to get coherent thought out of his mouth, 'There's a bit of a problem there. I don't have the spell components I need in my wand, so I have to get her home safely until I can prepare.'

'I'll help you!' she piped up eagerly, hopping down from the log and taking the petticoats from his arms. I can carry this lot; people will just think I'm taking my sisters' stuff to the wash house or something. It's definitely going to raise fewer eyebrows than you walking into town holding women's clothing.'

Henry had to agree she had a point. He looked down at the bird. 'Now, aunty, I'm going to take that blouse off, but you have to promise not to fly off or attack anyone. OK?' The goose regarded him with insolent eyes but remained still and quiet as he unbuttoned the blouse and slipped it up over its head. That done he pulled his own robes off and stashed everything wizardly away in his satchel. 'OK,' he said with a little more confidence as D.C. gathered up the last of his aunt's clothing. 'Do you need me to carry you?' He stepped towards the goose, reaching to pick it up, but it pecked his hands angrily away and started marching off towards town with a contemptuous ruffle of its tail-feathers. 'OK, fine. You can walk.'

The pair fell into step behind the goose as it waddled along the path.

'So … you gonna tell what's going on?' D.C. was clearly bursting with curiosity. 'Where are you learning real magic?'

Henry twisted his mouth sideways before eventually admitting, 'From the Wizard Royal, up at the castle.'

D.C.'s eyes widened. 'You've met Halcyon? How did you get into the castle? Blimey, H! How in the name of all things magic did you conjure that up?'

'Ah, well I've known him for years actually. I work up at the castle you see.'

The girl's eyes widened further and she halted in her tracks, gaping at him. 'In the King's vaults? You're an accountant up in the castle?'

'Yes, and my father used to be the Chief Accountant there so I would go with him sometimes to the castle when I was just a little lad.' He noticed that D.C. had gone very pale, her usual sparky attitude replaced by the look of a lost little girl.

'You knew my brother then?' Her voice was a whisper and it took Henry's ears a few moments to decipher the question.

'Your brother?' As he asked, memories started rolling over in his head, seemingly unrelated incidents bumping into each other and finding out they had something in common after all. D.C. *Hubbub*, she'd said that day at registration. Was one of the junior clerks down in the vaults named Hubbub too?

'Yes. Rowan. He was working down there for just over a year before he ...' She faltered, bad memories throwing a shawl of sadness over her. 'When he went missing on one of those stupid trade runs.'

Henry gasped in recognition. After his father had gone missing there had been several more attempts to trade gold coins for rare goods on the coast, but they'd sent lesser qualified accountants together with a junior clerk on the perilous journey to conduct them. He didn't remember much about Rowan Hubbub specifically as he'd only been working in the vault a few weeks himself when the whole office had watched the next pair of accountants go under a cloud of trepidation. He'd been young; not more than seventeen. A further eight hapless castle employees had gone missing before the King finally had to admit it was no longer economically viable.

Pulled out of her reverie by the gasp, D.C. was now looking at Henry with her own sense of unfolding recognition. 'Your dad ... he was the Chief Accountant? Before Colloid? That means ...' again the young girl faltered. 'Oh, I'm sorry Henry. It's bad enough losing your brother. Can't imagine what losing your dad feels like.'

Henry shrugged sadly and started walking along the path again. D.C. quickly fell into step beside him. 'It's one of the reasons I was so desperate to learn magic,' he said quietly. 'Whatever evil is lurking out there pouncing on unsuspecting accountants ... they can't just be allowed to keep doing it.'

'Me too!' The light was dancing in D.C.'s eyes again. 'And they're still out there somewhere H! All of them! Your dad, my brother. The bandits!'

Henry felt his heart skip as it always did when he allowed it to contemplate his father coming home one day. It wasn't something he allowed often any more.

They stood for a moment, staring back into the deep forest behind them.

'Maybe,' he said thoughtfully, before continuing to trudge along the path after the goose.

• • •

Once the pair had managed to herd the goose into the safety Mrs Flibbertigibbet's small home, Henry shut the door with a deep sigh. D.C. bundled her clothing on to a kitchen chair and went around the place pulling curtains closed.

'Won't that raise a few questions?' Henry said, remembering the way his aunt was always glaring out of the window at the world.

'Not as many questions as a bad tempered goose taking up residence,' she replied. 'Did you see the way old Mary and her crones looked at it when it waddled haughtily through their gaggle?'

Henry allowed himself to relax and smiled at the memory. He turned to the goose, considering. 'What does a goose need to survive the night? What do they eat? Seeds? Would you like a nice bowl of breakfast oats?' he asked it, feeling a little silly when it simply quacked crossly in reply.

'Grass and leaves I think,' D.C. said. 'Or insects ...'

The goose snorted, in so much as a goose can snort, and stalked away towards the bedroom in disgust.

'Oh my,' said Henry, the dread of anticipation overcoming him for when he finally gave his aunt a human voice again.

D.C. was filling a bowl with water. She placed it on the floor then took the herb garden from the windowsill to put beside it. 'That should keep her going. Though I hope for all our sakes she doesn't go crazy on the garlic plant.' She looked expectantly at Henry. 'What next?'

'Next I have to speak to Halcyon. Get the spell made and then come back here to face the music I guess.'

'When will that be?' D.C. was looking dubiously through the door to the bedroom.

'If Halcyon can make it for me while I'm at work tomorrow I can come back here right after. About six-o'clock probably.'

'Right.' D.C. stuck her hands in her pockets and grinned at him. 'I'll check back a couple of times during the day. Make sure she hasn't laid an egg or anything.' She chuckled at the look of dismay that barged into Henry's face at the thought. 'Don't worry, H. I'll keep things smooth here, you get the spell made and we'll meet up here at six-o'clock. I ... I can watch you do it, can't I?'

Henry smiled at the girl. It was a relief not to be going through this alone, he thought. 'Yes, of course. Thank you D.C. Really.'

'No bother H. That's what friends do, right?' She stuck out her right hand and he shook it gratefully.

# Chapter 8

The following day was disastrous. For starters it was a Monday, so everyone at the castle was in a miserable mood. When he'd explained to Halcyon about the mishap with his aunt, the old wizard had looked serious and said 'Oh dear. Oh dear, oh dear, oh dear ...'

'What? What 'oh dear'? We can reverse the spell can't we?' Henry felt a swell of panic beginning in his stomach.

'Well yes, of course we can. Never a question about that. But what then, I ask you? What then? Oh dear, oh dear, oh ...'

'Enough with the "oh dear-ing", OK?' Henry interrupted. 'If I can turn her back into a person everything's fine, isn't it?'

'Apart from the dreadful fuss she will make, yes. But then the inspectors down at C.R.A.S.S. are bound to hear about it. Knowing the range of your aunt's gossip-network that'll take, oh, about five minutes I should imagine.' The old man rubbed his scrawny grey beard pensively, as he always did when something was troubling him.

'The who?' Henry asked.

'C.R.A.S.S. The Council for the Respectable Advancement of Speculative Sciences. They're likely to be very upset. We've broken one of their chief edicts you see? "No person, or persons, should be turned into livestock without a really good reason, or written permission." And especially not your aunt, Henry. I'm afraid we're both in a lot of trouble.'

'But I didn't do it on purpose ... she snuck up on me! And anyway, why would you be in trouble? It was my stupid aim that did it.'

'Don't worry boy. Accidents happen and as long as you can demonstrate you acted swiftly and decisively to put things right the investigation will just be a formality. The trouble is ...' The beard was being tugged quite firmly now and began to curl up at the edges in protest of the man-handling.

'Trouble?' Henry's stomach was filling with dread again.

'I'm supposed to have filled out a mentoring licence to register you as my apprentice. It's a relatively new thing; damn bureaucracy. I never was much of a one for paperwork you know?'

'Will you get into a lot of trouble?'

'Oh, I should think so yes. Not that it'll affect me much. There isn't a lot they can do to me tucked away here in the castle. But your tutorage will have to stop I'm afraid, and neither of us will be able to use the magical supplies mail-order system for at least ten years.' The old man tutted. 'That's going to make it very difficult to practise high-level wizardry in a cost-effective way. Do you know how long it would take a man to collect half a cup of black sand-grains from the Amaranthine desert by hand?'

Henry blinked.

'Still,' Halcyon said shaking off his disappointment, 'best grab my spell book out of the back so we can put your old aunty back together again at least. Though I think you may not thank me for it when she gets that sharp tongue of hers back again, eh?'

Henry thought about the goose's sharp, jabbing beak as the old man shuffled off out back to retrieve the enormous spell book. Henry had an idea. 'Halcyon,' he asked when the old man returned, 'can't we use magic to make her keep quiet? A compliancy curse or something?'

The old man sucked on his teeth as he put the heavy book on his writing desk. 'Won't work I'm afraid, not permanently anyway. The low-level curse has a limited life, and your aunt's passion for gossip will make it very hard to stick. The high level spell is just too dangerous and was banned for human use almost three decades ago.'

Henry paced, looking at the book. 'Is there a spell that could make a person forget what happened?'

'Well certainly. There's a spell for every occasion.'

'Why don't I use that on her then? I could turn her back into a person and make her forget all about being a goose!' Henry was excited at the prospect of a resolution.

'Oh dear, oh dear ...' Halcyon began again, then noticed the thunderous look blooming between his student's eyebrows and thought better of it. 'Also against the rules I'm afraid, and likely to get us into even more hot water if they find out about it down at C.R.A.S.S.'

'But they won't find out. That's the whole point! She'll never know it happened, so she won't be telling a soul!'

'No, sorry. It's just not ethical. You can't go editing people's minds like that without so much as a by-your-leave, or at least a very good excuse ... and being denied the luxury of a mail-order foolscap-withers and shilly-livers doesn't cut it I'm afraid. Although, I will really miss their range of *Sorcerer's Sauce* ready-made potents. Very convenient, if a little pricey.'

'But, what about my training as a wizard?' Henry cried, close to despair.

'Hmm, yes I see your point. But it's just not right Henry.' Halcyon's tone was softer and more comforting now, but his resolve remained intact. 'I'm sorry lad, but no matter how troublesome your aunt can be, I simply can't condone such an intrusion into her mind. A good wizard has certain principles to uphold, otherwise constant misuse will turn the magic within you black and ugly, and we wouldn't want that to happen now, would we? It's a shame really. I was planning to get on to that part of the syllabus next week. Agamemnon's Almanac cites some very interesting examples of wizards going bad in this way. Although it's not good reading late at night I have to confess.'

This revelation didn't do anything improve Henry's disposition. 'But Halcyon ...' he started to argue, but the old man held his hand up towards the frantic accountant and shushed him quiet.

'No. You'll just have to find another way lad. Or live with the consequences.' And with that, apparently, the conversation was over.

After looking up the details for a *reversal charm* that would restore Mrs Flibbertigibbet to her usual, un-feathered self, Henry spent the next half an hour in Halcyon's chambers trying to memorise the difficult words of the incantation while the old wizard got the potent stewing in his cauldron. Since he had started studying, Halcyon hadn't allowed him to write the details of any of the spells down on account of how bad it would be if the wrong spell were to fall into the wrong pair of hands.

'Right, that should be ready for you once you finish work,' the old man said dropping Henry's wand into the bubbling pot.

'Work!' Halcyon's words struck Henry round the face like an affronted acquaintance. 'Oh no, now I'm going to be late for work too!' He quickly gathered up his things and headed for the door, tossing over his shoulder a cursory 'thanks' and a confirmation that he'd be back later in the day to collect his wand .

As Henry pelted along the stony cold corridors of the castle muttering anxiously to himself, Mr Colloid was pacing the entryway to the cavernous expanse of the vault, also muttering. But Mr Colloid's mutterings were of an entirely different nature. Whilst Henry's incomprehensible babble was mostly made up of words like 'oh no, not again' and 'I'm late ... so very very late', the utterances coming from Mr Colloid's mouth were more akin to the likes of 'five after eight, oh now he's going to be in trouble' and 'a shebble for every minute it'll cost him. Yes, it will!'

At precisely six-minutes-past-eight Henry came clattering noisily down the steps that led into his place of work, and screeched to a halt in front of the glowering Chief Accountant. The pinched face barring his way could barely conceal its twisted delight. For a moment they stood there, eyeball to eyeball, then Mr Colloid snapped his pocket watch closed with a theatrical clack.

Good afternoon Noble,' he sneered, as his reading glasses slid slowly down his long, oily nose.

Henry gave up before he'd even started. There was little point in trying to talk his way out of this one, and to be perfectly honest he didn't have the energy for it this morning. 'Sorry,' he mumbled sullenly into his chest.

'Not as sorry as me boy!' The gleeful tone in his voice grated on Henry like fingernails on a slate. 'And not as sorry as your poor family will be to learn that they're already eight shebbles light on their house-keeping this week. And it's only Monday morning ... Oh dear. Oh dear, oh dear, oh dear ...'

Henry had heard enough 'oh dear's to last him a lifetime. He resolved to have stern words with the next person who said it to him; it really was a very pointless thing to say. But he decided that diplomacy was the better part of valour right now, as Mr Colloid did not have a habit of taking challenges kindly.

He bit his lip and scurried over to his workbench and began busily counting piles of golden coins, hoping against hope that he could make it through the rest of the day without getting into any more trouble.

• • •

The rest of the day did, indeed, pass without event, although the quality of Henry's work suffered a fair bit from the stress of it all. This fact was confirmed by the disapproving frown on Bob Frugal's face as he marked up the young accountant's final figures on his slate. When five o'clock finally came Henry skulked out of the vault feeling pretty low. After collecting his fully prepared wand from Halcyon he headed straight towards his aunt's tidy little house on the corner of the market square.

D.C. was waiting outside, practically bouncing with anticipation.

'How is she?' Henry asked, not really wanting to know the answer.

'As mad as a nest of fire ants,' she grinned. 'Did you get the spell?'

Henry nodded. 'But I wish I didn't have to use it.'

'What? You'd leave her as a goose? Like, forever?'

'No, no,' Henry sighed heavily. 'It's only a temporary spell so she'd be her horrible old self again in a week or so anyway. It's just ...' He looked at D.C.'s expectant face. 'Once she tells everyone what happened it's going to put paid to my magic training. Something about an inspection and a licence not being filed.'

His heart warmed to the tangle-haired girl even more as she looked the perfect picture of how crestfallen he felt. 'Oh no. H! What can we do? Can't you use your magic to make her not tell?'

'I wanted to make her forget it, but apparently that's not ethical so Halcyon wouldn't give me the spell.'

D.C.'s face creased into a frown. 'Don't you have anything else? Something to shut her up? I'm sure I read about compliancy cursing in one of my books!'

Henry shook his head hopelessly. 'Those are all way higher level spells than I can do. Plus, you need to charge your wand with the right magical properties. All I have ready to go is the reversal spell and a tagging enchantment.'

Upon eager questioning Henry explained how the tagging spell worked.

'Hmm,' said D.C. thoughtfully. 'It's a shame you didn't have that on her already. How much does she know about magic?'

'Henry shrugged. 'As much as anyone else I guess, which is pretty much nothing. She's afraid of it, that's for sure. Why?'

A look of mischief flitted on to D.C.'s face. 'Well, if she doesn't know what hit her, how can she be sure of the consequences of flapping her lips about it?'

Henry felt his chest tighten with hope as comprehension surged through him.

She winked at him and nodded towards house. 'Let's do this.'

He knocked on the door tentatively.

'Aunty?' he called out uncertainly as he poked his head around the door jamb, D.C. craning to see in from behind him. Once his head had entered the house without encountering any major problems, his body decided to follow suit. But as he stepped gingerly through the door he felt a sudden, sharp pain in his leading ankle.

'Ouch!' He jerked his leg upwards to get it out of range of the painful experience, and his other ankle was treated to the same. 'Ouch!' By now Henry was hopping about the kitchen trying to rub his stinging ankles, at the same time as avoid further jabs from the bright orange beak of a very angry goose.

'Stop it! Ouch! Aunty, please ... don't bite. OUCH! Don't bite me any more!'

D.C. slipped through the door and closed it behind her, then filled a jug with water in the sink and promptly doused it over the furiously flapping bird. It spluttered and stopped dead in its attack, glaring at the young girl murderously.

'OK, look, I'm sorry about the goose thing.' He attempted to console the bird. 'But you did kind of sneak up on me ...' The goose squawked indignantly and lunged for his left ankle again.

'STOP IT!' yelled D.C. banging the empty jar meaningfully on the side of the sink. The goose went back to looking daggers at the girl. 'Look Mrs F. I realise you're upset. But Henry is here to fix you. Unless you want to spend the rest of your life as a goose, that is?'

The goose ruffled its feathers in the haughtiest way it knew how.

'Didn't think so. Right, H. Do your thing.'

Henry looked at the fat, white goose. 'Uh, do you think we should put her clothes on first?'

D.C. wrinkled her nose up at the thought of a naked Mrs

Flibbertigibbet materialising in the kitchen. 'Yeah. Probs a good idea.'

They placed petticoats and skirts carefully over a wooden chair, then stood the indignant duck in amongst them. Buttoned back up to the neck, the blouse was slipped over its head, wings directed into the sleeve areas. The pair surveyed their handiwork.

'She looks a goose playing at dressing up.' D.C. giggled.

The goose hissed at her hotly.

Henry emptied the contents of his bag on to the table. D.C. looked on, fascinated. Deciding the robe was unnecessary and would hinder a rapid escape once he was done, Henry jammed the pointy hat on to his head and assumed a casting stance.

'Now, I'm going to turn you back into a person,' he warned the goose.

'Nwack!' it swore at him.

The moment he started chanting the mystical words of the *reversal charm* inside his head, strands of white light began dribbling out of his fingers, turning pale blue as they approached tip of the wand.

D.C.'s eyes were wide. 'How did you do that?'

'Shush,' said Henry. 'I need to concentrate.'

D.C. shut her mouth obediently and stepped aside to give him room.

He drew his arm back in a flowing arc and then whipped the blue ball of light off the end. The goose's eyes widened with terror and then snapped tightly shut as it streaked across the room towards it. The spell hit home on its quivering, feathery chest, causing a sharp slapping sensation. The goose waited for a moment to see if anything else was going to happen. It didn't, so it opened its eyes and glanced down to take a look at its wings. To its immense relief the wings were hands again. Mrs Flibbertigibbet sat in the chair looking thunderously at her nephew. D.C. whooped with triumph. Henry just stood there in his pointy hat, his wand still held up to the ready.

'You wicked child!' she spat at him. 'You have the devil in you. I've always said it! Just you wait until your mother hears what you've been up to! Oh, but she probably put you up to it. HA! I'm on to you young man! You can't get your hands on my family's money that easily! I'll make sure everybody knows what you've been trying to do!'

Henry was stunned. 'Wha ... wha ...?' was all he could manage to articulate.

'Oh yes, you won't be allowed to get away with it!' the venom in his aunt's voice stung like a bee.

'H, what is she talking about?' D.C. had crept up behind him and was half-hiding as she watched the furious woman rearrange herself properly inside her clothing.

'I have no idea,' he said with complete honesty. 'Look aunty, I'm not after money. I didn't even know there was money. You snuck up on me when I was doing a bit of target practice. How was I supposed to know you were coming?' He was cut short by a loud and incredulous guffaw.

'I've been suspicious of you for a while now, in and out of those woods every day with that big bag slung over your shoulder ... Oh, don't think I haven't been watching you, you evil child!' She was red in the face now, and had got up and was advancing towards him menacingly. 'I saw you pacing circles round that clearing dressed up like some pagan freak, preparing to raise your evil spirit friends from the dead no doubt!'

She was almost upon him now, and instinctively Henry raised his wand to fend her off, the words of the tagging spell popping into his mind. Mrs Flibbertigibbet stopped dead in her tracks, her face filling with dread as she saw the light dribbling from his fingers to become a pulsing orange bulb on the tip of the wand.

'You wouldn't dare!' she accused. But seeing him wind up for a cast she realised he would, very much dare. Not wanting to be turned into a goose again she turned and fled for the bedroom, screaming like a mad woman. Henry flicked and the glowing ball of light left the tip of his wand, slapping her squarely on her retreating behind. She shrieked and threw her hands to her head in preparation for the inevitable. Nothing happened. She turned to face Henry again, looking uncertain.

'What have you done to me?' she said almost in a whisper, checking various body parts with her hands as she kept her eyes fixed firmly on her nephew.

'Nothing, yet.' Henry replied solemnly, feeling D.C.'s excited breath in hot little puffs on the back of his neck. He did his best to look as menacing as possible. 'But I have cursed you with an ancient and irreversible charm called the ... the *loose tongue hex!*'

Mrs Flibbertigibbet gasped, her hands flying to her mouth.

'You can live out a long and happy life,' he ploughed on, gaining confidence from the look of abject horror on her face. 'But be warned! Should you ever open your mouth to gossip about me, or my friend here,' he nodded back to D.C. proud of the fact he'd had the presence of mind to add that addendum, 'you'll be turned instantly into a weasel! And a weasel you will stay. There are no reversal spells for mean little tattlers.'

The old woman's eyes narrowed as she glanced between Henry and D.C. 'Get out!' she hissed.

Henry backed away unsteadily, the girl shuffling backwards behind him. His wand was vibrating ominously. 'Be warned!' he said as boldly as he could under such circumstances, waggling the tip of it at her as they slipped through the door. She continued to look daggers at him, but made no further sound.

Outside D.C. practically fell on to the floor with a strange mixture of laughing, crying and hiccupping with excitement. 'Oh my god, H! That was amazing! Real, honest-to-goodness magic!'

Henry looked about, nervously, pulling the tall pointy hat off his head and tucking it away under his jacket with his wand. 'I hope it's not the last I get to learn,' he sighed, but feeling himself buoyed by his friend's excitement.

The wand, still agitated by the proximity of its recent target continued to buzz angrily. At least he would always know when the interfering busybody was close by from now on, he thought. 'Come on.' He grinned at D.C. 'I think I owe you a ginger ale, only you'll have to come back to my house if you want to cash it in. My mum will blow her stack if she ever gets a whiff of that tavern on me again.'

'Really?' D.C. flushed pink with pleasure at being invited to the Noble household.

'Yeah, just stay away from anything breakable. We've had more than enough trouble for one day.'

# Chapter 9

His mother had been extremely surprised to see him come home with a young friend in tow. That surprise turning into an embarrassingly pink-faced level of delight when she realised it was a girl.

'Is that your girlfriend?' she probed gently later.

'No! Mother, don't be ridiculous!' His cheeks burned as his brothers picked up on the thread and started teasing him relentlessly.

'Ewww, Henry's got a girlfriend?' 'Who'd be desperate enough to go out with him?' 'How many heads does she have, Henry?'

Henry swore silently to himself about how he wished his mother would keep her mouth shut when the twins were about. But the whole incident passed with pretty much no more remark, so he figured he was at a net-advantage, consequences-wise.

A week went by and there were no reprisals from the people at C.R.A.S.S.

Halcyon heard no reports of an investigation into his working practices, and neither was anybody whispering and pointing at Henry as he passed them in street. It seemed their clever little rouse with Mrs Flibbertigibbet had done the trick nicely, thank you very much.

He'd passed by her house several times but never caught her glaring out of the window at him. The curtains had twitched though, and it gave him a smug glow to feel the wand vibrating deeply in his bag. In fact, Henry was feeling pretty pleased with himself altogether just lately, especially after Halcyon praised the quick thinking that had motivated Mrs Flibbertigibbet to keep her trap shut.

'Well done my boy! You see? That's the mark of a true wizard. Brain first; wand follows,' the old wizard had said tapping the side of his head with a gnarly knuckle. 'A spell is only as bright as its caster.' He'd glanced in disgust at a tall stack of freshly delivered boxes by the door labelled, *Sorcerers Sauce: Magic to the very last drop!*

'Well, I can't take all the credit. It was D.C.'s idea really.' Henry had decided it was best to tell Halcyon everything, including D.C. stumbling across the scene out in the forest.

'Yes, she's a canny one, isn't she? Well-read you said? I do like person who shows commitment.'

'Like? As in *like* enough to maybe train her too one day?' Henry ventured. He was beginning to grow quite fond of his new friend and was still feeling a little sheepish about keeping his magical secret from her.

The old man had stopped and looked at Henry thoughtfully. 'Well now, that's an interesting idea. I'm certainly a big supporter of wizarding diversity. Sadly, you can't become a sorcerer without a wand though, and I am fresh out of those. I tell you what? I'll keep my ear to the ground and if I hear of one going I'll try and snaffle it up for her. No harm in trying, I suppose?'

The elation Henry felt was two-fold; one that he could offer this thread of hope to his new friend, but also that he wouldn't have to share his magic-making classes *just* yet.

D.C. had been completely beside herself when he'd told her about the conversation later that week. Her eyes brimmed with tears as she laugh-wept, 'I can't believe you did that for me, H! The King's own wizard is really going to take me on as an apprentice?'

'Slow down, D.C. Remember, no wand, no wizarding. It might be years before he finds one.'

D.C. was jiggling about, clearly struggling to process the levels of excitement at the news. 'I can wait,' she said breathlessly, hugging Henry awkwardly. 'I can wait.'

Beyond this prospect she seemed quite happy to listen to his magical exploits, laughing and clapping as he told her about his progress. She appeared to be genuinely delighted her friend was getting to live out his dream. Both their dreams, Henry reminded himself frequently. He wasn't sure he would have been as magnanimous if the shoe were on the other foot. It made him admire her even more.

Whenever she could get out of her chores and babysitting duties at home D.C. would join Henry in the forest. He taught her the breathing exercises Halcyon had shown him and she practised casting techniques alongside him with a stick, pulling him up critically when he made a mistake. She'd tried really hard to get him to tell her the incantation of a spell, but Henry had refused remembering Halcyon's warnings about proper wizardly practice.

'It's not my place to teach you that, D.C. I'm sorry, I really am. But the words are useless to you without a wand to wield the magic anyway.'

'I know,' she'd whinged, eyeing his wand enviously. 'I just ... I'm just curious about the language. You know, what kind of words do spells use? Are they like regular words? Or just a jumble of magical sounds? How do you remember so many different verses?'

Unable to explain the strange texts in a way that would make sense to anyone who hadn't read them, he decided eventually to put paid to her badgering by revealing the words an enchantment. He figured the *reversal* spell he'd used to turn his aunt back from a goose couldn't do anyone any harm if it had nothing to reverse, so he spoke the strange words out loud to the wide-eyed girl.

'Wow.' She looked at him breathlessly. 'Just wow.'

Having her along for the ride got a bit exhausting sometimes, as she was always gushing on about some new magical book she was reading and the tips the author provided. But it made him learn faster and better, and it didn't look quite so suspicious tramping out into the forest with a friend. Having been a loner his entire life he was surprised to be growing extremely grateful for her company.

One Saturday not long after school term had started for his brothers and D.C. again, Henry was trudging the long path home from an excursion into the forest, his wizardly garb folded safely away in his bag. D.C. hadn't been able to come as she was looking after her little sisters, so he was completely alone. He loved showing off his spell casting to such an appreciative audience of one, but he had to admit it had been nice to have the chance to practise without any distractions for a change. Musing on his good fortune and congratulating himself on a marked improvement in his spell casting accuracy, he felt a sudden agitation in his bag; an agitation that could mean only one thing. Well actually, it could mean only one of three things; that one of his brothers or his interfering old aunty were close by. He spun around trying to figure out which direction they would come from. The forest was just starting to get thick here and couldn't see any obvious signs of life. Taking no chances, he dove behind a thick tangle of bracken and waited for the danger to pass. It wasn't long before he heard the soft murmur of voices coming from the direction of town.

'Edwina, it troubles me to see you this way.'

Henry gasped, then clamped his hands over his treacherous mouth to keep it quiet. It was Mr Colloid's cloying voice he could hear drifting through the leaves of the bracken, and a sideways stretch of his neck to peek round the edge of a large frond confirmed that Mr Colloid had been addressing Henry's aunt, Edwina Flibbertigibbet. It looked like they were holding hands.

'I've told you Neville, don't push me on this. I will not talk about that boy again. I just can't.'

'What has he done to you my petal? I thought we shared everything. You used to tell me all your troubles with the ridiculous comings and goings of that tiresome family. But ever since you said you might follow your nephew out into the woods to see what he was up to, you've been sealed up shut on the subject like a clam.' Mr Colloid's tone was soft and cajoling, the way one might speak to a child who won't come out from under the bed covers for fear of being eaten by monsters. Henry was torn between feeling incensed about the invasion into his privacy, and feeling delighted that the trick on his aunt seemed to have worked so astoundingly well.

'There are such better things to discuss Neville; like that dreadful girl, Maybelline Frost, whom I have it on good authority is arranging clandestine meetings with the bar tender from the tavern. Would you believe it? Honestly, I'm surprised her poor mother can show her face in public with all the carry on! Not to mention Mr Belcher from the Butcher's stall. I'd venture his relationship with that tavern is also very unhealthy. He could hardly see straight to cut me a side of pork yesterday afternoon, I thought I was going to end up with one of his thumbs. And it wasn't even three o'clock!' Mrs Flibbertigibbet's attempt at steering the conversation away from the dangerous subject of her nephew was short-lived.

'Have you ever seen Henry going in there again?' Mr Colloid's interest in him was beginning to sit badly in the pit of Henry's stomach, but judging by the silence that followed, his aunt had clearly decided today would not be a good day to test the *loose tongue hex*.

Undaunted by the lack of response, Mr Colloid pressed on. 'Look Edwina, we've been stepping out for, what? Four years now? And since that time I've been happy to sit and listen to you pouring your heart out about your dear, departed brother, rest his soul, and that dreadful family of his ...'

Henry blinked, and nearly gasped again. Mr Colloid's words seemed to slide round the tall, scraggy fronds of bracken Henry was crouching in and dig him in the ribs annoyingly. What gave that odious man the right to pry into his home life? He wanted to fly out of the thicket and pounce on the despicable duo. He wanted to pull out his wand, which was still buzzing away in his bag like an angry bee, seeming to egg him on, and brandish it at them menacingly. He wanted to watch them cower and squirm as he threatened to turn them into ducks.

They were practically opposite him on the pathway now. One good bound over the greenery and he would land on top of them.

Henry's murderous train of thought was interrupted by the exaggerated swish of a long, starched skirt, followed by the angry and deliberate stomping of a heeled boot. There was a split second's silence, and Henry held his breath.

'Look Neville!' his aunt spat menacingly at her companion, 'I will not be drawn into a conversation about that boy! We're supposed to be enjoying a pleasant stroll in the countryside. If you carry on interrogating me like this, I'll have no option but to walk home on my own!' The skirt swished again, then Henry heard the thud of two pairs of footsteps, beginning with the purposeful march of heeled boots and followed by the shuffling scuff of a soft-heeled pair trying to keep up. After they'd faded to silence the wand became still and Henry remembered to breathe again.

After about five-minutes more of skulking in the undergrowth he deemed it safe to poke his head out. Once he was sure there was no-one else there, the rest of his body followed. Quick as he could, Henry shouldered his bag and started trotting along the pathway towards town, glancing back over his shoulder occasionally in a haunted way. His mind was racing. Why had Mr Colloid been so interested in his business? And what on earth could the pair of them possibly see in each other? The thought of them even kissing turned Henry's stomach over, so he decided to concentrate on being outraged instead. He switched his stride from a 'hasty trot' to an 'angry clump', and continued towards the town fuming. It wasn't until he was almost all the way back to his house that he remembered he'd promised to stop in at the market on his way home to pick up some vegetables for supper. This recollection didn't exactly improve Henry's mood, but his feet changed their course obligingly, and began clumping a little bit harder towards the square.

The market was crowded and smelt of over-ripe fruit. Saturdays were always busy here because there was no activity in the square on a Sunday. The place was rammed with stallholders, all trying to out-shout each other in an attempt to persuade you that their 'almost too ripe to eat' produce was better than the next man's. Any space not taken up by the bellowing traders was filled with enthusiastic shoppers, all darting from this place to that, frantically scouring the horizon for that once-in-a-lifetime bargain that they would enjoy telling their grandchildren about when they grew old. Henry hated Saturday afternoon market. He braced himself and shouldered his way into the throng.

After pushing through to several stalls in the pursuit of a bunch of carrots and a turnip that could pass as almost fresh rather than just a complete bargain, Henry felt he'd earned a break. He made his way towards the fountain in the centre of the square where he could slosh his face with cold water and maybe treat himself to a peach from a fruit stall.

As expected, the throng thinned significantly as he moved away from the stalls, so he paid for a juicy peach and settled down to enjoy his fruit on the knee-high wall that contained the little fountain. The water splashed away happily in the background, and Henry began to feel some of the blackness in his mood slowly lifting. He watched the people busily stuffing their bags with fruit and vegetables, like ants gathering up the remnants of a hastily left picnic before a storm. Then, from within the crowd something caught his eye. A flash of white, then it was gone. Another flash, a little further to the left; this one lingering for a while, tossed about in the stampede of oncoming legs. Henry frowned and bit into his peach. The juice dribbled down his wrist then ran down his arm to take cover up his sleeve.

It wasn't long before the person distributing flyers came entirely into view, but it wasn't the incredibly round man he'd expected. This flyer dispenser was about Henry's height and age. In fact, Henry realised, he must be exactly his age since he recognised him from his old school class. He couldn't pin the age to an exact birthdate, since he'd never been invited to any of his birthday parties. But that didn't bother him in the slightest. Edmund Blight was no friend of Henry's, in any respect.

His eyes narrowed as they charted the course of the flimsy white leaflets through the heaving sea of shoppers. Wariness around Edmund was a habit he'd got into at school. A shy loner, Henry had spent his breaks gazing out of a window dreaming of magic and adventure rather than engaging in the rough and tumble of the playground. It made him an obvious target to bullies like Edmund Blight.

He and his friends were nothing but a bunch of fashionably-dressed terrorists who made school-life a misery for lots of kids. He watched as the older version of the boy who had tormented him flitted from side to side, digging the pieces of parchment into passing hands as he went.

He hadn't changed much in Henry's opinion. Still tall and fashionably tanned. Still swaggering in that infuriating way that only people who are very rich and incredibly stupid can really pull off. And still wearing his blond hair in that modern 'swept off the face into a greasy mop' look that reminded Henry of, well, greasy mops really. As Edmund drew near, Henry could see his face *had* changed a bit. He'd filled out in the cheeks and he appeared to have a pencil-straight moustache balancing comically across his top lip. This coarse brown caterpillar of hair curled up into a generic smile as the lips it rested on did the same, and before he knew it Henry found himself face-to-face with his childhood arch nemesis.

Henry's mind went blank, and it took him a while to realise that Edmund wasn't going trip him up; or goose him; or steal the chocolate cup-cake from out of his lunch bag. Although he felt an overwhelming urge to hide his peach behind his back. But Edmund was actually staring through him quite vacantly, with an expression of pleasant agreeability hung limply across his face to mask the emptiness underneath. In his right hand, which was fully extended and on an intercept course with Henry's, was clamped one of the familiar G.D.E. flyers.

'Hi,' Edmund said, coming to a halt in front of Henry. 'Can I interest you in a new and exciting career opportunity?' he recited from an invisible manuscript apparently about two-feet behind Henry's face.

Henry blinked. Edmund showed absolutely no recognition of the kid whose life he'd made so miserable back in school. 'With just a small investment of your time and money, you could be fulfilling your wildest dreams and more.' He paused robotically, obviously expecting some kind of response from Henry. 'Excuse me? Mister?' His face was closer to Henry's now, coming in for a better look.

'Hello Edmund,' Henry said.

It was Edmund's turn to blink.

'Henry …' Henry offered his name to trigger Blight's recollection. There was none. 'Henry Noble; from Miss Blither's class in school?'

Miss Blither had been their form tutor, and this new information gave Edmund's memory banks a jiggle. 'Whoa! Henry? I didn't recognise you. From school … Yeah. We used to call you Hen, right? Cluck, cluck, cluck?' He laughed. 'Those were the days, hey?'

'Yeah, right,' Henry muttered flatly. 'Hilarious.'

'So, you want to hear about these fantastic classes?' Edmund continued, spurred into a fresh burst of enthusiasm by the scent of an easy sale. 'Do you believe in magic?' Henry raised an eyebrow. 'I know, I know,' Edmund continued, mistaking his sarcastic look for disbelief. 'But I've just finished the course myself and I can tell you, it's spell-binding!'

Henry scowled at the face in front of him, despising the smug 'I've-just-made-a-really-clever-pun-but-you-don't-even-realise-it-yet' glint in its eyes. Those eyes were wrong to feel so smug. Henry understood the gag perfectly and it wasn't very funny.

'Seriously Hen, I'm a fully qualified wizard.' He held out his arms dramatically as if to prove it. 'I have a certificate and everything!'

Henry looked down at the leaflet being proffered and felt a sudden desire to call him out on it. Perhaps even make a big scene here in the crowded Saturday market so that no more dreamers like D.C. would be taken in by the sham.

'Prove it,' he challenged, affecting what he hoped was the air of someone who didn't much care for childish make-believes.

Edmund stepped back theatrically, raising his voice and sweeping his arm round to simultaneously grab the attention of the passing crowd and clear a small space by the fountain. 'The lad demands proof, ladies and gentlemen. Proof of the magic that stands before him.' He thrust his right hand inside his long black coat and produced a smooth stick with a flourish. Then with a graceful turn swept the pleated coat off his shoulders, placing it flat along the fountain wall in one balletic movement. 'Step aside, young master!' He elbowed Henry out of the way and leapt up on to the coat, lithe as a cat.

The milling shoppers stopped milling and assumed the form of a fledgling audience, slowly maturing into quite an acceptable crowd as the gaps between them began to fill up with people who had either noticed the commotion and couldn't resist stopping to stare, or simply wondered what everyone else was looking at. With another flourish Edmund produced a jet black cape from his bag full of flyers and tossed is aside with a thwump. Flyers slid out and across the cobbles. Henry looked up and Edmund was fussily tying the cape around his shoulders, flipping the sides out dramatically when he was done.

Edmund looked very much the part dressed in that magnificent swirling cape; he only lacked the pointy hat. The wand was entirely the wrong colour of course, but it wasn't likely anyone but him knew that.

'Ladies and gentlemen,' boomed the scarlet bellied bat standing atop the fountain wall. The crowd of suspended shoppers moved in a little closer encouragingly and Edmund sneered smugly at Henry before continuing with grandeur. 'I, the Mighty Blighty ...' Someone snickered at this and Edmund turned his attention sharply back to the crowd. 'I, the Mighty Blighty, will now levitate, right before your very eyes! I am, of course, available for weddings and birthday parties, please tell your friends.' He beamed a radiant smile at the sea of faces in front of him and a lethargic ripple of applause broke out. With a final stamping flourish on the small wall to engage his audience, he jumped down to the floor and then stood there, straight as an arrow, with the edges of his cape held up towards the sky impressively. The silky red lining of the cape gaped at the crowd, shimmering a glaring red brightness at them, drawing their eyes towards him like a snake hypnotising its prey. Then, very slowly Edmund began to draw his arms back down. As he did his feet raised steadily off the ground. A whisper of gasps started to ripple through the crowd as more and more people realised this. Before long the triumphant flyer-dispenser was floating a good six-inches above the cobbled square, his feet appearing to dangle in thin air. 'You see? Real magic! The kind of magic you can learn too if you sign up with Gorman Dizing Enterprises. Evening and weekend courses available,' he called as an aside to the one or two market stall workers who were showing an interest.

The crowd applauded and chattered about how unbelievable it was. Henry stood back, arms folded across his chest with an air of cynicism. 'Really? Real magic?' he said with as much sarcasm as he could muster.

'Deny your eyes if you like, fool. Reality speaks the truth! He was always slow in class, ladies and gentlemen ... Cluck, cluck, cluck, little Hen.'

A few of the girls gathering to watch tittered, though they weren't really sure why. Edmund flashed them a winning smile.

'Ha! You're about as magic as a box of bolts! I'm more of a wizard than you'll ever be,' Henry shouted angrily, grabbing the corner of the coat he'd laid on the wall and giving it a sharp tug. There was a low, grating crunch, and Edmund's left foot dropped three inches, tilting his body at an angle that made him look like a marionette in the hands of a puppet master who had just dozed off. Edmund shifted his body weight awkwardly, trying to keep his balance, but with a cry of alarm came crashing to the floor in a crumpled red and black heap. His collapse was followed by a large chunk of masonry that used to be pond wall. A flood of slightly green water whooshed across the cobbles, making the crowd gasp and step back as the top three inches of pond went in search of a new home taking a stack of the flyers with it.

'Hey!' someone from the crowd cried out. 'There's something attached to his shoes! It was hooked into the top edge of that wall there!'

Henry lifted the now sodden side of Edmund's cape to reveal a metal contraption hidden inside his excessive outerwear. 'This is the kind of magic you'll learn at Gorman Dizing Enterprises! Party tricks and shenanigans! And if you take out credit to pay for it you'll be a slave to their debt collectors for years!'

There was a murmur of disapproval building in the crowd. Underneath the crumpled cape, Edmund glared out with murderous eyes. 'You little ...'

He untangled himself from the contraption and flew at Henry in a rage, making the crowd gasp harder than ever.

Taken by surprise as he hadn't really thought this through to all its inevitable conclusions, Henry took the full weight of Edmund's tackle on his belly. The pair of them tumbled backwards and sploshed into the remaining water of the fountain where they splashed about trying to land punches of each other's slippery wet bodies. A woman screamed. A baby cried. And through the clamour of the scene Henry felt a rough fist curl into the back of his collar and he was hauled apart from the squalling Edmund.

Blinded for a few moments by the water in his eyes, Henry blinked until the person who had intervened came into focus. It was a large angry-faced woman in her forties. Hiding behind her petticoats was Peter Cosset.

'You hooligans stop it right NOW!' She threw the boys back into the pond and planted her hands on her hips. 'You're frightening the children, and goodness knows what bacterial Armageddon you've unleashed in that filthy pond water. We'll probably all be dead from marching-wiggots disease by sun-down!' She pulled a fresh hanky from her skirt pocket and wiped her hands distastefully. 'Peter, step back precious. Step back. Stay away from the nasty, germy water!'

Peter shuffled back, as did the rest of the crowd.

'Goodness, we'll have to scrub you in the bath for a week to get you clean!'

Peter looked plainly horrified and the crowd started to lose interest in the scene, realising it had probably reached its conclusion.

With one last angry splash at him, Edmund dragged himself to his feet and sploshed out of the fountain, gathering up his belongings. 'You'd better hope I don't run into you again little chicken,' he sneered through his now dripping mop of hair at Henry. 'It'll be a different ending when you don't have someone's mummy to save you.'

He stalked off through the crowd leaving a trail of anxious

squawks as he barged through unsuspecting shoppers in his sodden clothing.

'That went well,' laughed D.C. as she pushed her way through the crowd dragging a confused three-year old and a girl of about five behind her.

Henry sat in the fountain staring at her.

She laughed. 'Come on hero,' she said, attaching her clingy sisters to each other and reaching out her own hand to help him up. 'You can get cleaned at my house. We left Mum cooking a cherry cake and since she thinks the sun shines out of the top of your head right now I'm sure she will cut a large slice for you. You can borrow something from Rowan's things while we dry your clothes in the kiln room.'

# Chapter 10

The next day started like any other day. Henry had risen, as usual, at around five-thirty in the morning. After a tasty breakfast of ham and eggs, he'd picked up his lunch bag and bade his mother goodbye with a peck on the cheek; exactly the way he always did. Admittedly, he didn't get treated to ham and eggs every morning, but his brothers had helped chop firewood for an old neighbour the previous afternoon and been rewarded with a fat, juicy ham to take home. Apart from the ham then, everything seemed quite commonplace as Henry trod through the town towards his morning lesson with Halcyon.

Once he passed through the castle gates he wasted no time skirting the courtyard that separates the servants' quarters from the courtiers' rooms, heading straight for the spiralling towers at the rear of the building. Up the old stone steps, he doggedly trod, reminding himself of how little exercise he got working down in the vaults to make the ache in his thighs a little easier to ignore. He reached the sturdy oak door into Halcyon's chambers and, as usual, lifted the heavy iron knocker mounted upon it. It squeaked a half-hearted gripe about being called into action so early in the day, but nonetheless completed its task of slamming head first into the iron plate below without further complaint. The knock bounced off the stone walls, informing Halcyon his student had arrived. Henry waited.

After about two-minutes of waiting, Henry's daily routine made the first deviation from its normal, humdrum path. He knocked again.

Whilst Henry wouldn't normally be concerned about such an inconsequential deviation as having to knock twice on a door before it's answered, in all his time working at the castle he had never once come for his early morning chat and found himself lifting that door knocker a second time. An expression that drove worried furrows into Henry's smooth forehead corroborated that this was definitely something quite out of the ordinary. He waited for a reply to his second rap, staring at the door accusingly. The door stared back. Henry began shuffling his feet, biting down on his lower lip as his brain shuffled through his options to see if anything jumped out as the obvious thing to do. At both ends of his body the shuffling act proved ineffective, so Henry reached forward and lifted the doorknocker for a third time. He released it, and watched as it swung down, slamming noisily into the battered old plate. The impact sent an almost imperceptible ripple through the wood of the door; a ripple that exploded outwards and seemed to leak away into the stones and mortar of the walls. The chamber inside rang with the hollow sound of the door knocker's work. Then silence returned, and Henry could hear himself breathing.

He glanced along the corridor in either direction. To the left the stone stairs spiralled upwards unpromisingly, and to the right, they spiralled downwards in an equally uninspiring way. Henry turned his attention back to the door, which also remained unhelpful. He reached forward, this time to grasp the iron door-handle. Taking a breath to steel himself, he very slowly turned it. He could hear arthritic antique cogs clicking into place, followed by a solid clunk. With a much louder complaint than the door-knocker had made, the door eased inwards. Henry winced against the screech of its hinges, and checked the stairs in either direction again. He suddenly felt quite exposed in this stony-cold spiral. The stairs remained empty, so Henry peered inside the room and called out gingerly, 'Halcyon?'

Silence was the only reply.

Henry moved inside the room a few paces, coughed politely and tried again. 'Uhm ... Halcyon?' He looked around in case someone had left an explanation lying about.

He'd known the old wizard for almost over a decade. For the last two years he'd been coming here at the same time every morning before work. The tea would be waiting, as would Halcyon. He'd never known the wizard to even leave this room, let alone the castle grounds. He'd been a recluse since a nasty incident at the town fair when local yobs had pelted him with a basket of rotten fruit. He'd been right at the climax of his annual magical demonstration; a free performance he'd started putting on to combat the diminishing credibility of magic. A rowdy group of drunken revellers had become bored of his transformation spells, hooting and howling about how making butterflies from fruit was kids' stuff. What they wanted to see was Halcyon levitating a giant of a man who could hardly walk; making him fly way over their heads. The frustrated wizard had tried to explain that his wand wasn't equipped for that particular spell, not to mention the health and safety issues of levitating someone so ridiculously inebriated. He'd been forced off the stage by a barrage of sweaty, swollen fruit; backed up by a barrage of hurtful, narrow-minded insults about him not being magical at all. Henry was just five when the attack had happened, but he still remembered the look on the old man's face as he'd slowly gathered his belongings from the stage and made his way back through the curtain. He'd managed to maintain his dignity despite the bombardment of pungent produce hitting him as he retreated. But Halcyon had been so disappointed with society that he'd decided to boycott it altogether, and simply hadn't left his chambers since.

The room was dark and stuffy. The shutters were still closed against the day's bright assault, so it was lit only by a few surviving embers of the previous night's fire. As he grew accustomed to the dim light, Henry's eyes skimmed the surface of the room searching for abnormalities (other than the obvious, missing wizard). At first the search turned up a blank, but then Henry noticed that the ancient spell book, which was usually bound up in magical cloth and locked in a trunk deep in the old man's chambers to prevent it from falling into the wrong hands, was lying casually on the hearth. Its leather cover shimmered invitingly in the fire's glow. Henry stepped over and picked up the familiar book. He turned it over in his hands, enjoying the way the cover felt as it radiated heat collected from the waning fire. As he held it fondly, he noticed something else. There on the cover, almost invisible but for the darkness of the room, were some dimly glowing letters.

Henry moved away from the fire, deeper into the darkened chamber so as to make out the lettering more clearly.

*Time is short. Prepare well. The book will help. For goodness sake be careful! H.*

Henry stared down at the cover of the book. The faint golden lettering seemed to be fading before his very eyes. Whatever could it mean? Henry had spent the past four months eyeing this magical tome jealously, dreaming that one day he might be granted full access to its unearthly wisdom. Now, here he stood, alone in the old wizard's chambers, with what seemed like an open invitation to walk away with it. What should he do?

His brain started gathering his options up into a pack again, but before it could begin a shuffle he was distracted by the faint sound of clinking footsteps coming from below. Henry held his breath and listened. The footsteps were getting closer, and now he was picking up the deep murmur of distant voices. A small collaboration of cobbled boots was tramping up the spiralling staircase, their owners chatting casually. With no time left for thinking, Henry's body switched to autopilot. He stuffed the heavy old book under his arm inside his coat and started looking wildly about for an escape route. There was none. Henry's heart also seemed to be looking for an escape route. It clamoured inside the prison of his ribcage, beating hard with the rhythm of rising panic. His chest hurt. His head started to swim, ears pounding. The room began to turn and roll, like the deck of an abandoned ship and Henry realised that in his panic he'd forgotten to let go of his breath. He gulped in an enormous lungful of air and his head cleared a bit.

The footsteps were getting closer, and Henry was running out of time. Who knew what might happen to him if he were caught in Halcyon's chambers unaccompanied? He sped over to the door, poked one ear out into the corridor and listened again. Almost here … The owners of the boots were only thirty or so steps down from where Henry now stood, clutching the door frame as if it were a life raft. He steeled himself, then willed his own boots to make as little sound as possible as he flitted out of the room and up the stone stairs. He dashed around shadowy spiral estimating the position of the approaching feet by the sound they made, trying to keep a safe distance.

'Hey! The door's open, Chad,' said a deep voice. Henry kicked himself silently. The statement was accompanied by the sweeping metallic sound of short-swords being unsheathed.

Henry pressed his hot cheek against the cool wall in the centre of the staircase and continued breathing in shallow, even gasps. It sounded like castle guards, and Henry couldn't help wondering what they wanted with Halcyon.

More footsteps, and Henry could sense the soldiers moving in through the open door, poised and alert, their eyes dancing across the shadows to seek out any hidden menace. A familiar lazy creak followed by a wooden clack told Henry the shutters had been opened. The chamber must now be flooded with the brightness of the day outside. More footsteps. The opening and closing of various doors.

'Well, there's no-one here now. What d'you think we should do?' A sloosh of metal again suggested the swords were once more resting in their sheaths and Henry allowed himself a sigh of relief.

'Hmmmm ...' one of the soldiers contemplated.

'Do we still stand guard, or do we go tell the Captain about the door?'

Henry stumbled back up a few more steps as he heard a set of footsteps approach the door. He heard a 'sniff' echoing up the spiralling corridor and pushed himself further into the shadows that clung to the wall.

'You go. I'll stay here and keep watch.' The 'hmmmm' voice was calm and collected. Its words bounced off the grey walls suspiciously, and Henry had the distinct impression they were looking for him.

'Alright,' the other voice said, and a set of hasty footfalls became suddenly louder, and then began to drift back into the depths of the castle.

Henry stood, quiet as a mouse; quieter in fact because his lungs had once more decided it was time for a break. He willed them back to work and listened. Two soft footsteps; the clearing of a throat; and then the steady creak of the ancient door being swung back into place. Clunk.

Silence.

More silence.

Was the guard inside the room or out? Henry thought desperately about how to escape, and whether any of the spells Halcyon had taught him so far could help. As he pondered this dilemma he caught the sound of a tiny clink. Not much of a sound, but it was enough to tell him that the guard was outside the room. He was probably standing propped up against the battered old knocker, his eyes trained distrustfully on the dark shadows of the corridor leading upwards. Whatever was he going to do? The book stuffed under his coat felt warm and comforting, he hugged it to him and yearned for a solution to leak out from its mystical pages. The book grew hotter. Pretty soon it was becoming too hot to bear, and Henry had to stifle a moan as he slid it out from under his arm. The book cooled straight away and Henry cradled it in his arms. It had fallen open in his hands towards the middle, and Henry squinted against the shadows as he strained to read the text.

*Invisibility Spells*

*For centuries old, some of the greatest magical minds of our time have striven towards the ultimate goal of complete invisibility, and still we are no closer to finding a way.*

Oh great, Henry thought. Very helpful. But he read on …

*Whilst partial invisibility has proven to be a relatively simple art to master, it is useful as nothing more than a parlour trick to entertain young children, since a large portion of the body (approximately twenty to thirty percent in benchmark studies, depending on overall body mass) remains clearly visible. This phenomenon is believed to be, at least in part, due to the overriding effects of the Fundamental Confuddledom Theorem (consult the Alternative Physics Almanac for more information). But for those who find themselves in immediate peril, with no obvious means of escape …*

Yep. That's me. That's definitely me, Henry thought eagerly.

*… it may be possible to pass undetected through a limited space by casting a Concave Reflective Barrier\* in the direction of the impending danger. \* N.B. Consult appendix C for further details …*

…the paragraph ended. Henry turned quickly to the appendix in the back of the book to look up the *Concave Reflective Barrier*. It was on page 2733.

*The Concave Reflective Barrier spell (CRB)*

*This illusionary aide is a class fourteen spell, which can be used to conjure a real-time image of anything or anybody that the spell* caster can recall with sufficient accuracy. In this way an absconding wizard could pose as somebody else, or even just blend into the scenery. Though it should be noted this illusion will only work when viewed from the front of the casting arc.

Typical recall accuracy requirements;

Inanimate objects – 60 to 70%

Non-cognitive entities – 70 to 80%

Cognitive entities – 85% + (usually over 95% if comprehensible speech is required)

Essential Ingredients;

1 cup, essence of Monk weed

3 grains, Shadow dust

A good visual impression of the subject to be conjured

Optional extras;

The strength and duration of this spell can be increased by taking three drops of Doctor Hyperbole's Memory Enhancer (orally) just prior to spell casting.

Amidst the tension of his predicament, Henry allowed himself a moment of self-chastisement for not getting a bottle when he'd had the chance. He could use all the help he could get right now. But he did have his wand in his pocket, and it was fully charged up with Monk weed and Shadow dust as they were common components in the low-level spells he'd been practising with. So in theory he was charged up and ready to cast. The only thing he couldn't be sure of was how much of each was left, so it could be a short-lived bid for freedom.

He scanned the page, taking in the details of the charm. According to the book the illusion worked by projecting a memory into real space and time from the tip of his wand, making the objects contained in that memory appear solid and tangible from a certain direction. If he could conjure up an image of the empty corridor, an image he should have no problem remembering given that he'd spent the last fifteen-minutes standing with his face pressed firmly against it, he could slip undetected through the space behind the impression, right in front of the soldier's eyes.

His body tensed in objection to the outrageous plan, but his brain pointed out it was their only real option. It relaxed and agreed to get with the programme.

He slid his bag silently off his shoulder and smiled as he felt the familiar smooth warmth of the slender box against his blindly searching fingertips. Within seconds they'd popped the catch and were curling themselves about his faithful wand. The wand wasted no time and promptly dragged his hand eagerly upward, no longer an untamed stallion but rather a faithful hound tugging to be let off its leash. The image of the corridor fixed in his mind's eye, Henry glanced back down at the ancient pages of the spell book and began to think the strange, lyrical words of the short verse. Curling wafts of light began to drift from his fingers, turning orange along the shaft of the wand. But instead of gathering there in a tight ball, the shimmering glow spread out from its tip in a circular, curved dish. The dish grew rapidly, and before long was the size of two front doors, translucent in the darkness of the stairwell. Henry could see straight through the dish at the corridor in front of him. His confidence began to falter. Was it working? He jiggled his wand, weighing up his options. He froze in sudden horror as he heard the guard, probably alerted by the faint sound of movement up the corridor, leave his post and head towards where Henry stood.

'Hullo?' the deep voice questioned the shadows. The soldier drew his sword with the sound of steel against steel reminding Henry he was far from out of the woods yet.

Frantically, he continued thinking the incantation, pointing the tip of his wand down the stairwell. He squeezed his eyes almost completely shut and prayed the spell was working. He peeped, panic-stricken, at the downward turn of the stair. His breath caught in his throat as he saw the guard move into view.

He was in his late thirties, lean and angular with a clean-shaven face and a sadistic sparkle in his eyes. His right hand led the advance brandishing the tip of his short sword, his left hovering just above the hilt of his mace. It quivered with anticipation at being allowed to wreak havoc with the weapon at the merest hint of trouble. The guard stopped a few paces from the glowing disc projected from Henry's wand. Frowning, he turned and glared straight at Henry. Henry winced, readying for an attack. But after a long moment of inactivity it became clear the guard wasn't glaring at him at all. Thanks to the reflective barrier he was glaring at Henry's memory of the stairs; a memory he'd been quite careful to leave himself out of. The guard grunted, fingers flexing over the handle of the mace.

Very slowly Henry tiptoed back, pressing his body as quietly as possible against the outside wall of the stairwell, keeping the tip of his wand pointed directly at the guard. Instinctively he knew he didn't have much time, and not just because he was going to be horribly late for work if he didn't find a way past the guard. He was also pretty sure being caught here in the corridor, clutching a valuable book that didn't belong to him, would have far greater consequences than being docked a few shebbles from his pay pouch. He started to edge downwards, crab-stepping his way cautiously from stair to stair, rotating his body as he went to keep the wand's power between himself and the guard.

His left foot scuffed the corner of a step and he froze, his whole body rigid with the anticipation of discovery. The guard's head snapped round, eyes narrowing. They darted this way and that, confusion flitting across his brow. He was literally inches from Henry now and the tension was unbearable. The guard had only to reach out one hand and it could break through the flimsy illusion of the empty corridor and tweak the fugitive on the nose. Henry closed his eyes and prepared to meet his doom. But just when Henry thought he could bear it no more, there was a sudden thump from higher up the corridor.

He was so shocked by the noise for a split second he forgot to be terrified, and whipped his head round to see what could possibly have made it. Predictably, the guard was also interested in the answer to this question. He turned in a flash and began bounding furtively up the stairway three steps at a time; confident he was about to make an arrest.

Henry wasted no more time wondering what, or who had caused the thump that had saved him. He watched as the guard's trailing heel was swallowed by the constant curve of the corridor, then turned on his own heels and fled in the opposite direction, stuffing the wand and book safely back under his coat.

# Chapter 11

Henry didn't stop fleeing until he'd reached the safety of the dark, secretive passage that led off the central courtyard to the stairs down into the vault. Here he paused for a moment to catch his breath, and his senses. He had to hide the incriminating evidence before he met anyone else, so he slung his bag off his shoulder and reorganised the contents so he could cram the hefty spell book inside it. It was a little too big so Henry wrapped the fabric of his robe around the bit left sticking out of the top and hoped it didn't look too suspicious. It did look suspicious, to Henry anyway, but that was because he knew what it contained. He had to trust the flush in his cheeks wouldn't be broadcasting that information to the rest of the world. He slung the bag back over his shoulder and scuttled along the corridor towards his place of work a full half-hour earlier than usual.

Mr Colloid was already perched on his tortuous chair like a vulture. He looked up as Henry trotted down the stairs, narrowing his eyes at the young accountant. Henry countered with what he hoped was a cheery smile, but gave up when it felt like the sides of his face might crack. He dropped his eyes and headed over to his desk trying to keep his burgeoning bag out of line-of-sight from his employer.

'Noble?'

Henry stopped and turned, still fielding the over-stuffed satchel out of view. The two of them were alone in the echoing dimness of the vaults.

'What a pleasant surprise,' his employer smarmed. 'What brings you into the office so early on a Monday? Guilty conscience?'

Henry stood, unsure how to respond. Especially since he did, technically, have a guilty conscience.

Mr Colloid's eyes narrowed further as he watched the young man sweat and turn pink. 'What are you hiding, boy?' His curiosity was almost tangible, scratching and clawing for a way into Henry's mind. 'I know you're up to something. You might as well confess.'

Confess what? His magic training? Snooping around Halcyon's chamber? The spell book in his satchel? He decided on a one-word defence that would cover all possible options. 'Sorry.'

The irrelevance of this apology seemed to appease and bewilder the probing Chief Accountant in equal measure. Henry took advantage of his quandary and continued towards the counting benches. Once there, he tucked his bag under the table and settled down to start work.

What on earth had happened to Halcyon? Why were the castle guards patrolling outside his room? Variations of these questions ran amuck through his mind as he tried not to lose count of the coins in front of him.

Pretty soon the room filled up with other accountants. With every friendly nod of the head tossed in his direction, Henry felt his nerves returning to their normal state of calm. At around eleven o'clock he was just considering taking a break to stretch his legs when one of the castle's guards came clanking down the steps and approached the Chief Accountant. He whispered something into Mr Colloid's ear, whose usual expression of pinched sourness rearranged itself into a satisfied sneer directed straight at Henry.

'Oh really? How interesting,' Mr Colloid said still staring.

The guard's eyes followed Mr Colloid's line of sight, also picking out the hunched up figure of the young accountant across the room. Henry wanted to slide under the table to join his bag.

'Him?' the guard asked gruffly.

'Yes. But I'll see to it. You may go now.' The guard nodded a cursory nod and then clanked back up the stairs to continue doing whatever it is castle guards do when they're not apprehending criminals.

Henry's chest tightened as his employer fixed him with steely eyes. They knew about the book! How did they know? How *could* they know? Henry's brain rallied these pointless questions into a semi-organised gang that joined the other unanswered questions already running about. Together they formed the beginnings of a full scale riot inside his head.

Mr Colloid barked, 'Noble! Come here, and bring your bag. Mr Frugal, take down the boy's count. No point in wasting a morning's work.' Mr Colloid's voice was wet with contempt and Henry felt his cheeks burn as he gathered up his belongings and headed reluctantly over to the desk.

'Yes?'

'Well, well, well Mr Noble,' Mr Colloid oozed, 'I hope you don't have anything special planned for the near future. It seems you're going to be otherwise occupied.' He was eyeing Henry's over-stuffed satchel and Henry's stomach sank into the hollow space inside his trembling legs.

He gulped and tried to think of something to say, but without being sure what kind of trouble he was in his brain refused to play any part in the process. The best he could manage without its help was a couple of dry gulps and a tentative, 'Why's that?'

'I have a little job for you, Noble.'

A job? Henry's racing heart began to slow a little as it realised this wasn't a request for him to empty the stolen goods out of his bag and head down to the castle's dungeons to be placed under arrest. He felt the blood draining out of his burning cheeks, and loosened his death-grip on the satchel. 'Oh?'

'Yes, a little mission. The King's business. There's a large consignment of coconuts coming to port in Amalga in just under a fortnight, and we need someone to deliver the payment and oversee transportation back to Terratonia in time for His Majesty's birthday party.'

The optimistic feeling that had been stealing over Henry made a sharp about-face and started marching in the other direction. Naked dread drained even more colour from his cheeks. He was being sent on a mission. A trade mission. For the last nine accountants, including his father and D.C.'s brother, this had spelt certain doom. After the last failed mission two years ago there had been talk about sending armed guards with the party if the King ever wanted to trade on the coast again. Surely this meant he'd get protection?

'But not on my own, right?' he asked his employer with wide eyes.

The man sneered. 'Cosset will accompany you. I'll inform him as soon as he returns from the lower vaults.'

'But ... but what about guards? The bandits?'

'No-one to spare I'm afraid,' Mr Colloid said in a very unafraid tone of voice. 'They'll be far too busy making arrangements for the party. You can't be too careful when it comes to the King's safety.' He smiled unkindly. 'You should make it back just in time with the coconuts if you leave tomorrow.'

'Tomorrow?' Henry's head spun and he swayed back on his heels.

'I can see how bowled over you are by the trust I'm instilling in you,' Mr Colloid's tone mocked. 'You may take the rest of the day off to prepare for the trip. I'm sure you don't want to be late for the King's birthday so you'll leave at five-o'clock sharp tomorrow morning. I'll meet you here then with supplies and instructions. Oh, and with the gold. We mustn't forget the gold.' He was glowing with repugnant glee, and Henry felt his stomach turning to stone inside his legs.

'But ...' he started to argue, looking around at his colleagues for support. All the other accountants were being studiously oblivious to the exchange.

'Perhaps you'd rather I sent you home permanently? Your job here in the vaults terminated; your access to the castle reneged?'

Henry swallowed hard. No work meant his family would go hungry. He could possibly find another job ... but if he wasn't allowed back into the castle how would he discover what had happened to Halcyon and continue his magical studies? There was no question of it. He clamped any further objections shut behind bitter lips and turned leaden legs to the task of climbing the stairs.

As he walked along the corridor on the eastern side of the courtyard Henry's brain wrestled to make sense of the morning. Why was he being sent off with the King's gold without any protection? They had to know it was a death sentence. Did it have something to do with Halcyon's disappearance? He hardly knew Peter, but was pretty sure he wouldn't be much use in a fight against marauding bandits. Remembering how the boy's mother had pulled Edmund and he apart, part of him wished she was coming instead. Henry was distracted from this disturbing train of thought by a familiar voice. He froze and pushed himself into the shadowy corner of the cold outer wall of the courtyard, listening.

'You did a good job Chad, catching him on your own and all. Pity there's nothing we can pin on him. You thieving scoundrel, sneaking about the castle towers opening doors you've got no business opening!' It was the guards from outside Halcyon's chamber and they appeared to be flanking a person they planned on forcibly ejecting from the premises. Henry's eyes widened. Edmund Blight.

It must have been him up the stairwell earlier. But why? Was he responsible for Halcyon's disappearance? Henry was beginning to feel like he was reading a book that'd had every other page ripped out. He didn't understand anything going on right now. But that bully turning up here right after their confrontation in the square, on the morning Halcyon goes missing? That was just too much of a coincidence to be a coincidence.

Henry waited nervously for the trio to move out of sight towards a rear castle exit, and then swept along the corridor as quickly as he could without looking like he was running. He felt a rising swell of urgency as he recalled the words emblazoned on the cover of the spell book.

*Time is short. Prepare well. The book will help ...*

He must get to work immediately preparing his wand for the

direst of possible circumstances. Maybe this was going to be the end of him? Or maybe it was his chance to be a hero and solve the mystery of the disappearing accountants? This idea brightened his spirits enough to propel him into a swift trot as he left the castle through the grand portcullis, his brain beginning to make a list of all the things he should get done.

He knew that the bulk of the low to mid-level spells he'd been working with could be produced using various combinations of a few dozen key ingredients, but you had to soak them individually into the wand rather than mixing a finished potent. After checking his mother was out of the house and his brothers still safely in school, he got to work boiling up herbs and extracts in his peculiar-looking cauldron. It really was an ingenious invention. Divided into segments, with an enchanted channel running down the centre so that a wand could be in contact with the contents of all eight compartments simultaneously, it even came with a spell baked into the iron bowl that made it glow red-hot around any segment you filled. This allowed it to cook the strange soups inside without cooking anything that touched it on the outside.

As far as Henry could tell, there was no limit to the amount of magical ingredients the Malvern stick could store, at least not any he'd been able to scuff. But it was still a lengthy procedure; boiling up the individual ingredients he would need so that they could be mixed together from his wand in any combination during the casting of a spell. As the first batch bubbled away, Henry turned his attention to the book. He scanned the ancient pages for any hint about what new spells he might need on this journey.

*The book will help ...*

He placed it face up on the desk and looked at it. It stared back at him impassively. After a minute or so Henry broke the stand-off with an exasperated, 'Well, help then.'

The book shivered, then hopped, surprising Henry out of his seat on the bed. The front cover flew up and it landed open on page 344.

*The Classic Claustrophonic Charm – a convenient compression technique*

*This class twelve spell can be used to condense the contents of a trunk, or other solid container, so that it can be conveniently stored in a much smaller space.*

*Essential Ingredients;*

*2 tsps, Gnomic Balsam*

*2 grains, Feather Salt*

*5 drops, Revivification Potent*

*A pinch of cornflower blue*

*Directions: Simply enchant a suitable storage container and then fill it with items to be stored. (Note: Do not place items in storage prior to enchantment. It is the container you want to compress, not your belongings, and magical creases are extremely difficult to press out of your clothing.) Once the container is enchanted, compression can be triggered using the words of the application incantation, which should be repeated until your container has shrunk to the desired size for transportation or storage. Once reduced, the container will become incredibly strong, the physics of which involve a matter-to-volume ratio far too complex to explain in these pages. (For clarification consult The Alternative Physics Almanac by Professor Dictum). This will also help protect your possessions. To restore the container to its original dimensions, use the classic reversal charm, detailed on page 4025.*

*Special note: it is not recommended that you store any living person or animal in this way since the additional complication of reducing biological material makes it impossible to guarantee resurrection to normal proportions. This could leave a person or animal with an enormous head or very long legs for example. In the worst case scenario, they could remain trapped indefinitely in miniature form, which would no doubt make them pretty cross.*

Henry's attention was torn from the pages of the book by the sound of a slamming door that was swiftly followed by an angry buzzing coming from his wand. The liquid bubbling in the cauldron's segments shimmered with its vibration. He looked out of the window and for the first time noticed the late afternoon sun, just begging to tinge the scenery golden. The door must have been his brothers getting back from school. He slammed the book shut, making a mental note of the page it had shown him, and stuffed it under his bed.

He stood and checked the bubbling cauldron, then waved his hand over the enchanted rock he'd placed beside it, steeped with an *intellect deflector* spell. As he thought the familiar words of the ignition charm the rock began to glow a gentle pink, signifying that the magic was now active and the rock believed it was a miracle; at least enough to convince his brothers of it anyway. He could hear them squabbling as he made his way downstairs. They stopped as Henry appeared in the doorway.

'What are you doing here?' Will asked in an accusatory tone. 'Have those people at the castle finally realised what a numbskull you are and given you the boot?'

Bill giggled at his brother's quip and goaded Henry with a waggle of the spoon he'd been using to pry open a rusty box.

'No, I've been sent home to get ready,' Henry replied.

'For what?' the twins asked in unison.

Henry ignored them and began searching the kitchen for clean clothing to pack.

Bill lost interest in the exchange, retuning his attention to the old box they'd pulled out of the river earlier. But Will, still annoyed at having been beaten to the treasure by his younger twin, jutted out his chin at Henry. 'What are you getting ready for then, numbskull?'

Another snort of laughter from Bill.

'Not that it's any of your business, *those people at the castle* you love so much are sending me on a mission.' He felt a surge of resentment. His brothers had seemed to miss their father so little he couldn't imagine them being sad to see him go the same way.

Bill stopped wrestling with the box and looked at him. 'What mission?'

Something about the look on the boy's face fanned a cool breeze across Henry's temper. 'To Amalga. The King wants coconuts for his birthday party.'

It sounded so innocent when he spoke it out loud. Coconuts for a party. Hardly a life threatening mission, you'd think. But the identical looks of horror that slapped his bothers across the face confirmed it was anything but innocent.

Bill's bottom lip began to wobble and he looked much younger than his nine years. As usual, it was Will who spoke for them. 'Like Dad? Are you going away on a mission like Dad?'

At that moment the kitchen door opened and Mrs Noble stood

there. She glanced about the kitchen, clearly looking for a reason why her sons weren't bickering. Bill ran to her and buried his head in her stomach, sniffling. 'What is going on here?' she asked, patting her young son's head to comfort him.

Before Henry could answer, Will ran over and threw himself against her apron too. 'They're sending Henry away!' he cried with an amount of alarm that surprised Henry. 'They can't do that, can they Mum? Like Dad! They're sending him into the forest like Dad!'

Her face paled and she dropped the basket of food she'd just brought back from the market. A single apple toppled out and rolled across the floor.

She looked at her eldest son. 'What does he mean, Henry?' It was barely a whisper.

'I'm being sent to Amalga. Mr Colloid told me this morning. We leave at five o'clock tomorrow. Coconuts,' he finished lamely.

'*We* leave? How many guards are you taking?'

Henry could hear a desperate hitch in her voice and hated Mr Colloid even more for doing this to his mother. He thought briefly about lying, to make her feel better, but knew she would see straight through him before the fib had even left his mouth. 'No. Just a junior clerk and me. But we'll be OK Mum, I know we will. It's been over a year since the last attack.'

'It's been over a year since the last wretched trade mission!' his mother's voice was thin with hysteria. 'I won't let you go! You can't go! Why are they doing this, Henry? Coconuts? They're sending my boy off into danger for a bowl of party snacks? Well, no. Nuts to the King's coconuts! You're my son!' She was crying now, and Henry rushed to join his brothers at her side and put his arms around her.

'If I don't go they'll kick me out of the vaults. You know we can't eat if I don't bring home my wages.'

His mother's body was racked with a huge sob. She shook off her sons and lunged for the table, gripping its edge as she fought to control her rising panic. The three brothers stood together by the door, unsure how to console her.

Henry took a tentative step. 'A year is an awfully long time to go without anyone to rob,' he said. 'I'm sure any bandits have long since packed up to find more lucrative grounds.'

Getting her hitching sobs under control their mother sank down into a chair. 'I wish I could believe that Son.' She wiped at her eyes inconsolably with her apron.

'I can do this Mum. I've ...' He considered for a split second telling her about his early morning magic lessons. About the spell book and the glowing note from Halcyon.

His mother looked at him with teary eyes. They were eyes that begged him to tell her something that would reassure her; make her believe he could span the treacherous road to the coast and back again without befalling the same fate as everyone else. They were also the hurt and confused eyes of a woman whose heart was crumbling.

'Please be careful, Henry,' she wept softly. The twins moved past Henry to crowd around her shoulders, the three of them looking at him with doleful eyes. 'I couldn't bear to lose you too,' she said, drawing the younger boys too her with protective arms.

Under his family's tearful gaze, Henry made a silent promise to the world that he was coming out, wand a-blazing. And it had better not get in his way.

# Chapter 12

After packing up the rest of his personal belongings and grinding his way through a tortuously quiet family supper, Henry went back up to his room to load a new batch of ingredients into his cauldron. His brothers were so subdued he didn't think they'd be rooting him out to antagonise him, and even if they did he was beyond caring. What mattered now was gleaning as much information as he could from the book and cooking up sufficient spell components to make it useful.

He was startled out of his work by a soft knock at the door.

'H?' It was D.C.

Henry opened the door a crack and ushered her in. She took in the piles of ingredients and jars of extracts and looked at him seriously.

'So it's true.' It wasn't a question.

'How did you know?'

'We live a few doors down from Peter Cosset. He's going with you, right?'

Henry nodded.

'Yeah, you could hear the fuss his mother made right across town. Screaming and wailing like someone was trying to remove her insides with a spoon. Went raging off towards the castle and a few hours later was escorted back by a couple of guards. Whole town is talking about it; how she narrowly avoided a night in the dungeons trying to stop them sending her poor, delicate son off on a trade mission. Wasn't sure you were going too until I got here and saw the mess your mother is in.'

Henry's shoulders drooped at the thought and he turned to his cauldron on the windowsill. 'I know. I can't stand to see her like that. I just don't know what to say to make her feel better.'

D.C. placed a comforting hand on her friend's back and watched him work. 'So what spells are we taking?'

Henry stopped and turned to face her, awkwardly close in the confines of his bedroom. 'We?'

She stepped back. 'Of course, we! What did you think? I was going to leave you to get all the glory?'

'Glory?'

'Of course glory! When we find the criminals who've been terrorising our people and bring them back to the castle dungeons!'

'D.C. this isn't a game ... or turning nuts into field mice. There are dangerous people out in the forest.'

'But you're a wizard!' she enthused, indicating the garb strewn about his room.

Henry's cheek flushed. 'No I'm not. Not yet anyway. The limited number of spells I know are mostly harmless.'

D.C. looked down at the spell book now open at another charm on his desk. Henry leapt to slam it shut. She blanched. 'I'm not your enemy here, Henry.'

'I know. It's just ... I'm not even sure if I'm supposed to have it, and Halcyon has told me again and again not to let its magic fall into the wrong hands.' The words were out of his mouth and punching her in the ego before he had time to consider the implication.

'So, I'm the wrong hands?'

No! No ... it's just ...' Henry's hands flapped at his sides without much purpose.

'Fine. You don't want to share it, that's fine. But *you* have the spell book. You told me it contains all the spells in the known world. So, just learn something more deadly.' She straightened, the force of the idea washing away the recent slight against her character. 'I can help you! Come on, H. We can do this!'

'NO!' Henry's rebuttal came out fiercer than he'd intended. He'd been so wrapped up in preparations he'd forgotten how tense he was. 'Any spells I could use to fight off an ambush are way higher than I can cast yet,' he continued in a gentler tone. 'They need so much magic it'd take ages for me to form them. Pretty useless in the face of an ambush – one moment please Mr Bandit, I just need to make enough magic for this spell. Even if I could form one up in time I'd be more likely to hit a tree than a charging attacker.' D.C. had started shaking her head as if to stop his words from climbing into her ears. 'Besides.' He stepped towards her, but she stepped back on the defence. 'You saw the state of my mother. My two brothers are just as devastated, which is almost as unexpected as the trade mission. There are *eight* people in your house who will feel just as bad.'

'And it should be nine people!' she retorted in anger. 'We're not a family without Rowan. My brother is out there in the forest somewhere, and so is your dad! This is our chance to find out what happened!'

'I'm not even sure they're still out there, D.C.' Henry felt like he was admitting this to himself for the first time as much as her. 'It's been two years since my dad ...' he trailed off.

D.C. stared him down stiffly. 'Well I believe they are. And I believe we can bring them home. Even without magic!'

'I wish I had your confidence.' He sighed. 'But I'm not taking you with me. No arguments. It's just too dangerous. Anyway, don't you have school tomorrow?'

The girl blanched. She was still shaking her head, banishing negative thoughts as she backed towards the door.

'Wish me luck?' Henry smiled weakly, feeling awful.

'Good luck,' she mumbled through gritted teeth, then turned and stalked out slamming the door behind her.

Oh great, Henry thought as he returned to work at the cauldron. Now I've alienated the only friend I had left. He only hoped he would make it back from the trade mission so that he could go about mending some bridges. Somewhere deep inside he allowed himself to try on the notion that she could be right. That he could defeat the bandits and find the missing accountants out there in the wilds. He liked the way the idea felt, but it flopped about on his low self-esteem like an over-sized jumper.

Henry worked all through the night mixing together the herbs and potents he thought he might need. The ancient spell book continued to be helpful, flipping over pages to suggest several more spells. He learnt incantations for the *spectrum luminosity* charm, which lit up dark places like a candle, and *Fulcrum's Flabbergaster*, which could set a target spinning like a top (provided it wasn't fixed to the floor). It wasn't an especially dangerous spell, but as the author pointed out, it was handy for drying clothes quickly on a camping trip.

Once he'd done all the things he and the book could think of he piled his wizardly garb on the bed. He stuffed his robe and hat into the last remnants of space in his burgeoning knapsack, then looked at what was left of the pile. As he wondered how he was going to get it all up to the castle the pile of wizardly garb hopped. The heavy cauldron slithered off on to the floor, narrowly missing his feet, as the spell book elbowed its way open to page 344.

*The Classic Claustrophonic Charm.*

Of course! Henry looked around his room for a good-sized storage device to enchant. The only thing that was even vaguely suitable was his ink-stained writing desk, which had two big drawers, one on either side of the leg hole. He frowned. It wasn't ideal, but it was better than his huge teak wardrobe so he supposed it would have to do. He reminded himself of the enchantment and then fired it smartly off at the unsuspecting desk. The desk shivered as it absorbed the light from the spell, but made no other complaints.

At four o'clock the next morning Henry packed his magical equipment, including the spell book, cauldron and dozens of small bottles and pouches, into the spacious draws. Glancing around he grabbed some quills and bundled up a stack of parchment in a length of twine. He shoved those in too and slid the drawers shut. Then he held his wand over the desk and began reciting the words of the ignition charm. As he did the desk began to shrink. Over and over again he spoke the words of the spell, until eventually the desk was the size of something one might find in a dolls-house. It sat, looking quite lost in the big dusty space the grown-up desk had occupied. He picked it up and marvelled at the miniature perfection. He gave it a tentative squeeze. The twig-like legs seemed as sturdy as the book had promised. He guessed there might be a few raised eyebrows when his family entered his room and found the rather large desk missing. But that was another bridge he could cross when he got home ... if he ever made it home.

He stuffed the writing desk into a knapsack pocket and shoved his wand, tip first, into his inside jacket pocket. He tried a couple of quick-draws, fumbling the first few and trying out several different techniques and pockets before settling on a style. It involved holding his jacket out like a wing with his left hand while the right dove across his chest to grab the handle. He took a moment to admit Halcyon had been right. It was slower than slipping the wand out of the tailored slit in his robe. But it was still pretty slick and there would be a lot fewer questions to answer than if he turned up at the castle in his robe. He took one last look around his room. It was still dark outside, the night snoring away as if nothing was going on. He shouldered his bag and made his way down the stairs.

His mother was sitting by the stove. A delicious smell of baking hung in the air like a warm blanket and a stack of pancakes sat steaming on the table. She stood and handed him a large paper bag. 'Some food for the trip. I know they'll give you supplies at the castle, but I baked a few fresh treats to get you started.' She looked utterly miserable.

She didn't speak as she watched Henry munch through the stack of sweet pancakes. He willed himself to enjoy them, but in truth his stomach was already too full of worry.

'You be careful Henry,' she said later as she straightened his collar by the kitchen door and patted his bulging knapsack to make sure everything was secured.

'I will Mum. I double-promise.' She smiled at this echo from the past, an exchange that had become family tradition when promising to do something really important. That was back when times were happier of course. Then he kissed her on the cheek, as he always did when he headed out of the door for work. 'I'll be back soon.'

# Chapter 13

It was past twenty-to-five by the time Henry started trudging along the path leading away from his house and around the market square to the castle. He was running a little late, so he picked up his pace, feeling cold and alone in the dark and deserted streets. The weight of his belongings dug into his shoulders as if to remind him of the gravity of his situation. Everyone else was still safely tucked up in their beds, oblivious to his impending doom. As he walked, Henry started to see the warm glow of paraffin lamps and candles pop into existence at scattered windows. Through misty curtains he could glimpse the shadows of early-risers going about their early-rising business as if this were just another ordinary day.

He approached the castle fifteen minutes later and saw movement outside the portcullis gates. Three figures and a pair of four-legged beasts materialised out of the mist as the fingers of dawn stroked the horizon. The figures resolved into Mr Colloid, Peter Cosset, and one of the King's stable-hands gripping the reins of two of the shabbiest looking ponies Henry had ever seen. He nodded a greeting to Peter and the stable-hand, choosing to completely ignore the other man. Mr Colloid smirked through the crisp air. Peter's eyes were wide and haunted. He was wearing the expression of someone who hoped he was still dreaming. One of the ponies snorted and pushed its face against the terrified boy's bag, almost knocking him off his feet.

'How kind of you to finally join us, Master Noble,' Mr Colloid sneered dropping a heavy pouch full of gold and a bundle of wrapped parchment by his feet. 'You'll be needing these; maps, purchase orders, and a bag full of gold. Mustn't forget the gold now, must we?' Henry glanced down. 'Strap the pouch tight to your belt boy, we wouldn't want to lose it.' With that loaded statement still hanging in the air, the Chief Accountant turned on his heel and stalked back into the castle.

Henry stared at the items by his feet, then looked up at the stable-hand who smiled apologetically. 'They don't look like much, but they're willing and not too wild,' he said, cocking his head towards the dishevelled steeds standing behind him. 'I was going to turn out a couple of the fastest thoroughbreds but the Chief said the King didn't want to risk valuable horses on such a dangerous mission … ' The young stable-hand trailed off, realising by the fixed looks of horror on the two accountants' faces that this story wasn't helping matters. 'There's a shelter and bedroll packed on to your saddles. Brushes for the ponies too. Don't forget to rub them down each night or their backs will get in a terrible mess. Cook filled the saddlebags with enough supplies to last the trip. Dried meat and crackers. That sort of thing. There's a full water pouch too, but you'll need to stop and boil up more at the ponds along the track. Sorry,' he finished feebly, holding out the reins so that Henry and Peter could each take possession of a pony. His duties dispensed, the stable-hand also scuttled into the safety of the castle's belly.

What? No weapons, Henry thought. Not that he would know how to wield a short sword. But the King was happy to send two of his faithful accounting staff off like lambs to the slaughter, and yet didn't want to risk any of his thoroughbreds? Henry ground his teeth as he patted his ride tentatively on the neck. The shaggy chestnut drew its lips back into an enormous grin, then sneezed, spraying Henry's jacket with slimy white saliva. He sighed and glanced over at Peter, who was looking equally dubious about his own shambolic grey pony.

'Ready?' he asked.

Peter looked apprehensive, perhaps trying to work out whether a simple 'no' would suffice. 'I guess …' he managed eventually.

So they dragged themselves up into the creaky old saddles and kicked their mounts on into the dewy rising dawn.

• • •

About an hour out of town as the forest canopy began to do serious battle with the rising sun, Henry decided it was time to break the silence and get to know his travelling companion. They were going to be spending the next ten days together after all. Or they were going to be dying together Henry's brain reminded him forlornly.

'Your mum's pretty scary,' he said, hoping it sounded friendly.

Peter looked about like a startled rabbit as if expecting to be overheard. The thickening forest paid no heed, but the sight of it clearly didn't reassure him. 'She just worries about me,' he said still glancing about like a bird.

'Of course she does. Mine too.' Perhaps Henry could use this commonality to create a bond. 'She went crazy when I told her about the mission. Flipped her apron,' he fibbed a little.

Peter looked straight at him. 'Mine too. Did she go to the castle?'

'Practically had to hold her back. But Colloid said I'd lose my job if I didn't go and we can't afford to live without it.'

Peter chewed his bottom lip. 'Mum tried to hand in my notice, but they wouldn't let her. Threatened to throw her in the dungeon and take the house away. Some trumped up charge about unpaid death taxes she said.'

'Oh, I'm sorry,' Henry said, genuinely feeling it.

Peter shrugged. 'Dad died twelve years ago. I was only just four so I barely remember him. He was quite a successful tailor though, by royal appointment and everything. We were lucky because he left us the house and a little nest-egg, so mother is always telling me.' He looked sadly back over his shoulder as if hoping she might have followed them.

'That does sound lucky.' Henry felt a pang of envy and then pulled himself up and delivered a mental slap. Peter's father was definitely dead. He would rather have hope than money.

'What was that?'

The alarm in Peter's voice made Henry pull his mount up to a standstill. 'What?'

Peter made a shushing action and listened to the whispering forest.

There was a loud *crack* and they both whipped their heads round to stare into the thickening tangle of forest behind them. Henry's hand went instinctively to the inside of his jacket and he drew out his wand slowly, guiding the pony's head round with the other so that he was facing the direction of the sound. Peter looked at the shiny black stick but said nothing, his ears still scanning the undergrowth. They stood like that, their horses munching placidly on their bridles, as time stretched out.

When the forest uttered no more unexpected noises Henry forced himself to relax. 'It was probably just a dead branch falling.'

After a few more moments of intense listening, Peter seemed to accept the possibility. 'What's that?' he asked gesturing at the wand.

Henry swung his ride's head back around and looked at the black stick in his hand. 'Oh, you know, just a stick.'

Peter's eyebrows drew down into a frown. 'A stick?'

Technically it was the truth. Henry thought it was a bit too soon to go into any more detail unless he absolutely had to. He slipped it back into his jacket and urged his pony on with a kick. 'Come on Peter. The sooner we get there the sooner we get back.'

It was a hard logic to argue with so Peter pushed his own pony on with his heels.

As they rode through the morning Henry continued to try and get to know his companion. He learnt that Peter's father had died of an unexplained fever that had piloted him from healthy and happy to stone cold dead in under three days. His mother had been obsessed with illness and hygiene ever since. He drew a never ending supply of white handkerchiefs out of various pockets from time to time, fussing at his nose and dabbing his forehead in a way that suggested he'd picked up a lot of his mother's foibles. He was a year younger than Henry and had left school as soon as possible, going to work in the vaults as an antidote to his hay fever, which he said almost crippled him in springtime. In return Henry shared a few sparse facts about his own life, though he left out the bit about being a wizard and his father being lost on the very journey they were undertaking. He thought that might push the poor lad over the edge.

'So, what is the stick for?' Peter asked when they stopped for lunch.

Henry was investigating the baked goods his mother had packed, eyeing Peter's own much larger paper bag with envy. 'What did your mum pack?' he asked, avoiding the question.

Peter looked at the bag. 'That? That's my medications. They told her they'd pack supplies from the kitchen.'

Henry shook his head, feeling grateful once again that he was in his own shoes and not Peter's. He ripped a loaded ham sandwich in two and handed half to Peter, who took it and sat down next to him on the peaty floor. They leant against a log and watched their ponies chomping through foliage much in the way they were chomping through the sandwich.

'Why do you carry a stick?' Peter tried again as he brushed breadcrumbs off his lap.

'Protection?' Henry's answer sounded more like a question and Peter frowned again.

'How much damage can you do with a stick?'

'I dunno.' Henry made an effort to sound casual. 'More damage than without it.' He could see Peter's face contort as he tried to process this algorithm. 'Shall we?' He jumped up and stuffed the less-full paper bag into his saddlebag.

'I guess,' said Peter, and they stepped back up into their saddles.

The rest of the day passed without much note. Peter was still jumping at shadows, and as the forest canopy thickened, its floor softening underfoot, Henry felt the twitchiness rubbing off on him. Several times he jumped when he thought he heard a sound off in the bracken, his mind conjuring the image of a band of robbers tracking them through the undergrowth in a really unhelpful way.

It's alright, he reassured himself silently. They were way past the point where his father had been accosted. Perhaps they were going to make it after all? When the shafts of thin sunlight barging their way through the treetops started to turn golden, Henry judged it was a good time to stop and make camp. They picked a light clearing with a small pond to water the ponies, which they tethered to a strong branch before removing their saddles.

'You rub them down. I'll get camp set up.' Henry patted Peter's shoulder, then unbuckled both their saddle rolls and went to find a good spot to pitch the shelter. Once he'd banged struts into place and strung the canvass sheets between them he looked at their new home for the next couple of weeks. It wasn't going to keep much out but rain and the scatter of golden leaves making an early start on autumn.

He shrugged at the lean-to, telling it, 'worrying won't change anything, so I might as well get a fire going.' The crude shelter voiced no objections so he went off in search of deadfall.

A couple of hours later they were sitting beside the crackling yellow flames. Henry had shared two cheese sandwiches and a couple of sugar buns from his paper bag. Peter followed up the meal with a handful of pellets and a foul-smelling broth boiled from some herbs inside his own bag. It was almost completely dark and Henry could hear the sounds of the forest waking up. An owl hooted. A night-hawk replied. A bush somewhere just out of range of the glow of the fire, rustled creepily.

Just a breeze, Henry told himself, feeling not even the slightest puff of it on his skin.

'We're a tenth of the way there already, Peter. Nine more days like this and we'll be back in our own beds, snug as you like.'

There was a long moment of silence, filled only by the chattering of burning firewood.

'They say there are monsters out here,' Peter said eventually, eyes fixed on the fire.

'Who does?'

He turned haunted eyes on Henry. 'Everyone ... they say the accountants were taken by huge trolls. Other people too; several hunters and at least one mushroom forager.'

Henry let the fire do the talking while he chewed this over. The sound of a branch snapping somewhere deep in the shadows interrupted its monologue. Henry's heart jumped into his throat. He listened.

The crackling fire continued.

Feeling a bit foolish he looked at Peter seriously. 'You can't believe everything people gossip about in the square.' With an aunt like his, if anyone should know this it was Henry.

'It's true!' Peter said more urgently. 'Where my friend Penny works, the guards say the whole city was on amber alert because of troll sightings in the outlying trees of the forest. People are too afraid to go further than the edge of the meadow. Even the huntsmen travel in groups and always maintain a clear path back to open ground.'

Henry's brow crinkled. He hadn't heard any of this. 'It's just gossip, Peter. And not very good gossip or my aunt would have been talking about it too.'

Peter's cheeks flushed. 'Penny is not a gossip!' he defended. Realising how much he'd raised his voice by the surprise on Henry's face, Peter flushed a little harder then went back to staring into the fire. 'She said the guards told her. And she is not the type of person to gossip.'

Henry tapped his fingers on his bottom lip. Trolls in the forest? He glanced around but all he could see were the ghosts of trees at the edge of the fire's warming arc. He thought about what D.C. had said about the doll. *Chalk up another loss to the demons in the forest.*

The undergrowth rustled again and Henry pulled his bedroll up over his knees.

'They say no-one has come or gone through the Gateway Passage for two years. That the trolls are waiting to gobble you up ...' Peter's voice was almost dreamy as his expressionless eyes stared unblinkingly into the heart of the fire.

'OK, Peter,' Henry said, fear tightening around his vocal cords to give a sharp edge to his voice. 'That kind of talk really isn't helping.'

'But Penny said every security firm in Terratonia had been put on amber alert ...'

'Peter!' Henry's words came out sharper than he'd intended, making Peter flinch. 'That's as maybe, but talk is often exaggerated. Especially by bored guards who want to impress a girl. There might a few robbers about but this is a big forest and there is no reason to believe it's filled with monsters. We'll be fine.' Was he persuading Peter or himself, he wondered as his ears continued to dance through the night noises finding things to be scared of.

He rolled his coat up into a ball, thumping it into a rough pillow-sized hump. After so little sleep the night before and the constant stress of the day he felt exhausted. Pulling his blanket up over his legs he wiggled his body as close to the fire as he could without burning his nose. 'We should get some sleep. We'll rise with the sun and get this thing done as quickly as we can. OK?'

His reply was the rustle of bedroll and Peter shuffling up closer to the fire beside him.

Henry moved his hand to curl comfortably around the smooth handle of his wand, which was now slipped down inside his bedroll beside him. He stared blindly up at the sloping roof of their shelter, hypnotised by the rippling motion of a slight breeze caught underneath it. Just the wind, came a silent reminder from inside him, and he drifted off into an uneasy sleep.

He dreamt of battling a huge dragon with a cacophony of magic, and rescuing his father and all the other people from its stinking lair. The Henry inside his dream-world lit a fire of exhilaration underneath the thought of such an epic adventure. Somewhere deep in his subconscious he wished that waking-world Henry had this much courage.

• • •

Henry and Peter rose with the sun as planned, both anxious to get on their way. 'The sooner we get there the sooner we get back,' had become their mantra, helping them push on despite a growing sense that they were being watched. Henry knew by the way Peter kept darting his eyes about to search the undergrowth that he felt it too.

But once the day got going the sun burned through the lush canopy in shimmering spotlights that swung and swayed with the invasion of a breeze. They flickered and flashed across gold and red leaves as they drifted down from overhead, turning the place into a grotto of dancing colours and light. It was hard to imagine anything untoward happening on a day like today. Even the birds were in good voice as their ponies shambled along the stony track that leads north-west into the denseness of the forest. They were making good progress, managing to stay on the path despite its lack of recent hooves to trample the surging ground creepers. By late afternoon they'd reach the fork where the map told them they should cut east towards the deep gash in the Ribald mountain range known locally as the Gateway Passage. By midday even Peter agreed he was feeling a little more confident.

Henry was just about to suggest they stop at the next appropriate clearing for a bite to eat when his pony came to an abrupt halt, almost tipping him over its head. Henry grabbed a handful of mane and jiggled back into the saddle. He gathered his reins and kicked it on. The pony remained resolutely still. Henry frowned at the back of its head. Its ears were pricked forward, large nostrils flaring in nervous huffs. He glanced across at Peter, whose ride was behaving in a similar way. It was as if some unseen barrier had dropped on the path not ten yards in front of them. It was also the first time the ponies had exhibited anything more than lethargic tolerance since they started the trek.

Henry's skin began to prickle as he unsheathed his wand. He listened but heard nothing. He relaxed a little. But then his ears pointed out that the 'nothing' they were hearing included a complete absence of birdsong and his heart started to beat faster.

There was the faint sound of rustling somewhere further ahead along the track. Henry signalled at Peter to turn his horse around but before he could even start the turn there was a blood-curdling scream from behind them. The ponies whinnied in terror, having a sudden change of heart about going forward and bolted along the track away from the scream. Henry and Peter also yelled in terror, clinging on to pommels and manes in a bid to remain in their saddles. Up ahead something dropped down from a tree. A big something. A huge something in fact Henry noted with dismay. Equally dismayed the ponies both veered right, plunging into the unkempt tangle of the forest. They crashed their scrawny bodies through stands of grip-weed and flung themselves over fallen logs. Henry could feel the heavy knapsack bouncing on his back, making the business of remaining seated even more difficult.

Unearthly howls and hoots seemed to come from all directions, as if monsters were hiding up every tenth tree calling each other to the hunt. Each time the exhausted ponies slowed, thinking they'd outrun the danger, another howl would emit from the trees and the poor beasts would jerk their heads in the opposite direction and begin lumbering unseeing through the undergrowth again. Henry's legs were getting scratched and bumped even through his thick trousers, his knuckles white with the effort of remaining glued to his saddle. He could hear Peter whimpering and exclaiming about similar rough treatment behind him.

There was a deafening crack up ahead.

A large branch crashed down twenty feet in front of the fleeing pair. On it was standing a gigantic, hulking figure that paralysed both ponies and riders with fear. Unfortunately for the riders they weren't anchored to the forest floor by four hooves like the ponies, so both went flying over their mounts' heads, covering half the distance between them and the beast in a tumble of arms, legs and knapsacks. Henry slid to a halt on his stomach and was thwumped in the back of his head by his bedroll. His head spun.

He looked at Peter, who opened his mouth to scream as he took in the sight before them. But instead of a boy's yell, Henry heard the crazed screeching of ponies as their four-legged transport turned, literally on their tales, and galloped off in the other direction.

The creature roared and Henry joined Peter in gaping at the towering monstrosity. It was about eight-feet tall with dark green, mottled skin that hung in flabby folds along its jutting jowls. Its leathery hide oozed sweat and other unthinkable liquids from strange volcanic protrusions pocked across its surface. Its limbs looked powerful and strong; strong enough to break an accountant, for sure. Its horrific head was crowned with an unkempt explosion of dreadlocks like a nest of poisonous snakes.

Its eyes were the worst part though. They were black. Blacker than the blackest thing you can imagine, opening up to reveal a soul that was blacker still. Even its eyelashes curled away from the sight in an alarming fashion, turned grey at the tip with the stress of existing so close to such horror.

# Chapter 14

I couldn't even begin to explain the extent to which the creature they now faced was ugly. If I could, it would probably put you off your food for a week. Henry understood why the townsfolk had gossiped about trolls; although to be fair to trolls the macabon are considerably more unattractive.

For those not familiar with the legend, the macabon are one of the deadliest, most terrifying, and yes, it has to be said, ugliest creatures ever to have winked into existence. Some advanced humanitarians believe that 'ugly' is a somewhat cruel turn of term to use when describing an entire species, but it should be noted that the macabon don't really mind. As a race, they consider their looks to be the least of their current social problems. Plus, one can't escape the fact they are extraordinarily ugly.

This macabon now pinning the young accountants with its horrible stare was called Kig. He wasn't especially bright, as macabon go, but he was astoundingly ugly. He supposed this was one of the main reasons he'd become so good at his job, which mostly involved scaring people, murdering their families, and making away with their gold.

Ugly or not, Kig came from the Shangli forest settlement, three Kingdoms away to the west in the Fharrtherm Realm. Here he lived in a modest dwelling he shared with his wife, Karp, and his daughter Bokka. He missed his home a lot, despite how much he enjoyed his work. He'd been away from his family for over two years and would be missing out on all sorts of things, like his young child's first experimental torturing of baby animals. There was an art to pulling the legs off a puppy that only a father could really teach. But this assignment wasn't like the marauding contracts his agency usually sent him. Those were short-range expeditions plundering nearby towns and villages and stripping the gold from any grand buildings like castles places of worship.

Instead he and a group of fellow macabon had been sent to a tiny outpost in the Wastelands desert behind the northern stretch of the Ribald mountains. The camp was hot and dry, which were nightmare conditions if you wanted to maintain a good level of ooze on your skin. Added to which, Kig thought the rest of his team were complete idiots, which was really saying something coming from him. The brief was to stay out of sight, making sure nothing and no-one came or went from the town of Terratonia. It was a confusing brief, since one of the main reasons you'd hire the macabon was on account of their very scary looks. But the pay was amazing and they got the occasional tip off about travellers laden with gold, which they were sent out to seize and bring back to base. But the last year or so the action had dwindled away to nothing. The macabon crew patrolling the forest had become bored and listless. Kig had been considering jacking in the job for some time now. But then news had come a few days ago about more foolhardy travellers loaded with gold. And here they were, cowering in front of him.

Puffing out his horrendous chest, he peeled back thick, ugly lips, and growled a rank-breathed threat at the cringing humans. He revelled in the way his performance made their puny faces contort.

Getting into the swing of his work he pushed all thoughts of home to the back of his mind, which was that big so it didn't take long, and started towards his victims.

Since the macabon rarely leave the oppressive depths of the Shangli forest, neither Peter nor Henry had ever heard tale of such a cruel, heartless and utterly unpleasant beast as the one before them. If they had, they would've known that the macabon have skin as tough as old boots, making it almost impossible to pierce them with a spear. With arms like tree-trunks and knuckles that dragged along the floor when they weren't on the stampede, you'd be hard-pushed to get close enough to use a sword on them either. They would also have known that these destitute creatures have no sense of morality, feeling just as relaxed about torturing a puppy as they would be, say, handing out leaflets for the Shangli forest settlement annual recreation day and barbecue.

In truth this knowledge would not have been of comfort to Peter, given his current predicament and the proximity of the macabon. Neither would he be especially pleased to learn that the one and only thing these god-forsaken monsters fear is magic (since their species has no capacity to perform magic, and therefore possesses not the slightest defence against it). As Henry scrambled through the peaty floor in search of the wand he'd dropped tumbling from his mount, Peter's unblinking eyes stared the approaching terror.

After a few seconds that felt like hours, Henry spotted the Malvern stick just behind them. He shrugged the knapsack off and rolled back, closing his fist around its handle. The instant he did it whooshed up, practically pulling him to his feet until it stood, poised and quivering, at a forty-five-degree angle to the approaching chaos.

The chaos paused in its approach, regarding the wand with narrowed eyes. Peter scrabbled backwards to hide behind Henry's legs, eyes flicking from the beast to the stick which had halted the creature's advance. He blinked when he saw threads of delicate light starting to swirl and gather, pooling themselves elegantly in an orange ball around the tip. Peter's eyes gave up blinking and popped open wide. He watched as Henry drew back the stick, then flicked it in the direction of the monster. The orange light-ball flew from the tip and streaked like lightning in the direction of their assailant, exploding impressively on the trunk of an ancient tree about two-feet to its left. The hulking beast looked at the tree, taking a few steps back while he assimilated this new information. The enormous tree shuddered.

'Damn!' Henry was resuming a spell casting stance, but Peter's attention was snatched by the sight of several more of these lumbering trolls emerging from the undergrowth all around.

'Henry ...' he said in a shaky voice. 'It's the trolls ... just like Penny said ...'

'Not now, Peter.' The tip of his wand was loading once more with orange light. In his panic he could only remember the incantation for the tagging spell, which would be more than useless when the beast attacked. But the appearance of the wand had at least given it pause for thought for the time-being, and he couldn't just stand there doing nothing.

Seeing the new spell come into being and remembering how it had made the huge tree shudder, Kig had no desire to find out what it would do to a macabon. Neither did his colleagues who were watching this stand-off nervously.

'Be gone!' Henry shouted, hoping the creature understood and that his voice wouldn't break into a terrified squeak. He wound up to cast again.

This was enough to persuade Kig that this encounter was way above his pay-grade. He howled a warning of magic out into the forest and turned to run, Henry's spell chasing him into the trees like a ferret. As the lolloping beast was swallowed by the shadows, Henry saw the light hit it square on the behind. Kig yelped (in so much as a macabon can yelp), and clamped huge hands over his retreating backside.

'Wha … wha … what was that?' Peter allowed his staring eyes a couple of blinks. He glanced around to confirm that the fading sounds of trampled undergrowth was every one of those monsters retreating out of sight.

Henry stared after the sounds, then did something that was possibly the last something Peter could've expected him to do. He stripped off his coat and trousers.

Peter staggered to his feet and took a few steps back. The experience had obviously unhinged his companion's mind. Henry was now standing in the forest wearing just his long johns and boots.

Henry tore open the top of his knapsack and pulled out a bundle of rough blue cloth. 'I believe that we have just had a narrow escape from the very same bandits that have been plaguing our people for two years!'

'But, what were they? And how did you make your stick do that?'

'Those are two very good questions, Peter.' Henry paused to slip the rough blue robe over his head. He pulled the belt out of his discarded trouser loops and cinched it around his waist, hitching a billow of cloth up over it so he could see his boots once more. Next he attached the heavy pouch of gold to the belt. 'The answer to the first I have no clue of.' He was now rooting around inside his knapsack looking for something as he spoke. 'But I don't think they were about to invite us over for tea.' Finding what he was after he stood and shook the crumples out of a tall, pointy hat. He jammed it on to his head and grinned at Peter, picking up the black stick again. 'This …' He held it out proudly, 'is my wand!'

Before Peter could utter a reaction they heard crashing and cracking approaching through the bushes.

'Damn!' said Henry, cursing his useless brain for refusing to come up with anything more helpful the tagging charm.

Peter took a step behind Henry again as they watched the direction the sound was coming from with fearful eyes.

'Oh my gosh, oh my gosh, oh my gosh …' came the growing sound of a very un-monster-like voice. All of a sudden, D.C. burst through the trees, screeching to a halt as she saw the accountants. 'Henry!' She raced over to them and flung her arms around Henry, who stood there dumbfounded.

'What, in the name of all things magic are you doing here?' he managed eventually, peeling himself out of the embrace.

She looked embarrassed. 'I followed you. Oh, hi Peter.'

Peter waved a hesitant hand from behind Henry.

'Well you shouldn't have!' Henry was furious; well as furious as he could be, given how much adrenaline the last ten minutes had drained.

'But I did!' D.C. stuck out her chin in defiance. 'When I saw those monsters ambush you I followed as best I could but my donkey threw me, running off with all my supplies. I ran and ran towards the sound of those howling monsters. I thought I was going to find you dead.' She looked so crestfallen at the prospect, Henry felt his anger cool.

'You ... you ran *towards* the sound?' Peter was struggling to process this concept.

'Of course I did!' D.C. was emphatic. 'Henry is my best friend!'

Henry's anger hissed like a hot skillet being tossed into a bucket of water. 'What were you planning to do if you bumped into one of those creatures?' he asked seriously.

D.C. shrugged with one shoulder, looking a little sheepish. 'I didn't really have time to think that bit through.'

Henry looked around at their strewn belongings. 'Well, thank goodness you didn't. Those monsters were like nothing I've ever seen before. They would have snapped you in two like a twig.'

Peter flinched and clutched a handful of Henry's ample robe from behind him.

'I think I've seen them,' D.C. said, causing the accountants to look at her with surprise. 'In books anyway. They're called macaroons, or something ...' She wrinkled her nose, trying to remember. 'Anyway, they're one of the few living creatures with no magic to wield, on account of being too stupid to remember any spells. It terrifies them, so the legends go. Wow, Henry. What did you cast to chase them away?'

Henry's cheeks flushed. 'Just a tagging spell actually. It was all I could remember. It took quite a lot of effort too as my hat was still in my bag, so the first cast was way off target.'

Peter saw that Henry was smiling; actually smiling after the ordeal they had just been through. The girl who lived up his street was smiling back. Peter had no idea what either of them was talking about. 'Can we go now please? I'd like to go home.'

'Home?' D.C. was incredulous. 'Why on earth would we do that with such a juicy lead?'

Henry considered the idea it was evident she was about to propose. The beast has been tagged, so in theory he could instruct his wand to sniff out the direction it had fled in. They could follow at a very safe distance and discover the monsters' lair. But what then?

'Henry, we can't just leave those creatures out here terrorising the forest. Besides which, in case you hadn't noticed we're way off the beaten track in who knows which direction? Plus, we're two day's ride from home without a single ride between us!'

The evidence for the prosecution was mounting up. 'Well, I suppose it wouldn't do any harm to check out where they're hiding.'

'What?' It was Peter's turn to be incredulous. 'You're not seriously thinking of following those trolls into the woods?'

'Macabon,' D.C. said, remembering the name from her text books. 'Trolls aren't nearly as vicious.'

Peter glared at her. 'That's supposed to make me feel better, is it?'

D.C. shrugged and started gathering their scattered belongings from around the forest floor.

Henry put a hand on Peter's shoulder. 'Don't worry, we'll stay miles behind them. The spell I hit the beast with will let my wand point the direction we can find it.' He began scanning the ground about him, kicking piles of damp brown leaves and tangled limpweed aside until he uncovered a smooth stone with a flattish surface. 'That'll do,' he said placing it up on a log so that he could rest his wand on it without it snagging on any undergrowth.

D.C. was watching, a small collection of camping equipment and food supplies, that had flown from the saddles along with the accountants, stacked at her feet.

Henry stood back and thought a few carefully chosen words. The wand began to quiver, almost imperceptibly at first. It twitched twice, like a bloodhound sniffing for its prey, then swung round, tip pointing in the same direction as their hapless assailant had fled.

Peter blinked, still struggling to understand what on earth was going on. Not half an hour ago he'd been ambling along the forest track, chatting away about this and that with a mild-mannered accountant of no particular note. Now he found himself standing in a clearing with a man wearing long flowing robes and a tall pointy hat, who had the ability to make exploding light-balls eject from the tip of a fairly innocuous-looking stick. He was beginning to think he must have dozed off in his saddle and ensconced a bizarre nightmare. Assuming that wasn't the case though, he ventured a suggestion. 'Shouldn't we go home and get some back up first? Maybe a couple of hundred guards or something?'

'Or your mum,' smirked D.C. eliciting a glare from Peter.

'In theory, a good plan. But which way is home?' Henry felt a bit bad not revealing to Peter there were several tagging spells in place back home that they could follow with equal ease. But the thrill of adventure was catching light in his belly, fanned by D.C.'s enthusiasm.

Peter looked about dubiously. They were deep in un-trekked undergrowth. The canopy overhead was way too dense to see the position of the sun with enough accuracy to navigate by. He had to admit they could be lost out here for weeks before finding a familiar landmark. Home could just have easily been in one direction as the next. They were lost, with no means of transport and very few supplies.

Henry patted his arm. 'It's OK Peter. I'll keep us safe. As you might have noticed by now, I am a wizard, after all!' This pronouncement didn't get the reaction Henry was hoping for. The young lad stared at them both like a moon-fish. 'We'll just find out where they're hiding, and that should lead us to some kind of civilisation. Then we will go and get help. I promise.'

D.C. made a move to interject, but Henry waved her quiet and snatched up his wand. He could deal with what happened next when it happened. He shoved the wand into its custom fold in his robe.

The three of them shouldered the belongings they still had and started pushing their way through the forest, D.C. practically bouncing off the trees with excitement while Peter moved like a boy under a storm cloud.

# Chapter 15

For the rest of the day the three trudged on, deeper and deeper into the uncharted depths of the forest. As they trudged the trees grew bigger, taller and with more thickly gnarled trunks. Fat vines hung down from the canopy above, knotted with ancient swathes of moss. The forest floor itself was alive with a clamouring array of leafy vegetation, much of which neither Henry nor Peter had ever seen before. D.C. rattled off the occasional identification she remembered from one of her books. But much of it was a mystery to her too. The travellers seemed small and vulnerable inside the majestic embrace of the forest. A bird hooted and Peter, who had been dragging his heels, hurried to keep up with the others.

It was tough going in places, although the herd of terrified macabon they were trailing had done a reasonable job of beating a path with their blundering retreat. But with their ponies gone, as well as fighting off the advances of a thousand tiny barbs and sharp prickles which seemed to grab at them from every direction, their remaining supplies were getting hot and heavy on their backs.

Henry stopped suddenly and slapped himself on the forehead.

'What?' Peter was looking wildly about ready to run for cover.

'I'm an idiot, that's what! I know a way to make the going a whole lot easier.' He slid the knapsack off his back and stooped to riffle through a small pocket on the side.

Peter watched this search with growing curiosity, hoping-against-hope that it was going to turn up something a little easier to understand than the last bag-riffling he was party to. Finding what he was looking for tucked in the very corner of the pocket, Henry clenched his fist about the tiny object and pulled it out. He placed it carefully on the forest floor, then held out his wand above it and began mumbling under his breath. Peter gave up hoping this was going to make sense and watched in wide-eyed astonishment as a large, battered writing desk swelled out of the undergrowth. He gaped at this unlikely object as it inflated to full size, and felt his mind attempting to unhinge itself.

'Oh ... my ... GOD!' D.C. had dashed to the now full-sized desk and was running her hands over it, marvelling. 'A shrinking spell? Are you kidding me? How cool is that?' She turned to Henry, beaming. 'Why did you bring your desk, Henry?'

He pulled open a drawer and extracted a heavy leather book. 'Storage,' he said in a way that made D.C. 'wow' with comprehension and Peter 'eh' with confusion.

'We can shrink all our bags with the same spell!' D.C. exclaimed, tossing her own bag on the floor.

'Nope, sorry. Solid containers only. But I do know how to make them a lot lighter.' He riffled the pages of the book to check the words of the spell, then placed his boot on one of D.C.'s bag straps. He flicked the ball of yellow light that popped into existence at the tip of his wand at the bag, which rose up off the forest floor where it bobbed from the strap Henry was standing on as if it had no weight at all.

Peter's gaping skills reached an all-time high. D.C. 'whooped' and grabbed the strap from under Henry's foot.

'Be careful!' he warned, dampening her excitement. 'If you let go that's the last we'll see of that bag for a while. I used a more potent level fourteen *lifting charm*, so they should remain weightless for an hour. I'll just have to keep topping them up as we go.'

'Brilliant!' D.C. was prancing about like a ballerina with the formerly weighty bag strapped to her back.

Henry repeated the spell on the dazed junior accounts clerk's bag before D.C. helped put it back on him. Then it was Henry's turn and he slipped his arms into his feather-light knapsack. He smiled at Peter, who was still gaping at the old wooden writing desk. Henry hovered his wand over it and thought the ignition charm, making it shrink steadily back into the forest debris.

He stooped and collected it, shoving it into a side pocket of his robe. 'Shall we?'

They pressed on through the undergrowth as the afternoon above the treetops started to turn golden yellow.

• • •

Thirty-miles or so away, in the peaceful town of Terratonia, Mrs Flibbertigibbet was striding across the square, a very unpeaceful frown on her brow. Five-minutes earlier she'd been minding her own business gossiping with Mrs Meddling in the baker's shop, when her twin nephews had come bursting in. They were red-faced and out of breath.

'Aunty, quick!' one of them said. Mrs Flibbertigibbet was not sure which one. 'It's Henry!'

The one that wasn't speaking nodded along emphatically.

'What do you want?' she sneered, the innate fear of discussing her *other* nephew pulling at her guts. That little villain had been off in the forest for two days on that ridiculous mission for coconuts. While she wasn't enamoured with her brother's offspring (especially not *that* one), she had no desire to see them come to harm. She was, after all, a decent woman. Plus, they were the only living reminder of her beloved brother. She'd been furious with Mr Colloid for sanctioning such a doomed expedition given their budding romance. When she'd heard she'd marched up to the castle to confront him.

'They'll be fine, dear,' the Chief Accountant had smarmed, with an unfamiliar edge of impatience in his tone. 'They'll be back in ten days and we'll have a big party. I could hardly say no to the King's birthday wishes.'

'But why Henry?' She'd flinched as she pushed this name out through her lips.

'Because exactly *this*, dear,' Mr Colloid had pronounced, indicating her fractured state-of-mind. 'Plus, there needs to be a qualified accountant to sign off the purchase order, and I could hardly risk one of my more valuable employees.'

This slip of honesty had earned him a litany of angry accusations about risking one of her beloved brother's children and a promise that he wouldn't see hide nor hair of her until her nephew was safely back in the town.

The young boy in the baker's shop gulped air. 'The ponies! They came back without Henry or Peter. They were in a terrible state, frothing at the mouth and wild-eyed. The whole town saw them stampede through the square in a riderless panic!'

Mrs Meddling had gasped, her hands fluttering to her throat, presumably thrown by the idea there was gossip in town that only she and Mrs Flibbertigibbet didn't know about.

Now Mrs Flibbertigibbet was on course to break her earlier promise as she stomped back up towards the castle. She strode across the drawbridge glaring at the guards, a silent dare for them to try and stop her. They decided she was probably a woman best left un-stopped and looked up at the late-afternoon sky, pretending they hadn't seen her.

Along the cool dark corridors of the castle she strode, rehearsing in her head the withering speech she was going to deliver to Neville. Flying down the deserted passage leading to the vaults, she was just about to burst out at the head of the stairs when something made her stop dead. She heard Neville Colloid conducting a whispered conversation with some unseen person just on the other side of the archway through which she had been about to explode. With lightning reflexes honed by years of eavesdropping, she pressed her back against the wall and listened.

'Look, I can't make the figures look any better. Just tell the board that G.D.E. is expecting a large injection of capital in the very near future.'

'Capital?' The voice she didn't know was soft and conspiratorial.

'Yes, a nice big pouch full of gold is about to come into our possession. That should keep them happy for a while don't you think? Now get lost. I've told you not to contact me here at the castle ...'

Mrs Flibbertigibbet's bones almost jumped straight out of her skin as the cloaked figure of a man whipped past her hiding place and sped away up the corridor. She stood frozen, like a gargoyle bolted to the wall, until she heard the familiar slap of well-cobbled leather shoes making their way back down the stairs. Where on earth would Neville Colloid be getting a bag of gold? The only bag of gold she was aware had gone missing recently had been in the hands of her nephew, now also mysteriously missing.

    She breathed out a shaky breath. There was skulduggery afoot, and there was nothing Mrs Flibbertigibbet loved more than a scandalous mystery to unearth. She tucked the withering speech away in her memory for use at a later date, and then hurried back up the corridor in pursuit of the shadowy figure. All thoughts of her nephew were drowned in a flood of exhilaration from the familiar sense that she was on to a juicy story.

    • • •

Back in the forest, Peter was coming to terms with the ludicrous sight of his colleague, dressed in all the trappings of traditional wizardry, and his neighbour's kid, leaping over fallen branches and other obstacles with what looked like huge balloons on their backs. The three had made good progress since Henry had enchanted the weight out of their luggage, and Peter's overwrought brain had had time to gather up the loose ends of its fraying sanity and was now busily tying them back together with a good, strong knot. Every so often, when the trail became unclear, or branched off in more than one direction, Henry would stop and repeat the pointing ritual with his peculiar stick. Then they continued to trek on with Peter bumbling along in their wake. They must have covered about four more miles of grabbing, snagging undergrowth in this way when the weeds and bracken on the forest floor started to thin. Moss-wrapped rocky outcrops burst through its diminishing cover at rapidly increasing intervals, and as the ground sloped slowly up the trees became increasingly sparse. They could sense the looming bulk of a mountain coming from somewhere up ahead, and it cast an ominous shadow across the mood of the travellers.

Once they were clear of the forest's heaviest blanket of leaves, they could tell from the long shadows that it was rapidly approaching sundown. They needed to find a place to shelter for the night. Henry and D.C. were discussing whether searching for a small cave might be better than erecting the lean-to, when up ahead the shadowy forest resolved into a solid grey wall. It was smothered in tangled ivy and moss-vines. The wall, which should probably more accurately be described as the foot of a mountain, was broken dramatically right down the middle by a gaping black gash. The gash, which if pressed would also probably insist on being called a crack, was about ten-feet wide at the bottom, tapering away into a jagged hairline fracture about twenty-feet high at the top. Henry frowned and placed his wand on a smooth stone by his feet. After receiving its magical instructions, the wand pointed determinedly towards the crack in the mountain. The three of them looked at each other, then back at the crack. It really was a very dark crack.

'We'd better find somewhere safe to make camp,' Henry whispered, having no desire to walk into a creepy cave just as night was falling. 'And I think we should move a fair distance away from that cave. We don't want to form a welcoming party for whatever comes out of it in the night.' He got no argument from Peter, who was looking into the gaping mountain with wide staring eyes. D.C.

nodded too, so they turned to the left and started making their way along the mountain's edge in search of a suitable place to bed down.

After almost an hour of rambling along the mountain wall towards the sinking sun they found a reasonable spot where they all felt safe. They strung their remaining sheet of waxed shelter between a couple of large boulders and D.C. went off to find firewood.

There had been a heated debate between Peter and the other two about the wisdom of lighting a fire, given that they were supposed to be hiding from monsters. But when the thin sound of a wolf's howl had drifted down from the mountain he'd allowed himself to be persuaded they were far enough from the cave to light a small one.

It was not long before they had a nice little fire going, with their bedrolls spread neatly beside it. Henry was rummaging through the paper bag his mother had given him, pulling out half a dozen oat-biscuits and a chunk of heavy fruitcake.

'Not exactly a healthy meal,' he apologised as he handed the rations around.

'But yum!' D.C. took an appreciative bite out of the fruitcake.

Peter looked at his own supper miserably, giving his empty water pouch a rattle. 'What use is cake when we're going to die of thirst?'

D.C. scoffed through a mouthful of fruity goodness. 'Don't be such a drama duck! We can survive without water for days! Cake on the other hand …' She grinned and took another huge bite.

'Don't worry, Peter.' Henry was laughing at D.C. as he grabbed a small rock off the floor. He whipped out his wand, tossing the stone up and firing a ball of bright light at it as it rose through the air.

Peter put his well-practised gape to good use as he saw it transform into a translucent white lump.

'Good shot!' D.C. sprayed her lap with crumby cake in her appreciation of Henry's magic flair.

He caught the block of what was now, apparently, ice in a tin pan and plonked it on top of the fire. 'Give it a couple of minutes and you can make that awful tea of yours. As much as you like! The one thing you'll notice we're not short of is rocks.'

Peter looked about at the bleak landscape, grey and rocky. He couldn't deny the truth of that. 'Is that really ice? I mean real ice? That becomes real water when you melt it? How is that possible?'

'Simple physics. Well, magical physics,' D.C. replied in a matter-of-fact voice. 'Everything in the world is made up of atoms, and all atoms are made of the same three basic particles. Protons, neutrons, and electrons; just in different proportions depending what they're trying to be. A spell just rearranges the headcount inside the atoms, turning one thing into another from the inside out. Most low level transformation spells are only temporary, but if you alter the atomic arrangement again before it has a chance to change back, it will forget what it's supposed to be and stay the way you put it. Hence warming it up straight away to make water.'

Peter and Henry both looked stunned, although for entirely different reasons. While Peter was unravelling the string of words she had just spoken so he could sort them into a sentence that made sense, Henry was marvelling at her knowledge. She understood so much more magical theory than he did. He made a mental note to read more books in future.

'I've never seen anything like it,' Peter said, eyeing Henry's wizardly garb. 'Magicians usually only pull rabbits out of hats and saw their assistants in half.'

D.C. snorted again. 'That's not magic! Henry is a *real* wizard!'

A happy flush rose on Henry's cheeks. 'Well, more of a trainee wizard really. But it's pretty exciting.'

Peter shook his head. 'I thought all that stuff was just fairy tales for kids. You know? But those monsters were real.' He pulled his sleeve down to protect his hand as he lifted the now steaming pan off the fire. 'And this couldn't be more real,' he finished, sniffing the steam.

That night, for the second time in as many days, Henry fell asleep listening to the creaking and scratching sounds of the forest coming alive. Instead of a fluttering lean-to though, he was gazing up into a shimmering clear blanket of star-speckled sky. He lay there, hearing his two companions' breath become smooth and even as sleep overcame them. The duck-feather bedroll felt soft and comforting and he allowed himself to fan the spark of belief that things might work out OK after all. He drifted off into oblivion with a vague smile on his lips.

• • •

Terratonia was also asleep. At least, most of Terratonia was asleep. But here and there, a few scattered souls still burnt the midnight oil, or tossed and turned in their comfy beds fretting about some trivial matter as they waited for sleep to take them. Mrs Flibbertigibbet was also awake. But she neither burnt oil, nor lay in her bed. Instead she was creeping along the dark streets towards the glossy headquarters of Gorman Dizing Enterprises, her heart hammering.

The cloaked man she'd followed earlier had made his way back here, keeping his face shielded from the world with a billowing hood, as if he were allergic to the sun or trying to remain anonymous from the people he passed. She'd tracked him to the rear of the building where he waved something in front of a heavy black rectangle set into the wall. It swung outwards and he slipped through, slamming it shut behind him.

When she'd reached it a few moments later it was sealed up tight. It was smooth and metallic, with no visible signs of either handle or hinge. A casual observer would be hard-pushed to suspect it was anything more than an iron panel set in the otherwise uniformly whitewashed wall. But there was nothing casual about Mrs Flibbertigibbet's observations. She'd pressed her cheek against the cold surface and listened. Nothing. Just cold black leadenness. She'd looked to the left and right, trying to decide what her next move should be, then skirted the impressive building until she could peer in through the corner of one of the large glass panels encasing the magnificent lobby.

The long-legged girl had been sprawled behind the reception desk, this time plucking apathetically at a stack of unopened mail, tossing each envelope into an array of trays spread out before her. Mrs Flibbertigibbet decided that her usual trick of marching straight through the door as if she owned the place would suffice quite nicely against such a slip of a girl, so she'd straightened herself up and strode deliberately into the building. Without even looking at the girl on the desk she'd headed for the corridor leading off to the left, which she calculated would take her on the most direct route to the other side of that peculiar entrance.

'Excuse me? Hey, you! You can't just walk in there ... come back! BARRY!' The girl was not going to take it lying down, and was now screeching at Mrs Flibbertigibbet through the lobby.

The 'Barry' she had summoned appeared from a side room. He was dressed in the uniform of a security guard, though he looked to Mrs Flibbertigibbet like he could only just have finished school. He was tall and broad shouldered, with cropped hair and cold eyes. He'd moved to block the corridor Mrs Flibbertigibbet had been aiming for.

Realising she wasn't going to be able to sweep him aside with an icy stare she'd halted and eyed him with contempt. 'I'm here to see Mr Dizing,' she'd stated with authority, taking a few more steps towards the corridor.

The guard had lifted his arm. 'You can't see Mr Dizing without an appointment.'

'Then I'd like an appointment,' she'd scoffed.

'Only Mr Dizing can give you an appointment.'

'Well, how am I supposed to get an appointment from him if you won't let me see him?' She'd directed her most withering look at the guard. 'Now let me by or I shall be reporting you to your superior!' Mrs Flibbertigibbet had tried to press on through the arm, but it remained solid in its intention to keep her at bay.

'Mr Dizing *is* my superior, and I am acting on his direct instructions. I'm afraid you can't come through here.'

Determined not to be defeated, Mrs Flibbertigibbet had played her last card. 'Young man, do you know who I am?'

'I have no idea, but you're going to have to leave now. Unless you'd like me to throw you out?' He'd smiled an unkind smile.

Mrs Flibbertigibbet had trembled with indignant rage, but backed off a few paces and regarded the young guard with a scornful eye. 'Well, you just made a big mistake Mister. I happen to be a close personal friend of Mr Dizing, and when I tell him how you've been treating me ...' The guard took a couple of paces himself, towards the unwelcome visitor in the foyer, and Mrs Flibbertigibbet had had to admit that she was beaten; for now, anyway. She'd sniffed and tossed her head, then spun on her toes and marched out of the foyer and back into the street.

Several hours later she now crouched in the dark, concealed inside a shrub across the road from the glass frontage of the building. She smiled to herself whilst assessing whether there was anybody still inside. 'Ha! Think they can keep me away from whatever secrets they're hiding in there do they?' she said to herself. 'Well it takes more than a spotty teenager in a uniform to stop me! There's something very suspicious going on in that building and I'll get to the bottom of it.'

Barbara Meddling would be green with envy when she heard about whatever shady goings-on she unearthed. Then she melted back into the shrubbery and went in search of a quiet way into the building.

# Chapter 16

At about a quarter-past eight the following morning Henry placed a hand on Peter's shoulder and shook him gently awake. D.C. and he had already packed up their camp and there was a pot of watery oats cooking on the dying embers of the fire. 'You were so fast asleep we thought we'd leave you till the last moment.'

Peter yawned and sat up in his bedroll, confusion clouding his face as his brain tried to put the disjointed blocks of his world back in order. 'Oh. Right. Thanks.'

The steaming oats were thrust under his nose. 'Eat,' D.C. instructed. 'We'll all need our strength, even you, drama duck.'

'Don't call me that.' Peter snatched the tin of oats and prodded it with a spoon.

She huffed and turned to face Henry. 'I've been thinking. There's no way we can carry these through that crack.' She booted one of the knapsacks. It toppled over in protest.

'Yes,' mused Henry. 'We can rationalise when we get to the entrance. I can pack a few things in the writing desk too. There's a little more room in the drawers.'

An hour later they were back in front of the enormous crack, the bare essentials stuffed into downsized packs. They'd stashed the rest of their belongings in a small crevice not far along the mountain wall.

Henry held up his wand in front of him and edged towards the greedy blackness.

Peter gulped. 'Would now be a good time to tell you about this phobia I have about being in dark, enclosed spaces?'

D.C. made an exasperated noise but resisted the temptation of further name-calling when Henry shot her a warning look.

'Well, yes. These things are good to know – especially as we're about to enter a dark, enclosed space. How bad is it? Do you think you can go in?'

D.C. tutted and gave her pack another once over to check it was all strapped down tight.

'I ... I'm not sure,' Peter seemed nonplussed. 'What are the alternatives?'

'Wait here to be eaten to death by monsters,' D.C. said, losing patience. 'Or head back to Terratonia alone.' She looked up at the sun which had risen from the east, placing them somewhere along the northern stretch of the mountain range. She pointed roughly south. 'That way.'

Peter shuddered and looked over his shoulder into the dense, undeniably sinister forest, then back to the mouth of the cave; more sinister because of what it didn't reveal. He could hear his mother's voice in his mind, telling him to stay away from it, insisting he'd be paralysed with fear the moment he stepped into its overpowering darkness. He shook his head to shut her up. There was no way he wanted to be left alone. 'I'll give the cave a go,' he said, bravely shouldering his pack.

'Good stuff.' Henry smiled what he hoped was a reassuring smile; though to be honest he was feeling more than a little jumpy about the prospect himself. 'Just stay close to me. D.C. will bring up the rear. You'll be quite safe between us.'

As the three walked up to the mouth of the cave they noticed a rack of unlit torches and a big, messy bucket of burning oil propped just inside the entrance. D.C. was reaching out to grab one when Henry stopped her. 'I'll use the *spectrum luminosity* charm. I've already learnt it. It'll be a less conspicuous than a blazing torch, and a lot easier to extinguish in a hurry.'

She grinned as she watched him step into the cave holding his wand carefully between his hands. He seemed to be having a silent conversation with it. After a second it lit up like a pale green candle, spilling a constant flood of discreet light across the moody depths in front of them.

As far as they could see, which wasn't very far at all in the wand's gentle glow, the crack matured into a rocky tunnel leading into the heart of the mountain and goodness knows where after that. The walls were rough and damp, covered in green slime (or at least a slime that looked green enough in Henry's light). Peter felt his chest tighten as they followed the tunnel round a bend and the dwindling light from outside winked out altogether. It was cold and it was spooky, and he shuffled forward a few paces gathering up a loose handful of Henry's ample robe for comfort.

'How you doing?' Henry whispered over his shoulder.

'Oh, you know?' Peter replied, not able to think of anything more helpful to say.

He jumped as D.C. clapped a hand on his back. 'He's fine, aren't you P?' her confident voice echoed down the tunnel and Peter was tempted to shush her, but he bit down on his tongue and kept shambling on.

They continued this way for about half an hour, squinting into the shadows looking for danger. The large tunnel narrowed, the walls and floor becoming scuffed and smooth with the passing of many large bodies. A short while later it opened up into a yawning chamber of rock. They stepped out of the passageway and stood there, looking around in awe at the blackness that had engulfed them. They couldn't see the size of the chamber, since it was bigger in all directions than the understated glow from the end of Henry's wand. But they sensed its size by the drop in temperature and the subtle echoes of dripping water.

'Which way now?' D.C. whispered into the darkness.

Peter stared at the impossible black, breathing hard. There could be goodness-knows how many hidden exits out of a huge chamber like this, and taking the wrong one might leave them lost down here forever. He hiccupped in fright at the thought. The sound bounced eerily off every surface.

'There could be dozens of different exits,' Henry whispered as if he'd heard what Peter was thinking. 'Let's head a little way into the centre and then get another bearing with my wand.'

Peter gathered up a more determined handful of Henry's robe and stumbled after him, D.C. staying close on his heels. Ten yards in, Henry was about to start looking for a well-situated platform to place his glowing wand when he became aware of something moving the shadows. Perhaps it was nothing ... but there it was again. Just a fleeting glance of a dancing shadow, but enough to make the hairs on the back of his neck stand up. He waved at the two behind him to back up, and started reversing towards the tunnel. His eyes probed the darkness outside his wand's soft glow for any further signs of movement. A shadow flickered in the corner of his left eye. Henry whipped his head round, bringing his wand up in front of him to get a better view, then heard a sharp clacking noise, like the sound of wet sheets being shaken out before hanging on the line. He felt a whoosh of air as some enormous flying beast swooped at them from overhead.

Peter screeched, and Henry felt a bone-jarring tug on his knapsack as it was suddenly jerked sideways. Before his brain could work through all this information and suggest a course of action, he felt another pull in the other direction. He turned to see Peter clutching his robe with terror-driven determination. Behind, D.C. had thrown her arms around Peter's waist and was also hanging on for dear life.

'Henry!' she cried out. 'Peter, keep hold of him. Don't you dare let go!'

Just when Henry thought he had a handle on these shocking new developments and was about to start kicking and shouting, there was a sudden ripping sound and he flew unexpectedly back. The knapsack straps had been the first to submit in this deadly tussle and he landed on top of Peter, who scrambled out from under him in a panic.

'What was that?' The junior clerk's eyes were wild with fear.

'RUN!' was the only reply Henry gave as he heard the leathery flapping of large wings circle round in the darkness above them.

Peter didn't need to be told twice. Gripping each other's hands in the dark the three scrambled and tumbled back towards the mouth of the tunnel. Or at least, they thought they were running for the tunnel. But when they slammed into the edge of the cavern and found only a continuous layer of rock they realised with impending doom that their internal compasses had drifted. They'd missed the exit. As they started to clamber along the cavern's circumference looking for a safe haven, Henry heard the unmistakable sound of the creature's wings flapping, winding up for another assault.

He crouched beside the rocky wall. 'Get behind me!' he yelled, bringing his wand up to defend them. This act was more reflex than any real attempt at self-defence, since the luminosity charm was completely harmless. But it seemed to do the trick. Confronted by the spectacle of a glowing green orb thrust at it, the attacking creature swerved past with a strangled 'caw'.

'RUN!' Henry shouted again, running along the curve of the cavern wall, the green glow from his wand seeking out any bolt holes along it.

The beast circled the cavern somewhere up above creating a draught that tugged at Henry's robes with the flapping of its expansive wings. It observed the clumsy progress of its prey with narrowed eyes, then, seeing its chance folded wings back and lowered its head into a silent dive. They had no warning of the attack this time. The beast stretched out razor-like talons and made a vicious swipe at Henry as it plunged by. He stumbled and yelped as he felt the burning pain of tearing flesh. Then the beast was gone again, disappearing into the threatening black void about them. Henry pressed his hand against the wound on his left hip, wincing. It wasn't bad, just a nasty gash, but there was a long split in the side of his robe and his belt had been severed, both it and the pouch of gold flung off somewhere unseen into the maw of the cavern.

Hauling himself to his feet, Henry pressed his back against the wall and started muttering the words of a spell. The instant he began, the cool green glow from his wand was replaced by a swelling of hot, pink light flowing in waves from the fingers that grasped it. Henry wasn't entirely sure whether the *Fulcrum's Flabbergaster* he was conjuring would save them from this monster, but the spell book had reminded him of it again last night when he was mulling over preparations for the cave. It was a class twelve spell, so he would have to be careful with his aim, and inside the all-encompassing dark he would pretty much be firing blind.

He stood frozen, back up against the edge of the cavern and aware of his friends doing the same. He searched the dark with his ears. The unseen monster-bird-thing did another circuit. Henry could feel the subtle change in air pressure as it whooshed over their heads, and tensed for an attack. With another sharp clack of its giant wings the beast landed just a few yards in front of them. A huge beaked face loomed out of the shadow into the pool of pink light from the spell and made a jab at Peter. Henry lunged at it with the fully charged wand. The tip connected with the beast's head. A loud crack, and it shrieked with rage and fury as the ball of light exploded out and engulfed it. The light also engulfed Henry, who was connected to the creature by the wand. The fabric of his robe was snatched rudely from Peter's grasp as trainee wizard and beast were sent into a sudden ferocious spin; arms, legs, talons and wings all flying about as if caught in a typhoon.

Terrified, Peter dropped to his knees and brought his hands up to cover his face, peering through his fingers.

D.C. crouched beside him panting.

'Henry! H?!' she stage-whispered, though goodness knows why considering the racket coming from the spinning beast and accountant. Anyone, or anything within these caves would be very aware they were coming by now.

Once the *Fulcrum's Flabbergaster* had been spent, the gentle green glow of the luminosity charm returned to Henry's wand. They watched it gyrate like a Catherine wheel in the absolute darkness before flying in a small arc and clattering to rest on the cavern floor. It made Peter feel dizzy just watching it, so he closed his fingers and eyes up tight and began praying for a swift ending.

D.C. saw Henry stagger through the glow of the dropped wand, disoriented by his spin, then wobble off back into the shadows. 'Stay here,' she hissed at Peter, who never had any intention of doing otherwise, then made a dive for the wand.

Reaching it she gripped the handle with both hands. It leapt and bucked in her fist, sending violent shockwaves up her arms. Remembering the breathing exercises Henry had taught her, she tried to get hold of herself. 'Calm down,' she told the wand through gritted teeth. 'I'm trying to save Henry!' The wand stilled a little as if it had heard her, then swung round in a half circle dragging her arm behind it. A second later Henry stumbled into its pool of cool light, tripping over the hem of his robe which was now at least a foot longer than his legs.

She released one hand from the wand and used it to grab a handful of her friend, dragging him back towards the cavern wall. Her eyes scanned the dark for their attacker but couldn't pick anything out. Then she heard the heavy slapping of tough hide against rock, accompanied by another furious 'caw' and a thud as the unseen creature hit the floor.

Wasting no more time, she kicked Peter who was still cowering by the wall. 'MOVE!' she said, then hauled the stunned young wizard along the edge of the cavern, searching for an exit. A few feet along, the light cast by the wand was swallowed by a black hole and she shoved Henry into the mouth of a tunnel, barging herself in after him. Peter was not far behind, whimpering like a puppy.

Tucked back up in the relative safety of the enclosed space she allowed herself to breathe, adrenaline coursing through her body. The wand emitted a sudden sharp buzz and she let go of it in surprise. It clattered to the floor and came to rest against Henry's knees, upon which he was now crouched, recovering.

She glanced over her shoulder to check on Peter. He was standing dazed in the mouth of the tunnel. With a shriek she saw the dimly lit flash of a wing flapping just behind his shoulders. 'Look out!' But before Peter could react a talon reached into the glow from the mouth of the tunnel and closed over Peter's knapsack.

She launched herself at the terrified boy, grabbing the straps of his bag. Peter's eyes opened wide as he was jerked back, his head lolling drunkenly with the force. Wedging her feet against the rock D.C. hauled with all her might, the second deadly tussle of the day now well underway. Still woozy from the spin the dragon tried to get a better grip on the bag so it could yank this troublesome human from its safe place. One razor-like claw slit through the right shoulder strap and it popped off Peter's shoulder like a cork. Realising she would soon lose the battle of strength against such an enormous creature, D.C. let go of the strap still secured to Peter's shoulder and grabbed his free arm with both hands. She heaved at the young lad and he fell towards her, the bag ripped off his shoulder in an instant. D.C. heard the sound of a leathery slap as the creature catapulted back into the cavern and hit the floor, a small knapsack and flailing straps now it's only prize. It cawed with rage as the three of them scrambled backwards down the tunnel out of reach of snatching talons.

'What ...' Peter ran out of words as his mind replayed the last thirty-seconds in terror.

'I couldn't really see,' admitted Henry, still recovering himself.

D.C. was beside herself with hysteria. 'Dragon! It had to be! Crikey H! We just battled a real dragon!'

'It wasn't so much a battle as a tug of war,' Peter pointed out shakily, though he looked more than a little relieved.

'Whatever, we're alive!' she said, patting herself down to prove it.

'What now?' Peter asked.

They both looked at Henry. He swung the wand around scrutinising the space. 'It's not the same tunnel.'

'Well, that's good,' D.C. stated.

'How?' Peter asked in an incredulous tone.

'Don't want to go backwards!' D.C. waved at the mouth of the cavern.

'But how do we know this way is forwards?'

She didn't have an answer for that.

'It is.' Henry had regained his composure and was looking down at the wand on the floor, which quivered as it pointed along the tunnel away from the cavern.

'Whoop!' D.C. cheered, in a manner that the expression on Peter's face said was entirely inappropriate given the graveness of their circumstances.

Henry picked up his wand and looked down at his robe, which was pooled unhelpfully around his boots. 'I need something to tie up this robe, and I wouldn't mind getting a proper look at whatever is in there.'

Peter graduated from gaping to gawking. 'We are NOT going back in there! It'll kill us!'

'Don't worry, Peter,' Henry soothed. 'I'm just going to use a more powerful light spell. I'm sure Halcyon said there were grades of all the most commonly used functions. I just need to check in the book.' He was rummaging through his pocket in search of the desk. For one horrible moment he thought the rip in his robes might have spilled it out somewhere in the cavern, but his fingers came across it moments later with relief.

Peter looked at Henry stupidly as he placed the doll's house desk on the floor by his feet. He held his hand out over it and was about to start repeating the words of the reversal charm when Peter grabbed his arm and pulled it away. 'Wait!' he cried, his brain cottoning on to the obvious disparity his eyes had noticed. 'You'll crush us if you restore that thing to full size in here. Not to mention being unable to open the drawers.'

Henry blushed, relieved that in the green light of his wand Peter wouldn't be any the wiser. 'Of course.' He picked up the desk and edged deeper into the tunnel, which widened out quickly to a decent size. Once it could accommodate the desk, he placed it back on the floor and began the business of restoring it to size. Before long he'd opened the drawer and had the familiar spell book cradled in his arms, beginning to feel a little calmer. As usual he had no idea what he was looking for when he hooked his fingers into its binding and drew it open, but so far that hadn't seemed to be a problem. He looked down at the page it had opened on.

*Global Luminosity Charm*

*This class ten spell can be used when it is necessary to briefly illuminate a vast area. Note; Wizards should refrain from casting unless they are sure they're in a contained environment, since the resulting illumination of the entire universe could prove to be an overwhelming drain on resources (not to mention a bit of a shock for anyone who happens to be awake in the universe at that time).*

Once again the book had shown him the way. It was a simple spell, Henry already had the necessary components loaded into his wand, but he'd never attempted anything higher than a class twelve spell before and that had been devilishly difficult to aim. Still, as long as he got the magic right he didn't suppose aim would be a problem, since it would be pretty hard to miss a cavern so big when you're standing right at the door.

He memorised the chant while he unwrapped the stack of parchment, using the twine to hitch his robes back up to a manageable length. A few minutes later he had re-shrunk the desk and tucked it safely away. The three of them crouched close together near the mouth of the cavern gazing without focus into the absorbing dark.

'OK, let's see if I can do this.' Henry stood and started to concentrate on the words of the spell, ribbons of light spilling out of his fingertips and gathering into a blazing white ball at the tip. It was slow going and Henry had to concentrate really hard not to lose the thread of the chant, but eventually he felt a surge from the wand that he recognised as it telling him the spell was complete. 'Ready to see this dragon?'

D.C. was nodding feverishly. Peter shook his head slowly. Henry took up his spell casting stance and performed an almighty flip with the business end of the wand. He surprised himself with how smartly it snapped off the tip, streaking out into the cavern and bursting in a cataclysm of blinding light. Once their eyes adjusted to the shock they could see the huge chamber completely illuminated in a flat, white light, like a stormy landscape freeze-framed in a flash of lightning. It was round and maybe a hundred feet wide, with dripping limy stalactites hanging down from a domed ceiling approximately fifty-feet up. The towering ragged walls were laced with stringy green slime, and some kind of red fungus; the floor pooled with cold, stagnant water that nestled beside miniature reconstructions of the mountain they were trapped in. Peter, counted seven tunnel exits in total, as much to avoid having to look at the dragon as anything else. That made eight if you included the one they were in, with no way of telling which one led home.

Henry didn't notice any of these details about their environment. His eyes were drawn to the dome of the cave, knowing that a flying hunter would be perched somewhere up high ready to swoop down on its prey. What he saw had him transfixed for the entire ten seconds that the chamber was lit. The creature was like nothing Henry had ever seen. Settled on a rocky mound in the centre of the towering cavern, it had gigantic leathery wings and beak-like face. Its hide was a rusty red, with sharp horns jutting from the sides of its jaw down the entire length of its impressive backbone. The spikes grew longer and more lethal-looking as they went, tapering out along its tail which whipped angrily from side to side. The talons that had snatched Henry and Peter's bags were gripping its rocky perch so hard that rivulets of pebbles crumbled down from their embrace.

It glared down at the tunnel they were hiding in, then stretched expansive wings wide. One powerful flap launched the huge beast into the air. At that moment the light winked out. There was a furious caw and Henry felt a rush of wind as the dragon hurtled towards the tunnel. 'RUN!' he cried in alarm, but Peter and D.C. were already on their way, flailing along the tunnel as fast as their terrified legs would carry them.

# Chapter 17

'Flaming volcanoes, H!' D.C. exploded, much like a volcano herself. 'I can't believe it! What a beauty!'

'Yeah, shame the feeling wasn't mutual.' Peter continued to be dumbfounded by how excited the girl was about nearly being killed. 'Henry, we're never going to find out way home. There were eight tunnels leading off that cavern!'

The three were now moving steadily along the tunnel, Henry tripping over his hem every-so-often due to the parchment twine's poor performance at holding the robe up. 'If we keep following the tagging spell we shouldn't need to go back through there Peter. We can just exit wherever the macabons did and make our way along the mountain range until we hit the coast.'

'After we find out where they're hiding,' D.C. interjected.

Peter glared at her.

'Of course,' Henry agreed. He was beginning to feel like a referee in this trio. 'Come on now, the sooner we get there ...'

'The sooner we get back,' Peter finished despondently, bunching his fists into the folds of Henry's robe and following doggedly on.

They rounded a curve when D.C. cried out, 'Light! Up ahead. I see a light at the end of the tunnel.'

'You see, Peter!' Henry grinned, picking up his pace like a moth drawn to a lamp. 'We're nearly out ...' Then quite without warning the accountant and his tall pointy hat vanished in front of Peter's eyes.

An instant later Peter was pulled crashing to the ground by the bundle of rough wizard's robe he was still holding firmly in his fists. He cried out, wincing in pain as his knees exercised extremely bad judgement in coming down heavily on the rocky floor. He felt D.C. grab him round the waist with both arms, a feeling that was becoming disturbingly familiar, and haul him back from a tumble into the yawning hole that had opened up in front of them.

'Henry!' D.C. screamed right by his ear, leaving it ringing for several seconds.

Peter felt the cloth begin to slip through his fists. 'No! Oh no,' he cried.

'What?' D.C. was frantic. 'What, oh no, P?'

'I ... I can't hold on. It's too heavy. The cloth is slipping ...' A sudden force slammed him on to his stomach as D.C. flattened herself on top of him and reached over his shoulders to grab for some cloth. She leaned precariously far over his head as he watched the last few inches of robe slither through his fingers like a snake disappearing into a bolt hole.

'Oh no you don't,' grunted D.C. as she wound her own hands into the fabric, halting its departure.

They lay like that for a moment to be sure the situation was stable.

'Henry?' hissed D.C. 'Are you OK?'

The cloth in their grasp waggled side to side, and D.C. tightened her grip until her knuckles glowed white through the dark.

'Yes. I ... I appear to be upside-down be in some sort of hole,' came the echoed reply from Henry.

'It's OK. We've got you,' D.C. said. 'What can you see?'

Henry waved his glowing wand as best he could with his oversized robe hanging down over his head. All around were rocky walls much like the ones they'd grown accustomed to, only these ones headed straight down. He gazed into the impossible blackness of the hole, falling away to what could be impossible depths below. 'Not much.' His voice was a squeak.

He kicked against the wall of the chasm, which was poking unkindly at the fleshy cushion of his left thigh, and a rabble of crumbling rocks bounced their way past his head into the resonant darkness below. He held his breath and listened to their clattering passage, which faded away to infinity in a most alarming way. 'Uhm … do you think you could pull me up?'

Before Peter could think of a response he felt the weight on top of him shift as D.C. started dragging her knees up underneath her, still keeping tight hold of the robe. The wind was 'oofed' out of him as she sat heavily on his ribcage, then planted a boot either side of his head.

'Pull!' she instructed as she leaned back and heaved, wrapping more folds of robe around her forearms as they began to haul it up.

Still flattened on the floor, Peter helped as best he could until Henry's flailing feet reached the lip and he was almost booted in the face. By now D.C. was fully in control of the rescue operation and all Peter could do was lie there with his face pressed into the ground as a wriggling bottom, back and then shoulders were dragged unceremoniously over him out of the hole.

Once all of Henry's body was deposited safely back in the passageway D.C. collapsed in a heap to recover.

'Thank you,' Henry said to her in a shaky voice.

'You're welcome.' Peter grimaced, lugging himself back from the precipice and getting up.

'And you, Peter.' Henry stood and clamped the hand not holding his wand on the young lad's shoulder. 'I mean it. If you hadn't been holding my robe …' His voice trailed off as his eyes drifted to the gaping hole he had just walked straight into. 'I was just so focused on reaching that light.'

They all looked at the light now. So near. Henry pushed the glowing tip of his wand as far across the chasm as he could, seeking out the other wide. And yet so far. The light was completely swallowed by the hole as far as it could reach.

'What now?' D.C. asked.

'Well if that beast I hit with the tagging spell came through here there must be a way across.' Henry looked around at the unhelpfully ordinary tunnel walls surrounding them.

'Maybe it didn't,' D.C. said after a few minutes unfruitful standing around.

Henry shrugged. It was worth a try. If he missed a big fat hole in the ground, it was perfectly possible he might have missed a tunnel branching off. He placed the wand on a flattish hump of rocky floor and as the first few words of the charm entered his mind it immediately swung about and pointed back up the tunnel. He grinned at the girl. 'What would we do without you, D.C.?'

She grinned back in a blush of pride. Peter merely huffed and grabbed another determined handful of Henry's robe as the three of them made their way back up the stony corridor.

Fifty-feet or so down the passageway they noticed a large, dark crevice in the left-hand wall. A closer inspection revealed it to be a branching passage, and after confirming with Henry's wand that it was the route their attackers had taken they set off cautiously along it; Henry paying particular attention to the space in front of his feet.

...

Meanwhile, some seven-miles further north at the macabon outpost in the almost-empty Wastelands desert, a delivery was being made. Two sad-looking leather packs and a heavy pouch were dropped from a great height, narrowly missing a startled Kig who had been sulking outside the gold store, upset that he'd been put straight back to work after the raid. OK, the raid had been a total failure, and the Super had been livid. But a macabon had to eat. He scowled after the beast winging its way back towards its mountain hideout. There was even word around camp that the mysterious 'big boss' had flown in to deal with matters.

He stooped to examine the drop. Travellers' belongings and a pouch of gold. It seemed like the dragon had done what it had been put there to do, and the matter of the bungled raid was over. Kig felt a glimmer of hope. Being the one to bring news of this drop would no doubt play in his favour when it came to dishing out reprisals. He locked the bags away in the gold store and went in search of his boss.

He found him in the command centre, deep in conversation with a hooded human. Kig hesitated at the door. 'Excuse me ... Sir?'

His superintendent swung his huge head round, dreadlocks swinging. 'Whaat?' the macabon officer roared.

Kig swallowed hard and tried not to choke on his words. The head of the cloaked figure turned to observe him too. 'Somebody has been in the mountain passage ... the dragon just brought in a couple of bags and a pouch full of ... well, gold it feels like. Must be those traders from Terratonia.'

The human turned the rest of its body to face, Kig and growled, 'Oh? You mean the traders you fumbling idiots failed to intercept out in the forest? *Those* traders?' The voice was cold and made no attempt to hide the contempt it held for the current company.

Kig felt the hairs on his nose prickling, a clear sign that a macabon is becoming annoyed. How dare this puny human speak to him like that? Who did he think he was? He looked at his superior officer, who just stood there glaring at him from behind the man.

'Bring the bags to me,' the cloaked man snapped.

Kig continued staring at the Super, his simple brain trying to bang the square fact of being given orders by a human through the round hole of dawning understanding that this must be their mysterious 'boss'.

'Well?' came another roar from his superior. The cloaked man flinched in annoyance as the sound bellowed past him towards Kig. 'Do as the man say! Fetch the damn bags!'

As Kig dashed out, tent flaps snapping at his hasty departure, the cloaked man turned to scowl at the macabon superintendent. 'Those better be the bags we're expecting, and my dragon finished the job your boneheaded minions botched.'

The huge macabon stepped back into the tent wall trembling as the man drew a long black stick out of a fold beneath his cloak. Laying one last evil eye on the beast the man went to the table and swept away the parchments and office debris strewn across it. Drawing a shallow brass dish from another fold in his robes he placed it on the desk and then emptied a small vial of black liquid into it. He frowned down at the dish. The face he saw frowned back; his own face reflected with pin-sharp clarity in the mirrored surface of the liquid.

'Where are you then you little worm?' he hissed at himself. 'How did you find your way into the mountain passage?' He waved his wand over the dish and a wash of opaque light surged across the surface of the liquid, rippling his reflection until it was nothing more than a blur of random colour. The cloaked man waited, watching for the answer to his questions to be revealed in the diminishing shimmer of the glassy sheet. But when the contents of the dish returned to perfect calm it was his own face, instead of the face of Henry Noble, that was staring back at him crossly from below. 'What?! What's this? Blocked by a charm of some kind? Damn that interfering old wizard!' Enraged the cloaked man swiped at the dish, sending it clamouring into the corner of the room spraying its slick, black contents across the dusty fabric of the tent like a putrid wound. The macabon boss edged a little further away from the man as he began pacing the floor rubbing his chin. 'Damn him, damn, damn, damn!' he muttered to himself as he paced. 'He couldn't mind his own business, could he? Why couldn't he just disappear into the woodwork like the rest of them? I knew there was something going on. The question is, does the boy have the book? And how much of it can he use? If that interfering old fool has ... Of course he has! There's no way they could get this far without ...' His endless train of questions was interrupted by Kig clearing his throat from the flapping entrance. The cloaked man's head snapped round and he glared at the hulking figure. 'Yes?' he hissed.

'Uhm, you told me to bring the bags ...'

'And ... yes?'

'Well ... uhm, I brought them.' Kig held his two arms out with what was left of the straps of two knapsacks and a pouch of gold clutched in his fists.

The cloaked man rolled his eyes, exasperated. 'And you're expecting what, exactly? A pay rise? A medal? A rousing chorus of 'for he's a jolly good fellow'? Just drop the bags and get out of my sight you lumbering buffoon!'

Kig was taken aback. He might not be very bright, but there was no need for such an appalling display of bad manners. He dropped the bags exactly where he was standing and sulked out of the tent, wondering again what they were doing working for a human when it was normal protocol to murder and pillage them.

The superintendent was just grateful the wand had been put away again as the cloaked man stalked over to the pouch of gold and stooped to inspect it. He rolled it over in his hands, seeing the royal seal of Terratonia stamped on one side. Something resembling a smile slithered across his face. He grabbed the packs and tore them both open. Food; clothing; a couple of dirty bedrolls ... No evidence of magical activity. No spell book. He kicked at the empty leather sacks and started pacing the floor again. He must be prepared for the worst case scenario. He hadn't lived this long without learning that a few lost belongings didn't mean their owners were dealt with. He must assume the young accountant was still a threat and stamp on this whole debacle before it could do any more damage. It was time to return to Terratonia and batten down the hatches.

This decided, the cloaked man swept the wand out of his robe. The macabon officer cringed.

'Don't let anyone get in or out of this camp. And you'd better hope I can clear up the mess you've made because the alternative will see you hauling dead meat out of that town for weeks.' The shadowy man seethed beneath his hood. Over the years he'd learnt that *not* massacring entire communities made it a lot easier to go about your business. But he had the stomach for it if it became necessary.

The creature nodded dumbly, eyes fixed on the wand.

The cloaked man flicked the magical stick and the tip glowed a furious red, sizzling and crackling in the dry air. He touched it to the empty space in front of him, where Kig had been standing moments before, and drew it down. It seemed to rip a slash in the fabric of space as a gaping black hole opened up. The hole had ragged, surreal edges that smouldered with the energy of the spell. The cloaked man shoved his wand back into its pocket and stepped into the hole; taking a shortcut through another dimension to his private offices back in Terratonia.

As the last centimetre of his cloak was swallowed the broiling hole zipped up with a defiant sizzle. The macabon officer breathed a sigh of relief and then hurried out of the command tent to make sure all the guards were on high alert.

• • •

Back under the mountain, Henry and the others were still inching along a dark passage. Peter was beginning to wonder whether they would ever see the light of day again when they rounded a bend and came to a dead end. Henry tutted to himself and placed the wand on another flat stone to take a directional bearing. The wand pointed emphatically at the solid stone barrier in front of them. He frowned and scratched his head.

'What's up?' Peter whispered through the dark.

'I'm not sure. The wand seems to think we should walk through that wall …' He looked all around, but there was no obvious sign of a branching tunnel. He looked up above him, but saw again only the jagged rock that had been their constant companion for almost half the day now.

D.C. pushed past and placed a hand on the rocky surface barring their way, then felt the walls either side of them in the same way. 'It's a bit warmer,' she said nodding to herself. 'Could mean we're close to outside. But we can't get through solid rock.'

'Brilliant deduction.' Peter slumped against the wall, fumbling with his boot to empty the quarry of gravel it felt like had climbed in there.

D.C. flashed him a sarcastic smile.

Henry was tapping his bottom lip with the tip of his wand. It had been quite a while since they were in a section of passage wide enough to restore the desk so he could check the book, so he was running a quick inventory of the spells he already knew to see if any could save them backtracking.

'Turn it to ice and smash it?' D.C. suggested, spookily reading his thought-process.

'It's not a very strong spell, but we could do it in stages I guess? Let's see how much ice it makes.' Henry held his arm out to move his spectator away from the rock and fired a tight ball of magic at it from his wand. The light hit the stone and spread rapidly out, turning a door-sized chunk of the grey expanse a cloudy white.

'Nice! Plenty big enough,' declared D.C. grabbing a rock off the floor and slamming it hard into the icy plate. It shattered immediately and a large sheet of ice about as thick as a petticoat came down in shards. 'Hmm. Well this could take a while.'

Peter sighed deeply and moved back into the tunnel a few paces to sit on a boulder and put his boot on. As he sat he realised he was just on the edge of the orb of green light cast from the wand, and he didn't feel in the slightest bit nervous. Marvelling at the revelation that perhaps he wasn't so terrified of the dark after all, he almost spilled off the boulder on to the floor when it moved under his weight with a loud 'clunk'. Henry and D.C. jumped back and shielded their eyes against sunlight flooding in through a growing crack in the stone.

'Who did that?' Henry cried out, stunned.

'I ... I think I did,' Peter said, getting to his feet with his bootlace left untied. 'This boulder ...'

'Well done Peter,' Henry said clapping him on the shoulder as they all peered out. 'It seems like you're our chief secret trigger finder from now on then, right?' He put his hand up to shield his eyes and led them out of the tunnel.

The sun on their faces was warm and comforting after so long underground, but once his eyes had readjusted Henry didn't feel quite so comforted. In front of them, for miles and miles in every direction was the scorched and unchanging landscape of the Wastelands desert.

# Chapter 18

They stared out at the desert not speaking. The rippling sand stretched on and on like an endless yellow blanket, smothering the earth with its searing folds until it was swallowed up by the distant horizon in a glistening sea of heat haze.

Henry frowned. Surely they hadn't fallen *that* far behind the raiders during their passage through the mountain? He squinted off into the distance. He could see for twenty-miles or more in every direction and there wasn't even the slightest speck of movement out there. He looked at the ground for a trail left by heavy feet trudging through the sand. But the hot wind whipping across the desert had long since erased any evidence. Confused, he glanced about looking at the few rocks scattered against the mountainside before the perpetual sand ate everything up. Spotting a relatively flat area he placed his wand on it and held his hand out over it. It quivered and pointed straight ahead, out into the cruel vastness of the desert.

He jumped as D.C. breathed a question into his ear. 'What do you think?'

He looked out at the desert again. 'I think we're at another dead end, which at least means we're being consistent.'

'So, we're going home now, right?' Peter had come up beside the two. He pointed along the mountain wall to the east, 'It can't be too far to the coast, in the meantime Henry can keep turning these rocks into ice to keep us alive.'

D.C. pointed meaningfully at the wand, which still tremored, directing them into the desert.

'So what?' Peter shouted, losing his rag with this insufferable girl and her gung-ho attitude to danger. 'So we walk out into an *obviously empty* desert? With no food or water? Because a black stick told us to?'

D.C.'s face tightened. 'My brother is out there somewhere. Henry's dad too. We've come so far, we can't turn back. Not when there's still a chance they're alive.'

Peter's anger fizzled out.

'Look,' D.C. said, her face softening. 'The point is they can't have disappeared; those macabon things. Can't have got that far either.' She pointed at the horizon. 'So maybe there's a hatch somewhere to an underground lair?' She stooped to pick up a couple of rocks, shoving them in her pockets. 'We can load up with these for water and just head out a little way to see if we can find anything. We'll be fine, I promise Peter. A human can go three weeks without food ...'

'I do wish you'd stop trying to cheer me up with information about how quickly I could be dead.'

D.C. smiled. 'Are you on board then? Just a quick look around.'

Peter nodded. 'OK. A quick look.'

Henry felt a wash of affection for them as they busied themselves gathering rocks without another word. He decided against collecting any himself as the parchment twine was already struggling to keep control of his robe. He didn't think adding the weight of rocks to its workload would end well for any of them. Once Peter and D.C. had filled their own pockets they returned to Henry's side.

'Ready?' he asked, drawing his wand.

Peter looked down at his bulging, sagging pockets and sighed. 'Can't you make these rocks a bit lighter with your magic?'

'Sorry, Peter.' Henry put a friendly hand on the lad's shoulder. 'If I make them weightless they'll just float away at the first opportunity. What good would they be in the clouds?'

Peter shook his head and sighed again. He could also feel the rumblings of hunger fire up in his stomach. He pushed thoughts of his mother's roast lamb to the back of his mind then together they walked away from the mountain into the lost wilderness of the Wastelands desert. Henry brought up his arm to shield his eyes as a gust of wind flung a stinging assault of hot sand in his face, as if it understood it was being invaded and was warning them to turn back.

For the rest of the day they slogged on through the unchanging landscape. The sun continued beating its relentless path from east to west and as it began to slip down behind the golden, featureless horizon, Henry couldn't help wondering what his family were doing. Were they watching the sun go down over Terratonia wondering where in the world he could be? Had they already heard about the ambush and thought that he was lying dead in a ditch somewhere deep in the forest? He recalled how it'd been when they'd heard about his father's disappearance and wondered if his mother was sitting in stunned silence at the scrubbed kitchen table clutching her apron in her lap, a fat salty tear rolling down one ashen cheek. The thought of his brothers and her weeping at the news of his disappearance brought a lump to his throat that threatened to push its own salty tears out through his eyes.

He was startled from his reverie by a sudden angry vibration coming from under his left armpit. Henry froze. He knew that feeling well, and it always meant that trouble was close at hand. 'Hey!' he barked at his companions, who froze in their own tracks and turned to look at him. Henry had his wand out and was looking about wildly.

'What?' D.C. whispered, looking around herself now.

Peter looked perplexed. 'What?' he repeated, throwing his hands in the air.

Henry shushed him violently. He was staring at his wand. 'It only does this when a tagged object is within twenty-feet,' he whispered, lowering his body into a crouch and cast about looking for something.

Peter looked about too. There was nothing to see for twenty-miles in every direction, never mind twenty-feet.

'There must be a hatch around here somewhere,' D.C. said. 'We need to spread out and look.' She began creeping in arcs around the area, brushing sand aside in places with her foot.

Peter scoured the sandy vastness with his eyes but they found nothing. Not a hint. Surely if there was a hiding-place buried underneath the desert there'd be some kind of ventilation shaft? You'd see it sticking up out of the sand like a periscope. Plus, the bandits themselves would need to know how to find the entrance in this big expanse of yellow nothingness. Frustrated confusion took hold of his nervous system and started to pull it taut. He didn't expect a sign saying 'Welcome to the Bandits Hideout', but there'd have to be some kind of marker. He didn't see any of these things. He watched his companions stalking about like cats on the hunt. As far as he knew they'd both gone quite mad in the heat. He felt a bloom rising in his cheeks and something inside him snapped. 'There's nothing out there! Look!' he yelled, throwing his hands in the air.

Surprised by his outburst the other two stopped and shushed him again.

He strode past Henry into the desert, sweeping his hand along the horizon as if he were introducing them to an old friend who'd just arrived at a party. 'There is absolutely nothing out here to indicate …' and then quite without warning, Peter vanished.

D.C. stood there open-mouthed. 'Where'd he go?'

Henry gulped and held his wand up to the ready. 'Peter? PETER!' he called out to the empty space where his friend had been standing. He racked his brain for a good idea and must have caught it off guard because it delivered a great one straight away. 'Throw a rock at it.'

D.C. fished a large round rock out of her pocket and tossed it up once, testing the weight. Then she twisted, curling her arm back over her head for a good wind up and hurled the rock right at the spot their friend had ceased to be. It also vanished.

Henry looked at D.C. 'I hope for your sake he wasn't just standing on the other side of … of whatever is stopping us from seeing him. That rock would have knocked him senseless.' The wand still buzzed in his hand, as though encouraging them to press forward. Henry decided they needed a second opinion first, so retreated a few feet and started digging inside his robe for the miniature writing desk.

# Chapter 19

Peter floated inside a featureless pocket of peace and security. He was vaguely aware of a sense of unreality, but it didn't really bother him. Unreality can end up feeling like reality if you give it a chance. He could taste the familiar smells of childhood memories in the air. Cherry cake baking; freshly cut grass; crisp, clean bed sheets. Wisps of memories swirled in his vision too, like smoke curling into tantalisingly familiar shapes and sounds, but evaporating before he could put his finger on them. He felt a sudden pang of home-sickness, then heard his mother singing somewhere inside; inside the house that he felt must be just a breath away. Suddenly, he was looking up at clouds of billowing white linen hanging on the line outside his house. He caught glimpses of blue sky dressed in puffs of white cloud as the sheets flapped and snapped in the wind. It almost felt like he was standing on the bow of a sailing ship, grand sails billowing overhead. This thought turned his drifting mind to long-forgotten boyhood dreams of taking to the seas himself one day. He caught the whiff of a memory of his father reading him bedtime stories about great explorers and telling him he could be anything he wanted to be (to the scowling disapproval of his mother). He felt his chest tighten. When had that dream of sailing the world fizzled out? Did it die with his father? Memories of his father came flooding back in an overwhelming surge of emotion. He collapsed to his knees and started sobbing.

After what felt like the first ever really good cry over the loss of his father, Peter drew in three more hitching sobs and decided to pull himself together. Imagine someone catching him out here bawling like a baby? This thought pushed his eyebrows down into a frown as it raised a very important question. Where exactly was out here?

Getting to his knees he noticed the world was undulating, accompanied by the rhythmic sound of flapping sheets and creaking ropes. Beneath his knees he saw rough wooden boards, not the soft grass he'd been expecting in the garden. He stood and looked around, his astonished eyes confirming what all his other senses had been screaming at him; he was standing on the bow of a magnificent sailing ship. His jaw dropped, then reformed into a huge grin. An actual, real sailing ship? It looked just like the ones from his childish imaginings. The deck listed to starboard and he put his hand on a rail for balance, a glimmer of doubt seeping into his addled consciousness. What was he doing on a ship? What had he been doing before that? The deck rocked lazily, sails slapping a hypnotic beat in the gentle breeze. He gazed off the bow at the vast landscape of continuous blue sea, unchanging and featureless to the horizon. Like a sea of sand, only blue. His brain latched on to the thought of sand, as if it was a life belt thrown from another reality. But before he could ruminate on this any more he heard a voice from his past, distant but deeply familiar.

'Hello, Son.'

Peter turned and came face to face with his father, just as he remembered him as a little boy. 'Dad?' He reached out to touch the apparition, but instead of passing right through it his hand came to rest on top of a warm lapel.

The chest beneath the lapel shook as his father chuckled. 'You OK my boy?' He ruffled Peter's hair and without thinking the lad flung himself into his father's arms and sobbed a bit more.

Once he'd got what he hoped were the last dregs of it out of his system, he pulled a handful of hankies out of his pocket and cleaned himself up. He stepped away from his father, embarrassed. 'Sorry. It's just ... well, it's just been a really stressful day.'

'I know the perfect cure for that. Your mother is down in the galley cooking up a feast. Your favourite; roast lamb and minted potatoes. There's a steamed treacle pudding for dessert too. That'll put a smile back on your face.'

Peter blinked. That was the exact meal he'd been dreaming about not so long ago as he'd trudged through ... what had he been trudging through? He couldn't quite recall.

The sails flapped and his father stood right in front of him, taking him by the shoulders. 'Hop to it lad. We need to bring down the mainsail so we don't drift off course while we're eating. You remember the way I taught you?'

Without consulting his bewildered brain, which couldn't remember any such lesson, his body got automatically to the task of releasing the winch and looping the fall of halyard around a sturdy wooden cleat. He was about to interrogate his body about how it had learned all these strange new terms without running them past his brain, when his nose burst in with the announcement that dinner smelled delicious. It didn't take much after that for his stomach to stage a successful take-over. He was starving and had been dreaming about this meal all day. His stomach issued stern instructions to his body to stop dithering when there was treacle pudding on the menu, and Peter followed his father down into the galley for supper.

He was tucking into a third helping of sticky golden pudding when a question occurred to him. 'Where exactly are we heading?' he asked, custard dripping on to his chin.

'Where would you like to go, Son?' his father asked, smiling kindly.

Peter thought about this and couldn't really come up with an answer. It was such a long time since he'd allowed himself to dream this adventurous dream. But where on earth were they even starting from?

'Well, where would you like to be starting from, Peter?'

Peter frowned. This seemed like a surprising answer to get from a man he remembered as being quite logical, as you never got a choice about where you are right now. But more surprising was that he'd answered his son's thoughts.

Peter began to feel uneasy again. This wasn't right. His father was …

'Listen love.' It was his mother, moving towards him concerned. She wafted her husband away with a flutter of her hand. 'You look exhausted darling boy. You poor, poor dear … would you like me to make up your bed with fresh, clean sheets?'

Sleeping tucked up inside freshly laundered linen was still one of Peter's favourite things. It made him feel clean and safe; as if no badness could touch him. Even when the lights went out his nostrils were still filled with the scent of his secure little cocoon. He felt an intense desire to just settle into this pleasant new reality, where he felt safe and his belly was full for the first time in days.

'He does look tired doesn't he mother? I tell you what Son, we'll have a nice game of cards while your mother makes up the bed, then why don't we all get an early night?' He looked at his wife and smiled. 'Tomorrow we'll set sail and explore the world. We can even stop by your friend Penny's house if you like? Bring her along too.' He shot his son a cheeky wink that made his cheeks flush.

Peter watched his mother leave the galley through a door beyond the table. His father started digging through cupboards and drawers in search of a pack of cards. The galley was warm and friendly. On one side was a well-equipped kitchen with brightly polished copper pans hanging like bunting along the wall, swaying and chinking against each other with the pitch and roll of the ship. On the other side was a table that could seat up to six people along two wooden benches, and an assortment of furniture containing all the dining accessories he was used to at home. He had a moment to wonder if all ships came with such a well-equipped galley as he watched his father riffling a big dresser, tutting as he failed to locate the elusive playing cards. He turned to face Peter, a troubled crease tainting his brow. 'I can't seem to find them … do you remember what they look like?'

Peter stared at him, bewildered. 'What, the cards?'

'Yes. That's right.' He seemed relieved to have them named for him.

'You want to know what the cards … look like?' His father nodded in a strangely affable manner that made him look a bit gormless. Peter glanced around the galley to see if he could spot them and said, 'Well, they're a small box of stiff parchment, with different numbered symbols on each of them.'

'Ah, that's the blighters!' Peter looked back at his father's exclamation to find him holding a pack of cards triumphantly above his head. 'Found them!' he declared, somewhat redundantly. He plopped the box of cards down on the table and sat on the bench across from Peter. 'Shall I deal? What'll it be?'

The uneasy feeling was growing in Peter's bones, the sway of the lolling ship beginning to churn up the greedy meal he'd eaten. How did his body know how to sail a ship? Where had that pack of cards appeared from? There was something about his father too; something not quite right … He closed his eyes and yearned for anything that felt more straightforward to happen.

'Hello Peter.' Henry said.

Peter's eyes snapped open as a flood of memories slammed into him. The forest; the trolls; the desert. Not to mention the constant sense of imminent danger. He leapt up and edged around the table, backing away from Henry and his father.

'Son?' His father stepped forward, concern in his voice.

'No! Stay back. You're not my father!' The man looked hurt but stayed where he was. Peter was shaking his head as he backed towards the steps that led up on to deck. 'Yes, this is all very convenient isn't it? I think of home and I'm outside my house. I dream of a sailing ship and, pop, here I am. I miss my father and he just materialises, even though he's been dead for years …'

The Henry that had appeared beside his father made a move to step forward. 'Well done, Peter. You're getting there all by yourself. This is going to be easier than I hoped.'

'No!' The young lad felt panic rise and started climbing the steps backwards, holding Henry at bay with outstretched hands. 'I wished for something more ordinary to happen and suddenly you appeared. Out here, on a sailing ship? A boring accountant from work.'

Henry blushed. 'Well, we'll chalk that one up to the effects of the charm muddling your mind and I won't take offence. But we need to get out of here Peter. Will you at least give me a chance to explain?'

Peter replied by turning on his heel and fleeing up on to deck. The ship lurched suddenly to the side, tipped by a freak swell. Henry lurched with it and staggered to follow Peter up the stairs.

Outside the scene was very different from before. Fresh blue sky had been replaced by broiling black clouds, a furious gust snatching at the lashed down sails. Peter was caught off-guard as another freakish swell lifted the bow of the ship clean out of the sea, slamming it back down on its stern like a wrestler making a pin-down. Peter staggered and grabbed hold of the railing to keep from falling over.

'Peter! Peter wait!' It was the Henry impersonator, and he was advancing towards Peter with his hands held out in a deliberately non-threatening way.

'What's going on?' Peter asked. 'Who are you? And ... and ... and, well ... what's going on?'

'You're right Peter! You worked it out. Nothing here is real, except for me of course. It's all an illusion drawn from your deepest memories to keep you locked away in a netherworld.' The ship seesawed over another huge wave as the rapidly-awakening sea took umbrage at the way this conversation was headed. Henry joined Peter clinging on to the railing.

The younger boy edged further away towards the stern. 'I don't know what you mean,' he said in despair. 'I don't understand any of this.'

'It's magic, Peter!' Henry cried, as if that answered all questions.

'What magic? I don't want any more of your magic! Why won't you just leave me alone?'

The boy was wailing in competition with the rising wind now, and Henry had to raise his own voice to be heard. 'This isn't my magic, Peter. It was cast by a much more powerful wizard!' Henry's eyes danced with the thrill of this revelation. 'The spell book told us it's a class three charm! Class three! An illusion trap that conjures whatever your heart most desires to keep you from seeing the truth.' He stamped his foot on the wooden deck as the sea sloshed in from both sides. 'This ship is not real, Peter. That meal you ate? Just vapour. In reality you and I are wandering, glassy-eyed through a scorching strip of sand just outside whatever the spell is hiding. You could stay here inside the dream for days filling your belly with imaginary food and drink, but eventually you'd die of thirst in the desert.'

The wind picked up even more, howling through the giant masts above them. The ship swayed and creaked like an old wooden rocker in the grip of a violent earthquake.

Peter paled, gripping on to the railings with both hands. 'If this is supposed to be what my heart most desires, why is the weather turning? This isn't exactly what I'd call perfect sailing conditions.'

'It's a reaction to pollution. This illusion is built around you, Peter. The spell book showed me a protective charm so I could enter your dream without being affected, but I'm a foreign body as far as the spell's concerned. It wants to get me out.' As if to punctuate this point the huge boom chose that moment to break free from its tether and swing heavily across the deck in the turbulent wind.

'Look out!' yelled Peter, grabbing a shoulder full of robe and pulling Henry out of the way in the nick of time not to get swept overboard.

'Wow. Thank you.' Henry steadied himself on the railing, heart beating fast.

Peter looked at the robe balled in his fist and a strong sense of familiarity rose up from it. 'Your robe …' he said thoughtfully. 'Why would an accountant be wearing a robe? That wouldn't be ordinary at all.'

'There you go!' Peter encouraged. 'So unlike everything else in this world, I was not conjured from your imagination. Peter, please trust me and I'll get us out of here. Once we're clear of the barrier you'll come back to your senses and everything will make sense again.'

Peter's head was spinning. He wasn't convinced the world he was heading back to made much sense right now, but it was certainly preferable to dying of thirst in the desert, a prisoner in his own imagination. 'How? How do we clear the barrier?'

Henry looked up and down the ship. 'Well I entered at the front end, was that the same for you?'

'Bow,' Peter said.

'Eh?' Henry asked, wondering why Peter wanted him to bow.

'It's called the bow of the ship. And yes, I arrived there too.'

'OK.' Henry looked towards the rear of the ship which was bucking and writhing like a bad-tempered bull. 'I'm going to hazard a guess we need to leave through the back.'

'Stern,' Peter corrected.

'What? Oh yes … the stern. What do you say then? Are you up for it?'

'Up for what? Walking off the stern of a ship in the middle of a raging storm? Uhm … that'd be a no, thank you.' Peter looked incredulous.

'Peter, we have to do this. D.C. is waiting and we're so close to finding the hideout. You just need to have a little faith.' Henry held out a hand to his friend.

Peter reached out to take it. 'OK. I must be mad but, you win … I'll walk off the end of the ship with you, but you'd better be right about this!'

'It's what the book told me, Peter. You just concentrate on limiting your thoughts to this ship as the illusion is taken directly from your mind.' They were staggering towards the rear of the ship now, clinging on to the railing, each other, and anything else that came to hand. 'The last thing we need is for you to conjure up an enormous sea monster to attack us'

'Oh great!' Peter moaned. 'Now that's all I can think of.'

'Empty your mind. Think of absolutely nothing. You can do this Peter; I know you can!'

They continued shuffling along the deck, the violent storm battering them from every side in a most unnatural way until they reached the rear loading gate. Peter closed his eyes tight and tried to block out the image of them being dragged down into an inky sea by a giant squid. He reached out and grabbed an emergency floatation device, just in case, and started strapping it around his chest.

'No!' Henry cried through the screaming wind. 'You have to believe it ends here, otherwise you're just building more dreams to get snagged in ...'

Peter looked at his companion in disbelief, and then glanced down at the thrashing waves below. 'You're absolutely sure about this?'

Henry nodded, so Peter shrugged and tossed the device aside; in for a shebble in for a groat as they say.

Henry unbolted the loading gate and swung it open towards the raging sea. 'Together?' He gripped Peter's hand tighter.

Peter gulped one last time and willed the giant squid to go swim around in someone else's imagination, then they stepped off the end of the ship.

# Chapter 20

There was the sensation of falling. Peter could feel a hand still gripped in his own, but he couldn't see anything; didn't know *how* to see. Then he landed with a thwump on a packed sandy surface, rolling over until he came to rest on his back. He lay there, staring up at a cloudless, black sky, scattered with pinpricks of light ... Stars. Slowly, but surely, his brain was beginning to make sense of things again. He turned his head to the side, testing out various parts of his body to see if he could remember how to use them, then almost jumped out of his skin as he came face-to-face with the ugliest looking creature he'd ever seen. He cried out and rolled away from the horrible sight, scrabbling to his knees and making ready to run for it.

'Hey ... Peter, cool it bud!'

It was a girl's voice and after a second the memory of who it belonged to came back to him.

D.C. was crouching beside him, hand on his shoulder to comfort him. 'It's OK ... I think it's unconscious,' she whispered.

Henry approached, brushing himself off after the sandy fall. His wand was still buzzing in his hand like a trapped fly. He looked down at the huge macabon lying spark out on the ground. There was an angry red lump on one of its temples and a large round rock lay on the floor beside it.

'How?' Peter couldn't think of any more words.

'Lucky shot,' D.C. whispered back as if this should make sense. 'Come on, need to find cover before we get spotted.'

Peter didn't need to be asked twice. They scanned the surrounding area, which seemed to be a semi-permanent camp. Around the perimeter there were a dozen or so large, dusty tents (one of which was thankfully hiding the fallen macabon), and a few scattered wooden buildings. Lamps burnt inside some of the tents, and every now-and-then they could see silhouetted movement as bodies passed in front of the light. They ducked behind a shed not far from the fallen monster and peered out. In the middle of the camp there was a clearing with a more solid looking construction in its centre. It had sturdy brick walls and high windows with metal grills. The strong door was fitted with a heavy bolt and there was an empty chair placed beside it that looked big enough for a giant to sit in. On top of the tin roof a ramshackle chimney puffed woody grey smoke into the clear night sky.

Henry was about to ask the others what they made of the scene when a loud, flabby farting sound came from inside the shed they were pressed up against. They looked at each other in silent horror. Another fart, followed by a grunt and a snort, and then the unmistakable sound of a large body hauling itself to its feet. An unpleasant smell drifted through the cracks in the wooden panelling, and Peter covered his nose and mouth with his sleeve. D.C. made equally disgusted faces, gagging at the stench. It seemed they'd chosen to hide behind a toilet, and whoever (or whatever) was making use of it had a serious problem with their digestive system. This assumption was confirmed by a sudden slooshing sound as the shed's occupant flushed away its business. Peter grimaced. Henry was peering around the corner of the shed again.

As Kig left the latrine he belched and scratched his behind. He'd been on guard duty for almost six hours, moved from outside the gold store when the Super went on a rampage roaring at all of them to be on high alert, or else. He didn't elaborate on what the 'else' would be if they weren't on high alert, but Kig suspected it had something to do with the cloaked human and it had put him in an even fouler mood. Plus, he still hadn't eaten and it was playing havoc with his guts. He looked miserably at the canteen tent where most of his colleagues had already had supper. His shift would be over in ten-minutes though, then he could eat and grab some much needed rest. He crossed to the centre of the camp and sat down heavily in the chair by the bolted door. It creaked an objection but continued to do its job. Leaning towards the door he rapped on it and yelled, 'Lights out in fifteen-minutes people. Don't make me tell you twice.'

'What ... or rather *who* do you suppose is locked up in that building?' D.C. hissed in Henry's ear. By the rise of colour on her cheeks and the glint in her eye it was obvious what she thought. The missing accountants.

There was a sudden flurry of activity in one of the tents, then a small crew of macabon barged out of the flaps and made a beeline for where Kig was sitting.

'Have you seen Ajax? He's gone missing,' one of them asked the beast on sentry duty. 'Last seen doing his rounds a couple of hours ago.'

Kig looked up, disinterested. 'He's probably just fallen asleep somewhere ... did you check his bunk?'

'Checked it. You ain't seen nothing sitting out here?'

Kig shook his head, getting up hopefully. 'I'm happy to go and look for him, after I've had supper of course.'

'No, you need to stay here. We're going to do a circuit of the camp. See if we can find him.'

'What? All six of you? Can't just one of you take over so I can get some grub in my belly?'

'You heard what the Super said. High alert! You told us yourself that the ones who escaped in the forest had magic.' The search party all glanced around nervously at the idea. 'There's safety in numbers and you can't be too careful when it comes to dealing with wizards.' There was a general murmur of agreement and the small crew crowded off together in search of their missing comrade.

Kig slumped down on the chair and looked at his feet, sulking.

Henry swung round behind the shed and pressed his back against the wooden panels. 'They're looking for the one you hit with a rock, D.C.! It's only a matter of time before they find it ... and then they'll be looking for us!'

Peter wasn't at all pleased to hear this news. 'Should we hide the body?'

D.C. looked at the enormous dead-weight of the unconscious macabon lying a few feet further back from the clearing and the lack of decent hiding places. 'Doubt we could move it, even if there was somewhere to hide it.'

'How about the 'lifting' spell?' Peter suggested.

'No go, I'm afraid,' Henry replied. 'I used the last of the feather salt essence getting me and D.C. through that illusion trap unaffected. I'd have to set up my desk and spend several hours brewing more before I could cast another lifting charm. Something tells me we don't have that kind of time.'

'Wait ... maybe we *can* hide the body.' D.C. scuttled over to where the macabon lay and grabbed the rock, bringing it back to Henry. 'How about the *intellect deflector* that keeps your brothers from seeing your magical activity? Can you cast that one?'

Henry's frowning face smoothed with understanding, while Peter's crumpled into deeper confusion.

'You really are, quite brilliant in an emergency,' Henry said.

D.C. glowed with pride as he took out his wand and fired a bead of pink light at the unassuming rock. That done he did his own scuttling to place it by the macabon, holding his wand out over it and thinking the words of the ignition charm just as the sound of heavy footfalls and grumbling voices began to approach from the left.

Henry scooted across the sandy floor and slid down on his knees next to D.C. The three of them crouched in the shadows, backs pressed against the wall trying not to breathe. A small clump of huge bodies emerged through the dim outskirts of the camp. It weaved in and out amongst the tents and buildings kicking at empty buckets, as if they expected to find their absent companion secreted underneath one.

'Ajax, you numb nut, where you at?' one of them called out.

Peter wondered what Henry had done to the rock, and why on earth he thought it would hide the bulk of that monster's body. But before he could ask any questions the beasts had rounded the back of the tent where it lay.

'Hey! Look at this!'

Peter squeezed his eyes shut ready for the uproar as the body was discovered.

'Wow ... that's fascinating ... Uhm, what is it?'

The macabon were all gathered around the body of their fallen colleague, staring in wonder at the pink rock beside it. They seemed hypnotised, none of them taking their eyes off it, yet at the same time unwilling to get too close.

'I dunno ... anyone?' There was a general mumble of agreement that they had no idea what they were looking at and Peter let out a shaky breath. Whatever magic Henry had used it seemed to be doing the trick. They weren't even the slightest bit interested in the body.

'Kig might know,' one of the beasts suggested. Another, more urgent mumble of agreement and they rushed back to the centre of the camp to find him.

Kig was busy digging dirt out of his fingernails with the tip of his machete, still fuming at them for leaving him without any food. He looked up moodily as they approached. 'Did you find him?'

'Erm ... no.' Another mumble of general agreement.

'Really? No sign at all? Nothing out of the ordinary?'

The macabon search crew looked around at each other with blank expressions.

Kig eyed the group, somewhat puzzled. He was about to ask why they'd stopped the search if they hadn't found Ajax, but his stomach pointed out that this could trigger the start of another extensive search, delaying his supper even more.

'Oh well,' he said jumping to his feet, 'at least you tried. I'm going for food now and you know what the Super said about guarding this door. So one of you will have to take over the chair from me.' With that he strode across the camp in search of something to eat.

After a moment's confusion when they couldn't quite work out what had gone wrong, one of the beasts planted itself heavily in the chair by the door while the rest of the macabon drifted off in all directions, presumably to carry on doing whatever it is that macabon do in the evenings.

Henry turned to face his friends, smirking. 'Well that worked rather well wouldn't you say? Perhaps a little too well by the way they all wandered off so vacantly at the end.'

Peter nodded, relieved they'd evaded capture, so far at least. 'Now what?'

'We need to come up with a plan,' said D.C. looking at Henry.

'No kidding,' Peter hissed.

D.C. glowered at him through the shadows behind the latrine. 'We obviously can't take them all on together,' she continued ...

'Wait ... what?' Peter was aghast at the thought of doing anything other than running away.

'But we need to find a way to get into that building.' The three of them peered round the shed at the locked door across the camp with a dozy-looking eight-foot guard slumped beside it. 'Our only problem is the guard.'

'Oh really?' Peter gawked at the girl who had rumpled her face up to one side in deep thought. 'That's our only problem? Because for a moment I thought we were trapped in the desert with no supplies, surrounded by terrible monsters and with a dragon between us and home!'

Seemingly unaware of his disparaging remarks, Henry turned to D.C. with a look that hinted at mischief. 'Do you think you could knock that guard out with another rock, if I got you close enough to hit it?'

'Close enough to hit it? Are you crazy? You'd have to be just a few feet away.' Peter had raised his voice to emphasise the absurdity of the idea and the others both turned to shush him.

'What's the plan?' D.C. asked, pulling the rocks out of her pockets to find the best missile.

The plan was to wait for the camp to wind down for the night, then Henry would conjure up a *concave reflective barrier* to hide behind as they approached the lone guard. He assured Peter that as long as nothing snuck up behind them they'd be completely hidden from sight, and briefly explained the concept of the spell. Once they got within a few feet of the guard, D.C. would lob a rock at its head knocking it out cold like the other one.

'What if you miss?' Peter was digging up as many reasons to stay hidden as he could find.

D.C. scoffed. 'Miss? Unheard of! But if you want to make doubly sure why don't you throw a rock at it too?' She tossed one of the discarded stones to him and shoved a couple back in her own pockets figuring it wouldn't hurt to have extra ammo.

He picked it up and looked at it dubiously, but it appeared he'd run out of objections.

As they huddled behind the shed waiting for the diminishing sounds of activity to die out, Peter realised that the filling effects of the imaginary meal he'd eaten on board the ship had disappeared, and his stomach rumbled unhappily. After what seemed like forever, but was likely not longer than a couple of hours, Henry signalled he thought the time was right. He stood and assumed his casting stance and a translucent tangerine disc began to spread from the tip of his wand. It grew until it was big enough for them all to stand behind as long as they huddled up close.

Henry turned to Peter, smiling encouragement.

Please,' he sighed. 'Don't ask me if I'm ready. Let's just get this madness over and done with.'

Henry nodded and turned to D.C. who was practically climbing out of her own skin with the desire to get moving. Together they tiptoed gingerly out from behind the latrine.

They skirted the clearing with the locked building at its centre until they could approach the guard from one side. D.C. raised the rock to the crook of her neck, poised and ready to wind up for a throw. Then they crept out of the shadows to cross the empty space towards the building.

D.C. felt very exposed as she watched the dozing guard get closer through the shimmering haze of the magical barrier. Every now and then his head would slip too far to the side, threatening to spill him on to the floor. Then he would jerk it upright again with a snort, before allowing it to drift off in the other direction. They were less than ten-feet away from it now, almost against the side of the building, and D.C. could hear its breathing coming in deep, heavy rasps. She tightened her hold on the rock, rough edges biting into the fleshy pads of her fingers. Six-feet away now and they were edging along the wall, the guard momentarily obscured from view by the corner of the building. Then they were upon him, standing just a couple of feet away.

D.C. drew in a breath to steady herself then looked at Henry and mouthed 'Now?'

Henry nodded and she wound up for a good hefty throw.

At that moment Kig stepped out of the canteen tent. Having enjoyed a large meal he'd fallen asleep at the table, waking groggily with the imprint of a spoon pressed into the folds of his jowls. He stretched his arms in an extravagant yawn. Then out of nowhere, a large rock materialised. He heard it whistle through the air, watching aghast as it hit his dozing companion squarely on the head. He cried out in alarm as the guard slumped to the floor, no longer held in the chair by some small degree of consciousness. Kig rushed over to him, side-stepping the rock as if he expected it to jump up and attack him next. The guard was out-cold.

The young friends froze, pressing themselves into the shadows around the corner of the building behind the wand's protective barrier. D.C. looked at the rock still clutched in Peter's hand and gestured frantically at him to throw it. But before anyone could react there was more noise as macabons alerted by Kig's cry fumbled their way out of their tents to investigate. Before long the whole camp was gathered in front of the locked door and anxious chatter filled the air.

Henry ground his back into the wall as far as it would go, wondering how long he could maintain the spell that was hiding them.

'What happened to Garp?' one of the monsters asked.

'That rock,' Kig accused the rock. 'It materialised out of thin air and hit him on the head.' He was looking around in case of another attack. 'It's that human and his magic stick. I told you! We'd better get out of here before he comes back to get us!' A nervous murmur rippled through the crowd.

'What about the prisoners? The Super said nothing was to get in, or out,' asked another beast.

'And where is the Super now?' Kig asked, anger at the frustrations of his day coming out in a rush.

The mob looked at each other, confirming that their boss wasn't among their number. What they couldn't have known was that the macabon officer had decided several hours ago that he wasn't being paid enough to deal with a magic man, so had packed his bags and sneaked off home, planning an early retirement.

'Or Ajax? And now Garp?' Kig had the attention of the whole crowd now. 'Stay here if you want to go the same way. But I for one am fed up with this job. They never said there would be magic and I certainly don't want to be here when the one with the magic stick arrives.' There was another murmur, only this one had the undertone of agreement.

Henry's mind raced over the facts. The monsters that took his father were standing right in front of him. Three good paces forward and he could tap the closest one on the shoulder. They were huge, and intimidating and very, very ugly. But it appeared they were afraid of him. Henry Noble; the skinny boy who was most picked on in the playground at school. It was a powerful sensation. Making a rash decision he turned to others and mouthed, 'Follow my lead ...'

Peter's eyes snapped open and he began frantic gestures for his companion to stop whatever madness he was about to start. But it was too late. Henry straightened his back and edged out of the shadow around the monsters, keeping the wand barrier between him and them. Peter and D.C. had no choice but to press along behind him. Once he'd cleared the building and was standing in open ground behind the dithering gaggle of macabon he opened his mouth and bellowed as loud as he could, 'FEAR US BEASTS!'

The crowd, whose attention had mostly been on Kig by the locked door, swung a rapid about-face to where the shout had come from. They blinked in confusion as they glanced around the empty space, then there was a collective gasp as Henry extinguished the barrier spell and three humans appeared out of thin air in front of them.

The macabon crowd stared, astonished. One or two on the periphery looked like they might try running for it. Henry held up his wand and roared, 'Nobody move a muscle! I'm arresting you all in the name of King Maximal IV of Terratonia. If any of you move I'll turn them into a mouse, just like that rock over there!' A ball of light popped into being at the tip of his wand and he flicked it expertly at the rock that had knocked out Garp, thinking the familiar words of the charm he'd been using for target practice in the woods. The instant the bolt of energy hit the rock it exploded in a flash of greenish light, which disappeared as quickly as it had arrived to leave a rather fat rodent sitting in its place. The rodent looked at them for a moment, then burped and waddled away in the direction of the canteen tent. Henry watched it go, feeling a little guilty about winking such an unhealthy looking creature into existence. It must have been because the spell was intended for use on something as small as a colliwall nut, not a big hefty rock. But his little display seemed to have done the trick with the macabon, who were cowering against the front of the building all trying to avoid being at the front. Henry waggled his wand at one that had failed in this endeavour and said, 'Right, you. Unbolt the door … and no funny business, or you'll be dining on cheese from now on!'

The mob shuffled sideways to allow the trembling hulk who'd been picked out to approach the door.

'Hey, you!' D.C. had spotted a beast at the back of the group who looked like it was still considering making a dash for it. She raised a rock in her hand and waggled it at the would-be runner. 'You want a taste of my magic flying rocks too do you?' The beast clearly didn't and slithered back into the crowd.

Henry nodded at her gratefully and watched as the heavy bolt was slid back on the door. As soon as he'd completed this task the macabon dove back into the tightly packed wad of bodies and buried himself somewhere in the middle.

'No! WAIT! I wanted you to open the door too! Sheesh … OK, you do it!' Henry was pointing his wand at another macabon trying to sink into the crush behind him. A rough pair of hands materialised out of the crush and the unwilling assistant was shoved forward. Keeping a panicked eye on the wand in Henry's hand he sidled out and grabbed the door handle. There was a pause when it seemed like the whole universe must have forgotten to breathe, then the macabon flung the door wide open and bolted back into the crowd to hide.

The anticipation was tangible on every side; Henry and D.C. watching to see if their lost family would appear; Peter watching to see what new monsters would attack them; and the macabon watching for the first opportunity to run away.

The dark hole of the doorway began to fill with faces; prisoners who'd been listening to the sounds of the commotion outside with a growing sense of hope. Pretty soon the doorway was bunched up with people craning to get a glimpse of their rescuers. The men were thin and unshaven; all looking around at the scene with a mixture of haunted fear and dawning relief as it became obvious their captors had been subdued.

'Henry? Henry, is that you?' A man pushed his way to the front of the group now spilling out of the building.

Henry reeled. He'd recognise that face anywhere despite the fact that it was wearing the bushiest beard of all. 'Dad?' Henry's world began to sway and turn as his brain wrestled with the evidence. There stood Ernst Noble. His father. Very much alive and well; although in need of a jolly good shave. With this realisation Henry's world flipped over on to its head, leaving any remaining coherence he had to spill uselessly out through his ears.

# Chapter 21

As Henry fainted his wand sloughed into the sandy ground and lay there looking very much like an ordinary stick. The macabon crowd murmured, eyeing the dormant wand. Peter could practically hear them planning a stampede. D.C. was round the side of the throng trying to keep them in line with a threatening rock, but without the main attraction she was losing the battle fast.

Peter made a dive for the wand, planning to wave it at them as if he knew what he was doing and hope it would be enough. The instant his fist closed about the innocent-looking stick he felt a surge of power tearing through his nervous system. The wand jerked up, nearly ripping his shoulder out of its socket as his hand and arm were dragged after it. Next it zigged madly to the right, before zagging crazily to the left, dragging the out-of-control accounts clerk behind it. The macabon crowd pressed itself back against the building as the crazed wand danced before their staring eyes.

'Steady, Peter! Go easy on them.' D.C. was marching around to the front of the gathering. 'You see how mad you've made my friend?' she addressed the crowd with confidence. 'If you were afraid of my other friend's magic you should be doubly fearful of this one. They don't call him Terrifying Pete for nothing you know?'

Peter continued to be dragged around in a threatening performance of waggling, which became more erratic with the wand's growing frustration that this was pretty much all it could do without the addition of some magic.

D.C. had started waving at the bearded accountants to clear the entrance of the building. They scurried out and behind the spectacle of Peter flopping around in the wake of the angry wand. Henry's father rushed to kneel by his unconscious son. Still holding up the rock D.C. shouted at the macabon, 'In the building. Quickly! I can't guarantee we can hold him back. The only safe place is inside.'

The macabon fairly stampeded through the door, several times getting it so wedged with bodies they had to back up a bit to get flowing again. Once the last of them had vanished into the building D.C. shouted an instruction for someone to bolt the door and rushed over to help Peter, who was still thrashing about on the end of the demented wand.

She approached him with her hands out, like she was calming a cornered dog. 'Shhhh ... it's OK. You did good, but you can stop now.'

Peter was trying to figure out how to tell her he had no idea how to 'stop now', when the wand seemed to calm a little.

Breathing slow and deep D.C. reached out and closed her fingers over Peter's clenched fist, easing it open as she wrapped her own hand around the shaft of the wand a little further up. There was a jolt that racked both their bodies briefly then Peter's hand flew open. He collapsed on the floor, stunned. D.C. stood holding the wand out in front of her as if she expected it might turn around and bite her at any moment. Very slowly, she lowered it to the ground.

'Daisy? Is that you?'

Dropping the stick the last few inches D.C. stood bolt upright, scanning the faces around her. 'Rowan?'

A blonde-haired young man with an auburn beard pressed through the group of accountants and stood there looking at her like she was made of mist. 'Is that really you little Daisy-chain?'

Peter had recovered enough from his mistreatment at the hands of the wand to note the names behind the initials. He thought Daisy-chain was a pretty name, but he didn't suppose it went very well with her brusque nature.

D.C. was oblivious to anything other than the massive hug she was giving her previously lost brother.

# Chapter 22

It took D.C.'s joyful sibling ten-minutes to peel her off, by which time Henry had come round and was feeling rather embarrassed about having fainted. The air buzzed with the chatter of excited accountants asking about news of home. With his friends otherwise occupied with their own family reunions, the brunt of the attention fell on Peter.

'Are you sure you're OK now?' Henry's dad was asking, as Henry insisted on getting up. They'd done a good five-minutes hugging themselves once Henry's eyes had fluttered open.

'I'm fine Dad. It was just all a bit much and we haven't eaten all day.'

Ernst looked around the camp site, clearly a man used to taking charge of situations. 'Right, we need to get some food organised for you three and pack up the supplies.'

'Supplies?' asked Henry.

'Yes Son, we have to get back to town as quickly as possible.' A couple of nearby accountants had stopped badgering Peter for news and drew close as Ernst began issuing instructions to 'gather that' and 'get this done'.

Henry felt a swell of dread at the urgency in his tone. 'Dad?'

Ernst turned his attention back to his son and hugged him tight. 'It's OK, just taking precautions. We heard those beasts talking about having to murder the whole town if … well, if what turned out to be you and your friends, made it through the mountain.'

Henry gulped. 'Murder the whole town? What, Terratonia? Because we came through the mountain?'

'We don't know for sure, but it's a pretty good guess,' piped up one of the accountants. Henry's father shot him a look that said 'I wasn't planning on being quite so honest' and the man busied himself with the next job on the list.

'It's OK, Henry. It's not your fault.' He nodded at the locked building, from which there hadn't been heard a peep. 'I think you scared them pretty badly anyway. I doubt Terratonia will have any more trouble from those thieving bullies once the story gets out.'

Rowan and D.C. had joined them now. 'What are we going to do about them?' he asked looking at the makeshift prison, which didn't look strong enough to withstand a concerted escape attempt by the macabon.

D.C. raised her voice to a level that would carry inside the building. 'We'll station a guard outside the door with orders to use the vilest magic possible on any beast that tries to break free!' She winked at Henry as the sound of muffled gasps came from inside the building.

Henry's father laughed. 'Come on; let's get some food inside you. We can figure out what to do with them in the morning.'

A couple of hours later they were all sitting in the canteen tent listening to a buzz of excited voices discuss the prospect of home. A couple of the accountants had whipped up a roast chicken dinner from the macabon food supplies, which the bloated rat had already made quite a dent in. With his belly now full of real food, Peter was beginning to feel a little more human. He leant his elbows on the table and rested his head on his hands, watching Henry and his father talking feverishly close by.

'And your brothers? How are they?'

Henry pulled a face of mock exasperation. 'Oh, they're nine. You know? But mother says we're not allowed to throw them out, so we're stuck with them I suppose.'

His father laughed. 'Not being a younger brother, like I am, you won't be aware of the small print.' Henry looked at his father, confused. 'It's part of the job to make your older sibling's life a misery. Until the age of about fourteen, when you suddenly realise how much you have in common and become firm friends.'

Henry wrinkled his nose at the prospect of five more years of hell with the twins, despite their tears when he'd set out on this mission. 'Well, they've become a lot more manageable since I hit them with a tagging spell,' he admitted.

Henry's father had no need to ask for an explanation since he'd already heard the entire story of Henry's apprenticeship with the King's wizard and the subsequent rescue out here in the desert in some detail. 'I still can't believe you're training to be a wizard. You always used to talk about it but we thought it was just childish dreams. I'm so proud of you, Son.'

Henry glowed, then realised he'd done nothing but talk about himself since he'd woken from his faint. He'd answered his father's stream of inquiry about the four years of Terratonian life he'd missed out on without asking a single question himself. 'So, what about you, Dad? Why have they kept you here all this time?'

His father's face clouded. 'We don't know much. They just force us to do the books for what appears to be several huge multi-kingdom corporations. As you know, I was the first to be captured, thankfully Neville made it away safely. It was really scary at first, and I was *really* busy. But over the months more started arriving. The workload got heavier as the companies grew. Then after Rowan and Graeme it stopped. That must have been over a year ago?'

Henry nodded, wondering for the first time properly what it must have been like for them out here.

His father shook his head, visibly marvelling at the passage of time. 'We figured it was because the King had stopped sending trade envoys. Unless ...' He paused, glancing around to see who was listening, clearly about to voice an often discussed concern. 'Unless the reason there have been no new prisoners is because they found a way to get through?'

It turned out several people were listening and the room went quiet as Henry replied. 'No, no-one until me and Peter. We were the first sent since Rowan and Graeme, and as you know D.C. was a stowaway.'

Rowan, who was sitting at the same table with his sister, locked her head in the crook of his arm and tickled her with the other hand. 'Yes, and we're going to have stern words about that when we get home, aren't we little Daisy-chain?'

She squirmed crossly and a muffled 'It's D.C.!' came from the vicinity of his armpit. 'Her real name is Daisy, but I used to make daisy-chains when she was a baby and crown her with them. It kind of stuck. Everyone was happy until she turned eight and decided she wanted to be taken more seriously. From then on she wouldn't answer to anything other than D.C. unless it came with a bribe.' D.C. was still struggling to break free, horrified by how much of her history her brother was casually tossing on the table.

'How did you two meet?' Henry's dad asked, laughing at the struggle. He'd been impressed when he heard about their journey. The girl had shown pluck.

Her brother was also secretly impressed and was hugging more than head-locking by now.

'G.D.E.' D.C. said morosely, dragging herself free of her brother as she remembered the unpaid debt.

'What? Gorman Dizing Enterprises?' Rowan asked.

'The very one,' said Henry, intrigued. 'Do you know them?'

'It's the biggest corporation on our books,' Ernst said in a hushed voice so as not to alarm too many other accountants.

They all looked at each other across the table, wondering about the significance of this.

It was Henry who broke the silence. 'Mr Colloid has definitely got something to do with it. I heard him arguing with the board of directors at G.D.E. about cooking the books or something. And, I didn't want to worry you, Dad, after everything you've been through. But Halcyon ... he went missing from the castle just before we left.'

Ernst Noble looked shocked. 'The Wizard Royal?'

Henry nodded.

'So they have no magical protection,' D.C. said, wide eyes staring at imagined possibilities conjured over the table.

'What?' Peter's mind started spinning again as it always did when the subject of magic was raised. 'Why would they need magical protection?'

'Because it's the only defence against magic!' She stood, fists balled on the table as she summed up the situation. 'Whoever the boss is at G.D.E. they're running fake wizarding classes; most likely as a way of sniffing out *real* magical talent and turning it to the dark side! They could be building an army of evil wizards! And they're using slave labour to do the books!'

The surrounding accountants had started to take notice again and Ernst shushed her back into her seat. 'I'm sure it's nothing so dramatic.'

She glowered out from behind the unruly flop of her fringe but lowered her voice anyway. 'Someone is up to no good Mr Noble, and judging by the enchantment they surrounded this camp with, I'd say we're up against some powerful magic.'

Henry's father watched her silently for a moment, then nodded. 'OK, noted. I think we're all agreed we need to get back to Terratonia as quickly as possible and warn the King.'

'We need to find Halcyon too,' said Henry. 'He'll know what to do in a magical emergency.'

Henry's father gave him a reassuring pat. 'We've got enough supplies to last us at least a week, by which time we'll definitely have hit the coast and it won't be far to Amalga.' Several accountants were nodding agreement and going back to their own business since they already knew this part of the plan. 'Once there we can send a fast horse ahead to warn the King.' Ernst saw his son's face grow grave and deep with thought. 'Don't fret, Son. In ten days or so we'll be back home and things will get back to normal.'

Peter was also watching Henry's face, and the expression he saw blossoming gave him a sinking feeling.

'No.' The table all turned to query Henry's rebuttal. 'We can be there in three days if we cut through the mountain.'

'But the dragon,' Peter said, surprised by the sound of his own voice.

'We'll find a way to deal with it,' encouraged D.C. her brother squeezing her dubiously on the shoulder.

'How would we even find the entrance?' asked Ernst, who could still remember being dragged into the desert by his captors as a uniformly rocky expanse of mountain disappeared behind them. The accountants had discussed escape many times on the long nights in their prison bunk and the consensus had always been to head straight for Amalga.

Henry pulled out his wand and placed it flat on the table. He stood and held his hand over it, thinking the activation charm that would make it point towards Mrs Flibbertigibbet. The black stick quivered and sprang into life, spinning about to point tremulously towards the door of the tent.

'The tagging spell on your brothers?' asked his father.

'Uh, yes,' he fibbed, flushing pink. 'This will show us the fastest route home.'

'Uh ...' Peter had raised his voice. 'But the dragon?' he repeated, ignoring D.C.'s exasperated sigh.

'Henry's right,' said Ernst. 'The town is in danger and we can make it home in three days if we use the passage. We'll find a way to deal with this dragon when we get there.'

Pretty much the whole canteen tent was listening to the conversation again now, a thick blanket of apprehension hanging in the air.

'Time for bed then,' piped up Rowan, ruffling his sister's hair. 'There's a roster of accountants keeping an eye on the prisoners. We should start out for home at first light.'

Before he slept, Henry slipped away and found an empty tent where he could restore the desk and spend some time consulting the book. It showed him a few new spells, including a class twelve *slow-burning fireball* that would come in very handy when they reached the dragon's lair. He started the cauldron bubbling with a top up of key ingredients and then set an *intellect deflector* up beside it, just to be on the safe side.

That night he fell asleep in a huge macabon bunk listening to the steady flow of his father's breathing. In out. In out. His mind still swam with the news that he had his father back. He pictured arriving at their home, seeing the look on his mother's face; and yes, even the twins. A smile settled on his face as he drifted off and dreamt of defeating the fearsome dragon in the cave and returning home a hero.

• • •

The next morning, they rose early and before the sun had finished folding away the blanket of night from the sky everyone was gathered outside the locked building ready to leave.

'What do we do about them?' someone asked and they all looked at the building.

'It could a week or more before we can get any soldiers back here to arrest them,' Peter said.

D.C. frowned. 'They'll be dead by then.' She lowered her voice so the others had to lean in to hear her, 'We also want word to get out about Henry's devastating magical ability, right? If we can scare these monsters and all their friends off from Terratonia that has to be better than fighting them.'

Henry thought hard. 'We just need a few hour's head start,' he whispered to the huddle. 'They've seemed pretty convinced by magical threats so far. Maybe I can trick them into believing the door is enchanted? Then we can draw back the bolt and make a run for it before they pluck up the courage to test it!'

The huddle nodded its general agreement and Henry marched up to the door, giving it a confident rap. There was a muffled gasp from inside. 'Listen up you thieving bunch of petty criminals! We're leaving now, and we have far bigger things to do than come back and arrest you. So I'm going to enchant the door with a *disintegration devil* and then we'll pull back the bolt. The devil will only live for six hours, after which time I suggest you leave these lands and never come back. If you do, all manner of terrible, MAGICAL fates will become you. But, remember the *disintegration devil*! If you touch the door before it is gone you will be instantly disintegrated! Do you understand?' There was a murmur from inside and Henry demanded louder, 'DO YOU UNDERSTAND?'

'Uh, no ...' said a nervous voice.

'What?' Henry asked, confused.

'No, we don't understand ...'

'What's dis-inger-tate?' asked another confused voice carefully.

D.C. huffed. 'It means if one hair on your nose touches that door inside the next six-hours, you'll explode into a cloud of dust! KABOOM!'

There was a collective fluey-sounding gasp as the macabon all clamped their hands over their noses. 'OK,' said one of them through pinched fingers. 'We'll stay put.'

D.C. shrugged at Henry. All they could do now was see if the ruse had worked. Henry wound up to cast another tagging spell. The door shook with indignation at the unprovoked attack and they could hear heavy bodies inside the building pressing to the back of the room.

'Ready?' Henry's father said to them all as he reached to unbolt the door. They shouldered their packs and walked quickly out of the camp in the direction the wand had pointed.

Henry had loaded up on ingredients to make the simple shielding spell he and D.C. had used to get through the illusion trap, and as the accountants filed by he cast a quick spell on each of them to protect them. Soon enough, they were marching in a ragtag band across the barren desert towards the Ribald mountains. They stopped every now and then to check the direction with Henry's wand and by mid-morning they were standing in front of the secret entrance to the mountain tunnel. People scouted around looking for a trigger. Peter, who was rather enjoying the attention of all the gratefully rescued accountants, was busy instructing people to sit heavily on all the appropriate-looking boulders. Before long someone chanced across the correct rock and a section of solid mountain slid aside.

# Chapter 23

Peter looked at the dark mouth of the tunnel. 'Seriously, Henry,' he said stepping up behind his friend. 'What are we going to do when we meet that dragon? Please tell me you have a plan that doesn't involve D.C. running out into the cavern like a lunatic?'

Henry's chest tightened, then he heard D.C.'s voice in his other ear. 'I'm not so stupid as to run out and fight a dragon with my bare fists,' she hissed at Peter. 'But we do need a plan.' She twisted one cheek up in what Henry had come to recognise as her thinking face.

'Any ideas?' Henry asked when his father started calling accountants to the mouth of the tunnel and handing them lighted torches.

'Come on you three,' Ernst beckoned to the trio. 'We need Henry up front with the wand to show us the way.'

As they hurried after the accountants D.C. whispered, 'Dragons are afraid of magic, right?'

'They are?' asked Peter, saving Henry the embarrassment of asking himself.

'Yes, they are.' D.C. answered herself decisively. 'Because like the macabon we just met they have no magic in them, so have no way of defending against it!' She was warming to her idea now and looked at Henry and Peter as if they must know what she was talking about. 'Have either of you ever read a book?' she asked, exasperated.

'What do you mean they don't have magic?' Peter asked ducking into the tunnel behind Henry. 'They breathe fire don't they?'

'That's exactly why they *don't* have magic!' D.C. slapped Peter on the back making him hiccough in surprise. 'All living creatures have magic until they *forget* it,' she said into the echo-filled darkness of the tunnel swallowing them up. 'The macabon just forgot because they're stupid. But the dragons got so wrapped up learning to breathe fire they stopped using magic until it winked out for their species forever.'

Peter gathered up a comforting handful of Henry's robe and stumbled on through the tunnel behind him. 'So you're suggesting Henry scares the dragon with magic? That it will just step back and let us all escape?'

D.C. nodded.

'I think that's a terrible plan!' Peter was incredulous to see Henry appearing to contemplate it. 'How will we know which exit to take?' he demanded.

'We'll send a scout round with H, hidden behind that reflective barrier of his!' she cried, enthralled by the new idea as it hit her. 'We can check all the tunnels and come back and get everyone when we find the right one.'

'What's this *we* Daisy-chain?' Rowan, who'd been walking behind her put a hand on her shoulder. 'You are not going out into a cave to fight a dragon. Mum will kill me if you get eaten when you've only been under my charge for twenty-four hours.'

'What *charge*?' his sister sneered, not unkindly. 'I just rescued you! And I'm the only one who's got a hope of handling the wand if something should happen to Henry.'

As the team trudged on through the tunnel, this time lit with the flickering orange light of many torches, they contemplated their options in silence. By the time they approached the mouth of the cavern they had reached an unhappy consensus that this did seem like the best course of action. Ernst Noble had taken some persuading to let his son wander off into a darkness that might contain a dragon, but eventually had to admit the plan sounded like it could work. The group of accountants stopped well short of the chamber entrance so as not to alert the dragon to their presence and settled down to wait.

'Be careful,' Ernst said, holding his son's face close.

'I'll be fine, Dad.' Henry hugged him tight.

'You too pip-squeak,' Rowan teased D.C.

She punched him playfully on the arm. 'Just don't get into any more trouble while I'm gone.'

Then she and Henry edged along the corridor, a tangerine disc of shimmering light held out in front them like a shield.

As they crept out into the cavern, D.C. gathered up a handful of Henry's robes like Peter always did; just to stay close to him in the dark. Henry stopped and so did D.C. The pair of them stood there for a while peering out into the complete blackness. They listened for signs of a beast waking up, or perhaps clutching the rocks ready to pounce. All they heard was the dripping of ancient waterways bouncing off every surface. Once Henry's heart had stilled a little he nudged D.C. and they started edging around to the left. They tiptoed across the rocky ground, trying not to make a sound. While Henry kept his attention focused on directing the shield towards the centre of the cavern, for maximum possible concealment, D.C.

felt along the rocky wall behind them in search of the next exit. After a few minutes of crabbing slowly round like this her hand fell into a gap.

She tapped Henry's shoulder, jabbing a thumb towards the tunnel entrance behind them. He started shuffling them back into it. There were a couple of hairy moments when a stone was unintentionally kicked or they thought they heard something out in the dark, but they were soon backed far enough into the tunnel to be out of sight. D.C. breathed a huge sigh of relief and Henry got straight to the business of checking the wand for direction.

He watched it quiver, then his stomach lurched as it pointed back into the black mouth of the cavern.

'Damn,' said D.C. as if she'd been expecting them to find the right one first time.

Henry fired up the *concave reflective barrier* again. 'Ready?'

D.C. nodded and they moved quietly back down the passage to try the next exit.

The going was excruciating, but they were gaining confidence. There had been plenty of stopping and listening to empty sounds in the dark, convinced something was out there watching. But by the time they backed into the third tunnel they had to admit to themselves there'd been no concrete evidence that the dragon was out there.

'Do you think it's still out there?' D.C. asked, voicing the concern for both of them.

'I wish I knew.' Henry had bent to place his wand and was thinking the familiar chant. 'But if it is, we don't want it to know we're here until we're ready to make a run for it. It's a good plan D.C. A great one in fact. We just need to find the right exit and sneak back to collect the others. Then I'm going to throw every flash, bang and wallop I've got at the dragon while everyone makes a run for the exit.' He looked down at the wand and his heart leapt as he saw it pointing emphatically up the tunnel, away from the maw of the cavern.

'This is it then,' D.C. said, pulling out the blanket she'd brought in her pack and indicating for Henry to get going.

Outside the mouth of the tunnel Henry stopped, and D.C. spread the blanket on the ground as quietly as she could so they wouldn't miss the exit coming back. Henry concentrated on directing the shield out at the black nothing. Staring through the tangerine glow of the spell he couldn't see more than a few feet in front of them, but his ears picked out a sound further off and he froze. He nudged D.C. with his foot and she froze too, kneeling by his legs and listening with him. Somewhere deep in the swallowing dark, something was waking up. Henry heard the definite wet slap of smacking lips, and then a deep gravelly yawn echoed along the cavern walls. This was followed by a sound like a long roll of damp leather being unspooled.

D.C. slid to her feet at Henry's shoulder as they heard another long yawn plus an assortment of the kinds of sounds you'd expect to hear from a huge body that hadn't been stretched in a while. 'It's waking up,' she mouthed, gesturing Henry to get moving. The blanket would do, and hopefully the spectacle of magic Henry made would give them enough light to see by anyway. The third exit on the left. A forty second sprint at best she judged, and with the element of surprise still with them she was pretty confident they could all make it.

They crabbed slowly right, both staring blindly into the blackness as D.C. trailed her fingers along the wall to count off the exits behind them. Each time her fingertips felt empty space her body tensed, ready to snatch Henry back into safe cover if the dragon chose this moment to make a move. The rest of the time she just prayed for the next exit to come quickly because they were screwed if the dragon attacked here. So far they'd heard no more from the huge creature lurking out in the dark. They passed the second exit and their pace picked up a little, both eager to get back to the others and the safety of the tunnel. D.C. pressed her fingers a little harder against the wall to be sure she didn't miss it, but one of them caught on a cracked piece of jutting rock. It turned out that the rock had been waiting for an excuse to crumble for decades, and a large chunk of masonry dropped to the ground. The clatter ricocheted off the damp walls of the huge cavern in a most alarming way. They froze, pressing back against the wall and listened with fearful ears.

There was a loud clacking sound that Henry recognised from before as the beast taking flight so he indicated to D.C. to slide down the wall until she was crouching. He did the same, nestled up close to her, and tilted the glimmering tangerine disc up towards the ceiling a bit so that it hid them from above. Crouching like this, breathing hard but as quietly as possible, they listened to the dragon flying round. Henry could make out the sound of its heavy body landing on crumbling rock, where it would snuffle around and prod at things with whatever body part dragons favour prodding with. Henry wasn't entirely sure what this would be but he had a feeling D.C. would know. When these investigations came up empty-handed, or empty-clawed if you want to be fastidious, the beast would flap its great wings again and keep circling. Several times Henry felt a gust air as it flapped perilously close to them, seeking out the source of the noise.

He was just about to signal a suggestion they start making slowly for the tunnel again when the ground shook and there was the cracking thud of a substantial body coming to rest somewhere close by. The tangerine shield illuminated maybe twelve-inches in front of it, giving them extremely limited vision. Something would have to be three-feet away from where they crouched before they would have visual confirmation of its presence. Henry heard a huff of breath as the dragon snorted and sniffed at the air right by them. It was close enough for the smell of rank carrion to reach Henry's own nostrils. Fear rose up in his stomach like a swarm of flies disturbed from that carrion feast.

His mind started running through the spells he'd learnt the night before. Things the book had suggested when he'd been thinking about this very kind of scenario. He'd start with a slow-burning fireball, which should light enough of the cavern for him to see where the dragon was coming from. It would also hopefully give the beast one almighty scare. He recalled the way the dragon had shied away when he'd thrust the green luminescence spell at it before. If D.C. was right, Henry could hold the dragon off with loud threats, much like they had the macabon. The spell book had also pointed him towards the *celestial stinger* spell, which delivered a painful barb of sunlight to its target. It wasn't fatal by any means, but it was about as devastating as a class thirteen spell got. Henry didn't trust himself casting anything higher with enough accuracy yet. As a last resort he could cast the *Fulcrum's Flabbergaster*. If the beast was sent spinning like before they could run for freedom, although he had no designs on connecting himself with the spell this time.

The moment their cover was blown, he warned his body as it crouched in the almost-dark, it would have to leap into action casting these spells. D.C. would know to run for the accountants ...'

An eye loomed out of the black into the halo of orange light from the shield. It hung in the nothingness; a sly reptilian pupil prodding at the dark. A moist membrane of scaly skin flicked across amber irises as the eye blinked. For a moment it felt to Henry like the creature was staring right at him. But he remembered the same sensation from the castle tower and forced himself to keep perfectly still. He felt D.C. tense beside him, still crouched like a cat against the wall and clutching a handful of his robe for comfort. He hoped she was getting the memo about staying quite still until the last possible moment. There was still a chance it wouldn't find them. He watched transfixed as the eye faded into the black of the cavern and was about to breathe a silent sigh of relief when the eye was replaced by a nose. Its beaklike shape was crowned with one stubby but very sharp-looking horn. Nostrils flared as they hunted for a whiff of their prey. Henry stopped breathing, but it appeared the beast didn't find what it was looking for and after a few more sniffs the nose vanished out of sight. Henry waited to see what would happen next.

There was a sound like creaking leather and snapping kindling as the giant body straightened itself up and stretched its wings out wide, ready for flight. Henry couldn't see the beast but the sounds he was hearing were unmistakable. They'd managed to evade discovery and it was taking off to search elsewhere. He was just allowing his spirits to lift and turned to D.C. to share the feeling, when there was a blood-curdling 'caw' and a large clawed foot shot out of the blackness. It happened so fast all Henry could do was watch, his eyes cruelly spinning the speed dial right down, leaving the rest of his body to move in slow motion. D.C. opened her mouth to scream as the powerful foot slammed into her, but was winded into silence against the rocky wall. He reached to grab her as sharp talons snapped closed around her waist, a look of frozen horror on her face. Then there was a loud clack and a billow of air as his friend was dragged off into the darkness.

# Chapter 24

'D.C.!' Henry screamed, leaping to his feet and immediately conjuring a *slow-burning fireball*. He swung his arm back and hurled the spell towards the ceiling. It stuck on the rocky dome about three-quarters of the way up, forming a miniature sun that poured enough yellow light into the cavern to fill half of it well, the other half dimly. There was an angry 'caw' and the dragon, which had been heading back to its perch to finish the human off, skidded to a halt mid-flight. It turned with one huge flap of its wings and faced the fireball with hatred in its eyes.

Forgotten by the dragon, D.C. went flying from its grasp and fell, crashing into the rocky central mound. Henry winced as he watched her tumble to the ground like a discarded rag-doll, arms and legs flailing. She hit the bottom hard and lay there, quite still.

Henry's first instinct was to run to her, but he didn't know how long that fireball would hold the dragon's attention. The beast had landed back on its central perch now and was watching it roil and burn on the domed rocky wall with murderous rage. Moving to stage two of the plan, Henry conjured a *celestial stinger* and strode towards D.C. holding his wand aloft with the sizzling blue spell at its tip. He kept one eye on the dragon's eyes. The moment it stopped glaring at that fireball and turned its attention to D.C. or him, he would threaten it with the spell and if needs be give it a nasty sting on the belly, that being the largest place on the beast so he was most likely to hit it. He'd covered about half the distance to the crumpled girl when the dragon noticed the robed figure brandishing the magic stick marching towards it. It hissed at Henry, dropping its head. The spines along its back bristled, its thick tail swishing savagely behind it.

'You stay back!' Henry shouted assuming the casting position. 'We don't want any trouble. I just want to take my friends and get out of here.' He became aware of a commotion behind him. The rest of the party, alerted by the fireball going off, were pushing out into the cavern to see what was going on.

The dragon eyed the crackling wand, seeming to weigh up the threat with its darting amber eyes.

'Henry!'

Henry glanced round to see his father stumbling out of the tunnel. 'Stay back Dad! All of you. I think it's afraid enough of magic for us to get out of here, but it snatched D.C. and I need to get her.'

Someone cried out, he guessed it was Rowan, but he'd already returned his attention to the seething dragon in front of him. 'Just stay where you are ... Nice and easy ...' He had started treading forward again and the dragon, while it remained twitchy, made no move to object. Then just as he was getting his confidence up the beast issued a strangled 'caw' and stretched its wings wide to take off.

'NO!' Henry bellowed, firing the *stinger* off at its belly. The beast recoiled with a furious screech as the spell emptied its payload into the softest part of a dragon's body. Henry conjured another *stinger* and began to edge forward again, keeping his wand raised and eyes locked on the dragon. There was a scuffle of noise from closer behind him and he saw the dragon's attention snatched by whatever had made the sound.

'HEY!' Henry shouted again, bringing his wand arm up as if to cast. The dragon turned vengeful eyes back on him and hissed. A shadow flitted by in his peripheral vision. Rowan. He should have known the lad wouldn't leave his sister lying broken at the feet of an angry dragon's perch. Henry decided the best course of action would be to divert the attention of the dragon with his magic while Rowan grabbed D.C. and made a dash for the exit. He took up a spell casting stance again and waved his wand, still crackling with blue light. The dragon cawed and resumed its previous stance of hissing at Henry, bristling. 'Third exit,' Henry shouted at Rowan as he scooped D.C. up and raced past him. 'The blanket is laid down outside it.' He began backing away himself, using the sound of people being ushered through the cavern towards the exit to guide him. The dragon continued to brood, eyeing the wand with growing rage.

'We're all out Son, come on!' It was his father's voice, not far behind him. Dare he just turn and run? Trusting his legs to carry him out of here before that thing could attack?

Sensing his hesitation, the dragon decided it had had quite enough of this nonsense. It felt a murderous desire to snatch up the robed figure waving the magic stick, and break it into two pieces, perhaps three or four. It stretched out its great wings and Henry's inner dialogue about whether he should run for it or not found the conversation had dried up. He fired the *stinger* at the launching beast but missed. The crackling blue light dissipated harmlessly into the rock face behind it. His inner dialogue found its voice again and started shouting at him to turn and RUN!

The dragon folded its wings back and hurtled at him from the apex of the dome. Henry cried out and turned, lunging towards his father whose face was a mask of panic at what loomed behind him. Before he'd even stumbled three paces he was slammed into the ground face-first as the dragon landed on him heavily. For a moment he thought it was going to crush him to death, then he felt searing pain as it sank talons into the flesh of his shoulders. The weight of the thing lifted with a leathery clack, then bright spots of agony burst around the edge of Henry's vision as he was hauled into the air. He could hear shouts from his father and the other accountants but all he could do was hang numbly from the dragon's claws as it dragged him through the air, every beat of its wings delivering stabs of pain where it gripped him with sharp talons.

His brain grappled with the facts looking for a way out. What now? He was caught in the grip of a furious dragon who was, apparently, no longer afraid of his magic.

Time to move on to stage three. As soon as he got the chance, he would send the beast spinning with the *Fulcrum's Flabbergaster*. His face grew slack as that thought rattled around in his head for a few moments. What were the words of the chant? He went to slap himself on the forehead to jog the memory, but the searing pain in his shoulders reminded him sternly of his predicament. He rifled through his memory banks some more before having to concede that all his terrorised brain could recall right now were the words of the *reversal* charm.

His body was tugged sideways as the dragon swooped to land on its perch where it planned to get on with the business of dividing his body up into more pleasing pieces. Henry hit the rocky surface and cried out as the dragon jerked him cruelly to the right before tossing him into the air. He rolled through empty space, glad at least that the stabbing talons were out of his shoulders. But no sooner had his brain had time to register this thought than he was snatched out of the air by his left arm, from which he proceeded to dangle. In desperation he began muttering the words of the only spell he could remember, his wand hand flailing in the emptiness. The dragon paused and looked at its victim, watching the energy of a new spell pooling at the tip of its wand. It opened its mouth and cawed in a way that was too much like a laugh for it not to be laughing. The stale heat of its breath made Henry shrink back despite the bolt of pain this movement shot through his arm, where sharp talons were back to their favourite activity of puncturing his fleshy pink skin. The dragon leant in close and pulled the struggling accountant up so that their noses were almost touching.

For a moment Henry thought it was going to speak, but then it simply hissed at him.

Henry recoiled and the dragon pursed it lips as if it were about to start whistling. Instead, it blew a river of fire into the darkness beside Henry's head. Its claws tightened and he moaned. 'How about you put me down and I won't unleash this spell on you?' he tried one last time waving the fully loaded wand gamely over his head. But that just made the dragon laugh again.

Its longest talon, bored with the preliminaries and keen to get on with the mutilation, dug into Henry's forearm. He yelped and struggled away. He could feel hot blood dripping up his arm as the dragon's talon dug deeper. He twisted and turned, trying to break free. Instinctively his free hand, still holding the fully charged wand, sought out the cause of the pain to try and make it stop. The wand connected with the dragon's longest talon. There was a sudden, sharp crack.

Henry's body was shaken with the kickback of the spell, but the immediate pain in his forearm was gone. He looked at it. The arm was still seized in the dragon's claw, but he was astonished to note that the offending talon had disappeared. In its place a human toe waggled around. The sight was quite incongruous; a huge scaly dragon's claw with two-foot talons, and at the centrepiece a gnarled and wrinkly toe with a yellowing toenail and what looked-like a verruca on one side. The dragon also looked down at the toe and cried out. It let go of its victim, snatching its foot up to examine the damage. Henry proceeded to replicate D.C.'s earlier tumbling act down the rocky embankment and landed in a heap on ground.

His body screamed about the harsh treatment, but he sensed he didn't have time to worry about minor injuries. Staggering to his feet he cast around to get his bearings. He could see his father running at him from a dark hole on the opposite side of the cavern. He lurched towards the apparition, but tripped over the hem of his robe which had come un-cinched at the waist during the struggle.

As Henry tumbled in a muddled ball across the rocky floor, the dragon pulled itself together, screeching with rage. It lunged at the wand, which Henry had loaded once more with the magic of the reversal charm. He wasn't entirely sure why, but he was beginning to realise this was the way magic worked sometimes. The dragon landed heavily beside him. It had decided it was going to slice up this troublesome person with the claw that still had all of its talons, before reducing everything to a burnt pile of ash with its fire. Henry rolled over just in time to see the beast strike out with a razor-like talon, scorching his ribs as it gouged a fresh wound across them. Henry jabbed his wand at the beast as it thrust in for another assault. It connected with the dragon's leg just above its clawed foot, sending another shudder of power through Henry. The dragon screeched and looked down. There was a comical moment when they both stared open-mouthed at the spindly human lower leg that had replaced the dragon's mighty claw. Then the human leg buckled under the weight of the dragon's enormous body and it tipped sideways, landing in a graceless hump on the floor.

Henry backed away from the lopsided dragon, uttering the words of the *reversal* charm over and over again. The dragon sat there fuming, wondering how such a useless amoeba could have reduced its magnificent self to this. The wand now fully charged again, Henry took up the spell casting stance and prepared to launch another bout at his opponent. The dragon bellowed and took in one enormous lung full of air, then pursed its lips and propelled a jet of bright-hot fire at Henry. Without thinking, he launched the spell towards the approaching fire-cannon.

The two connected in an explosion of light, the magic from Henry's wand instantly turning the billowing heat of the dragon's breath into nothing more than a bad dose of halitosis; not terribly pleasant perhaps, but at least it is very unusual to be burnt to a cinder by halitosis. The spell seemed to eat its way through the inferno with relish and still had a little fight left in it when it reached the dragon's mouth. On making contact with its scaly lips the reversal charm spent the last of itself turning them into the lips of an old man; pink and moist and ludicrous in proportion to the rest of the dragon's face. Incensed, the dragon went to breathe another stream of fire at Henry, but changed its mind quickly when it discovered that human lips are not as fire-resistant as dragon lips. It shrieked with pain and indignation.

Although relieved he'd halted the attack, Henry was starting to have doubts about beating the dragon like this. He only had a limited supply of ingredients in his wand and it could take all day to put this dragon out of business if he was going to have to do it bit-by-bit.

Henry backed away from the dragon, which was dragging its huge bulk towards him with its remaining partially intact claw. Creasing his brow, he brought his left hand up to join the right one on the shaft of his wand and gripped it tight. He willed the magic to build fast enough to keep the beast at bay. As he thought the words of the reversal charm he felt an unusually powerful surge of energy from inside him. His head swirled sickeningly as he felt the words of the charm rushing round and round inside his pointy hat. The space between his arms was also caught up in a vortex of power, which was gushing out of his chest towards the tip of the wand in a tidal wave. This wave of energy didn't stop to gather its thoughts at the tip of Henry's wand like he was used to; there was no room for such magic to perch there. Instead it streamed from the thin black stick like a ribbon, groping out into the darkness for something to make friends with.

The dragon cowered, for the first time feeling rage melt away into fear, and tried to push itself backwards on its crippled legs. Seconds later the bolt of magic had found its mark and connected with the unfortunate beast's head with a sizzling blast. Light exploded outwards in a supernova.

Henry would have been quite impressed with himself if he'd been able to see what was happening, but his body was being racked with the force of a two-handed spell; way above his wizarding experience. Eventually it was all too much for him. The sheer force of the spell tore the rampant wand from his hands, flinging him backwards on to the rocky floor and knocking the wind out of his lungs. His head spun a few more swirly loops then everything was still again. He propped himself up on his elbows, heart hammering. He could see his wand lying on the floor a few feet away and was about to make a grab for it when he heard a cough. He twisted to face the dragon, tensing for an attack, and saw a craggy, old, but very familiar face looming down at him. Henry blinked, wondering if he might have hit his head harder than he'd thought when he fell.

'Well done Henry ... Well done!' Halcyon's face enthused. Henry slumped, stunned. 'Do you think you've got enough energy to restore the rest of me now?' Halcyon's face hobbled a little closer and Henry noted that it was actually Halcyon's head and the top part of his neck, attached rather incongruously to the enormous body of a dragon; that is, a dragon with one human leg and a big toe on the other foot. Henry blinked.

'It's OK,' Halcyon reassured. 'We don't have to start immediately, although these scales are pretty itchy to be honest. But we can do it a little at a time now that my head's back together again. You found that two-handed spell casting a bit wild I should imagine? But I must say you handled yourself splendidly considering how long you've been in training.'

Henry was struggling for words so just lay there, fish-bowling at the extraordinary vision.

'I make a formidable dragon; don't you agree?' Halcyon's face grinned as he spread the dragon's magnificent wings out behind him, flexing them to their most impressive span.

Henry's face turned pink. 'You tried to kill me!'

'Oh, yes. I'm sorry about that. But I wasn't feeling quite myself you see? It was a powerful spell that transformed me into a dragon; and dragons fly completely off the handle when they meet a wizard. They don't like magic you see. Did we not cover that in magical anatomy yet?'

'No, but I knew anyway. D.C. told us …' As the words slipped out of his mouth his brain slipped back into gear and he leapt to his feet looking around. 'D.C?' he cried out. The sound echoed off the cavern walls just as Henry's father skidded to a halt beside him, brandishing a flaming torch. He pressed his son behind him protectively and jabbed the torch at Halcyon's face.

The dragon with the wizard's head jerked back. 'Hey! Steady on Ernst old chap,' it said.

Ernst Noble stopped jabbing and gaped at the sight.

'It's OK, Dad.' Henry had placed a hand on his father's arm. 'It's just Halcyon, well some bits of it are just Halcyon.'

'Including the bit that does the thinking, thank goodness,' Halcyon interjected with a lop-sided grin.

'Where's D.C?' Henry asked his father. 'Is she …?'

'She's OK boy. Well, a few broken bones so not really OK, that was a terrible fall she had.' Halcyon had the decency to blush at least as Henry shot him a furious look. 'But she'll mend. Her brother is in the tunnel with her, splinting her up so we can keep moving and get some proper medical attention.'

Henry breathed out a sigh of relief and looked at the Halcyon-headed dragon. 'So, bit by bit then?' he asked taking up a spell casting stance.

'Yes please,' Halcyon replied. 'We'll start with the rest of this leg if you don't mind? I'm beginning to get cramp in my toe.'

# Chapter 25

Having laboriously turned each bit of Halcyon back into a wizard they were all now gathered around the exit tunnel discussing strategy.

'Who did that to you Halcyon? Was it this Gorman Dizing character?' Henry's father asked.

Halcyon frowned and rubbed his chin. 'I really don't know. I've been feeling unsettled for a couple of weeks now, so when I received a message to meet the King in the Oval Library I got suspicious; he hasn't asked for my help in years, you know? I decided to leave the book somewhere Henry would find it, just in case, and headed down for the meeting. I found the library deserted so I huffed crossly and turned to leave. That's the last thing I remember. I have got a rather nasty bump on the back of my head though,' he finished, rubbing the back of his head to prove it.

'We must get back to Terratonia as soon as possible,' Ernst said. 'If they took you from inside the castle the King could be in real danger.'

'And there's no-one in town with any magic,' D.C. reminded them fearfully, cradling a splinted arm. 'Who's going to defend them from whatever the evil wizard does next? Because let's face it, with the *illusion trap* and now this ... no-one is going to deny that's what we're dealing with here, right?'

'It could be,' Ernst conceded gathering up his pack and indicating for the others to do the same. 'But the dragon is dealt with,' he nodded proudly at his son, 'and we should be home in two or three days. Let's get moving.'

'What about a magical shortcut?' D.C. directed the question at Halcyon who took an involuntary step back.

Everyone else stopped what they were doing and looked at the old wizard too. Peter, who'd been a trembling wreck throughout the battle with the dragon and was still feeling pretty unhinged, stepped up close to Henry at the utterance of the word 'magical' and gathered a comforting handful of robe.

'Is there such a thing?' asked one of the accountants.

'Well, technically yes,' blustered Halcyon, caught off guard. 'But it's no good right now as I can't risk using any more transformative magic on myself until I've reached my chambers and can run some tests to make sure I'm all-the-way back to being human.'

'I'll go.' Rowan stepped forward and D.C. let out a strangled gasp that really wanted to be an emphatic 'No!' but didn't have the strength.

'No, I'll go.' This deeper voice belonged to Ernst Noble, who stepped in front of Rowan.

'Actually neither of you can go. The magical shortcut works by a creating a fold in the fabric of space and time. More of a crease really. It allows a wizard to open a gate to a conveniently compact alternate dimension, and step through to wherever he wants to go.'

'You cast it, I'll step through,' Ernst demanded.

The old wizard shook his head. 'You can't just go running off willy-nilly into other dimensions. A wand is the only reliable guide as they are uncannily good at navigating realities. If you don't have a good connection with one you can take through with you, you'd most likely get lost trying to find your way back and that would be the last anyone ever sees of you; in this dimension anyhow.'

'I'll go.'

They all turned and stared at Henry.

'No!' his father said firmly.

'Wait, Dad listen.' Henry was holding up his wand. 'I have a great connection with my wand. It'll get me safely through the gateway and I can run and warn the King! It'll take minutes instead of days, and I can get them to send horses and guards back to fetch you.'

The accountants looked around at each other. You could tell by the tortured expression on Ernst's face that he was rooting around for objections worth raising. But it did seem like a pretty good plan.

'OK,' Halcyon said eventually. 'Henry, I'll need to use your wand. Whoever bonked me on the head took mine, though they'll have the devil of a job holding on to it as I took the precaution of imbibing it with a cheeky little defence charm.' The old man chuckled as his mind played out whatever defences the wand would be deploying. 'No matter, it'll find its way back to me once we reach Terratonia. Do you have *feather salt* and *shilly-liver essence* loaded into this beauty?' He pried Henry's fingers from around the wand and took it in his own.

Henry nodded.

'Good, good,' the old wizard crooned, assuming a casting stance. 'The magic is simple for this spell, as you can probably tell by the common ingredients. But the distance you'll need to cover will make it a class five spell. Very complicated stuff.'

His face folded up into a concentrated frown and an arc of radiant red light went spinning from the tip of the wand. It hit the floor with a crash that shook their feet. When Henry looked down at the spot in front of him where the magic had hit, a circle of solid rocky ground had been replaced by a gaping black hole. It smouldered at the edges, as if the cavern was upset to have been vandalised in such a way. Henry looked at Halcyon.

The old wizard handed back the wand to his student. 'Don't forget this.'

Henry took the wand, and went back to staring into the smouldering hole. 'I just step through?'

'You just step through,' Halcyon agreed with a nod of encouragement. 'I opened the gate into my chambers. Sorry it's a down gate rather than an across gate. The tower is quite narrow and it's not a precise art. Didn't want to send you crashing out into the moat!' Henry gulped and the wizard tittered nervously. 'You should drop into my rooms somewhere from the ceiling.'

'Right ...' Henry said. Then he stepped into the gaping black hole.

Peter, who'd been watching this exchange through a haze of shock was dragged back to reality as his body pitched forwards. He glanced in horror at his treacherous fists, still bunched up in Henry's robe. He went to let go but was already toppling over, unable to right his balance. As he fell into the hole behind Henry he was aware of gasps and exclamations from behind him. Someone made a grab for his leg but it slithered through their grasp. Peter clenched his fists tight around the robe and clung on, squeezing his eyes tight shut too.

• • •

The instant Henry tumbled through the blackness of the hole his eyes were assaulted by blaring sunlight, which was streaming in through an un-shuttered window. He braced himself for the inevitable crunch as he hit the floor. The crunch didn't disappoint, but what Henry hadn't been expecting was the subsequent thump as something landed heavily on top of him.

'Ouch!' He rolled the heavy thing off him and sat up to find Peter looking dazed. 'Peter! What are you doing here?'

Peter blinked and tried to come up with a reasonable explanation. 'I was holding your robe. Force of habit I guess.' Suddenly he remembered Halcyon's warning about getting lost between dimensions and began checking himself over for discrepancies. 'I think I'm all here,' he said when he didn't find any.

Henry looked at the wand in his hand. 'I guess you formed a bond of sorts with it when you picked it up in front of the macabon?' The wand shivered its apparent agreement.

Peter shuddered at the thought of being bonded to that uncontrollable stick in any kind of way. He glanced about the room, suddenly looking very much like a young accounts clerk again.

'Alright.' Henry was picking himself up off the floor and brushing his robes down. The tall pointy hat, which was a remarkably good fit it seemed, sat snuggly atop his head. 'We need to get down to the dungeons and alert the castle guards … then I suggest we get right on over to the accounting vaults and have it out with Mr Colloid. It's Friday isn't it?'

Peter replied with a blank stare. Had it really only been three days since they'd started this crazy journey?

'Yes!' Henry answered himself, excitement agitating his features.

'So he'll be busy with the week ending ledgers. Boy, is he going to be surprised to see us!'

Peter sighed. Here we go again, he thought to himself as he hurried out of the door in the wake of his determined companion.

# Chapter 26

Down in the dungeons it was business as usual, and by that I mean half a dozen bodies in red uniforms were tossing playing cards into a growing heap on the table. A soldier with the keys to the cells hooked loosely on to his belt was dozing peacefully in a chair, a little too close to the cells for comfort.

Henry and Peter burst into the room and the card players looked up. 'Quick! We have to take Mr Colloid into custody!' Henry was red in the face. The card players stared at him blandly. The snoozing guard just snorted.

'I mean it! It'll take too long to explain, but you have to come with me to get Mr Colloid before he escapes. Hurry!' Henry was becoming panicked.

'Look,' one of the card players drawled, 'we can't just run about arresting people because some weirdo dressed in a raggedy dress and pointy hat has been out in the sun too long.' There was an amused rumble around the table.

Henry straightened his tattered robe self-consciously and struggled for more words to use on them.

It was Peter who finally found something to throw into the uncomfortable silence. 'We're the accountants. Sent to fetch coconuts? We were ambushed in the forest and some criminals stole the King's gold!' It was a rather simplistic synopsis considering everything that had happened, but it seemed to hit a chord with the guards. They sat up and looked at the pair properly for the first time. The lazy drawler placed his cards deliberately on the table and leant forward, peering at the two grubby-looking young men in the doorway.

'You're the accountants?' The guard was incredulous. 'My lord, we didn't think you'd be seen round here again. We were arguing for days about who had to go with you. Nine people already gone? We're not stupid you know?'

'Go with us?' Henry asked with incredulity to rival the guard's. 'We went alone!'

'Yes ... funny that. Mike and me were all saddled up, having lost a game of cards to decide who had to go, but when we got to the castle gates for the rendezvous at eleven o'clock this thin-looking man said you'd already left.'

'What? And you didn't come after us?' Henry was shocked.

'The scrawny guy said not to bother. Said you'd been given the swiftest steeds in the Kingdom and would be halfway to the Gateway Passage by now.'

Henry fumed remembering the lethargic ponies they'd been handed. 'Really?' he said through gritted teeth.

'Yeah.' The guard paled at Henry's obvious fury. 'He was an odd man to be honest with you. Gave us the creeps, didn't he Mike?' Mike nodded, a guilty flush colouring his cheeks as he also noticed how miffed Henry was. 'Well ... we decided that that was the matter over and done with, and we just kept our heads down, didn't we Mike?' Mike studied his feet and flushed a little harder. 'I suppose we should have come after you, if we'd thought that there was anything suspicious going on. But, you know ... well. It was kind of ... well there wasn't any real reason ... if you get my drift?' The guard's guilty monologue dribbled away into nonsense and he eventually realised he was no longer talking, so stopped opening and closing his mouth.

'Well, now we've cleared that up.' Henry's voice was barbed with a contempt that made the guards wince. 'Would you consider that bandits ambushed the King's envoy; the King's envoy that *you* were supposed to be guarding may I remind you? Would that fall into the category of something suspicious going on?'

The guards looked at each other and then nodded their agreement.

'Wouldn't it therefore follow that finding said envoy standing in front of you, having escaped the bandits' hideout and bringing news of a mole inside the castle,' Henry was warming to his theme as the guards watched him expectantly. 'Wouldn't the right thing to do, be to accompany said envoy into the vaults to arrest the mole; who also happens to be the Chief Accountant and the man who deceived you at the castle gates?'

Realising that arresting a suspect and potentially getting the gold back could deflect any unwanted attention from his own wrongdoings, the lazy drawler transformed miraculously into a proactive go-getter and leapt to his feet in support of the idea. 'Lead the way boy. Mike? You're with me.'

Mike threw his cards down on to the table and sheathed his sword, following the others importantly out of the dungeons towards the vaults.

They found Mr Colloid sitting in his familiar spot by the door, scratching long numbers into a thick parchment ledger that looked like it must've been in use for centuries. He looked up when he heard the clatter of armoured bodies descending into his domain. By the look on his face he wasn't expecting to see Henry and Peter.

He jumped to his feet and backed away from the approaching group, his hand fidgeting with his neatly knotted neck tie. 'What? What's going on? What are you two doing back here? And what on earth are you wearing, Noble?'

'Not expecting to see us again, eh Mr Colloid? Why's that then?' Henry glared at his employer while the guards frowned on.

'I ... you ... well ... not so soon, no. Good trip?' Mr Colloid snivelled.

'Good trip? Good trip!?' Henry's face turned pink with the ridiculousness of the enquiry. 'We've been leapt upon, roared at, clawed at and generally mistreated! We were nearly drowned out at sea and almost barbecued under the mountain!'

Mr Colloid looked from Henry to Peter to the two, burly guards, and then back to Henry again, who was beginning to seethe. 'All that in three days? I find your story quite preposterous.'

'Oh really?' Henry barked. 'Well how do you explain sending us off *six hours* before the armed guard was booked, and then *lying to them* about us being on fast mounts?' Henry was practically screaming now. 'Was it him, Mike?'

One of the guards nodded seriously. The man still gave him the creeps.

'And what is your part in the criminal activities of Gorman Dizing Enterprises?' Henry finished, pointing an accusatory finger at his cringing employer.

'I ... I don't know what you're talking about,' the accountant faltered, his eyes flicking about the room as if scanning for plausible explanations.

'Oh, don't give me that! I saw you inside the G.D.E. corporate headquarters talking to someone about fiddling the accounts. And all this time my father has been locked up, forced to keep the books for G.D.E. and we all thought he was dead!' Henry took a threatening step towards the older man and Peter took hold of his elbow to restrain him. By now the whole room had fallen silent. All eyes were on the commotion by the stairs and sweat was beginning to roll down Mr Colloid's cheeks.

'You're the only person who's ever escaped the bandits out in the forest ...' Henry accused. 'Very convenient that, isn't it? What happened out there two years ago Mr Colloid? How come you made it back when everyone else failed? What is your involvement with Gorman Dizing Enterprises? And come to think of it, who is Gorman Dizing anyway?' Henry ran out of questions.

It was the guard's turn to advance, caught up in the passion of the moment and still eager to blame someone else. 'Aiding and abetting the theft of the King's gold? Kidnapping? Slave labour? Not to mention shady accounting practices ... These are very serious accusations Mr Colloid. What have you got to say for yourself?'

Mr Colloid had reversed completely against the wall, his eyes darting back and forth between the guards and his junior staff. His fists clenched and unclenched as he struggled to come up with an alibi. 'It ... I ... It wasn't my fault!' He suddenly broke, sliding his back down the wall until he was curled up in a foetal huddle behind his large wooden chair. 'They attacked us in the forest ... they were terrible creatures! They caught me and threatened to kill me if I didn't go along with their plan. It wasn't my fault ... I was scared ...' He started to sob and Henry couldn't help feeling a kind of disgusted pity for the man.

'Take him to the dungeons and lock him up until the others get back,' Henry instructed the guards, who were only too happy to oblige and get this whole embarrassing mess over and done with as quickly as possible.

・・・

An hour or so later they had the paperwork completed, and the castle guards packed the two exhausted young men off home to rest with the reassurance that they would send a unit out to Gorman Dizing's offices right away. They also promised to send the King's guard to meet and escort the missing party of accountants back home. Henry scowled at Mr Colloid through the bars of his cell one last time and made his way out of the dungeon with Peter.

They left the castle and started making their way slowly along the path that led back into town. It was late in the afternoon, probably around four o'clock, and the streets were full of the usual assortment of Terratonia's citizens going about their usual Friday afternoon business. It was as if nothing had happened; that is, apart from the curious glances Henry's unusual attire was soliciting. Henry had to pinch himself to make sure something had. He ran over the simple facts in his mind and came up with the overwhelming majority vote that he couldn't wait to get home and tell his family. In just a couple of days Ernst Noble would be back and things could finally return to normal. He quickened his pace as his spirits lifted.

The market square was predictably busy, with zealous shoppers rushing this way and that in pursuit of the weekend's provisions. But as they skirted the hectic scene Henry's attention was caught by something else. Something that in this picture of perfect normality stood out like a sore thumb. His aunt's house, sitting neatly on the corner of the square as it always did, didn't look right. For starters, the regiment of window boxes she was so proud of looked a bit dry and thirsty. Then there was the fact the curtains were pulled shut, despite it still only being mid-afternoon.

Henry stopped and looked at the house. 'Peter? I just want to check something. Hang on a minute will you?'

Peter watched as Henry placed his hand in the fold of his robe where he kept his wand, and walked up the path to his aunt's front door. He knocked gingerly. 'Aunt Flibbertigibbet?' There was no reply, and his wand remained peacefully calm. Henry reached out and tried the handle. It turned in his grasp so he eased the door open and tried calling his aunt's name again. No reply. He stepped inside.

The air was dry and stale, as if the windows had remained shut for a few days at least. He made his way through the kitchen and peered into the front room. Nothing. Not a sign of life in the whole house. Where could she be? Henry was just about to make his way back outside when he heard a soft noise. His hand whipped the wand out of its fold and he pointed it in the general direction of the noise.

'Who's there?' he called out. He heard a sniff. It came from the bathroom, so he edged his way towards it. 'I know you're in there, and the house is completely surrounded! You might as well give yourself up now!' The sniff turned into a whimper and Henry felt his confidence grow. He rapped on the bathroom door and shouted at whoever was in there, 'Come on out now!'

'Please ... please don't hurt me ...' It was Mrs Meddling cringing in the bathroom doorway, clutching her apron to her stomach as if she needed to relieve herself.

'What on earth are you doing here?' Henry asked. 'And where's my aunt?'

'That's what I was trying to find out! I came in here to look for clues ... she's been missing for days you know?'

Henry frowned. He didn't like the sound of this and his aunt *had* been mixed up with Mr Colloid. 'Did you find any?' he asked the cowering town gossip.

'What?'

'Clues ... did you find any clues?'

'Oh, no ...' she finished lamely.

'Well get out of here then, and don't say a word about this to anyone. Mr Colloid has been arrested and we don't want Mr Dizing to get wind that we're on to him before the others get back from the forest.'

Wasting no more time on pleasantries, Mrs Meddling scrambled out of the doorway and beat a hasty retreat. She rushed up the garden path and past a bemused looking Peter, then vanished into the bustling market square desperate to find someone to tell.

# Chapter 27

A few moments later Henry came bursting out of the door and hurried up the path towards where Peter stood. When he reached his confused companion he popped the wand down on the floor and issued it with instructions to locate his aunt Flibbertigibbet, which it did with its usual enthusiastic flourish. 'Come on,' he said to Peter, and started marching away into the market, clearly on a mission.

'Hey! Wait! What? Where are we going now? And who was that lady who came out of the house? Henry? What is going on?'

Henry stopped and turned to face Peter, who groaned inwardly when he saw the blazing look in his eyes. 'To rescue my aunt ... I think. Or to arrest her. Either way, it's imperative that we find her before my father gets back. He's had more than enough to deal with these past two years!'

'But Henry ...' Peter looked scared again. He was just beginning to believe that they'd made it back home safely; was allowing himself to look forward to a lamb dinner tonight, since he felt sure his mother would be treating him to all his favourite things; and in a far more satisfying way than the last time.

Henry saw these thoughts chasing each other across his young friend's face and felt a pang of guilt about the way he'd dragged the poor lad into so much trouble during the past few days. 'Peter, I'm sorry. Of course, you go home. It won't take two of us to handle this ... besides, I have my trusty wand.' He waggled the wand at Peter to prove it.

Peter frowned. He wasn't sure why, but he thought it was a very bad idea to let Henry go off and do this on his own, whatever *this* may be. The frown dug itself in deeper and he shook his head. 'I can't believe I'm doing this ... but all right. Where are we going?'

Henry grinned. 'I'm not sure ... following the tagging spell I put on my aunt.'

'You put a tagging spell on your aunt? Henry, I worry about you.'

'It's a long story. But I think I know where it's going to lead us.'

'You do?'

'Certainly,' Henry said with an air of confidence that calmed Peter's frayed nerves. 'I think it'll lead us straight to the corporate headquarters of Gorman Dizing Enterprises. And I don't think Mr Dizing will be expecting us.'

· · ·

Sure enough, the wand led them straight to the glossy front entrance of G.D.E. They solicited a few curious glances along the way, which was hardly surprising given how Henry was dressed and that he would occasionally stop to spin a shiny black stick on the ground. But apart from that they made it across town with no further upsets. Once they reached the imposing building they hesitated, deciding on the best approach. Henry peered in through the giant, spotless front window, and his face reddened with the prospect of talking to the girl on the reception desk.

'Penny!' Peter cried from over Henry's shoulder, making him jump. 'The girl at the desk, THAT'S Penny Filigree, Henry.'

Henry looked at Peter. 'She's a friend of yours?'

Peter looked momentarily crestfallen. 'We went to school together since we were toddlers. Yes.'

Henry blushed as he realised what his shock had inferred. 'No ... I didn't mean. I just mean ... Well, she's really pretty.'

Peter flushed a complementary shade of pink. 'Yes, she is. But she's just a friend. Is it such a surprise she would like me?'

'Oh ... oh no. Peter. I don't mean that at all,' Henry said, mortified. 'I just ... well, I never know how to talk to girls.'

Peter looked at Henry like he was trying to figure out what species he was. Eventually he said, 'What about D.C.?'

Henry blinked. He opened his mouth to reply but his bottom jaw just hung there, unsure how to proceed without instructions from his brain, which was busy processing this new realisation. 'I guess you're right,' he managed in the end. 'I'm sorry. Plus it's great that you know her. Do you think you can persuade her to let us in?'

'I can try. Come on.' This time it was Peter's turn to lead the way, Henry still dragging his heels at the thought of having to even stand close to such a beautiful girl.

As they approached she looked up. Her customary disinterested glaze transformed into a friendly grin as her gaze touched on the familiar face in front of her. 'Pete!' Her gold-flecked eyes gave them a quick once over and her happy expression melted into a look of concerned recollection. 'Oh my days! You're supposed to be on that trade mission! Is everything OK? What happened? You look awful!'

'Gee, thanks!' Peter replied as lightly as he could.

She giggled and covered her mouth with her hand. 'I'm sorry. But you know how filthy you are, right? You're mother's going to be bleaching the kitchen for a week if you walk in the house like that! You look like you've been in a boxing match.'

'That's not too far from the truth to be honest,' Peter said. The girl cocked her head. 'Look, I'll tell you all about it later. But first, can we sneak into your building quickly? It's really important. We need to find your boss.' 'Mr Dizing? You'll be lucky! I don't know a single person who's actually seen the man; although apparently he lives in this building somewhere. Bit of a recluse so I'm told.'

Henry's heart was thumping and his ears pulsed with the sound of it. He was dying to ask this stunning girl all sorts of questions; questions about Mr Dizing; whether she'd seen Mr Colloid, or his aunt Flibbertigibbet in the last couple of days? But his brain seemed incapable of coming up with anything more coherent than 'wha, wha, wha,' so he decided to keep his mouth shut.

'Well, can we come in and have a scout round anyway? We promise not to cause any trouble. Right, Henry?' Henry nodded dumbly.

'Pete,' the receptionist said in a softer, more urgent voice. 'If something has happened you need to go and get help at the castle. You really do look terrible. It's not like you.'

Peter was taken aback by the concern in her voice. He'd had a secret crush on Penny since they were six-years-old. His cheeks coloured at the thought. 'Please, Penny. It's really important,' he said to change the subject with himself.

'I'm sorry Pete. You know they're already on amber alert but they've ramped it up in the last twenty-four hours ... I could look the other way but there's a guard on every exit out of this lobby and they've got strict instructions not to let anyone through without an appointment. Most of us think it's a bit over the top, but the guards love it.'

Peter glanced around the striking lobby. Sure enough there was an officious-looking guard standing at every possible route into the building. There was even one standing outside the entrance to the lavatory, although Peter couldn't be sure he wasn't just waiting for his turn to use it. He looked back to the girl behind the desk and leant in conspiratorially. 'Is there another way in?'

'Maybe ... there's a delivery entrance round the back somewhere. But believe me, security is pretty tight. And *you* should be getting a medical check-up. Or at least a damn good bath.' She smiled and then sat back in her chair with a guilty thunk as she noticed the guard by the toilet striding towards them.

'Everything OK Pen?' he called out. 'Are these vagrants bothering you?'

'No ... no, no Barry. It's OK!' She riffled through some parchment-work on her desk and dug a couple of slips out, pushing them into Henry and Peter's hands with a cheery smile. 'There you are, Sorcerer's Apprentice application forms. Only, I don't think you need to wear that getup until you're actually enrolled in the class, Sir.' She was talking to Henry, indicating his wizarding garb with a twinkle of amusement in her eyes. He almost swallowed his tongue with the shock of her direct attention.

Peter grabbed his arm, and plastered a similarly cheery expression across his own face. 'Thank you very much, Miss,' he said a little too loud, then spun his companion around and marched him towards the exit. Outside Henry relaxed a little. He looked down at the slip of parchment in his fist;

*Are you stuck in a rut?*

*Do you long for excitement, and crave respect from your fellow man?*

*Bring the magic back into your life ... train for a new career as a Sorcerer today!*

Henry felt a wave of déjà vu and threw the paper on the floor as if it had just bitten him. 'Let's see if we can find a way into this fortress then,' he said, and the pair crept around the side of the building in search of the delivery entrance.

Before long, Peter found himself crouching in a shrub with Henry breathing heavily at his side. They scanned the area for any hint of danger. They'd spotted a dark rectangle breaking up the monotonously predictable expanse of the back wall, and were trying to figure out if it was the delivery door or not. As they watched, the rectangle shifted, and the corner of a battered wooden crate poked itself out of the crack it had found, preventing the door from clicking back shut. The next thing to poke itself out of the door was a big, round bottom, followed up a split-second later by the rest of the incredibly round man. He was staggering under the weight of a second, identical crate. Once his considerable backside had cleared the door it slammed back against the first crate, which made splintering noises of complaint.

Henry looked at Peter then turned to watch the man disappear around the corner of the building carrying the crate. He spun his eyes back to Peter, a look of urgency dancing in them. 'This is our chance! Hurry!'

Before Peter could reason with him, his companion was off again, skittering across the ground that separated their bush from the propped open delivery door. With a groan Peter skittered after him. Reaching the door, they slipped inside, Henry pausing to take a look at what was in the crate. It was completely empty. Henry poked the tip of his wand inside the crate and rattled it around suspiciously.

'Come on Henry! He could be coming back any second!' Peter had no desire to be caught sneaking into this building, especially if it was owned by a powerful wizard. He'd had more than enough magic for one day, thank you very much. Henry frowned at the crate, then turned and fled up the corridor after his friend, hitching his robe up around his knees to keep from falling over it.

...

A little deeper inside the building Mrs Flibbertigibbet with thunder in her eyes was glaring across the table at a shadowy figure. She'd been held here against her will for almost forty-eight hours and was more livid than she could ever remember having been. 'You won't get away with this you insidious little man,' she growled at the person sitting opposite her.

'Oh really?' His tone was light, conversational. 'But you used to love my ideas. I thought we made such a wonderful team.'

She hissed at him and twisted her wrists against the rough twine biting into them, binding her to the chair. 'To think I trusted you once. But you won't get away with this!' The shadowy figure turned and leant in close enough for Mrs Flibbertigibbet to feel his breath playing across the hairs on her cheek. The corners of his mouth crept up into an ugly sneer and he began to chuckle in her face. She recoiled in disgust. 'They'll stop you, you know? I've seen enough evidence to have you locked away for the rest of your life!'

'HA!' The man slapped his thighs as if she'd just told a hilarious joke. 'Oh, you do entertain me dear. But seriously, I'll be long gone an hour from now, and so will all the evidence.' The man chuckled. 'No-one will be any the wiser, and I can continue working on my "grand plan" unfettered.' He straightened and looked around his plush office, heaving a heavy sigh. 'It's a shame to lose all this though. Took me over a century to build it up, you know?' he said to no-one in particular as he looked around the room. 'Things were going so well.' He swung to face her, eyes now blazing with malevolent rage. 'Until your interfering nephew got involved and spoiled it all for me!' He spat the words in her face. Mrs Flibbertigibbet winced. 'Still ...' he said, walking away and leaning on the mantle-piece in a pointedly-casual way. 'I shouldn't think you'll be bothered about that soon, since you're going to be disappearing with rest of the evidence.' The smile on his face made Mrs Flibbertigibbet want to gnaw through her restraints and leap across the room to slap it off, but she continued to sit there loathing him instead.

• • •

'Hey! Hey, you?'

Henry and Peter froze, their bodies rigid with anticipation.

'You're a bit lost aren't you?' The voice was non-confrontational and friendly, so Henry turned to face it. It belonged to a young man who must have been about the same age as him. He was wearing what looked like a caretaker's overall and pushing a bucket with a mop. 'Sorcerer's Apprentice?' he said looking at Henry.

Henry thought fast. 'Erm, no ... we were told that Mr Dizing wanted to see us. Do you know where we can find him?'

'What? *The* Mr Dizing? No idea ... I don't think anybody has. He's a very private man. Are you sure he wanted to see you?' The young man looked befuddled by the idea that someone as important and elusive as the big boss could be requesting an audience with these two grubby-looking individuals.

'Oh, well, it could just have been a trick by our class-mates,' Henry sighed in well-staged exasperation. 'What a bunch of idiots. You were right. We're in Sorcerer's Apprentice, Grade 1.'

Back on to familiar territory the caretaker relaxed visibly. 'Yeah, well, I'd get back up to your classroom if I were you. Security is crazy round here at the moment. We've all been put on red alert for some reason, and you don't want to get caught wandering around down here on your own.'

Peter stepped up and began tugging Henry along the corridor towards the centre of the building. 'We will, thanks! Sorry. Goodbye,' he called over his shoulder to the caretaker as they went.

The caretaker put up his hand in a friendly parting salute. 'And if you see anything suspicious along the way, make sure you report it immediately, OK? Don't forget ... Red alert!'

Peter barely contained a bark of maniac laughter at the absurdity of this exchange. Perhaps they should report themselves? He hurried up the corridor with Henry, rounding a corner before they stopped to catch their breath, astounded they'd got away with it. It was probably some minutes after five-o'clock by now and the place seemed practically deserted. The long corridors rang with the empty sound of silence and their own scudding heartbeats. After a few moments, Henry deemed it safe to dig his wand out of his robe and take another bearing on his aunt. The wand pointed encouragingly forwards into the building.

Inside the place was huge. It was a rabbit warren of branching corridors and staircases disappearing up around secretive corners, which made the going rather slow for Henry and Peter since they had to stop at every single junction and take another bearing from the wand. But they weren't disturbed again, which made the slow going a lot more amenable. Eventually they reached the end of a corridor two floors down from where they'd started, with two doors leading off into the unknown; one in front of them in the short wall of the passage, and the other to their right. Henry stopped and placed the wand on the smooth flagstones between the doors and uttered the words of his spell. Awakened from its state of rest the wand jumped into action, boldly pointing the way forwards through the tapestry-covered wall to their left. Henry wasn't expecting that. He made a face that explained this to the world, and then stepped over to the tapestry and pulled it back. There was another door behind it. Henry tried the handle. Locked. He looked about the corridor. 'No boulders to sit on here Peter, but apparently it's the right way.'

Peter looked at the locked door, then stepped up to it and started feeling along the top of the door frame. He covered the entire shelf, and then brought his dusty fingers back down and looked at them despondently. 'I thought there might be a key,' he shrugged. 'Well that's that then I guess?'

Henry blinked and rolled his eyes. He wasn't going to give up that easily, even if Peter wanted to. He dug in his pocket for the miniature writing desk. A few minutes later he had the spell book restored to full size and was reading the page it had fallen open on;

*Taking a shortcut through time and space is one of the most useful arts that any practical wizard can perfect. Not only can it provide a convenient mode of escape from whatever dire straits you might find yourself in, but can be of incalculable value if running late for a vital appointment. Most people believe (quite falsely) that such a magical feat must be very difficult to perform. It is in fact one of the easiest skills to pick up, yet conversely one of the most notoriously difficult to perfect as accurate targeting gets harder the further you wish to travel. Those students who are keen to learn more about the art of 'dimensional origami', can begin with incredibly short distances; say, just a couple of inches initially (although travelling this kind of distance is unlikely to be of any practical use, except for maybe passing through a locked door).*

Henry leant on the writing desk and looked at the door. Problem solved, he thought to himself, and began checking the details of the spell. Not long after, he had the writing desk back in his pocket and was winding up to perform his newly acquired spell. 'I'm going to make another fold in space Peter, just to the other side of this door. I don't think we should chance more than one of us going through it this time though, as it's only my first attempt at the spell. You wait here for me and I'll come back as soon as I can.'

Peter looked unenthusiastically up the long corridor. Wait here? On his own? But it was too late to protest. Henry had already unleashed his magic on the door, which was now replaced by a smouldering uneasy hole a lot like the one they'd fallen through before. A second later and Henry strode through it. It dissolved milliseconds later into a puff of negative thought, leaving nothing but a slight grubby scorch-mark on the tired wooden door panels in remembrance.

Peter stood there wondering what to do, then was startled by a sudden rusty click. He jumped back against the opposite door swinging his head from side to side in panic. The door-handle turned, then the door eased open and Henry's smiling, comfortable face popped itself around the door-jamb. 'There was a key, only on the other side! He must be in here already,' Henry whispered in triumph.

Peter followed him through the door into another long corridor, but he didn't feel anywhere near as triumphant as Henry knowing that there was a powerful wizard lurking around down here somewhere.

# Chapter 28

On the other side of town, deep inside the protective casing of the castle walls, seven guards slept like babies. Their breath came and went in rhythmic sighs that calmed the air about them, and caused their minds to stray to summer meadows and first kisses, and anything but the disturbing experience they'd just had. They were sprawled across the table and floor of the outer chambers of His Majesty's dungeons, resting as peacefully as if they were in their mother's arms despite their uncomfortable postures. On the other side of locked bars lay an empty cell, the keys to the padlock still swinging off the belt-loop of a dreaming guard lying prostrate under the table. On the back wall of this cell there was a grey smudge, as if someone had lit up a paraffin lamp against the whitewashed surface, scarring its skin with the visit.

...

Henry and Peter reached the end of another corridor, only this time there was just one door and no deceptive tapestries. Henry checked the direction with his wand anyway, he'd learnt by now that you couldn't be too careful. Sure enough it pointed towards the only obvious exit; straight ahead. Henry felt his stomach cramp up as he watched the wand point emphatically onwards. He experienced a moment of doubt about whether they'd taken on too much, but shook it off smartly when he felt Peter tugging at his elbow.

'Are we going in then?' Peter whispered. 'Only, if not, I don't have a problem with that either. I'm sure my mother could whip up enough roast lamb for you too if we ask.'

Henry sighed. As tempting as it was he couldn't just walk away. His aunt, indeed the whole town could be in mortal danger.

'I wish D.C. was here,' he said to himself more than Peter.

Peter winced. 'Yeah, well I'm sorry I'm not D.C.'

'No. I didn't mean ...' Henry felt awful as he read the hurt on Peter's face. 'I just wish we were all here, together. You know?' he said, back-peddling frantically.

'It's alright. I know I'm not brave, or quick witted. And your wand hates me ...' The wand shivered its objection. After all, it had pulled him safely through the dimensional gateway hadn't it? 'Let's just find your aunty and get out of here, OK?'

Henry patted him on the shoulder and stepped up to the door, fresh sweat prickling on his forehead. He took a breath to steel himself, and was about to close his slick fingers about the door handle when the wand started buzzing ominously. Henry snatched his hand away from the door as if it had stung him. He stepped back a few paces. The wand stopped buzzing. He pushed the wand towards the door and the vibrating started again.

'She's in that room!' he mouthed at Peter, gesturing towards the closed door.

Peter gulped.

Henry's brain had already started unpacking his options to lay them out on the floor. What spells did he know that he could use to fight off a malevolent wizard, just in case he should happen to bump into one? His brain decided to reserve judgement until it was given a little more information. OK, what kind of danger could he expect to find on the other side of that door? 'Leading question, and calls for speculation!' his inner dialogue piped up, determined not to be culpable if it all went badly from here.

'Henry, are you OK?' Peter's voice was quiet and urgent.

He nodded and gave up trying to extract an idea from his brain. His magic had seen them through this far. He had to trust he'd know what to do when he found what they were dealing with. Silenced by the notion that anything untoward from here on out could be fully blamed on magic, his inner dialogue shut up and allowed his hand to reach out and turn the door handle.

The door swung in to reveal a plush, expensive-looking room with a large marble fireplace dominating the opposite wall. An austere polished desk sat importantly in front of the fireplace, and sitting in a chair in a much less important way was a dishevelled-looking woman sitting with her back to them. Henry looked at the man and felt the rising terror drain out through the toes of his boots.

It was only Mr Colloid.

But how had he made it out of the dungeons while he was still under investigation?

Mr Colloid looked up, startled. He'd obviously not expected company, at least not yet, since Henry noted that there were a couple of large bags stuffed full of what looked like personal belongings sitting just inside the door. The Chief Accountant hissed at the intruders and reached inside his blood-red robe to extract a slick black wand.

'Argh! Bane of my life!' he cried, swiping a crystal tumbler off the table to illustrate his annoyance. It crashed on to the marble hearth and shattered into tiny fragments.

Peter winced.

The woman turned awkwardly in the chair and Henry noted she'd been bound to it tightly. 'Henry!' she shrieked on seeing her nephew in the doorway.

'Aunty!' Shocked to see his normally pristine aunt in such a state of disarray, Henry stepped towards her instinctively.

'STOP!' The man behind the desk roared.

Henry did, eyes flicking between his trussed up aunt and the Chief Accountant as his brain tried to decipher the scene.

'How did you get down here, maggot?' the Chief Accountant growled.

Henry folded his arms across his chest and put on a stern expression. 'That would be a good question for *you* to answer, actually. We left you locked up in a cell at the castle. How did you escape and make it down here before us? And where is Mr Dizing?'

The man across the desk looked momentarily bemused and then the corners of his mouth crept up into a kind of smile. This odd-looking expression very quickly became a chuckle, and before long he was holding on to his stomach cackling wildly. A passing onlooker could be forgiven for thinking his visitor had just delivered the punch line of the world's most ridiculous joke. Henry felt the swell of uncertain fear beginning to fill up his legs again. This man might be wearing the body and the face of the weasely Chief Accountant, but Henry couldn't help thinking that somehow Mr Colloid didn't look quite so much like Mr Colloid just now. It wasn't just the robe and pointy hat. There was something 'off' about his mannerisms. Mr Colloid continued to laugh uncontrollably for a few minutes while Henry and Peter stood there wondering what to say next. Then as quickly as the laughing fit had started, it stopped. Mr Colloid leant on the desk towards his intruders with a look of exaggerated boredom.

'Haven't you got it yet, fool? You're not a worthy adversary for one such as me!' he boomed. He spread his arms towards the ceiling as if addressing an arena of unseen spectators. 'How can this worm have caused so much trouble, eh?' The air about him seemed to darken and fizz with the power of his rage. 'Who's helping him?'

'Run, Henry! Go get help!' His aunt was writhing against her restraints and had turned back to glare at the man holding her prisoner.

He rapped her on top of the head with his wand. 'Shut up woman. Before I seal your lips shut for good!' he spat, silencing her at least for the time being.

Suddenly the significance of his employer wearing a long flowing robe and a tall pointy hat began to dawn on Henry. Intuitively he raised his own wand and started pleading with his brain to pitch in and think of something brilliant to do. The best it could come up with was the *Fulcrum's Flabbergaster* spell, which thank goodness he was able to recall the chant for this time. He assumed a casting stance and the words popped into his head. He wondered about risking another two-handed cast. One look at Peter's face told Henry that he should probably throw everything he had at this man right out of the gates, so he braced his feet in the doorway and grasped the Malvern stick in both hands.

The power was electrifying. His whole world was swept away in a torrent of energy, sending his muscles into spasms of violent objection. As the solid column of magic left the tip of his wand and stretched out across the room towards its mark it was all he could do to keep on his feet. Then with a sudden crack of explosive power, even that skill was taken from him as the world began to turn and spin, flinging any remaining strength he had into the furthest corners of the room. Faster and faster the world around him spun, a dizzy sick feeling punctuated with thumping pain as parts of his body collided with the wooden door frame. Through the violent turmoil, Henry thought he could make out laughter. A man's laughter. High and grating, and a little on the crazy side. He forced his left hand to break its grip on the wand, and continued spinning madly in the doorway for at least forty seconds before the effects of the spell died away. Then he slumped on the floor, bruised and battered, his head still spinning. There was a large gash above his left eye and he'd lost a boot. Peter was cowering a little further up the corridor, knocked there by a thrashing leg as his companion had whipped the air around him into a wild frenzy.

'You think you can beat me with your entry level offerings? Do you? HA!' the figure in red spat at him across the desk. 'I've been playing this game for more than four-hundred years! And you've been at it, for what?' He was advancing around the desk towards the still dazed accountant, talking as if to a particularly dense relative. 'A few months is my guess?' He turned his back on them scratching his chin. 'Against an opponent such as me that'd give you odds of ... oh, I don't know, let's be generous and say about ONE MILLION TO ONE?' The air crackled with hatred.

## A BOOKKEEPER'S GUIDE TO PRACTICAL SORCERY

The words hit Henry like a bolting horse, bellowed as they were from the very considerable capacity of Gorman Dizing's lungs. Gorman smiled to himself as he watched the accountant quivering in the doorway, a jumbled heap of tattered rags and battered bones. He was beginning to enjoy himself. He didn't often get the chance of a really good bellow these days, and bellowing was one of his specialities. It was a skill he'd perfected over the best part of three-hundred years of bellowing at anyone who came too close. But too much bellowing didn't sit well in the business world. So he'd decided to invent a number of more amenable personae through which he could manipulate his companies without doing quite so much bellowing. One particularly successful persona was that of Neville Colloid, who was able to keep a tight rein on all of the company finances, whilst at the same time lulling his opponents into a false sense of security through his insidiously spineless countenance. It was an ingenious disguise. Mr Colloid; the first person anyone ever suspected of ill-doing, and yet the last person you'd think could pull it off. He fancied himself as quite the conceptual performer when the chips were down.

Henry wasn't trying to conceptualise anything. His head was still reeling with the idea that his boss of the last two years might be a raving homicidal wizard. And how long did he say he'd been doing it? 'F ... f ... four-hundred years?' he stuttered, trying to do the maths but failing miserably.

'Why yes, boy. Didn't I mention it? I'm immortal! I know, I know. You're impressed, but it's too long a story for today.' He paced back and forth in front of the fireplace as he spoke, waving his arms in the air theatrically. 'You can't hurt me with your puny attempts at magic. Even if you did, by some miracle, manage to damage me. I just bounce back you see?' He bounced comically off the mantelpiece behind him to prove it.

Henry gulped. Immortal? How many spells did he know that could stop the unstoppable? The count ended in a disappointing zero. Well, if he couldn't stop him, he reasoned with himself, perhaps he could delay him for a bit. Give Peter enough time to get away and fetch help? He thought hard, vaguely aware of a poking sensation coming from one of the many secret folds of his robe. Inside the secret fold, the spell book (still trapped inside the miniature writing desk in shrunken form) was going crazy. During the past four days it had been constantly frustrated by its own failed attempts at attracting the attention of its keeper, and this particular occasion was no different. It slammed itself against the sides of the drawer that imprisoned it, causing the miniature writing desk to bob about excitedly in Henry's pocket.

But Henry was far too preoccupied with the figure in the red robe to take heed. He continued to think hard, oblivious. To fill in a bit of time while he waited for his brain to come up with the goods, he dragged himself to his feet and held his wand up like a dueller once more. Blood from the gash on his forehead was beginning to run into his eyes and he swiped at it crossly with a shabby sleeve.

'Halcyon will know what to do with you,' he said boldly, 'and he'll be here any minute!'

'HA! Not without this he won't be!' Gorman opened a desk drawer and pulled out what was presumably the old wizard's wand, wiggling it in the air at Henry antagonistically. 'That's one wizard who'll be travelling economy from now on!'

Without warning the wand leapt out of his hand. In a pop of yellow light, it transformed into a wasp and darted in, stinging the furious wizard on the end of his nose. Then it buzzed out of reach and settled on top of a bookcase where it turned back into a wand again.

'CURSE YOU!' Gorman Dizing raged. He'd still not been able to find the counter to that infuriating defence charm. Damn the old wizard Halcyon and his gnarly tricks. 'No wand means that tired old codger won't be getting back here for another two days at least,' he said, rubbing the beginning of red welt on his nose. 'I'll be long-gone by then. Spending my ill-gotten gains corrupting another sleepy town, I should imagine.'

'He'll find you ...'

'Ha! You just don't give up, do you? How's he even going to know who he's looking for? Eh? Since the only evidence about my involvement here is about to go up in flames, along with the only three people who've ever seen me being ME!' He laughed another maniacal laugh. 'No-one will suspect the feeble Mr Colloid even if they should stumble upon me.' The powerful man in the red robe shrank back on his heels as he said this, his demeanour changing from that of a commanding wizard into a snivelling pathetic accountant. 'There'll be no big search parties; no overenthusiastic heroes with a mind bent on revenge. Mr Colloid's not worth that kind of effort. I'll just melt away into the background, and soon enough it'll be business as usual for me.'

Henry looked desperately around the room for help. It was filled with an amazing assortment of expensive-looking furniture, but none of it looked like it was feeling particularly helpful. On either side of the fireplace, in front of which Gorman Dizing was standing, there were two large glass cabinets, stuffed full of glittering cups and awards. Henry felt something poking into his left hip again. A slight frown creased his brow. It was the miniature writing desk. An idea suddenly occurred to him. He brought his wand back up to bear and started mumbling a verse under his breath.

'Oh, oh, oh ...' Gorman was hopping from foot to foot grinning a lunatic's grin at Henry, pretending to be frightened. 'You gonna shoot me with your magic again? Oh, all right ... I'll give you a fair shot, but it's my turn next! Deal?'

He stood still now, arms held out to the sides to create a big cross for Henry to aim at.

Henry wound up for a shot, and sent a ball of swirling light spinning off the tip of his wand across the desk.

Gorman scrunched up his eyes, bracing himself over dramatically for the impact, but the spell went careering past him and into the glass cabinet to his right.

The doors flew open and all of the highly polished trinkets went avalanching out on to the floor with a tremendous clatter.

Gorman opened his eyes and turned to watch, exasperated, as the shimmering trophies tumbled noisily to the floor. Once the din had subsided he turned back to face Henry, scowling.

'Now look what you've done! I was very proud of those trophies. Right! Enough messing about. It's my turn!'

The wizard in the red robe assumed a purposeful-looking stance and flicked his wand towards the floundering accountants twice. In response, two sharp barbs of mustardy light screeched across the room towards Henry and Peter.

The pair scrabbled backwards as fast as they could, but it was never going to be fast enough to escape the stinging impact that hit milliseconds later. Stunned on to his backside once more, Henry blinked and tried to assess the level of damage before attempting to move. Initial reports were favourable so he decided to check out his extremities by patting them with his hands, never once taking his eyes off the grinning wizard in front of him. Again, everything seemed to be in order, so he pushed himself to his feet and glared at the man in the red robe defiantly.

'Ha! Not so tough are you? Ahh ...' This was an 'ahh' that suggested the ahh'er knew something that no-one else did and Henry felt his valour deflate. 'But that was just my first go,' Gorman continued reasonably. 'You had two goes, it's only fair. This next one's a killer. No really, you'll love it. I was just adding a little flavouring, if you know what I mean? Let's call it an appetiser? Now, I do believe it's time for the main course to be served!'

On saying this, he raised his wand. He fired off a tight little ball of bright yellow light towards a messy coil of twine by the desk, presumably left over from securing Mrs Flibbertigibbet to the chair. The light shot into the tangle of rope. It writhed with excitement. Henry watched wide-eyed as the fibres wriggled and squirmed in a very un-rope-like way. Swelling ominously it became smoother, its tattered, hairy lengths shimmering and glistening with a plump, rippling pattern of scales. They were the bright yellow colour of deadly poison.

By the time Henry realised the rope was turning into a snake the whole event was pretty much over and done with. He found himself staring at the biggest, most dangerous looking reptile he'd ever imagined (let alone seen). To make matters worse the snake was staring back. It raised itself on its long, fat body, standing at least six-feet tall with plenty of body still hooped beneath it. Henry watched, transfixed as it opened its mouth and tasted the air with its tongue. It obviously liked what it sensed because it stuck its tongue out again, only this time to lick its lips. Through a rising mist of terror Henry could hear his own heart hammering in his chest. Every inch of his body was telling his legs to run, but he seemed totally powerless to act. The snake's beady eyes fixed on him unblinkingly, draining his strength with their hungry stare.

'Henry?' Peter's voice hissing in his ear brought Henry back to reality with a bump. 'Do something!'

Suddenly his legs got the message. 'Run!' he yelled at Peter. The pair of them turned on their heels and fled stumbling up the corridor.

As it turned out, this was a pretty pointless exercise. This was no ordinary snake. It moved like molten lead across the floor. Mrs Flibbertigibbet's chair went flying with a careless flick of its tail as it went in pursuit of its supper. Hearing her cry out Henry looked back over his shoulder. He regretted it instantly as his toe snagged in the raggedy hem of his over-sized robe. He crashed to the ground with a sickening thud, and immediately felt the cold tightness of the snake's embrace creeping around his ankle. He was vaguely aware of Mrs Flibbertigibbet shrieking expletives at their attacker as he scrabbled along the corridor trying to free himself.

'Run, Peter. RUN!' he yelled kicking at the tightening coils. But Peter's reply was just a strangled snort as the snake whipped its other end through the air like a lasso and caught hold of him by the neck. Tighter and tighter the snake wrapped its deathly hug around them. Henry could feel his face turning red, veins swollen and throbbing from the restriction of his blood flow. His ears hammered with the pounding of his heart. It was becoming harder to breathe as his lungs were crushed under the weight of the embrace. It felt as though the life was being pressed out of him and he was aware of a hazy sense of disappointment about the way things were turning out.

# Chapter 29

Mrs Flibbertigibbet, who was lying uncomfortably on her side strapped to the upended chair, watched in horror as the scene unfolded. Her nephew, still dressed in shabby robes and clutching his wand, was struggling weakly against the constriction of the giant snake, but she could see that he was fading fast. His friend simply hung lifeless inside a crushing coil, his head lolling against the thick body of the snake.

'STOP!' she cried out at Gorman, who was chuckling to himself as he watched the performance.

'Oh but I'm having so much fun. Why do you want to spoil it for me? You're always such a party-pooper,' he teased.

This made her furious. She wanted to slap his face so hard that he'd be wearing his nose upside-down for a week but the searing burn of the ropes around her wrists reminded her once more that she could do no such thing. She would have to come up with another idea, and fast.

'I thought you wanted this to look like an accident!' she screamed at him suddenly. This got his attention. 'Not much of an accident if they find those two half-digested inside the belly of a giant snake.'

'STOP!' It was Gorman who cried out this time, raising his wand and sending a belt of deep blue light streaking across the table towards the writhing serpent. It collided with the snake's skull just as it was making ready to wrap its jaws around Peter's lolling head.

Blue light flooded along its scaly length, turning it instantly from a snake of poisonous yellow into a brilliant electric blue ... and suddenly its appetite for accountants was gone. It shrank back reluctantly. Loosening its coils it turned to glare at the man in the blood-red robe.

'In here.' He gestured at the seething reptile, and it slunk into the office dragging its prey. It deposited them in a heap amongst the fallen trophies, and then coiled itself neatly around them before sulkily turning into a piece of rope, binding them together, back-to-back.

'Curse you. I won't let you ruin things for me now.' Gorman glowered at Henry and Peter as they started to come round on the floor. 'I would love to watch you die a slow and horrible death for all the trouble you've caused. But the old baggage is right. Less questions to answer means less people looking for me.'

'Why, you ...' Mrs Flibbertigibbet was speechless with rage at being called a baggage.

'Oh, shut up you old BAGGAGE!' He kicked at the chair she was tied to.

'You won't get away with this.' Her teeth were gritted, barely contained rage sizzling around her.

He bent to face her. 'Oh? Why's that?' His tone was that of an insolent teenager.

'You just won't. You can't go round killing good people and not get your comeuppance! The world doesn't work that way.'

'Good gracious, are you really that naïve? Because the bad guy never wins? Pah! I *have* won! Don't you see? This isn't a stupid fairy tale where the handsome knight will gallop in and rescue you from the "wery bad man".' He used a sarcastically babying tone that made her cheeks burn. 'No, my dear lady. I'm afraid this is the end for you three. Good little citizens of Terratonia, trussed up like turkeys at the scene of a very nasty fire, or at least that'll be the scene in about twenty-minutes. The only people who even *know* you need saving are two days walk away. You do the maths!' Gorman broke out into another peel of maniacal laughter. 'Now, where were we?' he said at last. 'Ah yes, I was about to make off with the loot, leaving you all to perish in a tragic blaze; most likely started when some thoughtless executive tipped hot ash from his cigar into the waste basket.' He slid another drawer open and produced a fat cigar, which he lit by tapping the tip with his wand.

Throughout this exchange, Henry had been struggling against the biting tightness of the twine. He still had hold of the wand but with his arms pinned uncomfortably to his sides there wasn't a lot he could do with it. It seemed the more he struggled the tighter the binding became. He had no idea what to do next, but he knew he had to do something.

Trussed up beside him, Peter was having his own internal struggle. He felt utterly useless, like he had for most of the trip. Pretty much the only claim he could make against their progress so far was the ability to sit on a rock successfully. What would D.C. do?

'Fight!' her voice barked inside his head.

'What with? I'm tied up on the floor having been half strangled by a snake in case you hadn't noticed!' he screamed at her internally.

His image of her, which was actually a lot scarier than the real D.C. he noted with some dismay, leaned in close to his face. She looked very serious as she said quietly, 'With anything you can get your hands on.'

'Hey, you ... Colloid, or Gordon ... or whatever your name is ...' Henry had decided to play for time, hoping something brilliant would turn up in his ideas bank while he wasn't looking.

Gorman threw his gaze to the ceiling and turned with exaggerated annoyance to face the young man on the floor. 'Are you still here?'

'I don't understand,' Henry said, twisting his arms to see if there was any give in the rope. 'If you're such a powerful wizard, why don't you just magic all the evidence away? Surely there's no need to burn down the whole building?'

'Oh honestly, Henry! Get with the programme. I'm trying to persuade people that there's no such thing as magic here! Now don't you think a large part of the skyline simply vanishing from sight might raise a few eyebrows? Get people poking their noses in? Eh? No. I believe an unfortunate fire might be a tad less suspicious, don't you?' He turned and marched back towards the fireplace, clearly becoming bored with this pointless exchange.

Henry stopped struggling. 'But why? What have you got against magic?'

'Well now, if I told you that I'd have to kill you.' Gorman stopped suddenly, turning to face the tethered accountants with a look of comical thoughtfulness. 'But then, I'm already going to kill you, aren't I?'

He smiled and walked back to them, hunching down in front of Henry. 'All right then ... why not? It is rather a good plan, even if I do say so myself. You see magic is a powerful tool. In fact, it's *the* most powerful of *all* the tools we have available to us. If you don't have magic you're bound to miss it. The dragons learnt that the hard way, although I believe the macabon don't have the intelligence to miss it. Anyway, I digress. The reason that magic is so important is that it's the one and only thing that can be used in defence of magic, as you've probably already learned, Henry. So, in a world where magic is the stuff of poetry and make-believe, how powerful do you suppose a skilled wizard in possession of the only remaining Malvern stick on the planet could become? Shame about the Malvern forest though. It had such a pretty blossom in the springtime, but it had to go.'

'You destroyed the Malvern forest?'

Gorman sat back on his heels, affronted. 'Officially? No! It was a forest fire.' He leant forward again, eyes sparkling with a conspiratorial glint. 'Unofficially ... yes.' He snickered at Henry as if sharing an inside joke. 'Not a very environmentally conscious act, I'll admit. But I couldn't have people running about all over the place with magical sticks to remind them of their heritage, now could I?'

'So that's why you've been running those ridiculous fake wizarding classes in the evenings?' It was all falling into place for Henry and he didn't think it was such a great plan after all. He decided to say so. 'What would you say if I told you your plan is a load of rubbish?'

Gorman sat back on his heels again, genuinely affronted this time. 'What would *you* say if I turned you into a frog?'

'I'd say you're a coward who's too afraid to hear the truth.'

'No ...' Gorman said slowly. 'You'd say RIBBIT!'

Henry recoiled as Gorman bellowed into his face, but continued on bravely, his brain still clamouring for a good way out of this mess. 'Your empty words can't hurt me!'

Gorman's eyes narrowed. He leant in close to Henry's face and hissed at him with venom, then the furious wizard leapt to his feet, marching towards the fireplace muttering in disbelief. When he reached it he placed a steadying hand on the mantelpiece and turned to face the trussed-up accountants, breathing heavily. His eyes were black and thunderous, fists clenched with frustrated rage.

'So, sticks and stones may break your bones, but not my words eh? Well, we'll have to fix that, won't we?'

He raised his wand into the air dramatically and whipped it in a circle above his head a few times. Thunderous grey light began to gather in a sinister cloud above his pointy hat, crackling and sparking with malice as it grew in size and density. Before long there was a fairly impressive storm cloud of dark swirling light hovering over the mantelpiece above Gorman's head. It moved with him as he crossed the room back to where Henry was sitting and leant in close.

'Boo,' Gorman whispered into his ear, and as he spoke a fork of angry white lightning struck out at Henry from the cloud, biting him viciously on the shoulder and causing both he and Peter to cry out in pain and alarm. It felt to Henry like being belted with a white-hot anvil, the static heat from the blow sending his body into involuntary spasms as it racked itself through his muscles. Gorman stood back, watching him squirm in agony with a satisfied smile. 'A little extra heat won't make any difference will it Henry?'

Henry screamed again as the piercing electricity struck him in his stomach, tearing him apart inside with its unrelenting torture.

'Oh now we're having fun, aren't we?' Gorman asked the writhing accountant, another bolt of terrifying power shooting from the cloud in Henry's direction. This time the evil magic walloped home on his chin, sending a shuddering crack of pain up through his jaw and along the sides of his skull, clearly looking for a way into his head to melt his brain.

Peter felt Henry's body go limp against his back. He'd managed to fill his fists with a couple of heavy blocks that had been used to mount shiny cups. Quite what he was going to do with them was another matter, given that he was wrapped up tight in a barrel of rope with his barely-conscious friend at his back. He tightened his sweaty hands about the marble blocks and began praying for a miracle.

'Oh. Is he dead already?' Gorman gave Henry's leg a kick and another shard of lightning forked out, juddering the limp body of the young accountant. He moaned and lolled to the other side. 'Not quite, but no more fun I see. Ah, well ... all good things must come to an end as they say.'

He turned a cheery smile on Mrs Flibbertigibbet. 'Now my dear ...'

The woman screeched as a fork of electricity shot out of the storm cloud and stung her on the behind. 'Oops, sorry!' he sang jovially, waving his hand through the dark mass above his head. It dispersed into nothingness. 'So, as I was saying; as much fun as this has been, which isn't much at all if I'm honest, it's time I was elsewhere.'

He was about to conclude his business, knocking the cigar out of the ashtray and making his way swiftly through another dimension to a sleepy little town he'd had his eye on six-kingdoms west, when he heard the crackle of magic. He turned an incredulous glare on spent accountant. 'You just don't know when you're beaten, do you?' he said with a note of grudging admiration.

Repeating a familiar verse in his head, Henry straightened his back and pointed his feet towards the enemy, bringing both hands to bear on the shaft of his wand. He took aim between his knees in one last ditch effort to cause some damage, or die trying.

Gorman shook his head and held his own wand up, clipped delicately between forefinger and thumb to prove a point. The stream of green light coming from the tip of his wand connected with the stream of pink light from Henry's in an almighty *kaboom*. In an instant the pair of accountants bound up together on the floor began to spin like a cyclone had grabbed them.

'Wonderful thing, the *duplexagonal reflector*,' Gorman said over his shoulder to Mrs Flibbertigibbet as he worked. 'You see, a wizard as powerful and experienced as I, need only think the vaguest of thoughts and this spell will reflect lesser magic straight back upon the caster. Using their own magic against them, do you see? There's a poetic justice in that, I think. And it illustrates my point about magic combating magic rather nicely. In this case, with some very amusing results.' He watched as the whirling accountants spun madly, kicking up all manner of glittering trinkets and display cabinet relics as they went.

'You monster!' Mrs Flibbertigibbet turned away from the scene, unable to watch her nephew suffer any more.

Gorman laughed. 'He's only got himself to blame. If he would just … stay … DEAD!'

But then suddenly, and quite without warning, something went very wrong for Mr Gorman Dizing.

Just as he was beginning to get bored with torturing these pathetic, insignificant mortals, he was struck brutally on the top of the head by an extremely solid object moving at quite considerable speed. It was one of the marble trophy stands, flung out of Peter's grip as they spun at great speed on the floor.

If he were a mortal man it was a blow that would have killed him, but luckily for Gorman Dizing he didn't have to worry about such annoying trivialities as death any more. He did, however, have to deal with the fact that the flying chunk of marble had knocked off his pointy hat. The resulting fluctuation in the force of his spell caused his delicately clipped wand to be jerked out of boastful fingertips.

It skittered across the jumble of display cabinet debris and came to rest not far from Mrs Flibbertigibbet's nose. She squirmed away from it distrustfully.

Gorman Dizing screeched an unearthly screech as he watched it go, and then howled with rage as Henry's two-handed *Flabbergaster*, now running unchecked by any sort of magical retaliation, got to work quickly with the business of spinning its new victim around like a top.

Gradually the two young men on the floor ground to a clattering halt. The mad spin had loosened the rope enough for Peter to struggle out, but Henry was still connected to the whirling Gorman Dizing by a stream of lavender energy that shook his wasted body like a rag-doll.

'Henry! Henry, you got him. Let go of the wand!'

Through the haze of his dilapidated consciousness Henry got a sense of what Peter was yelling at him, and wrenched his left hand from its grip with some considerable effort. He lay in the trophies exhausted, every part of his shattered body deciding it was throwing in the towel for good.

Peter got up and watched the spinning red wizard apprehensively, the second marble mounting-block clutched in his hand. 'He's slowing down Henry! Henry, what next?'

Henry propped himself up and said, 'The cabinet ... Peter, push him into the trophy cabinet.'

Peter looked doubtfully from Henry to the glass cabinet. Surely that wasn't going to hold a grown man for very long? But since he didn't have any better ideas he approached the staggering, turning wizard cautiously and shepherded him towards the cabinet. The *Fulcrum's Flabbergaster* spell had pretty much worn off now, and Peter gave him one last hard shove. He fell back into the cabinet in a dizzy heap and Peter closed the door, leaning on it and breathing hard.

'Stand back, Peter.' With a supreme final effort Henry dragged himself over to the cabinet wincing in pain. He raised his wand until it was hovering about twelve-inches away from the cabinet doors and began reciting a verse.

Gorman came to his senses to a fishbowl view of a world that was growing larger. Central to this picture of reality was a huge wand, which together with the hand that was holding it was also growing at an alarming rate. He roared and went for his wand but realised it was lying on the floor in front of his desk, which was also getting bigger. He felt his rage turn inwards as he realised what was happening. TRAPPED! Why did he have to show off in such a foolish way? Now he was stuck inside a shrunken glass cabinet with no means of escape, for what could be a very long time. Curse that damn idiot Noble! This was *not* how he'd expected things to turn out. And his head was really going to get chilly at night with no hat to keep it warm.

'I don't believe it!' Peter cried staring at the tiny glass display cabinet in amazement. 'You did it!'

'*We* did it Peter … I'm so glad you were with me.'

'Well, to be honest I think I might have been channelling D.C.'

Henry laughed. 'Whatever it was, it worked.' He looked around the room, feeling a little stronger. There was a pointed cough and they both remembered Henry's aunt, who was still lying bonded to the chair. She was glaring at the two of them in what looked like a combination of horror, confusion and relief. 'Aunty? Are you OK?'

She nodded, watching the wand in his hand nervously. Henry realised that it was still buzzing like an angry bee, and it had a tendency to swing round and point in her direction if he wasn't paying attention. Through all the excitement he'd completely forgotten about the tagging spell. He spoke a few words of command into the wand and it buzzed one last time in protest before lying quietly still again, the combination of its link to Mrs Flibbertigibbet forgotten. For the time-being anyway.

# Chapter 30

When news got out, which didn't take long thanks to Mrs Flibbertigibbet's network of gossipy friends, the kingdom was ablaze with talk of the brave youngsters who'd rescued their loved-ones from the trolls in the forest and foiled an evil wizard. Rumour had it they'd locked the wizard away in a tiny glass display cabinet that they could all go and gawk at in the castle if they needed further proof. By teatime the next day there was a queue of eager proof-seekers stretching all the way out of the castle gates and halfway across the drawbridge. The constant glare of giant eyeballs didn't do anything to improve Gorman Dizing's mood.

Henry, however, couldn't have been happier. He was bruised and battered, but this just added colour to his stories of heroic deeds as he regaled them to his astounded family again that night.

'I can't believe you fought a dragon!' Will enthused.

'And wrestled a snake!' Bill admired.

'Well it all sounds very dangerous to me. You could have been killed,' was his mother's offering to the fray, which dampened the mood somewhat.

Henry turned to her in the flickering lamplight and took her hands gently in his. 'But I wasn't mother. And father will be home tomorrow and everything will be OK again.'

She smiled and reached out a hand to stroke his cheek. 'Yes. You did a wonderful thing, Henry. Really quite astounding and I'm so very proud and grateful.' A tear rolled down her cheek, but she was smiling as she drew Henry into her arms and hugged him like she might never stop. A few seconds later he felt the double-thwump of his brothers joining in on either side of them. Henry laughed and threw his arms around all of them.

...

On hearing news of the lost accountants, the King decided to bring his birthday party forward to celebrate their safe return. As people gathered in the castle they talked in hushed voices about how it was going to be the most spectacular affair the kingdom had seen in thirty-years ... except anyone under the age of thirty, who just thought it was going to be the most spectacular affair the kingdom had ever seen. True to the King's rather gaudy tastes, the grand hall was festooned in a thousand bright decorations. It certainly helped to create a festive atmosphere. Henry and Peter were, of course, the guests of honour. Wherever they went the air buzzed with grateful excitement.

In just a few hours D.C., Halcyon, Henry's father and the others would be home, and then the party would really begin. A regiment of the King's personal guard had been dispatched yesterday morning with instructions to bring them straight to the castle. The whole town had turned out in their finest to get a glimpse of the two courageous young men who'd returned their missing people to them. Henry's chest swelled with every friendly pat on the back or enthusiastic shake of the hand that came his way. In amongst the bustle he spotted his mother. She was standing across the hall with her two younger sons clasped firmly to her sides, chattering with a group of people hovering by the entrance. The group milled in a tight circle glancing anxiously from each other to the hall outside, and then back to each other again. They were waiting for husbands, brothers and sons. Henry felt hot, happy tears prickling his eyes as he watched them hug each other and weep with joyful anticipation. Perhaps sensing his gaze, his mother turned and caught his eye, gesturing for him to join them.

'Henry, there you are. Lucy, this is my son, Henry. She wanted to meet you.' His mother put an encouraging hand on his shoulder.

Henry stepped forward and shook the hand of a young woman clutching a toddler to her breast. 'Thank you. Oh thank you so much! Did you see my Jesse? Is he OK?' The toddler squirmed in her arms, grizzling.

Henry had no recollection of meeting a Jesse, exactly. But there had been so many people and so much going on. He was about to open his mouth and deliver a non-committal, 'He's fine,' when he felt a hand on his other shoulder.

'Lucy? Lucy Drummer?' It was Peter, smiling at the woman and reaching out to tickle the baby. It squirmed in a less bad-tempered way and stopped trying to escape.

'Yes?' She looked at Peter with haunted eyes. Eyes that had got used to expecting bad news. It was a look Henry knew well from his own home.

'Yes, Jesse is fine. Though he's fairly bursting at the seams to meet this one.' He delivered another carefully aimed tickle and the infant giggled. 'You had a girl then?'

The woman's eyes brimmed over with grateful tears. 'Yes. Jessie,' she said to the youngster in her arms. 'Meet the boys who've rescued your daddy. You're going to meet him soon.'

'You named her Jessie too?' The baby cooed as Peter continued to enthral it with threatenings of tickly fingers.

The woman flushed pink. 'I didn't know ... I wanted a reminder ...' Her eyes brimmed with fresh tears.

'Could get confusing when your husband gets home,' Peter pointed out.

'We'll cope.' The woman smiled, swallowing back her emotion. Reassured by Peter's words she went back to staring out of the door, occasionally pointing at things to keep her daughter's attention focused.

By now other people in the group had seen the exchange and were pressing forward to offer their hands in gratitude. Henry noticed his aunt bunched in amongst them, and tensed as she pushed through the crowd.

'Ah, Henry. Yes, he's the one who defeated the evil wizard. My nephew you know? He's very good with magic,' she announced to the group matter-of-factly. 'We're all very proud of him.'

Henry looked at his mother in stunned silence. For a moment they both just stood there gaping, then her face broke into a radiant smile that lit the air around her. 'Yes, we are very proud aren't we?' She beamed, and the group all cooed and clucked.

Henry's cheeks flushed pink as Mrs Flibbertigibbet continued to boast while his mother beamed on. Although Henry couldn't help noticing his aunt threw plenty of her own anxious glances out of the grand entrance to the hall.

He felt a tug on his sleeve. It was Bill.

'Is Dad really on his way home? Did you see him ... honestly?'

Henry nodded and Bill hugged him again. It still felt weird, but he was getting used to it.

Peter whispered into his ear. 'I could quite get used to this hero stuff. But you know who is just going to die for it?' Henry frowned and Peter blanched, realising what he'd said. 'Not die, as in *die*, you know? Sorry, bad choice of words.'

Henry smiled. They'd been through a lot together in the past week, an awful lot. 'Yeah, D.C. is definitely going to enjoy the attention. I think she struggles to get heard at home sometimes, what with having so many sisters.'

'A brother too now,' Peter grinned.

And a wand, Henry thought resting his hand on the polished case he'd tucked away in his bag. Just as soon as Halcyon had given it a once over to cleanse it of any malignant magic.

Wanting to keep the few remaining Malvern sticks safe he'd also tried to collect Halcyon's wand from on top of the bookcase. But after three near misses from an angry wasp's stinger and a *lot* of bookcase climbing, he decided it might be best left for the wizard's return. A guard had been posted on the door to the office to make sure the wand stayed safe until then.

'Peter, thanks for putting up with all this. I know magic isn't your thing. It took a lot for you go through that mountain, and then into the desert; not to mention sneaking into that big ugly building on the other side of town.'

'Hey. You're not getting all misty-eyed on me are you?'

Henry laughed. The Peter standing in front of him was such a different Peter to the one he'd worked with down in the vault all those ... all those *days* ago. Could it really only have been a few days? It seemed to Henry as though he and Peter had aged a good deal more. This thought made him uncomfortable.

'What are you going to do now?' he asked Peter to change the subject.

'Oh I don't know. I might just enjoy the attention for a while, see if I can get a date with Penny Filigree. She seems to have a twinkle a little past the friend-zone in her eyes when I see her now.' He grinned sheepishly at the admission.

'Will you go back to work? I mean in the vault?' Henry asked.

'I think so, yes. Things should be better without Mr Colloid; don't you think? And with your father as Chief Accountant; what with me having risked my neck to save him and everything, I was hoping he might think about promoting me early. What do you reckon? Will you put in a good word?'

Henry blinked. It seemed strange that things might just return to normal. Even stranger that Peter should to want them to. 'But what about what we've seen Peter? Monsters and madmen! Don't you want to learn more about the mysteries of the world?'

'No way! Henry, I'm not like you and D.C. I like to daydream same as everybody else. But that's all they are. *Daydreams*. I went along on this trip firstly because I had to or we'd lose the house. And then because it was safer to stay with a man carrying an explosive stick than run off into a forest full of monsters on my own.' Henry wilted at his words and Peter touched his shoulder smiling. 'But I followed you into the desert because I trusted you. You're going to make a great wizard one day. That takes a special kind of courage that I don't have. I'd rather be growing vegetables and raising a big family, that's all ... But hey! You'll always be welcome at my table when you get the chance to pop by and tell us of your adventures. I take it you won't be carrying on in the castle?'

Henry laughed. 'Well, not the vaults anyway. But if there's one thing this whole episode has made clear its that we need to train up some real wizards for protection, and to make sure we don't forget how to use magic.'

Peter prodded his friend in the ribs. 'Just stay away from trophy cabinets in future, OK? Hey, talking of which ...' Peter nodded towards the miniature trophy cabinet displayed in a much larger version of itself across the room. 'Do you think he knows what's going on? I wonder how much he can see from up there. I hope he has to watch your dad and the others walking in through the door, knowing that there's nothing he can do about it.'

Henry was about to reply when he realised his friend's attention had been caught by something over his shoulder. He followed Peter's gaze and saw Penny Filigree, leaning against a table laden with finger-food. She was smiling at him coyly. Henry could see it was pointless trying to converse with his friend now, and was just about to tell him to go over and talk to her instead of mooning across the room, when he was almost knocked off his feet as someone slammed into him.

'Oh ... ooh, ooh ... sorry. Did I hurt you?' It was the guard, Mike, who'd helped them arrest Mr Colloid (or should that be Gorman Dizing?).

Henry brushed himself off and shook his head. The guard frowned and Henry thought he looked strangely vacant. Still frowning, the guard leant towards Henry and took him by the shoulders, more to steady himself than anything else. 'Listen,' he said. 'You don't know what we're celebrating here do you? Only, I seem to have lost touch a bit. What day is it?'

It was Henry's turn to frown. The guard must be drunk. 'The missing accountants are returning home,' he explained slowly to the vacant face in front of him. 'Mr Colloid has got his just deserts. Oh, and its Sunday.'

The guard looked more confused than ever ... 'Who?' he managed eventually. 'When?'

But Henry had already been whisked away by another pair of congratulatory hands that wanted to introduce him to their partner's congratulatory hands on the other side of the room. The guard staggered on in search of somewhere to sit down, slamming heavily into several more people, and finally a massive glass trophy cabinet by the door.

The cabinet rattled alarmingly as it swayed against the force of the knock, sending trophies, cups and other glass display cabinet paraphernalia toppling over on sparkling shelves. Rocking dangerously back and forth with everything else was one piece of paraphernalia you wouldn't expect to find sitting in your average glass display cabinet. It was itself a perfect, miniature glass display cabinet. Sitting inside it fuming was a perfect, miniature wizard.

Gorman Dizing looked testily out at the busy crowd through his cruelly clear fishbowl view of the world. 'Go on ...' he urged the tiny cabinet as it tottered back and forth. 'Fall over. Smash the glass and set me free. I deserve a lucky break after all the bum deals I've had lately.'

But despite his persuasive tone-of-voice both cabinets, large and small, righted themselves again. The tiny wizard slumped on to the floor in a huff. He rubbed his bare head and tried to cheer himself up with the thought that at least all these smiling faces would one day be dead and buried; a deep rot eating away at their inane grins as nature slowly decomposed them. He, on the other hand, would live forever. This whole affair was just a minor set-back. Then he settled himself down in the cabinet for a very, very long wait.

# About the Author

Kate Russell is a technology reporter, writer and gamer, who has spent the best part of five decades in the tireless pursuit of refusing to grow up.